GAT[illegible]
SHADOWS

GATE OF SHADOWS

CAMBRIDGE GOTHIC – BOOK 2

Mark Wells

A CAMBRIDGE TALES BOOK

First published in Great Britain in 2021 by Cambridge Tales Ltd

A catalogue record for this book is available from the British Library.
ISBN: 978-1-9160284-2-5

Formatting by Polgarus Studio

Cambridge Tales Ltd
115c Milton Road
Cambridge CB4 1XE
www.marknwells.com

IN MEMORY OF

SAM FITZSIMMONS
1996–2020

Gothic Scholar and Captain of
St John’s College Rugby Club,
“The Redboys”

Prologue

Alfonso woke, the sun hot against his back and neck, drawing him out from the blessed darkness of sleep. Blinking, he saw the scarred surface of the red wall mere feet away. As he stared, the serried ranks of grooves came into focus, row upon row, filling one side of the cramped cave in which he lay. Six notches and a slash, repeated again and again, thirteen times in total.

Had it really been that long? Thirteen weeks since he'd been brought here, bewildered and confused, and deposited like a bag of refuse on the ledge outside?

Alfonso remembered peering at the alien landscape and being terrified by the precipitous drop, hundreds of feet, to the valley floor below. But that was nothing compared to the horrors that awaited him when darkness fell.

The harpies had come for him that first night, their winged outlines visible against this world's many moons, swooping like bats out of the night. Alfonso had retreated within the narrow confines of the cave and watched in terror as they fought to get at him, their gaping maws mere feet away. Only the span of their wings had saved him, their broad shoulders unable to enter the cleft into which he had crawled.

It hadn't been until dawn, when the first of the twin suns had risen above the horizon, that respite had come. The surviving harpies had returned to their caves or clung limpet-like to cliffs, their bodies becoming dormant during the day. The remains of those they had left behind had littered the entrance to his cave, but not for long.

Alfonso had watched in disbelief as the suns' rays had touched those dismembered bodies. A pallor had fallen over them, their composition changing before his eyes until, their life force long gone, they crumbled to dust. All that had remained of his night of terror was the fine powder that covered the floor of his cave.

This was when Alfonso, exhausted but alive, had made the first entry of his makeshift diary. He'd carved his mark in the wall using a fragment of bone he'd found in the corner of his cave beyond the reach of the sun. The crude mural had become a testament to his survival in this brutal and alien world.

So once again, Alfonso raised his stiff and aching body from the floor to repeat that daily ritual. But as he reached into his tattered pocket for the stylus of bone, a shadow fell over him, blotting out the marks on the wall.

"My, you have been busy, haven't you?"

Alfonso spun around. A hooded figure was standing in the entrance, her hunched silhouette framed against the bright sunshine, just as she had all those weeks ago.

"Mother Mary?"

"And who else would it be?"

"You… You are early."

The woman snorted. "We have work to do." She peered past him at the wall. "If you can spare the time that is."

Alfonso rose to his feet, but something made him stand his ground, though what, he couldn't be sure. An instinct to protect his territory perhaps, if that is what this meagre crevice could be called. Or an unwillingness to move until he'd made today's entry. Either way, it cost him.

The staff struck him in the stomach before he knew it was moving. Even as he doubled over, another blow caught him in the side of the head, knocking him flat. As he lay there, a bony hand grabbed his hair and pulled his head up. He found himself staring into those wild green eyes. Human eyes still, but sharing the same alien intensity that he'd seen in the creatures here.

"You dare to challenge me, boy?"

"No… I didn't mean…"

Before he could finish, Mary yanked him up with surprising strength and hurled him out into the sunlight. Alfonso fell, sliding across the ledge and coming to a stop in a cloud of pale dust, inches from the precipice. As he attempted to get up, he felt the base of the staff slam into his back, pinning him to the floor.

"Be careful, boy." The menace in those words was unmistakable, and Alfonso lay still.

The ledge on which he lay was cut into a column of red stone, hundreds of feet high, dwarfing the land around. From here he could see a meandering line of tall stone columns, snaking away down the valley carved by the river that flowed between the towering cliffs. Through the settling cloud of dust, Alfonso fancied he saw movement in the lee of the columns. Harpies were gathering in the shadows before the twin suns stilled their bodies once more.

"I meant no harm."

"Harm?" She snorted. "You cannot harm me, boy."

The pressure from her staff increased, and Alfonso willed himself to relax, knowing that the more he resisted, the more she would push.

"Besides, Olga here wouldn't allow it, would you, dear?"

Before him, a figure rose on wings that fanned out in a wide arc, blotting out the sun. Part-human, part-harpy, Mary's eldest daughter glared at him with undisguised hatred, her fierce eyes burning with an amber glow.

"It would be the last thing he did," she hissed.

Though Olga had inherited her mother's resilience to the sun's rays, her powerful body was that of a harpy with taloned claws that were as vicious as her nature. Most of the many scars that now covered Alfonso had come from her clawed feet.

Not wanting to provoke either mother or daughter further, he dropped his gaze and was rewarded by an easing of pressure from the staff.

"Come, boy, you've lazed about long enough. We can't have you getting soft. Up! You have work to do."

With a glance towards Olga, Alfonso rose to his feet. It was only then that he saw Katya, her sister, hovering nearby on wings turned golden by the sun. Her face bore the same striking features as her sibling. However, Katya's eyes were darker, and her thoughts were unreadable as she stared at him across the void.

With a flap of her wings, Olga glided forwards, and Mary stepped from the ledge onto her daughter's back. Though hundreds of feet above the valley floor, neither showed the slightest concern. Moments later, mother and daughter were soaring upwards. The old woman's hood flew back, releasing a tangle of white hair that streamed behind her in the rushing wind.

"Bring him!" she called.

Alfonso turned to see Katya angle her wings and swoop towards him. He just had time to avert his face before she reached forwards with her iron-hard claws to pluck him from the ledge. His stomach lurched as she swept him out over the valley towards the others.

Alfonso closed his eyes, trying to blank out the image of that dizzying drop beneath him. Instead, he focused his mind on the one thing that gave him the strength to endure the nightmare of his existence: the memory of his family.

Unseen by Mary, their names were carved in an alcove at the back of his cave. The place where he cowered at night when the harpies came. He traced his fingers over the engraved letters in those darkest of moments. For if he was to die, he wanted them to be the last names he uttered.

"Mama, Papa, Raquel," he said.

Alfonso felt the claws tighten, and he glanced up to find Katya staring at him. Their eyes met, just for a moment, before she returned to gazing at the distant speck in the sky.

Beating her wings with renewed force, she soared after her mother and sister, leaving Alfonso alone once more with his thoughts.

Chapter One

Giles ploughed on through the chilly water of Porto Pollença Bay, his feet beating a steady rhythm as he swam back to shore. The black bodysuit gave him some insulation from the cold. Still, twenty minutes into the swim, he was beginning to lose feeling in his fingers and toes.

Glancing ahead between strokes, he spotted the white tower of the Vidal residence set back from the beach, partially obscured by the trees of its compound. Adjusting direction, he headed towards it, wondering if their guard dogs were watching him through the bars of the gate. *If so, they'll be the only ones*, he thought.

The Christmas Eve celebrations across the island of Mallorca had gone on well into the early hours of the morning. It had been quite an introduction to Raquel's family. Her mother, aunts, and cousins were doing their best to make him welcome, despite his lack of Spanish and their indifferent English.

Raquel had started out as his translator. But this had soon lapsed when the subject of Catalan independence had reared its head. Giles had been left bemused by the quick-fire conversation as the verbal jousting had played out in front of him. Though he'd noticed that he wasn't the only spectator.

Raquel's father, a short square man with a boxer's face and fists to match, had said very little. The patriarch had sat at the head of the table spearing food with his fork and glowering at the newcomer with his one good eye. Giles had asked Raquel about her father's disfigured face before they headed off to their separate bedrooms, his being the guest room in the courtyard, hers at the top of the tower.

"The Police," she'd said.

"You're joking."

"I don't joke, Giles."

Which was true. Not after that night on the Chapel Tower when they'd found her brother's torn and shredded jacket among the bones of the harpy's eyrie.

Picking up the pace, he stretched out with each stroke. When his fingers finally touched the sand, he pushed himself up and shook his mane of blond hair.

"Bracing!" he said, grabbing his towel and looking out over the peaceful bay. His home in London seemed a world away right now, which was just fine as far as Giles was concerned. Spending Christmas with his parents in Fulham and hearing another pitch about how much Cambridge graduates could earn in the City, was enough to put a dampener on any festive spirit.

No, this was a much better option, he thought as he headed back across the sand to the Vidal's compound, where three faces stared out at him through the bars of the gate. "Don't you think?"

The dogs wagged their tails. Since his arrival a few days earlier, the three German Shepherds had become accustomed to Giles's presence in the guest room adjacent to the kennels. Chara, the matriarch of the pack, would often sit with him in the evening, her muzzle resting on his lap while the pups played. Now the younger two whimpered in excitement as he unhooked the latch and stepped inside.

"Shh," he whispered, glancing towards the sleeping household. "We don't want to wake the others."

While the pups licked his salty fingers, he looked at the tall white tower where the Vidal family slept. Raquel's bedroom was on the second floor, her open window visible above the canopy of her parents' balcony below. A seasoned night climber back at Cambridge, Giles was familiar with scaling buildings undetected. From what he could see, the Vidal's tower looked a good deal simpler than the one he'd climbed over New Court last term.

As the pups scampered off to play beneath the trees, he turned to the matriarch.

"What do you think, Chara?"

The dog cocked her head to one side, her dark eyes never leaving his.

"Mum's the word, eh?"

Wrapping his towel around his shoulders, Giles headed towards the house. Standing underneath the balcony, all he could hear was the distant rumble of snoring. Levering himself up, he paused to listen for movement before swinging his legs over the balustrade. The tiled floor felt cold as he edged towards the window and peered inside.

The room was in darkness, but he could make out the shape of a large bed and two lumps beneath the crumpled duvet. The snoring seemed to be coming from the bigger of the two. Stepping back, Giles looked up at the canopy. It looked sturdy enough, he decided. Resting a hand against the wall for balance, he stepped up onto the stonework and paused.

The snoring had stopped.

Looking into the compound, he saw the German Shepherd watching him, ears pricked, and wondered if she had noticed it too.

The sensible thing to do would be to head back down. But that was not a word Giles used very often. Reaching up, he took hold of the canopy's horizontal support strut. He was about to pull himself up when Raquel's mother stepped out onto the terrace, arched her back and yawned.

Giles froze and watched as the woman padded across the tiled floor. She wore nothing more than a thin cotton nightdress which hung to her knees, exposing sturdy calves and an ankle tattoo of barbed wire. Reaching the low wall facing the sea, she produced a box of cigarettes and put one to her lips. Only then did he spot the little ceramic bowl and lighter left there for this purpose.

Just great, he thought.

Raquel's mother lit the cigarette and, taking a deep drag, spotted the dog below her.

"*Ola*, Chara," she said.

The dog stared at the woman, and Giles willed the animal not to give him away. If Raquel's mother saw a man in a black bodysuit hanging there, she'd probably have a heart attack.

No, the only way out of this was up, and soon too, before she turned around.

"You want one?" said Raquel's mother in English.

Oh crap, Giles thought. But before he could respond, Raquel's father stepped out onto the balcony.

"Is a filthy habit, woman," he replied, strolling over to join her. The man took the offered cigarette and blew out a long plume of smoke.

"Why didn't you speak to the poor boy in English?" Mrs Vidal asked.

"I prefer to keep my eye on him."

"You are not alone," she said, looking down at the dog. "Hey, Chara. You've been keeping an eye on our guest, haven't you?"

The dog barked and wagged its tail. Then Giles saw Raquel's father move his free hand to his wife's buttock and give it a squeeze.

"Hey, stop that!" she said as he wrapped her in a bearlike embrace.

Giles took his chance. Using the ironwork like a parallel bar, he swung up until he was able to plant his right foot on top of the canopy. Levering himself upright, he swayed for a moment before twisting his body flat against the tower. Below him, the giggles and deep throaty rumble became louder.

"Not here, El Toro."

"No?"

"No, I want you inside..."

"So do I."

Mrs Vidal's delighted chuckle was followed by the sound of hurrying footsteps over the tiles. The voices became muffled, and moments later, Giles heard the creak and groan of the bed. Heart thumping in his chest, he pressed his forehead against the wall.

I bet Santa doesn't have to put up with this sort of thing, he thought.

As the creaking noises from the bedroom increased, he edged along the top of the framework to Raquel's window. Climbing up onto the sill, he dropped down into the room.

Raquel started up from her pillow, and stared at him, eyes wide.

"Giles?" she hissed. "Are you crazy?"

"For you," he whispered, tiptoeing across the room. Unzipping his bodysuit, he slipped under the duvet alongside her.

"Ugh! You are all wet! Like a..."

His kiss stopped her protest, the heat of her lips warming him far more than any towel could do. When they broke apart, Raquel wrinkled her nose.

"Like a fish. You taste of salt."

"You, on the other hand, my dear, are delicious!"

He kissed her again, gentler this time. When they parted, her eyes studied him.

"Why you do this swimming?"

"A dip in the sea is a Christmas Day tradition in England. Invigorating, don't you think?"

"In-vig-orating?"

"Wakes one up."

"For me, that is coffee."

"That too," he said. "But this is much more fun."

"You are mad, you know that?"

"You know what they say about mad dogs and Englishmen?"

"Mad dogs?"

"Never mind." He began playing with a strand of her hair. "I'm just glad I'm here."

"Me too."

She nestled against him and stared at the family photo next to her bed.

"I miss him," she said. "So much…"

Giles didn't need to ask who she meant. He looked at the young man, standing between her parents, an arm draped over his sister's shoulder.

"I'm sorry about your brother."

"Why?" she asked. "It was not you who took him."

Her sadness punctured the happiness he had felt moments before.

"What hurts most, is that in here," she took his hand and placed it over her heart, "I feel that he is still alive."

Giles didn't know what to say, so he kept quiet.

"I know it sounds crazy," she continued, "but I do. Alfonso and I were *simpatico*."

Raquel's eyes implored him to believe her. Part of him wanted to. But she was talking about something he'd never experienced. No one had ever been that close to him. Certainly not his parents. The nearest thing he had to a brother and sister were his friends Ying and Trevor, but after the last term, even that relationship was now strained.

The reason he was here in Mallorca though was his hope – his need, even – to feel something more profound than friendship. Giles took her head in his hands and stared into her eyes.

"Listen," he said. "What happened last term was crazy, so I'm not going to argue."

"You think it's possible too?"

"I don't know. But there is someone who might."

"The Professor?"

"Gupta knows more than he's letting on, that's for sure."

"So, you'll speak to him?"

Her stern features softened, just for an instant, and Giles saw a lost and desperate girl staring back at him.

"Yes, Raquel, I will."

Wrapping her arms around his neck, she pulled him to her. Breathing in her hair, Giles noticed the small crucifix on the wall above her bed. The crowned and bleeding head looked down at him, and he felt something stir inside. What it was, he couldn't be sure, but he was surprised how much it moved him.

When Raquel released him, her usual intense expression was back.

"You know what I want now, Mad Dog?"

"What?"

"I want to in-vig-orate."

Giles raised his eyebrows.

"Not that!" she scowled, pushing him off. "Coffee! Before my parents wake."

"Won't they want to sleep in this morning?"

"Not unless they can smoke in their sleep." Raquel rolled out of bed and slipped on her dressing gown. "Come on, we need to get you dressed."

Giles felt for his towel, but it wasn't on the bed, nor could he see it next to his crumpled bodysuit on the floor. Frowning, he tried to remember when he'd last had it. He was sure it had been around his neck when he'd clambered onto her parents' balcony.

"Hurry up," said Raquel, opening the bedroom door. Bending down, she picked something up from the staircase landing. "Giles, is this yours?"

She held out his towel, still damp from the swim but now neatly folded. Giles thought back to that moment on the balcony when he wondered if Raquel's mother had seen him.

"Crappity crap."

Chapter Two

Nick reached for the phone by his bed and held it up to check the time. In the dim light of his bedroom, he could make out the crazy spider's web of lines from a crater in the centre of its lifeless screen.

"Oh, for f…!" Nick began, but caught himself in time.

His mum didn't like swearing, and the walls of the terraced house were paper thin. Gingerly, he lifted up his tee-shirt and stared down at his ribs. The livid pattern of a boot tread was clearly visible, and there were more bruises on his forearms, where he'd blocked most of the blows. But the lump on the back of his head was a painful reminder of one that had got through.

Easing himself out of bed, he stepped over the discarded clothes that were strewn across the threadbare carpet, and crept along the hallway in his boxers and tee-shirt. Thankfully, at this time of the morning, the bathroom was empty. As he stood over the toilet, he checked his urine for signs of blood, and was relieved to see there wasn't any.

The same couldn't be said for his hands though, which were a mess. The knuckles were scuffed and swollen from the couple of shots he got in before he went down. As he held them under the cold tap, his reflection in the mirror showed that he'd paid a heavy price for doing so. His top lip was cut and swollen and there was a bruise forming under his left eye from the blow that had floored him.

"Never go down, Nick, you know that," he chided himself.

There was a frantic knock at the door.

"I'm busy," he said.

"I'm bursting!" Charlie replied.

"Can't you use the outside one?"

"It's snowing."

Nick sighed and unlocked the door. "Don't mind me," he said as the portly figure of his brother hurried past to get to the toilet.

"Shut the door, will you?" Charlie said.

Nick pushed the door closed and returned to the sink. "Would you like me to wipe your arse too?"

"Not likely, I don't know where your hands have been."

After he'd finished, Charlie replaced the lid and sat down.

Nick rolled his eyes. "Can't anyone get a little privacy around here?"

"You're not in Cambridge now, in case you hadn't noticed."

"We share bathrooms there too, only people tend to leave you alone to wash in peace."

"I'm being peaceful, aren't I? Just chatting. Best place for it. No chance of being disturbed."

"That's what *I* thought until you barged in."

"My, aren't we sensitive this morning? Heavy night?"

"Sort of."

Nick splashed water onto his face, cupping some into his mouth and swirling it around before spitting it out. There was a thin trail of blood in the bowl.

"Bro, have you been fighting again?"

Nick reached for the towel, but seeing that it was pale pink, decided against it. Instead, he pulled up his tee-shirt to dry his face.

"Bloody hell, Nick! What's that on your ribs?"

"Keep it down, will you?" he said, dropping his voice. "And mind your language."

"You look like someone's been using you as a doormat."

"I tripped."

Charlie shook his head. "Schoolboy error, going down."

"Tell me about it."

"How's the other guy?"

"Better than me."

"Anyone I know?"

"I hope not."

"So, what happened?"

Nick sighed. "It was down at the club." Most holidays, he cleaned tables at the Working Men's Club to pay for his rugby subs. "Being Christmas Eve, Big Jim asked me to stay late to clear up."

"And?"

"And they were waiting outside."

"They? How many?" Charlie asked.

"Three or four. Hard to tell really. Must have known I'd have a Christmas bonus."

"Did you recognise any of them?"

"No, but they knew me. 'Oxbridge tosser', I think was the phrase."

Charlie grunted. "Eloquent as always."

"What do you mean?"

"Sounds like the Football Factory."

"The what?"

"Just some idiots who got suspended from school."

"For what."

"Being gits."

Nick looked at his brother, but Charlie didn't elaborate.

"Hey, is it OK if I use your phone? Mine got smashed."

"Sure. Who are you calling?"

Nick hesitated. "A friend."

His brother raised an eyebrow. "No name, then? Must be serious."

"We're just friends."

Charlie snorted. "Sounds like a heartbreaker."

"The voice of experience, eh?"

"With a body like mine, trust me, 'just friends' is my middle name."

"I'll bear that in mind," said Nick, heading for the door.

"And I'd cover your arms if I were you. Mum's not good with bruises at breakfast."

"Right."

Charlie shut the door behind him, and Nick heard the latch turn. For a moment, he stood in the silent corridor as a thought formed in his head. How would his brother know about covering up bruises?

Frowning, he headed down the corridor. Charlie's room was cramped with barely enough space for the desk tucked in the corner. Whereas Nick's walls were covered with pictures of sports teams and trophies, this had posters of superhuman warriors and shelves filled with ranks of carefully painted toy soldiers.

Charlie had been an avid wargamer for as long as he could remember. Nick had dabbled himself once, but with rugby training and his part-time job, any free time he did have was taken up with studies. Besides, his brother's hobby wasn't cheap, requiring him to do two paper rounds to fund it. Still, it wasn't going to win him many friends at school. The opposite in fact.

Was that what he meant by bruises at breakfast?

Nick heard a buzzing noise and saw the mobile phone vibrating on the desk. He looked at the screen.

Swipe to open message

He hesitated, then did so. A Gif appeared showing Santa Claus dropping his trousers to reveal the words: MERRY CHRISTMAS LOSER!

Nick's breathing became very still as he stared at the figure performing the lewd gesture. Then from down the corridor, he heard the sound of the bathroom door creak open. Scrolling to the top of the screen, he hit the delete button as Charlie entered the room.

"All done?"

"What? Yeah, thanks." Nick handed the phone back and Charlie checked the screen.

"She's not going to be sending me love messages, is she?"

"No, I don't think so."

"That's good because there's only so much fan mail I can take."

Nick looked at his younger brother, standing there in his misshapen pyjamas.

"What?" said Charlie.

"Nothing."

"In that case, unless you want to stay and discuss your minefield of a love life, I'd like to get dressed."

"Right," said Nick. But in the doorway, he stopped. "Charlie?"

His brother sighed. "What now?"

"You fancy doing some hobby with me over the holidays?"

Charlie stared at him. "What, painting you mean?"

Nick shrugged. "Some gaming too, maybe?"

His brother's face lit up. "But what about your studies?"

"I'll cope."

"Your call. But I'm warning you, my Orks don't take prisoners."

"What makes you think my Space Marines will?"

Charlie grinned. "I'll see you at breakfast."

Back inside his room, Nick leaned against the door and stared at the law books on his desk. He thought about his broken mobile and the Santa message on his brother's phone.

"Tossers," he muttered under his breath, and reached for a long-sleeved top.

Chapter Three

Annabel stood at her grandmother's kitchen sink, washing up the last of the dishes from Christmas lunch. She glanced down at her phone for the umpteenth time that day and wondered why Nick still hadn't returned her call. After leaving him a voice message first thing, and two further texts during the morning, she couldn't understand what was keeping him. Didn't he know it was just her and her Gran this year?

Stop it, girl, she thought. *He'll call.*

Outside, a deep covering of snow lay in drifts against the drystone wall, a legacy of the weather front that had followed her train from Cambridge to Yorkshire earlier that week. Though the snowstorm hadn't hit by the time she arrived at Hebden Bridge, the sight of the person standing on the station platform had left Annabel in no doubt that it was due.

One of Gran's favourite sayings was "There's no such thing as bad weather, only unsuitable clothing". Based on the sturdy walking boots, heavy-duty Barbour jacket, and fur-lined hat she'd been wearing, Gran was expecting a blizzard. Still, the old woman's face had lit up like a summer's day when she'd seen her granddaughter.

"Annabel! So good to see you, my dear!"

"And you, Gran," she'd replied, hugging her.

When they'd pulled apart, the former nurse had cast a professional eye over Annabel's face.

"You look tired! Busy term?"

"You could say that."

"Good, I'm looking forward to hearing all about it. Come on. Let's get you home."

By "home", her grandmother had meant her little hillside cottage above the old mill town. The old woman had lived there for as long as she could remember. Now, it had become her home too.

After the death of Annabel's family last year, Gran had first come down to her parents' house in Surrey, while she finished her A levels. But once her place at St John's College had been confirmed, they'd put the house on the market. Neither could face the prospect of rattling around the old family home over the holidays. Though Annabel worried that the ghosts of Christmas past would follow her even here.

As if anticipating this, her grandmother had made a long list of festive chores which she'd pinned to a cork-board in the kitchen. And so, while the snow had fallen over the subsequent days, they had thrown themselves into getting the place ready, only venturing outside to retrieve logs for the fire.

By the time the big day arrived, the cottage had been transformed. Traditional decorations adorned the walls, garlands of holly hung from the rafters, and the Christmas tree, wrapped in fairy lights, glittered like a shooting star.

Rising late, they had spent the morning in the kitchen preparing lunch and listening to carols from King's College on the radio. The meal itself had been jolly enough, with both of them wearing hats and groaning at the dreadful jokes from the crackers. But afterwards, as Annabel had set about the washing up, her thoughts had returned to Nick and his strange silence.

"So, Annabel, tell me what lectures are like?"

Turning, she saw Gran standing there, a dishcloth in hand as she removed a cluster of soap suds from a large saucepan.

"Oh, they're pretty full-on for NatScis," Annabel said, grateful for the intervention.

"NatScis?"

"Sorry, Natural Scientists. I'm a Bio NatSci. We have lectures on the New Museum Site in town. Most afternoons we have labs there too. When we're not having Supervisions, of course."

"And what are they exactly?"

"Weekly grillings by our subject Supervisors. We tend to have them back in College. Most Fellows host Supervisions in their rooms."

"Sounds fun."

"Not when you don't know your stuff. With three students at a time, there's nowhere to hide. In my first one, I hadn't realised my Supervisor was the co-author of the textbook we should have read."

"Oh dear."

"Don't worry, Ash and Brian covered for me."

"Ah yes," she said, smiling, "how are they both?"

Gran had met Annabel's two Supervision partners at the start of the last term. Ash and Brian were the sort of socially awkward, hyper-intelligent beings that thrived in the academic hothouse of Cambridge. Immersed in their studies, they rarely engaged in chit-chat about family and home life. Which was just fine as far as Annabel was concerned.

"They sent their best wishes," she said, smiling at the memory of the two text messages she'd received that morning.

Hi, Annabel, Ash here. Merry Christmas! Any snow in Yorkshire? None here but fingers crossed. Seeing Brian later. Making a Lego Millennium Falcon together. May the force be with us, haha! Hope you have a great day, say hi to your Gran!

Brian's, by contrast, was a model of brevity: a snowman emoji.

"That's kind of them," said her grandmother. "Anyone else?"

"Katie. She sits opposite me in the boat."

"You're still rowing then?"

Annabel heard the surprise in her voice. They both knew how close she had come to drowning when the American oarsman, Brett, had taken her out on the river at the beginning of term.

"The boat club was short of coxes," Annabel explained, "so I couldn't really let them down."

The truth was, no one had asked Annabel to get back in a boat. Certainly not the College boatman, Blades. He'd witnessed the accident and had helped drag her and Brett's lifeless bodies from the water. No, it had been Annabel's decision to get back on the river. And she remembered the old boatman's approving smile when he'd seen her sign up for the women's novice crew. That same expression was on her grandmother's face now.

"How's that tray coming along, Annabel?"

"Almost done."

"Excellent. In that case, I'll put the kettle on. We should just have time to open our stockings before the Queen."

Annabel gaped at her, knowing the Hamiltons usually opened presents after the monarch's annual address. The old woman shrugged.

"Well, it is Christmas, after all."

"Don't worry, Gran. You had me at stockings."

Taking a wire wool pad, Annabel gave the roasting tray a vigorous final scrub, removing the last vestige of goose fat before placing it on the drying rack. Wiping her hands, she took the phone from her pocket and checked it once again.

Still no message from Nick.

"We can go outside later if you like," her grandmother suggested, handing her a steaming mug. "Take some photographs for Nick."

"Why would we do that?"

"Show him what Christmas in Yorkshire looks like. In case he wants to visit."

Annabel frowned.

"We're just friends. You do know that?"

"Of course. Just a thought."

"He'll be too busy. You know, with his… family."

Annabel hadn't meant to say the F word. It had crossed her lips in a moment of weakness. Images came to mind of her dead sister and parents, laid out in the hospital mortuary, alongside the other driver from the accident. They had been on their way back from Oxford, with Annabel waiting at home, eager to hear Serena's stories about her first term at Balliol College. Stories they would never now share together.

Annabel felt her eyes mist up and gulped her tea, burning her tongue.

"Ow, that's hot," she said, blinking away tears.

"I'm sorry, Annabel," said her Gran, unable to hide the sadness in her voice, before recovering. "But tea should be hot and strong. Like a good man!"

"Gran!" Annabel laughed, taking the opportunity to wipe her wet cheeks.

"Come on, dear, let's see what Santa's brought us, shall we?"

They headed through to the "Snug" as her grandmother liked to call it. The corner room with its low timbered ceiling, comfy armchairs and wood-burning stove was aptly named. The addition of Christmas decorations only enhanced the homely feel.

After putting her mug down on the coffee table, Gran reached for the two stockings hanging above the fireplace.

"This one's yours, I think," she said, handing the fatter of the two to Annabel.

"What have you been putting in here, Gran?"

"Me? Don't you believe in Santa?"

"Not for a long time."

"Honestly! I had the chimney swept just last week."

Annabel smiled. "Thank you, Santa."

Rummaging around inside, she couldn't help feel a tingle of childlike excitement.

"Oooh, what do we have here?"

Annabel extracted a satsuma, and then one of her Christmas Day favourites, a Terry's Chocolate Orange.

"You know me too well, Gran!"

"Well, we all have our weaknesses. Mine's After Eight mints."

Next out of the sock came a book. Turning it over, Annabel read the title and frowned.

"*The Hitchhiker's Guide to the Galaxy*?"

"Don't you like it?"

"No, it's great. Just a bit unbelievable, that's all. You know," she hesitated, "people being transported to other worlds and all that."

"Douglas Adams was a Johnian."

Annabel stared at her.

"Was he? I didn't know that."

"Anyway, I just thought you might like something a bit lighter than a textbook to read over the holidays."

"Good thought, Gran. I'll give it a go," she said, reaching to the bottom of the stocking and feeling something soft.

"What's this, then?"

Annabel pulled out a blue beanie with the St John's College crest on it.

"Wow, Gran! Where did you get this?"

"I ordered it from Ryder and Amies. You know, the shop where we bought your College gown. I hope it fits."

Annabel put it on, pulling the band over her ears.

"It's perfect! Thank you so much, Gran. Just what I need for those early morning outings on the river."

"Good, I'm glad you like it. Now, are you going to keep that orange to yourself, or am I allowed a piece?"

Annabel offered her the satsuma.

"I meant the chocolate one."

Rolling her eyes, Annabel peeled back the wrapper. The rich aroma of dark chocolate wafted around the room. At that moment, her phone began to vibrate in her pocket.

"I wonder who that can be?" Gran said, smiling.

Annabel stared at the screen and felt her heart quicken. Ignoring her grandmother's arched look, she took a calming breath and put the phone to her ear.

"Merry Christmas, Brett!"

Chapter Four

It was just before midnight on Christmas Day when Professor Ravi Gupta turned off the lights to his Second Court room in St John's College and locked the door behind him. The contents of his canvas shopping bag clinked together as he descended the spiral staircase, the worn timber steps creaking under his weight.

On the first floor landing, he caught a hint of coal dust in the air from the hidden bunkers located beneath the leaded window. These supplied the fireplaces in the Fellows' Combination Room, the magnificent sixteenth-century long room, where he and his colleagues had taken lunch on Christmas Eve.

The Fellowship's final gathering of the year had been a convivial affair, made all the more enjoyable by the presence of Aurelia. The Portuguese waitress had been serving him meals for almost thirty years, and though their relationship had never blossomed beyond menu choices, Ravi had long hoped that it might.

So when, at the end of lunch, Aurelia had wished him a Merry Christmas, the sudden surge of joy had left him flustered. By the time he'd mastered his emotions and turned to wish her the same, the waitress was already heading back to the Butler's pantry with his plate.

Even now, a day later, he felt deflated at that missed opportunity. His one chance to engage her in conversation before the festive break and he'd messed it up. As he had done so many times over the years.

"You old fool," he said, as he descended the final set of steps and slid his rickety wooden room indicator to OUT.

Ravi paused in the relative shelter of the stairwell's archway to look out across Second Court. The latest cold front had brought with it the first heavy snowfall of winter. A smooth white blanket now lay across the immaculate lawns, save for a couple of mounds where the snow had drifted against the KEEP OFF THE GRASS signs. Not that these prohibitions served any useful purpose today, he reflected. The students and tourists were long gone. Except for him, the College was deserted.

Well, almost, he thought with a smile.

Adjusting the faded College scarf his friend Robert had given him all those years ago, Ravi set off for his last errand of the day. Though a far cry from the ice-covered slopes of his native Nepal, the frozen cobbles underfoot were treacherous, and he trod with great care. It wasn't until he reached the gritted path, that the going became easier.

Ravi turned into a covered passageway and emerged into Chapel Court where the windows of the College Library lay in darkness for once. Instead, the pretty little square was illuminated by fairy lights hung from the trees on the far side of the court. Their pale blue glow added a magical touch to the academic heart of the College, and his spirits lifted, if only for a moment.

His eye was drawn to paving slabs in front of the Library entrance. Memories of that night at the start of term came flooding back – when something far heavier than snow had fallen from the Chapel Tower. The wounded harpy, diving to save its precious egg, had smashed into the flagstones. The impact had sent an explosion of calcified remains into the air that had clung to the tower's walls like a funeral shroud.

Though the subsequent storm had washed any lingering trace of the creature away, the crater had taken the College's maintenance department days to repair. For Ravi, no amount of new stonework could erase the memory of that final keening screech. Even now, as he stared at the tower rising up into the night sky, he felt a shiver that had nothing to do with the cold.

"Bad memories?"

The voice made him spin around, the bottles in his bag clinking as his hand reached inside his jacket pocket. Framed in the passageway stood a squat, gowned figure. How the person had come within a few paces of him without making a sound, he could not fathom. But when Ravi saw the impish smile on the man's face, he understood.

"Master!" he said. "You startled me."

"Forgive me, Ravi," said Dominic Lester, Master of St John's and former senior intelligence officer at MI5. "I was on my way back from the neighbours after dropping off a present." He waved towards the distant spires of Trinity College. "A bottle of College port for my opposite number, to make sure she had something decent to drink over Christmas."

"Very neighbourly of you," said Ravi.

Trinity's well-stocked wine cellar was almost as legendary as its endowment.

"Well, it is the season of goodwill, after all," said Lester, stepping out of the passageway and staring up at the Chapel Tower.

"The peregrine falcons are still around then?"

Ravi remembered that a pair had been seen hunting from the gargoyles.

"I believe so," he said.

"You're something of an authority on raptors, of course," said Lester, continuing to stare skywards.

Ravi shot him a look. The Master was well aware of what had happened earlier that term with the creature. Indeed there was little the man didn't know about what went on in College. But Lester had still not forgiven Ravi for taking matters into his own hands and destroying the harpy, nor for involving the students who had first discovered it.

Still, as Master, he had done his best to cover things up, laying the blame on corroding Victorian ironwork for the damage to the Chapel rampart. He had then commissioned the Domestic Bursar to conduct a full structural survey to keep the press and insurers onside. But Ravi's role in the incident had put a strain on their relationship, and he could hear the edge in Lester's voice.

"It is protected, isn't it, Ravi?"

"The bird of prey, you mean, Master?"

Their eyes met and they both knew he was referring to the portal.

"I believe so, yes," Ravi confirmed, remembering Robert's assurance that it had been sealed.

"That's good to know," said Lester. Then the smile was back. "I must say, the falcons have been doing a marvellous job of keeping the pigeon population under control. I've hardly seen any on the lawns recently."

"I'm sure the gardeners are delighted."

Lester snorted. "Well, mind how you go, Ravi, these courts can be lethal."

"Thank you for your concern, Master. Merry Christmas."

Ravi waited until the former spy had disappeared through the far passageway leading to the Master's Lodge. With a final glance at the tower, he made for the shelter of the Chapel cloister.

Ahead of him, he could see lights glowing in the Forecourt Lodge. If he was lucky, Bert, the Head Porter, would be there with some of his wife's excellent mince pies. Besides, he was in no rush. There was no one waiting for him at home in his terraced house in Newnham.

As he approached the lodge, Ravi was pleased to see a familiar figure standing under the clock. Pushing the door open, he held up the clinking bag.

"Merry Christmas, Bert!"

******

Outside in Chapel Court, the wind whipped up the snow, sending ghostlike flurries dancing across the lawn before settling back onto the shifting surface of white. Far above, on an outcrop of stone, a pair of sharp eyes peered down at the scene.

The falcon tensed, spotting movement in the air. A bat flittered out from the eaves of the tower, its black outline visible against the white lawn. The peregrine flexed its wings to dislodge the icy flakes that had collected during the long minutes it had sat motionless on the gargoyle's back. Then it sprang from the lofty perch and dived for its prey.

A heartbeat later, a grey hand reached out and plucked the bird from the air. The falcon screeched in alarm, but cold fingers clamped over its beak, silencing the cry. The hand tightened, crushing the life from the creature. The bird's wings continued to flap until, with a sickening crunch, they lay still.

The hooded head leaned over the lifeless body, bending down so that the cowl almost touched the feathers jutting from between its fingers. Barely audible over the whistling of the wind, it sniffed its catch. Moments later, the Trinity clock began striking twelve o'clock and, unobserved by anyone, the last festive bird of the day was consumed.

Chapter Five

St John's College still had a thick covering of snow when the first of its residents returned after New Year. Rosy-cheeked students gazed in wonder at the pristine white lawns as they dragged bags and suitcases across gritted paths on the way to their rooms. By the evening, many could be found heading for Second Court to catch up with friends in the Buttery and College Bar.

Ravi stood at the foot of his staircase and stared at the procession of figures, tramping through the snow. Though Cambridge looked serene and beautiful in its winter wardrobe, it felt so much more alive, as he did, once the students returned. Adjusting the collar of his gown, Ravi couldn't help but feel a spring in his step as he set off across the court for the Fellows' Lobby and his first formal event of the new term.

The Domus Feast was a popular event among Fellows keen to return to normality after a week of over-excited children and endless party games. His late friend Robert jokingly referred to the sight of the many gowned figures heading back into College as "The Great Escape".

As a resident in College, Robert had prided himself on being one of the founding members of the "Escape Committee", rallying the troops for the New Year get-together in the Fellows' Combination Room. His absence this year would be keenly felt, not least by Ravi, who couldn't remember celebrating the New Year without his friend.

When they had first met as freshers some fifty years earlier, Robert had invited a homesick Ravi to spend the winter at the Mackenzie family gathering in Edinburgh. This had proved to be something of a crash course in Scottish culture as Robert's larger than life mother took Ravi to her not inconsiderable bosom.

For the shy Nepalese boy, the noise, laughter and boundless goodwill of the Mackenzie clan had literally swept him off his feet. And after a week of memorable meals, walks and parties, he'd returned to Cambridge with a sore head, sore feet and a debt of gratitude that could never be repaid.

After Robert's parents had passed away, their son had taken it upon himself to organise New Year festivities in Cambridge, booking meals, arranging gatherings, and organising activities. One of their favourites was hiking out to Grantchester for the traditional barrel-rolling championship.

Robert had loved this event, which was a thinly veiled excuse for the village's four pubs to organise a day of drinking that started early and finished when the beer taps ran dry. The Scot had even competed one year when a member of the Red Lion's team had failed to turn up on time. Ravi smiled at the memory of his friend charging down

Grantchester's high street, his barrel careering between the protective straw bales as the crowd roared him on.

It was that evening, after Robert had consumed most of the Red Lion's winning magnum of Champagne, that they had first discussed the possibility of finding life in the cosmos. Standing in a Grantchester meadow, staring at the stars, this fanciful idea had grown into an obsession in Robert's case, one that had driven him to his death.

Ravi stared up at those same stars now and, with a nod to his friend's memory, adjusted his gown and pulled open the door of the Fellow's Lobby. Warm light flooded out from the Green Room where the rest of the guests were assembling for pre-dinner drinks. Convivial conversation greeted him like an old friend, and he felt that familiar sense of belonging once more as he entered the room.

Fifty or so Fellows were already gathered. They were standing in clusters or sitting in the window seats, their black gowns contrasting with the pastel shades of the walls. A few heads turned his way and smiled or nodded their welcome. Ravi responded in kind as he edged his way through the robed figures towards the drinks station.

This was a mahogany table set against the wall between two leaded windows. Its polished surface was laid out with glasses and a selection of wine, sherry and bottles of sparkling water, arranged on a silver platter. Ravi helped himself to sherry and made a note against his name on the leather-bound ledger for the appropriate deduction to be made from his College account. That done, he took a fortifying sip and turned to face the room.

"Evening Ravi," said Peter Norton, a genial theologian whose unruly hair had gone prematurely grey. This was thanks in no small part to his brood of six children and the equally pressing demands of being the College President.

Elected every four years, the President had the unenviable role of handling the concerns of the Fellowship and representing their views to the Master. Robert had once quipped that the incumbent required the diplomacy of a Foreign Secretary, the firmness of a judge, and the patience of a saint. Ravi felt that Norton scored highly in each of these areas, but three years into his tenure, the man looked a good deal more careworn than when he had first taken up the mantle.

"Good evening, Peter," said Ravi, raising his glass. "How is the family?"

"Biological or academic?"

"Both?"

"Over-indulged, tiresome and irritable," said Peter. "The children, on the other hand, are fine."

Ravi smiled. "I'm glad to hear it."

"Jean and I discovered some years ago that the secret to a harmonious Christmas is a wide selection of Pixar films, a couple of 1000-piece jigsaws and copious quantities of Lego."

"Something to try with the Fellows perhaps?" Ravi suggested.

The President's careworn face lit up. "Now that's a thought! I'll suggest it at the next Council meeting."

The door opened, and they turned to see a tall, striking woman enter the room.

"Perfect timing," said Peter. "Here's someone I want you to meet."

The President led him over to the new arrival.

"Ravi, let me introduce you to a new member of the Fellowship. This is Dr Dutour, who joins us from the École Normale Superieure in Paris. That's right, isn't it, Gabrielle?"

"*Oui*, Peter, though we tend to call it the ENS," said the woman, smiling and extending her hand. "Professor Gupta, so pleased to meet you." Her dark eyes, magnified by black-rimmed glasses, bore into his.

"Please call me Ravi."

"Gabrielle is a physicist," said Peter.

"I am replacing Professor Mackenzie," she added.

It was an innocent remark, but to Ravi it felt like a slap to the face. Recovering, he managed a smile.

"Yes, of course. Your field is theoretical physics if I recall."

"Indeed, something I shared with my predecessor. In recent years, Professor Mackenzie and I collaborated on several projects. Did you not work with him also? I have read some of your papers from the 1960s. Very intriguing."

Ravi felt a tingle of alarm at this.

"That was a long time ago," he said. "Our areas of research later diverged."

"A shame," she said. "Why was that?"

Ravi was not expecting such a direct line of questioning. "Oh, you know how it is. Different interests, sources of funding..." he said, deflecting.

The President, spotting his discomfort, interrupted.

"Gabrielle, may I introduce you to the Senior Tutor? He's been hoping to speak with you about the law students. They have been without a Tutor since poor Robert left us."

"But I know nothing about the law," she said, switching her penetrating stare to him.

"Ah, well, at Cambridge, Tutors are responsible for the emotional rather than academic needs of their students. For that reason, we find it best if they come from a different discipline. Ravi here looks after the Natural Scientists for example."

Gabrielle glanced in surprise at Ravi before turning back to the President.

"Is it a lot of work?" she asked.

"That depends on the students, though it does come with a stipend and an enhanced entertainment allowance."

"Can I choose my own wine? This one is not nice."

Ravi noticed a couple of nearby Fellows glare in her direction.

"Tutors," said Peter, dropping his voice, "can order from the Fellows' wine list. Perhaps we can move over here so I can explain how it works. Please forgive us, Ravi."

"Not at all," he said, grateful for the intervention. "It was lovely to meet you, Gabrielle."

Her magnified eyes swung back towards him.

"And you, Ravi. I look forward to talking more about your research."

Ravi inclined his head. "Enjoy your evening."

As he watched them, the President guided Gabrielle towards a quiet corner of the room. Ravi had a sinking feeling in his stomach. The last thing he wanted was this forceful scientist asking questions about his early research. Particularly when he and Robert had spent half a century trying to keep their findings secret.

"That bad, eh?"

Ravi turned and found Dr Esdee Jones standing alongside him, looking out across the room.

"Only, you look like a guy who could do with a stiff drink."

"Happy New Year to you too, Esdee," he said, smiling at the handsome black woman whose gown looked a lot less moth-eaten than his own. "A gin and tonic wouldn't go amiss perhaps."

"Good luck with that, fella. I could do with a shot of bourbon, but the Fellows' Steward would have a fit."

Ravi could imagine. Some things were just not done. "So," he said, "how are you finding the role of Dean?"

Jones, a criminologist from Harvard and former public defender turned academic, had been the obvious choice for the role after Robert's death.

"Interesting."

"A very English response, forgive me for saying."

"Damn! Really? This place must be getting to me."

"It has a habit of doing that."

"Let's just say that some of the things the students get up to would be enough to drive anyone to drink. You know a Giles Chamberlain?"

"Our paths have crossed, yes," he said, thinking, *What's he done this time?*

"I've got the University Proctor's office wanting me to throw the book at him for some stunt he pulled last term."

"Nothing too serious, I hope."

"Hell no, just high jinks. But they want us to make an example of him."

A gong sounded, and the Fellows' Butler appeared at the Green Room door.

"Ladies and gentlemen, please make your way upstairs to dinner."

Ravi caught sight of Gabrielle Dutour looking at him from across the room. He turned towards Esdee.

"Shall we? Only I'd be interested to hear your views on punishment vs community service orders."

"Sure. But we'd better hurry. I want to get a seat close to one of those fires."

"More English by the day," Ravi replied.

Her deep chuckle made him smile as they headed for the door.

Chapter Six

It was late when Nick, weighed down by his backpack, trudged through the Forecourt Gates of St John's College. The train from Mansfield had taken longer than he'd expected, the snow causing problems on the line.

When it had finally arrived at Cambridge station, the queue for taxis was so long that Nick had decided to walk instead. By the time he'd made it back to College, his feet were freezing, and the new trainers he'd received for Christmas were soaked.

Not a great way to start the term, he thought as he pushed open the glass double doors and stepped into the warmth of the Forecourt Lodge.

"Mr Wood. Welcome back."

Bert the Head Porter stood behind the counter.

"Hi, Bert. Happy New Year."

"Happy New Year to you too. Have you had a good break?"

"Yeah, good. You?"

"Too quiet for my liking. Still, it's good to see the students coming back. Plenty of Redboys I see."

"Rugby training starts tomorrow."

The Porter nodded. "I thought so. I saw a few red jumpers heading over to the Bar earlier."

"Yeah, I'm running late. Listen, I was wondering if I can pick up my things from storage?"

"Of course." Bert turned to the Porter sitting at the bank of CCTV screens. "Shirley, can I introduce you to Mr Wood, one of our first-years. Shirley's just joined us this term."

"Hello, Mr Wood," said the woman, her broad, pleasant face breaking into a smile.

"Nick," he said.

"Nick here very kindly offered up his room for interview candidates in December," continued Bert. "We stored his belongings in the New Court cellars. Would you mind unlocking the door for him, Shirley?"

"Sure, no problem," she said, getting up from the desk. "I'll get the keys."

A few minutes later, Nick and Shirley headed over the Bridge of Sighs, its covered roof offering them some measure of protection against the elements. When they reached the New Court cloister, they turned towards B staircase, which stood in the corner of the square, its entrance light casting an orange glow over the surrounding snow.

Once inside, Nick stamped his trainers on the flagstone floor, as much to restore some circulation to his toes as to remove the compacted ice from their treads. Shirley blew on her hands and looked around the cavernous hallway.

"So where are these cellars then?"

"Over here," he said, leading her over to a doorway tucked behind the main staircase.

Once Shirley found the relevant keys, she unlocked the heavy door, and a damp, musty smell wafted up from below. Nick was reminded of the horror movies he and his brother used to watch at night when his parents were out. The ones where they'd yell at the heroes not to enter the darkened cellars, armed with nothing more than a torch. He saw Shirley pull a flashlight from her pocket.

"Here," he said, reaching over and switching on the cellar lights.

"Oh, right," she replied. "That's good."

They descended the steps to a landing with three archways leading off it.

"Which way now?"

Nick looked around. The last time he'd been here, he was loaded down with boxes and Bert had led the way.

"I think it might be this one on the left."

They headed down a narrow passageway that led to a small room with a set of steps running up into the dark. There were patches of moss on the brickwork and the sound of water lapping above them.

Shirley shone her torch. "Is that the river up there?"

"Could be," he said.

They climbed to a small landing and saw the steps descend down to a low arched doorway. Moonlight reflected off the water beneath the rotted timbers.

"Some sort of loading bay," he suggested.

"So, no storage boxes then."

"Sorry."

Returning to the hallway, they took the second archway, which led them into a labyrinth of different rooms and corridors. After coming to several dead ends, Nick recognised a network of old pipework running along a wall.

"It's this way, I think."

Following the pipes through a series of passageways, they found themselves in a large room, the walls lined with storage racks. These were piled high with boxes and crates, some covered in mouse droppings, including an old, battered trunk with R.T.F.M. stencilled on the side. Nick had seen those initials before and was trying to remember where when Shirley called out.

"Nick, is this it?"

Turning, he saw the Porter standing by two cardboard boxes with the name "WOOD" marked on the side.

"How d'you work that out?"

"Oh, I don't know. A wild guess, I suppose."

Taking a box each, they retraced their steps through the cellars, emerging at the B staircase entrance. Shirley made sure to turn the lights off before locking the door.

"So, where's your room, Nick?"

"Cripps."

Nick led her from New Court to the 1960s accommodation block at the back of the College. Arriving at A Staircase, he paused to switch his room indicator to IN before heading up to his room on the first floor.

The large bedsit with its metal-framed windows and whitewashed walls looked just as it did when he'd left four weeks earlier. Though he had to admit it smelled a good deal fresher: the odour of drying rugby kit had been replaced by the smell of disinfectant and freshly laundered sheets.

"Thanks, Shirley. You can leave it there."

The Porter set the box down on the desk and peered out at the river flowing beneath the window.

"Nice view," she said, staring towards the College Library and snow-capped Bridge of Sighs.

"A bit different from home," he said.

"Where's that then?"

"Mansfield."

"In the Midlands?"

"You know it?"

"Did a stint there in the 1980s," she said. "During the miners' strike."

"Maybe you bumped into my dad."

"Was he a copper?"

"No, a miner."

"Oh," she said. "Quite possibly."

Nick smiled. "I'll see you around, Shirley. Thanks for your help."

After the Porter had left, Nick dumped his backpack on the bed and hurried out. While he knew the Redboys would be waiting for him in the bar, he wanted to head up to Annabel's room on the top floor and explain why he hadn't been in touch.

Arriving on her landing, Nick was greeted by a deep base thump coming from one of the rooms. He'd just begun knocking on Annabel's door when the neighbouring one swung open and loud music filled the landing. A girl in leather trousers staggered out, the front of her blouse stained red from her neckline down to her exposed navel.

"Piss off, Colin, that wasn't funny," she shouted over her shoulder.

"Come on, Naomi, I was just trying to help," came a voice from inside the room, sounding more amused than concerned.

"Idiot," she said as the door swung shut, muffling the raucous laughter.

For a moment she just stood there, leaning against the doorframe. Long blond hair hung in front of her face as she peered down at her ruined top. Nick was about to ask if she was all right when she looked up.

"What are you staring at?"

But before he could reply, the door swung open again, and another student appeared in the doorway.

"Naomi, it was just a…"

He stopped on seeing Nick. The girl lurched away from him.

"Leave me alone, Colin!"

"Come on," he said, grabbing her arm. "It was just a bit of fun."

"Let go of me!"

"Come back inside."

"No!"

Nick stepped towards him. "She said no."

The boy glared at him. "This doesn't concern you."

Nick took another step forwards. "That's where you're wrong."

Colin let go of Naomi's arm and turned to face Nick.

"Who the hell are you?"

"A friend," Nick said, though there wasn't an ounce of friendship in the way he said it.

The two of them stood facing each other as the bass thumped through the concrete floor.

"Well, friend, I suggest we ask Naomi what she thinks."

Nick just kept staring at Colin.

"It's OK," said Naomi, her voice calmer now. "I'm just going to get cleaned up."

"There you go," said Colin. "The lady has spoken. So why don't you just run along, friend."

Nick stared at him before turning to the girl. "You sure?"

She nodded. "Yeah."

"You see," said Colin, smiling. "That's all settled then, isn't it?"

Nick didn't feel it was settled at all. Naomi must have sensed it could still kick-off, because she said, "Go back inside, Colin. I'll be there in a minute."

"Sure thing, gorgeous." His eyes never left Nick's. "I'll let everyone know you'll be along shortly. After all, the party's just getting started. For invited guests only, of course." He gave Nick a mirthless grin. "Good night, friend."

Backing into the room, Colin disappeared inside. Nick stared at the closing door, aware of the blood pounding through his temples. From somewhere far away, he heard Naomi say, "Thanks." Turning, he realised she was still standing there, watching him.

"You don't have to go back in there," he said.

"Yes, I do." She sighed. "It's my room."

"Do you want me to clear them out?"

"That's not going to go well, is it?"

"Depends," he said, thinking back to the club in Mansfield. "I've dealt with worse."

"For me, I mean. They're my friends."

"Even Colin?"

"He's just protective."

He shrugged. "Your call."

"I'm fine." She smiled and nodded at the other room. "Were you looking for Annabel?"

"Have you seen her?"

"She left with some tall American. They were heading for the Bar."

So Brett's back, Nick thought.

"Right, thanks." He turned for the stairwell.

"Hey, I don't know your name?"

"Nick," he said. "Nick Wood."

"Thanks, Nick."

"No problem." He hesitated. "It's Naomi, right?"

She nodded. "Naomi Clarke."

"You're sure you're all right?"

"I'm fine."

"OK, I'd better go."

"I'll see you around, Nick," she called after him.

As Nick descended the stairs, he didn't feel right about leaving Naomi. Still, it was her choice. And though he would have loved knocking the grin off Colin's face, he didn't fancy getting into trouble with the Dean. Not on his first night back. Besides, he had more pressing concerns.

Last term, Annabel had been captivated by the handsome oarsman from Yale until a rowing accident had seen Brett return to the States for treatment. With the former Olympian back on the scene, how would she react to him now, he wondered?

By the time he reached the ground floor, Nick was already jogging, his footsteps keeping time with the thump, thump, thump of the fading music.

Chapter Seven

Annabel was hit by a wall of noise as soon as she stepped back into the Bar. A roar of laughter came from a group of rugby players sitting around a table covered by half-empty beer glasses. All were wearing red jumpers, some so patched and torn that their shirts were visible through the gaping holes. The College crest could still be made out on most of them, though in some cases it had been stitched, sewn or stapled back on.

Not that this seemed to bother the assembled gathering, who were more concerned with the destination of a ping pong ball bouncing among the glasses. As cheers and groans chorused around the table, Annabel saw a familiar figure standing at the Bar, his red jumper stretched to breaking point across his back.

"Hi Trevor," she yelled above the din, and a bearded face turned towards her.

"Annabel!" The third-year wrapped her in a bear hug and lifted her off the ground. "Happy New Year!"

"Happy New Year to you," she said as he deposited her back on the ground.

"Didn't expect to see you here. What brought you back so early?"

"Boat Club," she said, pointing to the group gathered among the alcoves at the far end of the room. "First outing is tomorrow."

"Who are you rowing for?"

"W3," she said, meaning the women's third boat. "After Novices, I thought I'd try out for Lent Bumps."

"Good for you. Ying said we needed more freshers this year."

"I didn't know Ying rowed?"

"May Bumps only. Doesn't enjoy the cold winter outings."

Annabel looked around for his girlfriend. "Is she here tonight?"

"No. The ADC lot are plotting at The Maypole."

Annabel remembered that Ying, like Giles, was a member of the University's Amateur Dramatic Club.

"Giles too, I take it? I thought they were great in the pantomime!"

"He's due back from Spain, but with this weather, who knows?"

"Oh, so he spent New Year with Raquel?"

"Christmas too," said Trevor, raising a meaningful eyebrow.

"It's serious, then?"

"With Giles, who can tell? Let's just say I wouldn't go buying a bridesmaid outfit just yet."

"Point taken."

"By the way, have you met Gareth?"

He turned to the man-mountain standing next to him, who was loading jugs of beer onto a tray.

"Hey, Gareth! Can I introduce you to Annabel?"

The big man turned and gave her a cheerful smile.

"Ah yes, you're Woody's girlfriend?"

"Just friends," she corrected.

"My mistake," Gareth said, looking around. "Haven't seen him, have you?"

"No, I haven't," she said, feeling a knot tighten in her stomach.

"Well, if you do, tell him he'd better not be late for training tomorrow morning."

"Now the University Varsity match is over," Trevor explained, "Gareth can play for the College again."

"I see," said Annabel.

"You'll have to come along to Cuppers," said Gareth, talking about the inter-College knockout competition. "With Freshers like Woody, John's should have a good chance this year."

"Let's hope so," said Trevor. "It's my final year, so I'm hoping to bow out on a high."

"Anyway, better go," said Gareth, lifting the tray over Annabel's head. "I see supplies are running low! Nice meeting you, Annabel."

"And you!"

The Welshman made his way towards the rugby table and was greeted by a chorus of cheers.

"I'd better join him," Trevor said, loading jugs of water onto another tray.

"What are those for?"

"Captain's round," said Trevor. "A protocol we agreed with the Dean. Senior players like Gareth and me are on the water, so no one has to drink beer if they don't want to. Ensures it all stays harmless." He dropped his voice. "And given what we've got planned for training tomorrow, they'll all wish they'd stuck to water. Start as we mean to go on."

"I see," she said.

"So, if you see Nick, you might want to warn him." He gave her a wink. "Right, I'd better go."

Edging past her, Trevor carried the tray to the table as the ping pong ball landed in a glass of beer and a huge cheer went up. Annabel saw Aden, a well-built Fresher, stand up with his glass to take the applause.

Shaking her head, she turned to look around. There was still no sign of Nick, so she headed back to the boaties' table at the other end of the Bar.

Brett was wedged in the corner surrounded by a crew of female rowers. The place next to him where Annabel had been sitting was now occupied by Clarissa, the long-legged stroke of W2. She was looking up into the big American's handsome features, hanging on his every word as he made a sweeping motion with a plate-sized hand. When he saw Annabel approaching, Brett stopped and gave her the sort of smile that wouldn't look out of place in a toothpaste commercial.

"Make room there, ladies," he said, shuffling away from Clarissa, whose smile faded when she saw who was returning.

Rising from his seat, Brett reached across the table. Taking his hands, Annabel found herself lifted over the collection of glasses and deposited next to him. Face flushed, she noticed a few envious stares from the others.

"Have I missed anything?"

"Just showing the gals the catch and draw," said Brett in his easy Southern drawl. "Firm and smooth."

There was an audible sigh from one of the first-years, which Annabel pretended not to notice.

"So, you're still planning on coaching us this term?"

"Are you kidding? Racing crews down a narrow, twisting river trying to bump the boat ahead of them? I wouldn't miss it for the world!"

"We don't technically have to hit the boat in front," Clarissa said. "Just overlap until they concede."

"Where's the fun in that?" Brett said, grinning. "Bumps is the name, so bumps is the game!"

There was a good deal of laughter at this, though Annabel thought Alice, who rowed at Bow, looked a little uneasy at the prospect of ramming into the stern of another boat.

"No chance of you going for a Blue then?" Clarissa asked when the noise died down. She was of course referring to the Oxford and Cambridge Boat Race, where an Olympian like Brett would have been a shoo-in, if not for his head injury last term.

"Not this year," said Brett, tapping the faint white scar just below his hairline. "But who knows. Next year maybe?"

"You're staying on then?" Annabel asked, surprised.

"My Director of Studies has agreed to an extension to complete my Master's."

"That *is* good news," purred Clarissa, playing with a strand of her long hair.

And not just for Brett, Annabel thought.

"So you'll be seeing a lot more of me, I guess." He grinned. "On the towpath, I mean."

This time there were a good deal more giggles than laughs, and Annabel could understand why. Having Brett as a coach would make those early morning outings all the more bearable. Indeed, she might even welcome the sound of the alarm clock for a change. The American gave her a mischievous wink and Annabel felt her cheeks grow warm. Embarrassed, she looked away and found Nick staring at her from the entrance to the Bar.

"Oh, dear," said Clarissa, her voice cutting across the other conversations around the table. "Someone doesn't look very happy."

Annabel shifted in her chair as Nick continued to stare at her. Like the snow that flecked his hair, the look he gave her was anything but warm.

"Annabel, isn't that your boyfriend?" Clarissa asked.

"We're just friends," she replied, annoyed and embarrassed by the question. But the conversation had already faltered, and her words carried far further than she intended. A few heads turned towards Nick, who stood there, his pallid skin adding to his grim demeanour.

"Clearly," remarked Clarissa.

Before Annabel could respond, a roar of "Woody!"

boomed out from the far end of the Bar. Trevor emerged from the crowd and advanced on the new arrival.

"Better late than never," said the Redboy captain, ushering Nick towards his teammates, who had begun singing the theme song to Toy Story. "Come on, you've got some catching up to do."

Around the boaties' table, the conversation picked up, people having to speak louder to be heard above the singing. Clarissa turned with a satisfied smile to her neighbour and began discussing Erg times. Annabel just sat there feeling deflated.

"Who was that guy?" asked Brett, looking towards the rugby table.

"That's Nick," said Annabel. "He's on my staircase."

"Good looking fella," Brett said, but Annabel barely heard him above the refrain ringing around the College Bar.

"Boy, you've got a friend in me,

Yeah, you've got a friend in me!"

Chapter Eight

Arriving late from the airport, Giles dumped his bags in his room and set off for The Maypole, where he'd promised to meet Ying and the others. The pub, which was just around the corner from the ADC Theatre, was a popular haunt for the Camdram crowd, not to mention the many students living in College hostels by Jesus Green.

First night back and he expected the place would be busy. Even as he approached from Park Street, Giles could see people were already standing outside. Though many of these were smokers, huddled in groups and stamping their feet against the cold, there were plenty of regulars too.

Must be rammed inside, he thought, as he hurried past the human smokestacks and pulled open the door.

The fug of hoppy beer and warm bodies that greeted him was a welcome change to the arctic conditions outside. That and the hubbub of cheerful laughter proved a heady combination. By the time Giles squeezed through the tightly-packed throng and made it to the counter, he had a broad grin on his face.

"Evening, Giles," said the dour-faced barman who was

busy pulling a pint. "Good holiday?"

"Invigorating, Dave," said Giles, thinking of his last night with Raquel. "You?"

"Bit quiet."

"You see, I knew you'd miss me."

Dave snorted. "So, what'll it be?"

"A pint and a Scotch. Separate glasses."

The barman raised an eyebrow.

"Medicinal," Giles explained. "It's freezing out there."

"You're not wrong there," said a person behind him.

Turning, he found a young woman blowing on her hands. Her long brown hair was dusted with snow, and her cheeks had that rosy glow from standing too long in the cold.

"Hi," he said, wondering where he'd seen her before. "Can I get you a drink?"

"I'll have a whisky if you're ordering."

"Another Scotch please, Dave."

"Thanks," she said as the barman headed off.

Giles frowned. "Have we met?"

"You don't remember?"

He was usually so good with faces. But he just could not place hers. She watched him suffer for a bit longer before putting him out of his misery.

"Come on, Giles," she said, switching to a perky Essex accent, "there was me finking you Latin scholars had such good memories."

"Jane?"

The former College waitress, now free of her gothic makeup and peroxide blond bob, smiled back.

"Took you long enough," she said, reverting to what he assumed was her usual voice.

"Sorry, it's just with the hair... your accent... Well, I just wasn't expecting to see you again, that's all."

"I should be flattered, I suppose. In my line of work, it pays to blend in."

You're not kidding, Giles thought, eyeing the young Special Branch officer. The previous term, she'd been part of a surveillance team keeping tabs on Julian Schiller, the sinister Swiss philanthropist funding research programmes in Cambridge. It was only after the man had been arrested that Giles had had any inkling of the former waitress's undercover role.

"So, you're still... doing research?" he asked.

"Just tidying up a few loose ends before the trial."

"Good luck with that," he said.

After seeing Schiller hold a blade to Raquel's throat, Giles hoped the man would be sent down for a long time. Their drinks arrived.

"Cheers," he said, clinking glasses.

Giles savoured the burning sensation as the Scotch went down. Jane though just sipped at hers.

"So," she said, "were you in Cambridge over Christmas?"

"No, I've been staying with Raquel."

"Oh? How is she?"

"Pretty good, considering."

Jane, who had been one of the last to see Raquel's brother alive, nodded.

"I can imagine Christmas would have been tough for her and her family."

"It was," he said, studying her over his glass.

"Listen," he said, "this may sound weird, but there's been something troubling me."

"Go on."

"Afterwards… you know, when everything was cleared away from the Chapel Tower. Was there any sign of Alfonso's remains?"

He'd half-expected her to dismiss his question out of hand. Instead, Jane's eyes never left his.

"No, Giles. Nothing."

"Don't you think that's odd?"

"You tell me." she said, taking another sip of her drink.

"Frankly, yes." Giles thought about the nest of bones, "So none of that other… debris was from him."

"Just that jacket," she said.

"Right, the jacket."

Something didn't add up, and he could tell this woman thought so too. While everyone else in the bar continued their conversations, the pair of them stood there, sipping their drinks. Finally, Jane broke the silence.

"Listen, I need to go. Perhaps we can continue this conversation another time."

"You're staying around Cambridge, then?"

"I'll have to come back, now and again."

"How do I get in touch with you?"

"You don't," she said. "I'll contact you."

"How?"

"I know where you live."

"Of course," said Giles, remembering the time she had

come to his room last term.

"Don't worry, I'll knock first," she said, smiling.

"That's good to know."

"Thanks for the drink, Giles."

She leaned in and, for a moment, he thought she was going to kiss him on the cheek. Instead, she whispered in his ear, "Gupta holds the key."

Before he could ask what she meant by that, she turned and disappeared into the crowd. As Giles stared after her, he caught sight of someone waving at him from the other side of the saloon. Justin, the College's organ scholar, was sitting with the Choir in their usual corner, "lubricating the larynxes" as they were known to do.

Giles raised his beer in greeting. Justin pointed to the ceiling and mouthed the word "Ying!"

Of course, Giles thought, remembering the reason he was here. Giving his friend the thumbs up, he made his way through the crowd holding his pint aloft and out of harm's way.

Upstairs was no less busy, though most people were seated around tables. He spotted Ying was over by the far wall, surrounded by half a dozen familiar faces. She stood up and waved.

"Giles! Over here!"

"Widow Twanky!" Someone called out, referring to the pantomime dame he'd played at the ADC before Christmas.

"Oh, no, it isn't," he replied.

"Oh, yes, it is!" they chorused.

"I see none of you have lost your sense of humour over

the break," he said, returning hugs and handshakes.

Ying leant over the table and gave him a pouty kiss.

"Thought you were a no-show," she said with an admonishing look before resuming her seat.

Giles edged around the table and found a space by the wall.

"Just flew in."

"Trouble with the flights?"

"Flights were fine. It was the train from Stansted that was the nightmare, what with all the snow."

"Yeah, well, you're just in time," she said. "We're about to decide what play we're doing this term."

"Excellent!" He stared at the others. "Nothing too dull, I hope?"

"Some people wanted to do Shakespeare again," said Pippa, a linguist who was just back from her year out in Germany.

"But after the success of the panto," said Saul, a mathematician, "we thought we might do something a little less high-brow."

"And not too heavy, time-wise," said George. "Engineers have exams straight after Easter."

There were groans from the others, followed by an argument about who had the worst workload. With everyone doing different subjects, this was not unusual. Finding time for rehearsals among Supervisions and essays was a constant struggle.

As Giles watched the animated conversation, his mind returned to the former waitress Jane, wondering once again how he'd failed to recognise her. Shaking his head, he took a sip of beer and noticed Ying studying him over her glass.

"OK guys!" She raised her voice to be heard. "We've been through this all before. I'd like to hear what Giles thinks?"

"Hold on, he turned up late remember," protested Saul. "How come he gets a say?"

"Because he's buying the next round," Ying purred.

"Oh, harsh," said Giles.

But it was clear that the others didn't think so. A barrage of drink orders came his way.

"OK, OK. But before I get those, you going to have to tell me what play you've decided on."

"*Pygmalion*," said Pippa.

"What, *My Fair Lady* without the singing?"

"That's the one," Pippa confirmed.

"So, who's going to play Eliza Doolittle?"

"What me, guv'nor?" Ying fluttered her eyes at him. "Being a Londoner an' all."

Giles snorted. "I can see Professor Higgins is going to have his work cut out there. So, who has drawn the short straw then?"

"You mean playing the upper-class, pompous, know it all?" Ying asked.

"The very same."

All heads turned towards him.

"Oh, you're kidding."

"Come on, Giles," said Pippa, "you're made for it."

"Thank you very much!"

"You know what I mean. You'll be brilliant!"

The others began weighing in with flattering reasons as to why he should do it: an iconic role, his last year, a great send-off and other such platitudes. Giles waved these away, all too conscious of his promise to Raquel to discover her brother's fate.

"Guys, I've got a research project to finish, not to mention the small matter of a dissertation to write up. I haven't got time."

"Giles Chamberlain," Ying said. "You're not trying to tell us you've got too much on?"

"Well, yes, I am, actually."

Their loud laughter made heads turn on other tables.

"What?" he said, looking at their incredulous faces.

Wiping her eyes, Ying said, "Giles, you could do all that stuff, and learn the lines of every part, in your sleep."

"Lucky sod," said George.

Ying fixed Giles with a look. "Yer not scared, are yer guv'nor?"

Giles scoffed. "Scared? Me?"

"Sounds like you are."

"Yeah," agreed Saul. "Has Giles finally met his match?"

"What," said Pippa, "upstaged by a girl, you mean?"

"A flower girl no less," added George.

"Now, hold on…" Giles began.

"I fink it's true, me friends," said Ying, putting her hands on her hips. "He's not man enough to handle me."

Giles rolled his eyes, but the others began chanting, "Shame! Shame!"

"Oh, very well," he said, holding up a hand. "I'll do it."

"Yes!" Pippa yelled.

"Drinks all round, me lovelies!" Ying grinned, sliding her glass across the table. "That'll be your round, Professor Higgins!"

******

Sometime later, they left the pub and headed for the ADC Theatre. Giles and Ying said goodbye to the others and turned towards home. Despite the salt that had been spread over the pavements, the latest snowfall made the going treacherous. That and the fact that Giles's final round of whisky chasers "to keep the chill off" had left Ying somewhat unsteady on her feet.

"So, Giles," she said, leaning on him as they slithered along, "How was the lovely Raquel?"

"Sends her love," he said. "She was asking when you and Trevor wanted to visit?"

"Not until after finals. Mum will kill me if I mess them up."

"That's what I love about your mother."

"What, that she's a homicidal maniac?"

"That she cares," Giles said, reflecting on his own parents' indifference.

Ying slipped on the ice, almost dragging him down.

"Steady!" he said, hoisting her upright.

"Tricksy, this ice stuff," she said, "very tricksy!"

They continued on their meandering way towards the squat, circular shape of the Round Church, its snow-covered roof resembling an igloo. Up ahead he saw the spiked iron gateposts of St John's College Forecourt. Behind these rose the Chapel, its tall tower disappearing into the night sky. The memory of wings, claws, and a gaping maw came back to Giles, and with it an uncomfortable feeling that they were being watched.

Glancing up at the snow-capped rooftops, he half expected to see a creature perched there, tracking them from above.

"Who's that over there?"

Ying's question threw him, and Giles looked down at her, confused.

"What? Where?"

His companion was staring along St John's Street towards the Great Gate entrance.

"Over there," she said, waving an arm at the small patch of snow-covered lawn in front of the Chapel.

Giles looked, and noticed a dark outline in the shadow of the buttresses. He stopped and stared, aware of how silent the street had become.

"Chamberpots!"

The yell from behind them made him jump. Ying spun round, slipped and pulled them both down onto the compacted snow. A chorus of laughter rang out. Peering back, Giles saw a cluster of figures approaching from the direction of The Maypole.

"Don't get up on our account!" said Justin as he led the rest of the Choir towards them, his voice echoing off the surrounding buildings.

Smiling, Giles felt the tension ease and began getting to his feet.

"Sounds like this lot are in good spirits," he said, helping Ying up.

"Gin, probably," she said, dusting snow off her backside.

"My Giles, you certainly know how to sweep a girl off her feet," Justin quipped.

"It's a gift. You should try it sometime."

"I prefer a more formal approach." The organ scholar offered Ying his arm. "Shall we?"

"My, a proper Gentleman," she replied, switching to a cockney accent and giving Giles an outrageous wink.

"Come on, my fair lady," he said, taking her other arm and leading her through the Forecourt gates. "Let's get you home."

As they passed the ranks of bikes, half-hidden by snow, Justin began to hum.

"Show me the way to go home, I'm tired, and I want to go to bed."

The tune was taken up by a couple of voices behind him.

"We had a little drink about an hour ago, and it's gone right to our heads!"

More members of the Choir joined in.

"Wherever we may roam, o'er land or sea or fall."

The deep bass sound of the baritones kicked in.

"You will always find me singing this song, show me the way to go home!"

As they approached the Forecourt Lodge, Ying and Giles joined in while Justin conducted the others with his free arm. Pushing through the glass doors, Bert looked up from his copy of the Cambridge News as they rose to a final rousing chorus.

"SHOW ME THE WAY TO GO HOME!"

"Good evening, Gents," said the Head Porter, peering at them over the top of his reading glasses. "The Maypole was it?"

"Indeed, Bert," said Justin. "They've missed us apparently."

"No doubt takings were down over the holidays."

"I don't know what you mean."

"Well, looks like you've been making up for lost time. And picked up a couple of new members by the looks of things."

"Heaven forbid," said Justin. "Giles here has a voice like a scalded cat. Ying, on the other hand, is welcome to join us at any time."

This was greeted with shouts of endorsement from the others.

"In your dreams, boys," Ying said.

"Don't say we didn't ask you. The offer's there any time," Justin replied with a grin as they began filing out. "Good night, Bert."

"Good night, Gents. And mind you keep the noise down," he called after them as the doors swung shut. Shaking his head, he turned back to Giles and Ying. "Now then, what have you two been up to?"

"Plotting," said Ying.

"Sounds ominous."

"This term's play, Bert." She put an arm around Giles. "You are looking at my new leading man."

"Not a Dame, then? My wife and I rather enjoyed your Widow Twanky."

"Why thank you, Bert." Giles bowed. "But no, I've hung up my corsets, for good."

"I see, so what will it be this term, then?"

"*Pygmalion*," announced Ying.

"George Bernard Shaw, isn't it?"

Ying beamed. "It is!"

"So, I take it you'll be Professor Higgins," he said, looking at Giles. "And the lovely Eliza Doolittle?"

"That'll be me, guv'nor."

The Head Porter nodded. "Well, let me know the dates and I'll make sure I go along."

"Ow, thank you Bert."

"Anyway, I'm glad I bumped into you, Giles," said the Porter. "You have an important meeting in the morning."

"I do?"

"The Dean. I put a note under your door. She'd like to see you first thing."

"What for?"

"Didn't say, but she didn't look happy. I wouldn't be late if I were you."

"That doesn't sound good," said Ying. "What have you been up to this time?"

"Search me? I've only just got back. Unless…"

"What?"

"There was that lecture on the last day of term."

"And?" There was a warning note in Ying's voice.

"It's a long story. I won't bore you with it now. I'm sure it will all be fine."

"Well, I'd have an early night if I were you," Bert said.

"The Dean is expecting you at eight, sharp."

"Come on, you," said Ying, linking her arm in his. "Best get you home." She waved at the Porter. "Good night, Bert."

"Good night. And don't forget, Giles. First thing, remember?"

"I won't. Good night."

Stepping out into the frosty air of Chapel Court, Giles found Ying looking up at him.

"Don't say anything," he said. "A storm in a teacup."

"You've met the new Dean, have you?"

"Well, no. I can't say I've had the pleasure just yet." His previous dealings had been with her predecessor, the late Robert Mackenzie, who he'd always rather liked.

"Trevor said she's a real ballbreaker. She read him and the other captains the riot act last term."

In the distance, they heard cheers coming from the College Bar.

"Sounds like Trevor's taken her advice to heart, then."

Ying groaned. "It would be just like the big oaf to get Deaned too."

"Shall we go and rescue him?" Giles suggested.

Ying cast him a sly look. "Depends if you're buying, guv'nor?"

Giles inclined his head. "When you put it like that, my dear, how could any gentleman refuse?"

******

While Giles escorted his leading lady to the Bar, the last remaining late-night revellers either headed off to the clubs in town or retired to their beds. As they did so, an eerie quiet fell on the approaches to St John's College.

The darkened windows of the surrounding buildings looked on its closed gates with glass-eyed indifference and, for a while, nothing stirred to disturb the picturesque scene. Even the air was still, the only movement coming from the crystalline creep of night frost over its metal railings.

When a wintry peace had descended over the snow-covered lawns, the shadow by the Chapel wall shifted, and a hooded figure peered up and down the deserted street. After checking the way was clear, it turned and, placing pale hands against the stonework, began its vertical climb back into College.

Chapter Nine

The mobile phone vibrated and buzzed like an angry insect on the bedside table. Annabel managed to extract an arm from the tangled duvet. She groped for the off button, pressing it until silence descended. For a few moments, she lay there face down on the pillow, knowing she had to get moving before the insidious forces of sleep drew her in again.

In rooms similar to this, all across the College, eight other girls would be dragging themselves from their beds and staring bleary-eyed at watches or digital displays. Faced with the prospect of a near-frozen river, would they, like her, be wondering what madness had driven them to sign up for rowing this term?

Probably, she decided. But there was no backing out now, least of all for her. No cox meant no outing, and a gruelling session on the ergs instead. That was not going to happen on her watch.

Annabel kicked off the duvet and rolled out of bed, her bare feet curling up as they touched the cold parquet floor.

Right, she thought. *Warm clothing. Lots of it. Ready… Go!*

Five minutes later, she stood in front of the mirror,

wrapped up to the eyes in multiple layers of lycra and polyester fleece. She pulled on her new College beanie and stared at her reflection.

"There's no such thing as bad weather," she said, mimicking her grandmother's Yorkshire accent, and headed for the door.

On the way down the stairs, she passed Nick's landing and tried not to think about that awkward moment seeing him in the Bar the night before. And in front of Clarissa too, of all people.

That girl really knew how to press Annabel's buttons. And she was all over Brett, poor guy. So, so annoying. She made a mental note to avoid sitting next to her again at future Boat Club socials.

Hurrying along the Cripps walkway, Annabel ducked into C Staircase and took the steps down to the bike store in the basement. As she unlocked her bike, she thought about Nick. That look on his face in the Bar still made her squirm. And she'd been so looking forward to seeing him too.

Sure, she'd been annoyed that he hadn't called her over Christmas or even answered her texts. But maybe something had happened at home. Something he couldn't or wouldn't talk about. Or someone. An old flame perhaps? The thought made her shudder. No, Nick wouldn't do that. Not Nick.

Annabel decided she'd go and see him on her return. Clear the air over breakfast and start afresh.

Good plan, girl, she thought, rolling her bike up the ramp. *Now, let's get this show on the road.*

Although it was only a five-minute cycle to the College

boathouse, she was glad of her new hat. By the time she'd pulled into the driveway and locked her bike to the railings, her nose was like a block of ice. Cupping her hands, she blew hot breath onto her face as she slithered down the ramp.

The Lady Margaret Boat Club was housed in an old timber clad building with distinctive scarlet doors. Annabel was surprised to see that these were still closed and there was no sign of life. Blades the Boatman was usually here by now, getting everything ready for the early morning crews.

Wandering down the slipway, she looked downriver towards the other boathouses. These appeared as quiet as her own. The same was true of the traditional narrowboats, moored on the opposite bank, motionless save for wisps of woodsmoke rising from their soot-blackened chimneys.

A sudden splash made Annabel jump. From the shadows under the old Victoria Bridge, circular ripples fanned out across the river. Fascinated, she watched as the rings rolled towards her, expanding with perfect symmetry across the still surface. They had almost reached where she was standing when two bright beams of light swept across the water, banishing the shadows. Turning, Annabel saw the boat club's minibus trundle down the snow-covered driveway and come to a skidding halt. The driver's door swung open and Blades climbed out.

"Happy New…" she began.

"Get away from that edge!" he yelled.

"What…?"

"Move," he said, striding towards her, with a torch in hand.

Annabel did as she was told, surprised by his reaction.

"Sorry. I just heard a splash, that's all."

"A splash? Where?" The Boatman stared past her at the ripples now retreating back across the river.

"Near the bridge. I couldn't see where exactly."

Blades shone his torch over the surface, but didn't say anything. He looked as if he was searching for something.

"Blades? Is something wrong? It's just you seem a bit upset."

Frowning, he turned to her, and Annabel was shocked by the intensity of his gaze. Finally, his expression softened.

"Sorry." He sighed. "I was just worried, that's all. Seeing you so close to the edge. You know, with all this ice."

"Oh, OK," she said, though something about his explanation didn't ring true.

"I'd best put some more salt down. You've got an outing I take it?"

"Yes, first one this term. Brett's taking us out."

"Is he now?" he said, glancing once more at the water before turning to the boathouse. "Best get things ready then."

Once inside, Annabel went to collect her equipment and life jacket from the cox room on the first floor. By the time she returned downstairs, there was a tall figure waiting for her.

"Morning, Annabel!"

In the confined space of the old Boathouse, Brett's smile, like everything else about the American, seemed larger than life.

"Morning," she said.

"Looking forward to getting out on the river?"

"Yeah," she lied, as other members of the crew began arriving. One or two looked a little bleary-eyed, though each seemed to perk up on seeing their new coach.

"So, who else are we waiting for?" Brett asked, looking around.

Annabel checked the other familiar faces. "I don't see Stroke," she said, referring to Katie, a first-year lawyer who had spent the last term sitting opposite her in the stern of the boat.

"Here I am!"

To her surprise, Annabel saw Clarissa enter the boathouse. She gave Brett a bright smile as she joined the huddle, the others parting to make way for the new arrival. Annabel just stared at her and noticed that, while most of them looked like they had just got out of bed, the third-year had somehow found time to apply makeup.

"Ah yes," Brett said, "I forgot to mention that Clarissa has kindly offered to join W3 this term. With Katie doing such a good job in the Novices, the women's captain was happy to give her a run in W2."

There was a buzz among the rest of the crew and smiles for their new Stroke, who stood there looking immaculate in matching top and leggings.

"OK, then," said Brett. "Let's get the boat out on the water. I'll see you outside."

As cox, it was Annabel's job to issue instructions to the crew when performing the tricky manoeuvre of moving the boat from its storage rack and out onto the river. While this was something that Annabel had done countless times last term, having a senior oarswoman like Clarissa at Stroke made her nervous. And with Brett watching too, she wanted to make a good first impression.

Their boat, a white shell with red trim on the bow and stern, was stored on the racks, sandwiched between two other eights. After the squad lined up alongside their respective stations, Clarissa turned to her.

"Don't forget the chocks."

Annabel bit back a retort, knowing full well this was the first step in the procedure.

"Got it," she said. "Chocks!"

The crew removed the small wooden wedges under the hull of the upper boat to raise its riggers out of the way. And before her new Stroke could speak again, Annabel called out, "Hands-on! Sliding on three. One, two, three!"

If Clarissa was surprised by Annabel's brusque manner, she gave no indication as the crew slid the boat out on its metal supports.

"Lifting on three. One, two, three!"

Eight pairs of hands lifted it clear.

"OK, let's take her out. Go."

The crew walked the boat down to the water's edge, where Blades stood waiting, having just spread another layer of salt over the compacted snow.

"OK, ready. Heads on three. One, two, three."

As one, the crew swung the boat over their heads, each member moving to stand under it. Clarissa was facing

Annabel now, her cheeks blowing out as she and the others took the strain. Their eyes met, both knowing this was the tricky part. They were standing inches from the edge of the river with £25,000 worth of College equipment suspended above them. Annabel gave the command.

"Roll her in!"

The crew swung the boat over and down in a graceful arc.

"Gently," she instructed as they bent over and laid the boat with a quiet slap on the surface of the river.

"Good job," said Brett. "Get her rigged up while I head over to the towpath."

Half the crew went off to get the oars, and Annabel saw Blades give her an approving nod.

"Not bad," said her new Stroke.

"Thanks," she said.

"Not you, him."

Clarissa was watching Brett mount his bike and set off up the ramp. "So, what's the story with you and our American friend?"

"What do you mean?" Annabel asked as the other turned back to her.

"How come an Olympic oarsman is coaching a College boat. A bit unusual, don't you think?"

"Not really," said Annabel, feeling her face grow warm. "He's just a friend, that's all."

"Another one?"

"Sorry?"

"That rugby player. What's he called, again?"

"Who, Nick?"

"That's the one. You've got quite a friendship group there."

Before Annabel could respond, Brett called from the opposite bank.

"Come on Cox. Let's get everybody on board!"

Flustered, she called back, "OK, Coach!"

Once everyone was in their seats with the oars secured, they pushed off. The smooth fibreglass shell glided over the surface of the water, and Annabel adjusted the rudder cords to line them up in the centre of the river.

"Cox," Brett said, "I want you to take them out slowly until we get past the boathouses."

"Got it," she replied.

"Stroke?"

"Yes, Coach?" said Clarissa, turning to give him a dazzling smile.

"Keep it slow and steady. I want everyone to concentrate on getting the timing right. No rushing."

"Slow and steady," said Clarissa, and turning to Annabel, "sounds good to me."

Annabel couldn't believe this girl.

"OK, Cox, take them out."

Focusing back on the boat, Annabel spoke into her head microphone.

"Right, girls, let's make this a good one. Come forwards!"

The crew slid forwards as one, extending their arms so that their blades lay flat on the water.

"Ready!"

They squared their blades.

"Light pressure, go!"

Annabel felt a thrust in the small of her back as eight blades bit into the water. The crew drove their knees down and drew the oars into their chests. There was the swish of release as the blades came clear and the boat cut through the water. Clarissa came forward again and repeated the stroke, the rest of the crew following her lead.

In the quiet of the early morning, Annabel listened to the creak of riggers and the splash of oars as they established a steady rhythm. All thoughts of Nick and Brett faded away as she focused on the eight women in front of her. It was clear that Clarissa knew her stuff, and Annabel could feel the crew match her confident stroke.

"Looking good, ladies!" called Brett from the bank.

Peering ahead, Annabel could see crews from other colleges still getting their boats ready. For the moment the river in front of them was empty.

"OK, girls," said Annabel. "Let's show them what a top Maggie crew looks like."

Faces set, they rowed past the other boathouses, their blades catching the water in perfect unison. Annabel called out the rhythm as LMBC W3 glided by, leaving eight symmetrical puddles in their wake.

And between these, a few feet behind its red-tipped stern, an indistinct trail of bubbles tracked the boat's progress, unnoticed by anyone, least of all its preoccupied cox.

Chapter Ten

Legs burning, chest heaving, Nick stumbled on with the dead weight of Aden's body over his shoulders. Behind him, he could hear the others chasing, their footsteps muffled in the snow.

"Come on, bro," gasped Aden in his ear. "You're almost there."

Five steps, four steps three, two, one, done!

Nick sank to his knees beneath the rugby posts, his training buddy rolling off his back to lie in the snow alongside him. Other pairs came staggering up and collapsed across the line near them. For a while, he just knelt there on all fours, sweat stinging his eyes as he sucked in deep lungfuls of frosty air. Next to him, Aden looked wrecked, his barrel of a chest heaving up and down.

"Let that be the last..."

Nick felt the same way, though he didn't trust himself to speak. All through the holidays, he'd been looking forward to running out on the playing fields again. But with snow covering the pitches, Trevor and Gareth had organised a fitness session instead. And it had been a beast. Shuttles, pyramids and sprints, always in pairs, with little or no time for recovery, just like in a game.

As he fought to keep the contents of his stomach down, Nick regretted those beers the night before. He should have stuck to water as usual. But after seeing Annabel cosying up to the good-looking American, he'd not held back.

Dumb, dumb, dumb, he thought.

Mind you, he wasn't the only one who was suffering. Nearby, the half-back pair of Sam and Kyle, the comedians in the squad, were both doubled over, unable to utter a word, witty or otherwise. Elsewhere, bodies were sprawled in the snow or bent over, saliva or worse frozen to their lips. Trevor, who still looked relatively fresh, jogged over.

"OK, boys. That'll do for today. Gather round!"

Nick saw Aden close his eyes and mouth what he suspected was a silent prayer of thanks to the heavens. A shadow fell over them, and he looked up to find Gareth standing there. The University Blue looked fresh as a daisy.

"How are you boys doing?"

"Fine," Nick lied.

"Come on. The Skipper wants to talk."

Nick got to his feet and held out a hand to Aden, who took it.

"Cheers, bro."

Together they headed over to join the other players, gathering around Trevor.

"In a huddle, boys. You know how it's done."

Linking arms with Gareth and Aden, Nick joined the circle around their captain, steam rising from their sweat-stained tops.

"Remember today, boys. If we want to win Cuppers this year, this is what it costs. Fitness wins matches. When it gets to those last twenty minutes," said Trevor, "we need to be ready. Same intensity. Same commitment. Because of sessions like this."

Nick stared at the others, faces dripping with sweat, and saw their eyes lift towards their captain.

"We've not won Cuppers since I've been here, but this year's going to be different."

He had their attention now.

"We may not be the biggest," he looked at Gareth. "We may not be the fastest," he stared at Nick. "Good-looking, maybe," he smiled at Aden.

"Thanks, Skipper."

"But we will be the fittest. And we will keep running to the final whistle. Agreed?"

"Agreed!" Nick responded with the others.

"So, this is what we're doing. Three mornings a week. Everyone together. As one. Redboys!"

"Redboys!" they shouted.

"And again, Redboys!"

"Redboys!"

The fierce growl made the hairs rise on the back of Nick's neck. He felt a togetherness here, not just from the press of bodies, but from the sense of brotherhood that they were forging. Something they would need for the campaign to come.

Trevor must have sensed it too, because he smiled. "Good stuff, boys! Same time Thursday morning." And this time there were no groans.

The circle broke up as people went to retrieve discarded tops and hats. Nick turned and began walking with Aden towards College, the Chapel Tower visible in the distance. Gareth came over to join them.

"How are you doing, boys?"

"You really want to know?" said Aden.

"Rough," admitted Nick, "after last night."

"Ah, yes," said Gareth. "Water next time, perhaps?"

"Hell yeah," said Nick.

"Teetotal from now on," agreed Aden. "At least until the final."

"I'll hold you to that," said Trevor, who had jogged up behind them.

"No problem, Skipper. I wouldn't want this finely tuned body looking flabby as I run out."

"For your army of admirers, you mean?"

"You got it."

They crossed Queen's Road and entered the main College site. As they walked between the avenue of lime trees, Gareth and Trevor began discussing training drills. Aden turned to Nick.

"So, how was Christmas?"

"OK, I suppose."

"That good, eh?"

Nick sighed.

"My brother's having problems with some kids at school."

"Oh yeah?"

"Yeah. Me being here doesn't help."

"I get you, bro. My mum misses me too."

They walked on in silence.

"Still," Aden added, "she wouldn't have it any other way."

"How so?"

"Went mental when I got in. Never seen her so happy. I bet your brother was the same."

Nick remembered Charlie's celebration around the kitchen table and smiled. "Yeah."

"So, we got no choice, have we?"

"What do you mean?"

"We smash it, bro! Make 'em proud. Show them it was worth it. Know what I mean?"

"I suppose so."

They crossed the little bridge over the Bin Brook, where the paths diverged, and Nick stopped.

"Hey, listen, I'm going this way," he said, indicating New Court.

"You're not coming to the Buttery, then?" Aden asked. "I can almost smell the bacon from here."

Nick shook his head. Given the state of his stomach and his finances, he wasn't sure he could manage a full English. Besides, he wanted to catch Annabel and explain about his phone.

"I'll see you Thursday morning."

"Seven o'clock, right?"

"I'll be there." Nick turned towards the Eagle Gate.

"And remember, no beer!" Aden called after him. "I don't want you slowing me down!"

Nick made his way back to Cripps A Staircase. He had just reached his landing, and was wondering if Annabel would be up yet, when he heard footsteps coming down the steps. Glancing up, he half-expected to see her hurrying to breakfast, but saw that it was Naomi instead.

Annabel's neighbour was wearing riding boots, roll-neck jumper and a navy blue trench coat. Nick thought she could have come straight from a cover shoot for Vogue magazine.

"Oh. Hi, Nick" she said.

"Hi," he replied.

"You're up early."

"Training."

"Of course."

There was an awkward pause as Nick stood there, feeling grubby in his sweat-soaked rugby gear. "Listen, I…" he began, but she interrupted him.

"Did you find her?"

"Sorry?"

"Annabel. Last night?"

"Oh. Yes, thanks."

Naomi nodded and there was another long pause.

"Nick, about last night," she said, approaching him. "I just wanted to say thanks."

She stopped so close that he could smell her perfume.

"No problem," he said, aware of how much he must stink.

"No, I mean it." She reached out and touched his arm.

The sound of footsteps coming up the stairs made them both turn. Annabel appeared fresh-faced in her rowing gear, and stopped dead. Nick saw the colour drain from her cheeks.

"Oh," she said. "Sorry, I… didn't mean to disturb you."

Naomi smiled. "Don't apologise, Annabel. I was just thanking Nick for last night."

Annabel stared. "Last night?"

Naomi looked embarrassed and turned to Nick. "Anyway, you were great. Thanks."

"No problem. Any time."

Then she was skipping down the stairs, coat billowing behind her. Annabel stared after her, and when she looked up at Nick, her mouth was a thin line.

"Sorry about that," he said. "Listen, I'm glad I caught you…"

Annabel cut him off. "I'm late."

"Oh, I…"

She strode past him.

"Wait, Annabel…?" Nick began again.

But she was already hurrying up the stairs. He listened to her fading footsteps until they were cut off by the sound of a door slamming. Nick was left alone on the stairwell wondering, not for the first time, what the hell had just happened.

Chapter Eleven

A piercing white light flooded his eyes, and Giles raised a hand in front of his face.

"Giles Chamberlain! For the last time, get up!"

Blinking, he peered through his fingers at the figure standing by the curtains of his Second Court room.

"Rose?"

"Who else would it be?" said his bedder, looking down at him, hands on hips.

"What are you doing in here?"

"Bert told me I had to get you up and looking presentable."

Giles thought for a moment. Bert? Then he remembered his appointment with the Dean.

"What time is it?" He asked, sitting up.

"Half-past seven."

"Oh, thank goodness," he sighed, laying back down.

"You're not in trouble, are you?"

"Not really," he said, hoping he was right. "I've got a meeting with the Dean at eight."

"In that case, you'd better get a move on," said the bedder, heading for the door. "I'll leave you to get changed, but if you're not ready in a quarter of an hour, I'm coming back in, dressed or not."

The door closed with a thud. Giles eased himself up, his empty stomach grumbling. He shuffled up his sloping floor towards the bathroom cupboard concealed behind the wood-panelled wall and didn't bother looking in the mirror. After last night's session, it wasn't going to be pretty. Instead, he spent the next few minutes brushing his teeth, and splashed water over his face and hair until it hung in damp blond curls around his ears.

By the time Rose returned, he had managed to clean himself up and was dressed in jeans and his one decent shirt, sitting at his desk reading the Dean's summons.

Dear Mr Chamberlain,

I have received the attached from the Faculty of Earth Sciences regarding an incident on 4th December at the Mill Lane Lecture Theatre.

I would be grateful if you would attend my room at C1 Second Court on Tuesday 18th January at 8.00am to discuss the matter in person.

I look forward to seeing you then.

Sincerely yours,

Dr E. Jones

Dean

C1 Second Court.

There was a two-page report attached, including a statement from the Professor whose lecture he had hijacked before Christmas. Reading through the transcript, he noted that the complaint hadn't come from the lecturer herself, but from an unnamed student.

"How are you doing?" asked Rose.

"Just reading the summons."

"Well, at least you look half-decent," she said. "Come on, you need to go."

Giles folded the note and rose from his chair.

"Thanks for waking me up, Rose," he said, grabbing a fleece from his wardrobe.

"Don't thank me, thank Bert. And mind what you say to Dr Jones. I clean her rooms too, and she doesn't strike me as a person who'll take any nonsense."

"Would I do that?" he said.

Rose ignored him. "Just take your punishment and get on with the rest of the term."

"You sound like my defence lawyer."

"I'm warning you, Giles," she said, wagging a finger.

"OK, OK," he said, holding up his hands. "No funny stuff. I get it."

"I hope you do. I don't want you messing up your final year."

"I won't. Trust me."

"Hmph." Rose didn't sound convinced.

Giles stuffed the summons in his pocket and headed for the door. Pausing in the doorway, he turned to his bedder.

"Rose, do you think I have time to buy flowers?"

"Sorry?"

"Or chocolates? Flowers or chocolates. I can never decide."

"Giles..." he heard the warning in her tone.

"For Bert, Rose. As a thank you."

"I... What?"

"Don't worry, I'll ask the Dean. See what she thinks."

He gave the bedder a wink and closed the door before she could reply.

Jogging down the spiral staircase, Giles emerged onto the snowy whiteness of Second Court. He was greeted by a snowman that he and the rugby boys had made after Trevor had escorted Ying back to her room. Breathing in the cold air, he felt his spirits rise as he headed across the square, whistling the theme tune of Frozen.

The wooden name plate at the foot of C staircase confirmed that Dr E.R. Jones was IN. Uniquely in Second Court, the Dean had an entire staircase to herself as the other floors were taken up by the Fellows' Lobby and Combination Room. Giles always felt this was a deliberate ploy to ensure miscreants had time to contemplate their fate as they climbed the well-worn steps.

In his case, the state of his stomach was of more immediate concern. By the time he reached the top of the stairs, his insides were sounding like First Court's plumbing.

Let's hope this doesn't take long, he thought as the Trinity clock began chiming the hour and he knocked on the door to the rhythm of Let it Go, Let it Go.

"It's open!" came a voice from within. Twisting the brass doorknob, Giles entered.

Like many of the rooms in Second Court, the Dean's office shared the same wood panelling as his own. The difference was that this room was huge by comparison. Its carpeted floor stretched the entire width of the building and was twice as long with hallways leading off it. The fireplace dwarfed his own, and facing it were two large sofas on either side of a coffee table that was the same size as his bed.

Giles turned to the desk that was covered in books and facing the window. Sitting in front of it on a high backed leather chair was the room's only occupant, peering at a computer screen and writing notes on a yellow legal pad.

"Happy New Year, Dr Jones," he said. "You wanted to see me?"

Her head turned, and her dark eyes studied him.

"Take a seat, please, Mr Chamberlain. I'll be with you shortly."

"Of course. Take your time."

"Oh, I will," she said with emphasis.

Too late, he remembered his bedder's warning. *Strike one*, he thought.

While he went over to sit on the nearest sofa, Dr Jones continued to study her laptop screen and make notes. Giles placed her summons on the coffee table and stared at the surroundings.

Bookcases lined the room, their shelves bowing under the weight of legal tomes, the gold embossed lettering on their spines glinting in the morning sunlight. Framed photographs hung on the walls, showcasing an immaculately dressed Jones standing with various dignitaries, including Police Chiefs, District Attorneys, and politicians.

In front of Giles, a stack of Harvard Law School coasters sat on the coffee table alongside a bowl of nuts and an industrial-sized set of nutcrackers. *A nice bit of subliminal messaging*, he thought, reinforcing Rose's view that this was not someone to be messed with.

The Dean closed her laptop with a snap and rose from her chair.

"Can I get you a glass of water, Mr Chamberlain? You look a little pale."

"No, I'm fine thanks," he said, not sure if his rather delicate stomach would cope with anything just now.

As she crossed the room to sit on the sofa opposite, he noticed a gold crucifix hanging from a chain around her neck and made a mental note not to use any words that might offend a churchgoer.

Settling back in her chair, Jones placed the legal pad on her lap and a pen between her manicured nails. For a moment, they both stared at each other across the coffee table. Giles thought she looked like a pitcher sizing up the incoming hitter.

OK, lady, he thought. *Let's play ball.*

"So, Mr Chamberlain, no doubt you will have read the report I sent you."

"I have, Dr Jones, thank you."

"I wonder whether you would like to explain yourself."

"In what way, exactly?"

"Why you thought it would be acceptable to turn up to a lecture at the Faculty of Earth Sciences... buck naked."

Giles was about to point out that he didn't turn up naked. He had removed his clothes towards the end of the lecture. But with his bedder's words ringing in his ears, he decided to leave that one. Being pedantic at this point in proceedings was not going to do him any favours.

"I was raising money for charity."

"Charity?"

"Yes, a local homeless charity, Winter Comfort."

Dr Jones stared at him.

"How, exactly?"

"I'd set up a Facebook campaign where people watching the video could make donations." She made a note on her pad. "I also had an affiliate link to generate additional revenue every time the video was downloaded from YouTube."

More notes. "I see. And what was this campaign called?"

"We All Like Fig Leaf Pudding."

She glanced up from her pad.

"That was the melody on the video," Giles added, beginning to hum the tune.

"Thank you, Mr Chamberlain," she said. "I am aware of the carol."

"Of course," he smiled. "I was hoping it would appeal to people's festive spirit."

"And did it?"

"I like to think so."

"So, how much money did you raise?"

"Just short of £7,000," he said.

"£7,000," she repeated.

"Well, £6,986.55 to be precise."

Dr Jones wrote the number down.

"My goal was £1000, but once the algorithms kicked in, it really took off."

"As did your clothes."

"Well, yes. Apart from the fig leaf."

"The fig leaf?"

"Hence the campaign name. I thought that once word got around, anyone searching for keywords like 'fig leaf' or 'pudding' would find the donation page. As it was, the 'pudding' contingent – mainly middle-aged housewives – proved particularly generous."

"I see," said Dr Jones

It was all true, of course. He had the Facebook analytics and Just Giving receipt for Winter Comfort to prove it. Though he'd noticed that none of this had appeared in the official report from the University Proctor's office. *Perhaps they aren't on Facebook*, he thought.

Giles found that the Dean was studying him over her glasses, so he gave her his most earnest smile. He was half-hoping this would provoke her into asking for evidence. That would be a home run for sure.

However, when it came to poker faces, Dr Esdee Jones was up there with the best. Giles couldn't tell whether he'd hit the ball out of the park or been caught on the fence. So, it was with some degree of anticipation that he waited for her response. When it came, the curveball was well disguised.

"I can appreciate you wanting to support a homeless charity, Mr Chamberlain. Given the winter we've just had, I wish more people would."

Here comes the but, he thought.

"Needless to say, your methods have not endeared you to the University authorities. The Proctor's office has been in touch with me asking that I send a strong signal to the student community to discourage these sorts of antics."

Giles felt the first tingle of unease at this, made worse by his stomach making a noise like a cow in labour.

"Sorry," he said.

Jones just stared at him.

"Have you ever been to Detroit, Mr Chamberlain?"

"No, I haven't," he said truthfully.

"My folks were dirt poor. They had no money to finance our studies."

Giles decided to keep quiet, wondering where this was going.

"I used to get up early to go clean at a local boarding house before school. Afterwards I'd return and iron sheets. You ever iron sheets, Giles?"

"My dress shirt," he said without thinking.

"I bet you did," she said, and there was a hard edge to her voice that told Giles he'd just swung again and missed. *Strike two.*

"One thing you learn when you clean after other people," she continued, "is that all those hours doing repetitive tasks, give you plenty of time to think. Helps you get clarity and perspective. It did for me anyway."

She looked at one of the portraits on the wall of a young Dr Jones with an academic gown and mortarboard.

"By the time I was sixteen, I knew I wanted to go to College, and when I had the opportunity, I took it. With both scrubbed hands."

Giles looked at her manicured nails and raised an

eyebrow, realising too late that she'd seen him do it.

Oh crap, he thought, *strike three.*

"Forty hours community service," said the Dean.

"Forty hours?"

"Five hours a week for the rest of term should satisfy the University authorities."

"But I have play rehearsals," he said, thinking of what Ying would say when he told her.

"I would have thought that after last term's stunt, most people would have seen quite enough of you by now."

Giles just stared at her. Forty hours was a serious amount of community service.

"I'm sure that Housekeeping will have plenty of jobs to help you reflect on the choices you have made. I'll be asking them to send me an attendance record each week, so make sure you don't let anyone down. Is that understood?"

"Yes, Dr Jones." He was too shocked to argue.

She rose and headed back to her desk.

"Good. And I'm sure I won't need to tell you, Mr Chamberlain, that I don't expect to see you here again this term. If I do, you may find that I have lost my sense of humour."

Giles got to his feet, trying to recall any hint of humour in their conversation.

"And Mr Chamberlain?"

He turned and saw her sitting at her desk, peering through her glasses at the laptop screen.

"Get some food inside you. You sound like a sick dog."

Giles closed the door behind him and headed for the Buttery, feeling a good deal more sober than when he had arrived.

Chapter Twelve

Ravi leaned over the Kitchen Bridge and peered down at the river, hardly daring to breathe. A thin layer of ice had formed along the banks, its glassy surface reflecting the pale sky above as he waited for the intruders to appear.

Sure enough, the first of the Canada geese emerged from the shadows, gliding over the water, oblivious to Ravi's presence. It was not alone. More followed, forming a silent procession slinking towards Trinity's distant grounds.

As if sensing his hostile gaze, the matriarch glanced around and spotted him. A warning honk caused the others to arch their necks and stare back at Ravi who rose from his vantage point to glare after them. More honks followed as they recognised their long-standing adversary.

As a member of the Gardens Committee who walked the riverside path most mornings on his way into College, Ravi was all too aware of the menace these creatures posed. The amount of foul-smelling excrement each bird was able to produce never ceased to amaze him.

For decades he had encouraged the Committee to wage a non-lethal campaign against these trespassers. A whole arsenal of countermeasures had been deployed over the years, from bank-side fencing to ultrasonic alarms. However, it wasn't until this autumn that the College gardeners had come up with an unlikely but highly effective solution. A plastic coyote, the native predator of the North American wilderness, had been deployed in different locations along the banks.

When Ravi and the other members had first been told of the plan, there had been a good deal of scepticism.

"It'll just end up as a trophy in some student's room," one Fellow had remarked, and the Domestic Bursar had asked whether it came with a money-back guarantee. However, they had agreed to the proposal, more in desperation than in any genuine belief that it would work.

Fido, as he soon became known, made his first appearance in November, and much to the Committee's surprise, he proved an immediate success. Not only did the geese begin giving the St John's grounds a wide berth, but they also migrated instead to the unprotected lawns of its neighbour, Trinity College.

So, while the New Court Paddock was soon restored to pristine condition, Trinity's Backs now looked and smelled like an avian latrine. An unforeseen, though deeply gratifying, consequence of the new countermeasures, as far as Ravi was concerned.

As the unwelcome flotilla disappeared around the bend of the river, he turned to stare across the unsullied white of the Paddock. This was now populated by a recently formed fellowship of snowmen and snow-women. One of the sculptures, he noticed, bore an uncanny resemblance to the Master. His cheery demeanour was captured to perfection, even down to a pipe protruding at a jaunty angle from its mouth.

What Dominic Lester would make of it, Ravi had no idea, though he suspected the man had enough sense to leave it alone. Removing it would no doubt result in a more exaggerated caricature appearing the next day.

Though I'd have to set my alarm a little earlier to get to work on it, Ravi mused.

The clang of a gate disturbed his thoughts. In the distance, he could make out a group of red-topped figures entering the College grounds via the Queen's Road entrance. Spotting Nick among them, Ravi realised it must be the rugby club on their way to breakfast.

Probably wise to get in ahead of them, he thought, and set off for the Buttery. On entering the College's self-service restaurant, he wondered if Aurelia would be at her usual station behind the Servery. However, he was surprised and not a little disconcerted to find the far less welcoming sight of Gabrielle Dutour waiting inside.

Wrapped in a long coat, she stood on her own by the serving area, peering at her mobile phone. For a moment, Ravi wondered if he could turn back and beat a hasty retreat. But then those large, black-rimmed glasses looked his way, and she called out to him.

"Professor Gupta!"

Given that most of the early morning regulars preferred a quiet start to their day, a few heads turned at this startling breach of etiquette. Aurelia, he noticed, was one of them, raising a disapproving eyebrow from behind the cooked breakfast counter. Ravi did his best to affect a gracious smile.

"Good morning, Gabrielle, what an unexpected surprise."

"The Master told me you eat here most mornings."

"Did he now?" said Ravi, making a mental note to give that particular snowman a good kicking on his way home.

"And, as we were unable to talk more last night, I decided to join you here."

"Of course," he said, picking up two trays and offering her one.

"Is not necessary, I drink only coffee at this hour."

"I see," he said, returning hers to the stack.

"I cannot understand this full English Breakfast that the British love so much," she said. "All that disgusting fat and grease. It cannot be good for you."

Ravi saw Aurelia raise a second eyebrow, which was never a good sign.

"Good morning, Professor. Your usual Full English?" She said, with particular emphasis.

"Yes, please, Aurelia."

Wielding her spatula with brutal efficiency, the waitress filled his plate with bacon, poached eggs and baked beans before handing it over the counter.

Ravi, who had burnt his fingers on more than one occasion, held out his tray, and she deposited the sizzling plate on it. Gabrielle stared at its contents, but thankfully declined to comment as they moved on to the beverage section. Aurelia stalked them on the other side of the serving area.

"Earl Grey tea, Professor?"

"That would be lovely."

"Do you have coffee?" Gabrielle asked.

"Of course." Aurelia indicated two Thermos jugs on the counter.

"No cafetières?"

"We have those too if you want."

"What coffee do you have?"

"You want decaf?"

"*Non*, I meant what origin?"

Ravi winced. Even the most hipster of students had learned long ago not to ask that question.

"Colombian."

"You don't have Ethiopian?"

"No."

"Kenyan?"

"No."

"Any other kind of coffee?"

"No."

Gabrielle shrugged. "Colombian is good." And oblivious to the minefield she had just stomped through, she headed for the seating area.

Adding two cups to his tray, Ravi waited by the checkout while the waitress prepared their drinks. When she returned with his pot of tea and Gabriele's cafetière, he thanked her and escaped before the rugby club arrived. He found Gabrielle sitting at a low coffee table at the far end of the Buttery, and set the tray down before sinking into the armchair opposite.

"So, Ravi," she said, "about your research. I find it intriguing."

"How so?" said Ravi, who was still wondering how to tackle his cooked breakfast from this prone position.

"You publish a series of illuminating papers on Everett's theory of multiple universes, and then you abandon that line of research altogether."

"Oh, I'd hardly say that."

"What? You didn't abandon it?"

"No, I meant that the papers could hardly be described as illuminating. Just a few fanciful ideas from a couple of young academics."

"You and Professor MacKenzie?"

The mention of his friend's name always came as a shock.

"Well, yes. Robert and I enjoyed bouncing ideas around."

"Did you also 'bounce ideas' when Robert revisited your work last year?"

"No, we didn't," said Ravi, trying to hide the edge in his voice.

"Why not? Hawking's M-theory had just been published, and Everett's work couldn't have had a better endorsement. Weren't you keen to get involved?"

"Not really. I always felt that without empirical evidence, our ideas were only speculative."

"But that is my point, Professor," said Gabrielle, her large eyes accentuated by the thick lenses. "Professor Mackenzie suggested to me that he might be able to produce such evidence."

Ravi didn't like how this was going. He bought himself some time by pouring tea.

"Won't your coffee be ready now?" he asked. "If it's like tea, I wouldn't let it stew too long."

Gabrielle stared at the cafetière as if seeing it for the first time and busied herself with plunging the filter and pouring a cup. Ravi used these precious seconds to regain the initiative.

"Gabrielle, may I ask what the ultimate aim of your research might be?"

"The use of wormholes for inter-dimensional travel."

"A noble quest, indeed," he said, managing a smile. "But more the domain of science fiction than academic study."

"You didn't seem to think so in the 1960s."

"We were young back then. Besides, we found no evidence that wormholes could be identified, let alone used in any practical way."

"That is not what Robert suggested to me. Quite the contrary. He felt there was much to be learned from your early work."

"What makes you think that?"

"The papers he prepared for a conference last year."

"Ah, yes, Robert mentioned CERN."

"Not CERN, Ravi. Geneva. He was scheduled to speak there in December."

This one got straight through his defences, and Ravi just sat there, stunned.

"You did not know?" she asked.

"Robert never mentioned it."

"I'm surprised. There were many interested parties lined up to hear him."

I bet there were, Ravi thought. He wondered who Schiller might have invited.

Before Gabrielle could say more, a large contingent of rugby players entered the Buttery and headed towards the Servery. Ravi noticed her frown at the disturbance.

"Perhaps it would be better to continue our conversation in quieter surroundings," he suggested.

"Yes, you are probably right," she said.

Rising from her chair, Gabrielle looked down at his tray.

"But you haven't finished your breakfast," she said, indicating his untouched plate.

"I've rather lost my appetite."

"I'm not surprised," she said, wrinkling her nose. "All that grease cannot be good for you."

Picking up his tray, he was taking it to the collection racks when he heard someone call his name.

"Professor Gupta!"

Turning, Ravi saw Giles approaching them.

"I hope I'm not disturbing you," he said, smiling at Gabrielle. "Only, I was wondering if we might have a chat." He gave Ravi a meaningful look. "On a personal matter."

"I see," said Ravi, relieved by this unexpected intervention. Adopting a serious expression, he turned to his breakfast companion.

"Forgive me, Gabrielle. As a Tutor, I'm sure you'll understand."

Dutour stared at Giles, and for an awful moment, Ravi wondered if she knew the boy wasn't one of his tutees.

"*Bien sur*. I understand. I will send you those papers we discussed."

Ravi smiled. "I look forward to reading them."

Gabrielle nodded and, glancing at Giles, headed for the door. Ravi let out a sigh and turned to find the student studying him with a quizzical smile.

"Tutor, eh, Professor?"

"It's a long story," said Ravi. "Let's just say, I owe you one."

Giles grinned. "Do you mind if I get myself something to eat? They'll stop serving shortly."

"Not at all, you go ahead. I'll find us a table."

Ten minutes later, Ravi stared with satisfaction at his empty plate, while Giles polished off a bacon sandwich.

"So, Giles, you said you had something you wanted to discuss."

"I do, Professor. It concerns Raquel Vidal."

Ravi tensed. "Raquel? How is she?"

"Christmas was difficult."

"I can imagine."

"The thing is, Professor, she wants to know what happened to her brother."

Ravi shifted in his seat. "We know what happened to Alfonso."

"Do we though?"

Ravi frowned. "I'm not sure what you mean."

"We never found Alfonso's remains."

"We all saw his jacket…" he began, but Giles interrupted.

"His remains, Professor. Nothing was ever returned to the Vidals."

"Perhaps they weren't able to identify his…"

"No, Professor. There was no trace whatsoever of Alfonso Vidal. Nothing."

Ravi didn't understand how Giles could know this, but the boy spoke with absolute certainty. For the first time since that dreadful night, he felt a seed of doubt form in his mind. It must have registered on his face because Giles nodded.

"So, if he's not in this world, then he must be somewhere else."

"You think his remains were taken through the portal?"

"Who said anything about remains?"

Ravi stared at him.

"How can you even think that? You saw what the creature did to its other prey."

"Yes, but none were human."

"That doesn't mean Alfonso is alive."

Giles shrugged. "Raquel is convinced that he is."

"Giles, I'm sorry for Raquel, truly I am. But I doubt very much Alfonso could have survived his encounter with the creature. And even if he had and it had taken him…" he glanced around, "to the other place, there is no way he could be alive now."

"But how can we be sure?"

Ravi stiffened. "The gate has been sealed and will not be opened again. The Master was quite clear on that point. As am I."

Giles studied him, but Ravi met his gaze. Eventually, the younger man shrugged.

"I had to ask, Professor. For Raquel."

"I understand, Giles, truly I do. But I cannot help you I'm afraid."

"Understood." Giles sighed and looked towards the rugby players who getting ready to leave. "Listen, Professor, I'd best be off. Things to do and all that."

"A busy term, no doubt."

"You're not wrong there," Giles said, rising from the table. "The Dean's got me doing Community Service for most of it."

"Really?" Ravi said, remembering his conversation with Esdee Jones over dinner.

"No rest for the wicked, as they say."

"I've never thought of you as that, Giles. A rebel, perhaps, but not wicked."

"Must be losing my touch, then," he said with a wink.

Ravi watched as Giles went over to join the rugby boys filing out of the Buttery. There was a burst of laughter.

"Deaned already, Chambers? Must be a record!"

The door swung shut, leaving Ravi to mull over the implications of their conversation. Had Alfonso gone through the portal? Could he still be alive? Surely not. No one could survive in that other world. It was a death sentence. It had to be, or else...

Frowning, he rose from the table and took his tray to the racks for the second time that morning. Ravi was so wrapped up in his thoughts that he didn't even notice the smile Aurelia gave him as he headed for the door.

Chapter Thirteen

Yawning, Giles trudged around North Court, jabbing with his litter picker at the cigarette butts nestled among the flower beds.

Now in his third week of community service, he had a pretty good idea of where the smokers congregated in College. The areas outside the Buttery, Bar, Hall, private dining rooms and Library were particular hotspots. Still, he'd also found mounds clustering around several student windows and staircases. He wondered if the Dean was aware that his morning reparation was also covering the tracks of a good number of fellow wrongdoers.

It wasn't just cigarettes Giles collected. In addition to the usual takeaway containers, plastic cutlery and beer bottles, he'd found gloves, scarves, hats and even the occasional shoe. The black bin bag he held in his hand swung from the weight of five courts' worth of items, which he'd been collecting since Rose had roused him out of bed at eight o'clock.

As Giles headed back into Chapel Court, he reflected that the only detritus dwindling in quantity were the pigeon remains. At the beginning of term, there had been a good scattering of carcasses over the white-covered lawns. But now that the snow, and snowmen, had melted away, so too had the daily dusting of feathers. Glancing up at the Chapel Tower, he wondered why that would be. The Peregrine Falcon couldn't have gone vegan, could it?

"So, Professor, how's your student coming along?"

Turning, he saw Trevor emerge from his staircase.

"What?"

"Eliza Doolittle. Or Ying if you prefer."

"Oh, the play, you mean?" Giles sighed. "I'm not sure. She's a pretty bad case, I'm afraid."

"Tell me about it," said Trevor. "Seriously though, are you enjoying the role?"

"Yes, it's fun."

"I thought it would suit you."

"The stage, you mean?"

"No, being a Professor."

"Very funny, Trev," said Giles.

"I'm not kidding," Trevor said, looking around. "You're made for this place."

"You mean I don't cook, clean or wash for myself?"

"That too," said Trevor. "I've always thought your bedder was a saint."

"Devil, more like. Rose practically threw me out of bed this morning."

"My point exactly. This place is like a boarding school for grown-ups."

Giles snorted. "Trust me, it's a lot more civilised here."

"But you have thought about it, haven't you?"

"Not really," said Giles, though this was not strictly true. When challenged by his parents about his intentions after Cambridge, he had once said he was thinking of staying on to do a PhD, safe in the knowledge that this was one of the few things they would consider an acceptable alternative to a career in the City.

"Well, you should," Trevor said. "You're on for a first, aren't you?"

"Pretty much. Just my dissertation to do really."

"Like I said. Three years for your doctorate and you'd be unstoppable. Or is it insufferable? Probably both."

"I don't know, Trev. I'm not sure that's me."

"So, what then?"

"I thought I might head off to Mallorca. Learn Spanish, teach windsurfing, chill."

His friend snorted. "You'd be bored stiff. Listen, I know Ying wants to see you settled, but that's her dream, not yours. Not that I'm complaining, mind you."

"Yeah, you struck lucky there, my friend."

"True, that girl saved my life, in more ways than one," said Trevor. "But your scholarship was no fluke. If anyone's got what it takes to make it here, it's you, mate."

Giles stopped and looked at his friend. "I thought you studied English, not psychology."

"You don't think reading the great writers helps you understand people?"

"Fair point," said Giles, remembering why his friend made such a good rugby captain.

"Just think," said Trevor. "In forty years, you could end up like him."

Giles turned and saw Ravi's hunched figure emerge from the Second Court passageway and head towards the Library.

"I don't know," he said. "Gupta's all right."

"On his daily pilgrimage, I see," said Trevor.

"To the Library?"

"Every morning, regular as clockwork. You can set your watch by him."

Giles watched as, sure enough, the Professor disappeared inside the revolving door.

"I'd better go," Trevor said. "I've got a lecture."

Giles smiled. "Thanks for the career advice."

"As I said, something to think about," said Trevor, turning to go. "I'll see you around."

"You will," said Giles, watching his friend head off. "And tell Eliza, Professor Higgins is expecting her to be word perfect this evening."

Trevor raised a hand in acknowledgement before disappearing into the Forecourt Lodge.

Giles stood there for a moment thinking about what his friend had said. Not about his future, which he tried to think about as little as possible, but about the Professor's mysterious visit to the Library each day. Why would an astronomer with a lab at the Cavendish be spending so much time in the College Library?

"Only one way to find out," he decided, and he hurried off to the Housekeeping Department to drop off this morning's haul.

A few minutes later, Giles crossed the Library lobby to the reception desk, where a bald head was just visible above the raised wooden counter.

"Good morning, Mr Weston!"

The College Librarian looked up and peered at him over a pair of half-moon glasses.

"Mr Chamberlain. This is an unexpected surprise. What brings you here?"

"You know what they say, Mr Weston. Start as you mean to go on."

"Given that you're partway through your third year, might this be regarded as rather a late start?"

"What was it George Eliot said? It's never too late to be what you might have been."

Mr Weston nodded. "She did indeed."

"Anyway, I thought I'd come and check out a few books. Final year and all that."

"Archaeology, isn't it?"

"Right again, Mr Weston. I have a dissertation to finish."

"Of course. So, does that mean we will be seeing more of you this term?"

"I expect you shall."

"In that case, I shall warn my colleagues about the stranger on the second floor."

"I take it that is where the archaeology section is?"

"It is, Mr Chamberlain," said the Librarian, reaching behind the counter and producing a floor plan. "Have one of these. I wouldn't want you getting lost."

"Heaven forbid," said Giles, taking the map and heading

for the circular staircase. "Though I may be some time."

"Take as much time as you like, Mr Chamberlain. It's why we're here, after all."

Giles climbed the stairs, glancing down at the guide and seeing that the astronomy section was on the Mezzanine floor. This was deserted, so he checked the first, second and third floors as well. The Professor was nowhere to be seen.

Standing in the law section on the top floor, he was about to head downstairs when he saw movement in the arched windows of the Old Library. The seventeenth-century building extended out from Second Court all the way to the river. Through its elegant leaded panes, Giles saw a hunched figure moving between the tall bookcases on the upper floor.

"There you are," he said to himself, watching as the Professor disappeared from view behind an alcove. "Damn."

Giles was about to find a better vantage point when the shadow appeared again, now on the ground floor moving back towards the entrance. Hurrying downstairs, he arrived on the mezzanine in time to spot the Professor emerging into the lobby. The old man strode towards the exit, a troubled expression on his face.

"Have a good day, Professor," said the Librarian.

"And you, Mr Weston," he replied with the briefest of smiles before heading out through the revolving door.

Giles descended to the lobby and approached the counter, where Mr Weston stood waiting for him.

"So, Mr Chamberlain, you found it then?"

"Yes, the archaeology section was just where the map said it would be."

"That is reassuring."

"Tell me, Mr Weston, I noticed that the Old Library is not listed on the plan."

The Librarian raised an eyebrow. "That is because few students have cause to consult the Special Collections. Is there a particular text you are interested in?"

"No… I just thought that, as I was doing the tour, it would be remiss of me not to visit that too."

The grey eyes studied him above their cropped lenses.

"It would indeed," said the Librarian, closing the book in front of him and rising from the desk. "In that case, why don't you follow me?"

Giles blinked. "Are you sure it's not too much trouble?"

"It is no trouble at all, Mr Chamberlain. As you can see, this early in the day, we are hardly overrun."

Taking up the unexpected offer, Giles followed the Librarian through a series of interconnected exhibition spaces to the Old Library foyer. This was a screened-off area of the lower library with a long reading table opposite a tall desk. There, one of the College archivists sat, studying her computer screen.

"Good morning, Andrea."

The woman looked up and gave the Librarian a bright smile.

"Good morning, Mr Weston."

"I'm just giving Mr Chamberlain here a brief tour of the upper library."

"Of course. If you would both just sign in."

The Librarian took him over to a small table on which

sat a ledger, its lined pages crammed with entries. Taking a pen, he entered the date, time, his name and signature. Giles did the same, scanning the other listings and noting Professor Gupta's spidery signature throughout.

Looking up, he saw the Librarian watching him.

"Shall we, Mr Chamberlain?"

"Of course, why not?"

Weston led him through the fireproof partition into the lower library.

The first thing that Giles noticed was the smell, musty and stale with a hint of old wood. Then there was the silence as they walked between towering bookshelves stretching almost to the ceiling. At the far end of this maze of accumulated knowledge stood a circular metal staircase guarded by a wrought-iron garden gate.

Swinging it open, the Librarian smiled.

"After you, Mr Chamberlain."

Giles began to climb, the whole structure creaking and clanking as he did so. When he emerged onto the upper floor, he found himself facing the huge oriel window overlooking the river and the Bridge of Sighs. Breathtaking as this was, it did not compare to what greeted Giles when he turned around.

Roughly one-hundred feet long and thirty feet wide, the upper library of St John's College had been, for most of the eighteenth century, the most extensive library in England. Though it had since been overtaken by other institutions, Giles could see why it had once attracted monarchs, noblemen and academics from all over Europe.

Row upon row of carved wooden bookcases flanked a carpeted walkway that disappeared into a stone archway in the distance. Velvet display cabinets ran down the centre of the aisle, each containing historical manuscripts and books on temporary display. On the nearest one stood a brass telescope, its polished metal surface directed towards an ornate crest mounted on the far wall.

In comparison to the musty and oppressive ground floor, the upper library seemed light and airy. Filtered sunlight seeped through the UV screens on the south-facing windows, adding a mystical quality to the place. It was hard for Giles not to feel awed by the visual splendour and the sense of scholarship that hung in the air.

The Librarian looked at him. "Your first time here?"

"Yes," he replied, staring around at shelves laden with leather-bound volumes, their embossed titles dulled by age. Weston followed his gaze.

"There are 32,000 books in the upper library alone," the Librarian remarked as he wandered over to the nearest bookcase.

With great care, he eased open two hinged panels set in its side.

"Catalogued by hand when the Old Library was built in 1628."

Giles approached and stared at lines of flowing script, applied by a fine quill nib all those centuries ago.

"The tall bookcases are original, the crests acknowledging the founding benefactors. The dwarf bookcases," Weston said, indicating the smaller ones in the middle of each alcove, "were added as the collection grew. They were later raised in height to accommodate extra donations."

Giles saw how the new additions had been incorporated into the layout. He shook his head in wonder, and the Librarian smiled.

"A special place, don't you think?"

"Awesome."

"An overused word at times, but I have to agree with you."

"You must enjoy working here, Mr Weston."

"I consider myself very fortunate."

"I can see why Professor Gupta likes to visit."

The Librarian looked up at this.

"I spotted his name on the register," Giles explained.

Weston nodded. "The Professor visits us most days."

"I assume there is a good astronomy section here," said Giles, gesturing at the brass telescope on the nearby cabinet.

"Why yes." Weston smiled. "That particular instrument belonged to Sir Fred Hoyle, one of our College's great astronomers. Though he wasn't the only one. John Couch Adams, Sir John Herschel... Why, even John Dee, personal astrologer to Elizabeth I, was a Johnian."

"And all their papers are here?"

"A good many of them. Professor Gupta has become something of an authority on their work. So much so that I have loaned him my former office here in the upper library." He nodded towards the distant archway, and Giles understood how he'd lost sight of the Professor earlier.

"That is good of you."

"Well, I find my time is better spent advising our younger members on their research activities." He peered over his glasses at Giles, who remembered the tip Weston had given him last year about climbing New Court.

"And much appreciated it is too, Mr Weston."

The Librarian nodded. "Besides, the Professor keeps to himself. Some nights, we have to remind him that it's time to leave. Lost in another world, he is."

"Sorry?" Giles said, wondering if he'd heard him correctly.

Mr Weston smiled. "Books, Mr Chamberlain. They can do that, you know."

Their eyes met, just for a moment, before the Librarian turned back to the staircase.

"Now if you will forgive me, Giles, I need to get back to the front desk."

The use of his first name was almost as surprising as the conversation they had just had.

"Oh, right," he said, glancing towards the distant archway. "Of course."

"But I encourage you to come back at any time," said Weston, pausing at the top of the stairs. "Scholars are always welcome."

"Thank you, Mr Weston," Giles said. "I intend to."

Chapter Fourteen

The lecturer switched off the monitor and smiled. "Have a good afternoon! I'll see you all next week."

There was a momentary pause while her flagging audience processed this. Then, on cue, conversations broke out across the packed lecture hall as students reached under desks, stuffing pads, pens and computers inside backpacks.

With a weary sigh, Annabel closed her laptop and sat back in her chair. Three hours of chemistry, physiology and physics was a tough gig four weeks into the term. Too tough for some.

In front of her, she saw one or two heads rise groggily from arms they'd been resting on long before the final bell. The Professor glanced at a boy a few rows down from her who had been asleep for the last ten minutes. Nudged by one of his neighbours, his head jerked up and he stared around, a bewildered expression on his face. Annabel hoped that the lecturer wasn't one of his Supervisors.

Rising to her feet, she arched her back, which was still stiff after another early morning outing cramped in the cox's seat. She couldn't wait to get outside for a stretch and some fresh air. Cramming a hundred students in a lecture hall for hours on end created a biosphere whose organisms didn't bear thinking about.

Glancing around, she spotted Ash and Brian in the front row, packing their things away. As usual, the seats either side of them were empty.

Ash, who was something of an eco-warrior, maintained a one-shower-a-week policy. Brian, dressed in his customary black greatcoat, lank hair hanging over his shoulders, appeared to have extended the principle to something considerably longer.

Then again, most students had a natural aversion to sitting in the front row, so her friends usually had the benches by the podium free to themselves. Not that the lecturers seemed to mind.

Ash hung on every word, scribbling notes energetically with coloured pens for the mind-mapping technique he'd once tried to explain to her. Brian, by contrast, simply stared at the lecturer, making the occasional pencil entry in a small leather book. Annabel had only ever seen him refer to it once in a Supervision, given his ability to recall whole lectures verbatim.

Turning around, Ash spotted her and waved, employing his full arm, swaying it back and forth above his head like a drowning man signalling for assistance. Annabel smiled and, slipping her laptop into her lilac Cambridge Satchel, rose from her seat. They waited for her at the bottom of the steps, Ash smiling and Brian staring at his shoes as she came down to join them.

"Hi, guys," she said. "How was it for you?"

"Great," said Ash. "What about you?"

"I was struggling a bit at the end. Fancy getting some fresh air?"

"Good idea."

Ash fell in step beside her and Brian tucked in behind as they joined the crowd of departing students.

"So what are you two up to this afternoon? Labs again?"

"Not today," said Ash, looking excited. "Big day."

"What's that then?"

"Punting!"

"You're not serious," said Annabel, pushing through a set of double doors. They were met by a chill wind, a reminder that winter had not released Cambridge from its grip. "I can't imagine that it would be much fun in this weather."

"Oh, we're not going out on the river."

"So, where then?"

"The Punt Society. We're doing annual maintenance!"

"And that involves…?"

Too late, Annabel realised her mistake as Brian's voice whirred into action.

"Last term we hauled the punts from the river and stacked them in the punt store. Now we're stripping away the bitumen, paint and varnish and sanding down the runners…" The monologue continued for another minute as he described the repairing, painting and varnishing stages in some detail.

"I see," said Annabel, when he finally stopped.

"Of course, there's a lot more to it than that," Ash added.

"But we're still new and learning the ropes."

"Chains," said Brian.

"Sorry?" said Annabel.

"We don't use ropes," continued Brian. "They fray on the moorings. We use chains to attach the punts to the quayside. With brass and stainless steel padlocks to prevent corrosion. And we mitigate the risk that keys are dropped by attaching wooden floats."

"Sensible," she said.

Annabel wondered if that was why the College punt poles were made of wood. But she had the presence of mind not to ask. The thought of Brian holding forth about oiling and polishing poles as they walked among other students didn't bear thinking about. She saw Ash smiling at her and, not for the first time, wondered if he could read her thoughts.

"You should come along some time," he suggested. "It's not all hard work, you know. We have plenty of time to chat while waiting for the paint to dry."

"I'm sure you do."

"We have a kettle and a large supply of tea and biscuits."

"Biscuits, eh? What sort?"

This was all Brian needed.

"Digestives, obviously. But we've also tried jammy dodgers, custard creams, hobnobs, chocolate bourbons, rich tea, ginger nuts..."

While he continued running through the options, they left the New Museum Site and turned into Pembroke Street. It was only after entering Free School Lane that he stopped.

Quite literally, in fact, causing other students to step around them. Annabel turned to see what the problem was.

"Brian? What is it?"

"I'm not sure Jaffa Cakes can be classified as a biscuit."

Annabel stared at him before looking to Ash for help. But he was frowning too, apparently giving the matter serious consideration. More students filed past, glancing at the three of them as they stood there in the middle of the pavement.

"Guys, we're causing a holdup."

Still, Ash and Brian remained standing, lost in some sort of silent philosophical debate.

"Maybe we should just get some and see?" she suggested.

It was as if someone had flicked on a light switch. Ash's face brightened.

"Great idea! Nothing like empirical evidence."

Without warning, they began walking again, with Annabel hurrying to keep up.

"Annabel, why don't you come this afternoon?"

"You know what guys, I might just give it a miss today. What with the rowing and everything, I'm a bit behind with work."

"Oh, OK," said Ash, sounding disappointed. Then he perked up. "What about our next social?"

"When's that?"

"This Sunday. We're transferring the punts back into the water, so most of us will be there, including Brett."

"Brett?"

"Brian asked him."

Annabel looked back at the figure behind them, whose

head seemed to shrink further into his coat as they turned into King's Parade and caught the full blast of the wind. She remembered that he and Brett had formed an unlikely friendship last term after discovering a shared interest in aircrews stationed around Cambridge during the war. The idea of spending time working alongside the big American without Clarissa around was appealing.

"Sure, if you need an extra pair of hands."

"Great!" said Ash. "We meet at 10.00am and should finish in time for a pub lunch at The Punter."

"Sounds perfect."

"Would any of your crew be available to lend a hand?"

"I think they'll probably appreciate a lie-in," she said, reluctant to give Clarissa a chance to muscle in.

"Oh, OK. Well, perhaps you could ask Nick if he can come along?"

"Nick?"

"We need six people to lift a punt, but it's best to have eight."

"Oh, right. Well, if I see him, I'll ask."

Ash gave her a funny look. "Annabel?"

"Yes?"

"Are you and Nick OK?"

Annabel was so surprised by this, she didn't know what to say. "Why do you ask?"

"Only I don't see you two together anymore."

"Oh, that," she said. "It's just that he's busy. You know, with the Redboys."

Ash frowned.

"The rugby team," she added by way of explanation.

"I know who the Redboys are," he said.

"Of course, sorry."

Annabel felt a hot flush rise in her cheeks, and for once she was grateful for the chill wind. They continued in silence until they entered the relative shelter of Trinity Street. Out of the corner of her eye, she thought she saw Ash mouth something to Brian. Then, out of nowhere, the latter spoke up.

"Maybe Nick can bring the Redboys with him?"

"That's a good idea, Brian," agreed Ash, and she shot him a look. "To lift the punts, I mean."

"Four more people should do it," Brian said.

"To free up time for a tea break!"

"And Jaffa cakes," added Brian.

"More hands make less work…"

"Guys!" Annabel stopped and turned to face them, "I'll ask Nick, OK?"

"Oh, OK," said Ash. "Thanks."

Almost in a whisper, Brian asked, "And the Red…?"

"And the Redboys," she said. "Happy now?"

"Well, yes," said Ash. "That would be great."

"Good!"

Annabel set off once more, leaving the other two to hurry after her. Striding past Heffers Bookshop, she wondered why she hadn't just told them the truth. That Nick had dumped her for some long-legged fashion model. Instead, she now had to go cap in hand and ask her ex for a favour.

"Just great," she said under her breath and heard the

footsteps falter behind her. Glancing back, she saw their sheepish expressions and immediately felt bad. By the time they reached St John's, she knew she had to say something.

"Listen, I'm sorry guys," she said, pausing outside the Great Gate. "It's just, well, girl stuff."

Ash's eyes widened into something close to panic and Brian's features went rigid, suggesting some sort of internal systems overload.

"Not that sort of girl's stuff," she said. "Look, is the Buttery still open?"

Ash blinked. "The Buttery?"

"I'm in serious need of chocolate, right now. How about you?"

"Erm, we like chocolate, don't we, Brian?"

"Dark chocolate, not…," but he saw the look on Ash's face. "Yes, we like chocolate."

"Good, come on then," she said setting off into First Court, "I'm buying."

Chapter Fifteen

Nick closed the Criminal Law textbook and stared at the lever arch file containing printouts of his lecture notes. Almost halfway through the term and the work was piling up. With an essay due that day, he had spent all afternoon in the College Library checking the case law, and he'd just found three judgments he hadn't taken into account. Still, with the deadline looming, Nick didn't have time to make more changes.

At least I'll have them ready for my Supervision with Dr Jones, he thought.

If there was one thing he'd learned in his short time in Cambridge, it was not to turn up to a Supervision unprepared. Particularly one conducted by a former litigator. That was an experience to be avoided at all costs.

Glancing at his watch, Nick saw that he only had a few minutes before pre-dinner drinks with his new Tutor. Hitting ENTER, he sent the document to the printer in the Library lobby. Grabbing a PLEASE LEAVE card, he placed it on the desk and headed off down the spiral staircase, two steps at a time.

For once, the machine gods were smiling on him, and his essay printed off without a hitch. Barging through the revolving door, he hurried from the building to the Forecourt Lodge.

"Evening, Nick," said Bert. "In a hurry, I see."

"I have an essay due for Dr Jones."

The Porter reached under the counter and produced an internal envelope.

"Here, I'll add it to the pile. She hasn't collected her post yet."

"Great. You don't happen to know where Dutour's rooms are, do you? I've got a Tutorial."

"Ah yes, there have been quite a few lawyers asking that tonight. Straight across the court," said the Porter, pointing to an archway on the other side of the square. "Past the College offices and take the stairs to the top floor. Dr Dutour's rooms are in the attic."

"Thanks."

"Oh, and Nick, no running in the courts, there's a good lad. Only the Dean's a stickler for that sort of thing."

"Right."

Nick left the lodge and, sure enough, spotted Esdee Jones on her way to collect her mail. Making a point of strolling across the court, he disappeared inside the doorway and sprinted up the stairs. On the top landing, he followed the signs up a circular wooden staircase to a tiny hallway. There he heard the sound of muffled conversations behind a door marked "Dr G.V Dutour - Please Knock and Enter".

Nick did as instructed and stepped into a crowded room,

full of people holding wine glasses and canapés. A few faces turned towards him, including Katie, one of Annabel's friends, who gave him a bright smile. Others, mainly second- and third-years, he had seen around College but didn't know by name.

Nick peered around the room, which was very different from the grand New Court set his previous Tutor, Professor Mackenzie, had occupied. With its vaulted ceiling and windows overlooking the surrounding rooftops, the apartment had a bohemian feel. While the shelves were mostly filled with books, the furniture was contemporary, all pale wood and fabrics, with modern lamp-stands in each corner of the room.

"*Bonsoir.*"

A striking woman with large-rimmed glasses edge through the crowd to welcome him. She wore a black dress with bold white patterns and held a glass of red wine.

"Dr Dutour," he said. "Nick Wood."

"Ah, yes," she said, shaking his hand. "A first-year, no?"

"That's right."

"Pleased to meet you, Nichola," she said, dropping the s. "Your colleagues have already made a start on the wine. Can I get you a glass? It's good, not from the College cellar."

Nick would have preferred beer, but being late, he felt that he couldn't refuse.

"Please."

"Help yourself to the *hors-d'oeuvres*. The *saucisse de Toulouse* is very good," she said, heading off to get his drink. "Or we have some cheese over there."

Nick looked around and saw a coffee table covered in

canapés and what looked like a bowl of mottled eggs. The cheese was on a side table on the far side of the room, surrounded by a group of students.

With a shock, Nick saw that one of them was Colin, Naomi's boyfriend. The third-year's face darkened when he recognised the new arrival, and a couple of his friends glanced in Nick's direction. The silent standoff was only broken by a cheery greeting.

"Hi, Nick!"

Turning, he saw Katie and Darius, another first-year, the latter holding a plate piled high with food.

"Hi," he said.

"So, what do you think?" Katie asked.

"About?"

"Our new Tutor?" She picked up one of the eggs and began peeling off its shell.

"We've only just met," Nick said.

"She's a bit full-on," mumbled Darius through a mouthful of sausage.

"You think?"

"Don't worry, you'll see," said Katie, dipping her egg in a bowl of salt before popping it in her mouth.

"Watch out, she's coming," whispered Darius.

Dr Dutour returned, holding out a glass.

"There you are, Nichola. Tell me what you think."

"Thanks," he said, taking the glass and peering at its dark contents. His host watched him, her large eyes magnified by the thick lenses. Nick took a sip and suppressed a shudder at the flavour.

"Good, *n'est ce pas*?"

"Unbelievable," he said.

She nodded. "It is rare to find someone who can appreciate a good Bordeaux. Complex but satisfying, like a legal judgment no doubt?"

"Indisputably," said Darius, raising his glass and taking a healthy slug himself.

"These canapés are delightful, Dr Dutour," said Katie. "It is good of you to go to so much trouble."

"It was nothing. I'm sure Professor Mackenzie did the same."

"Hardly," said Darius.

"Did he not?"

"Mackenzie's Tutorials consisted of beer and sandwiches, followed by a game of room cricket."

Their new Tutor looked aghast. "What, no wine?"

"I think there might have been a bottle of sherry," said Katie.

"For the ladies," said Darius, imitating a Scottish accent.

"*Incroyable*," said Dr Dutour. "I thought it was a Tutor's role to look after your non-academic needs, is it not, Nichola?"

"Well, yes..."

"And what is more important to the soul," she continued, "than a good Merlot?"

Two pints of lager and a packet of crisps, Nick thought, but he decided not to share this preference with his host.

"Sounds good to me," said Darius, raising his near-empty glass.

"*Bon*! That is agreed," said Dutour. "When the President first asked me to be your Tutor, I wasn't sure. But I can see now why I was chosen for this role."

She looked around the room at her tutees with a new sense of purpose, then froze as something caught her attention.

"*Non*! Do they not know how to cut Brie?"

Dr Dutour headed across the room to accost Anita and Hamish, the two first-years she had caught desecrating the cheese.

"See what I mean," said Darius, keeping his voice low. "Full-on."

Relieved it hadn't been him, Nick was about to admit as such when someone knocked his wine arm from behind.

"Oh, dear," came a voice from behind him. "Can't hold your drink?"

Turning, Nick saw it was Colin.

"Watch it, you…"

"Nick, the carpet!" Katie gasped.

Nick looked down and saw big blotches of red wind splattered across the pale material.

"Quick," he said, setting his glass down on the table and grabbing the stack of paper napkins. "Get me some salt and sparkling water."

"Sparkling water?" Darius asked. "You're sure?"

"Mum says it's great for stains." The door opened behind him, and Nick turned in time to see Colin step outside.

"See you around… friend."

Before he could respond, Katie handed him the bowl of salt. "Here!" she said.

Nick turned back to the carpet and poured the contents of the bowl onto the stains. Just then, Darius returned carrying a green bottle.

"Will Perrier do?" he asked.

"Thanks," said Nick and poured the liquid over the salt. Fizzing, the little white mounds began turning pink.

"Wow," said Katie, impressed.

Nick waited a moment or two before using the napkins to scoop up the darkening crystals. The stain was still visible, but most of the pigment had gone. Nick poured more sparkling water and dabbed at it again.

"What is this!"

Conversation faltered and Nick looked up to find his Tutor's pale face staring down at him.

"I'm sorry," he said in the silence.

Dutour's gaze moved from the carpet to the table, where Nick saw a dark red ring on the pale wooden surface.

"Really sorry," he said.

The woman turned to look at him, her face unreadable. Then she shrugged. "At least not much has gone to waste."

Nick wasn't sure he'd heard her correctly. "Sorry?"

"With wine this good, that would be a tragedy. Don't you agree?"

"I suppose," he said.

"Definitely," said Darius, chipping in.

"It really is delicious," agreed Katie.

The tension in the room eased, and a few tentative conversations started up again.

"Tell me, Nichola, how is it you know about carpet stains?"

"My mum," he said. "She works in catering."

"I see." Dutour sounded impressed. "Is her restaurant successful?"

"She's very busy at the moment," he said.

"Wonderful. Any particular dishes you would recommend?"

"Honestly?"

"Of course."

He shrugged. "Toad in the hole."

"Ah, yes. *Cuisses de grenouilles*! An excellent suggestion, Nichola. I shall order some next time."

Darius began to choke on his wine.

"Are you all right, Mr Levy?"

Darius, his eyes watering, managed a nod.

"Come, let me get you a glass of water. This bottle is empty." She led him away as Nick turned to Katie.

"What's up with Darius?"

"He's fine. Just thought it was funny, I expect."

"What?"

"Our Tutor ordering frogs legs for you," she said.

Half an hour later, the three of them stepped out into Chapel Court.

"Well, that was interesting," said Katie.

"I'll say," said Darius. "What with Hamish and Anita despoiling the cheese, and Nick here redecorating the furniture, it was a lot more entertaining than I expected."

"I thought I'd blown it," said Nick, who still couldn't believe how Colin had set him up.

"Seems like you managed to win Dutour over in the end," said Katie. "Quite the charmer, Nichola!"

"Thanks for your help back there."

"You should thank your mother," said Darius. "Perrier was a masterstroke. Must remember that for the May Ball."

"Where did she learn that one?" Katie asked.

Nick hesitated. "Mum's a school dinner lady."

Darius stared at him for a moment before slapping him on the back. "Brilliant!"

Katie smiled. "So you weren't kidding about Toad in the Hole!"

"Like I said. One of my favourites."

"What are you lot cackling about?"

Turning, they saw Hamish and Anita emerge from the staircase.

"Begone, foul fiends!" Darius crossed two fingers and held them up in front of him. "It is the Butchers of Brie."

"Don't blame me, it was Hamish," said Anita.

"No, it wasn't!"

While the others argued, Darius turned to Katie.

"Fancy a post-match debrief in the Bar?"

"I think I'll give it a miss," she said. "I'm rowing tomorrow,"

"Yeah, I've got a game," said Nick.

"Fair enough. I'll stay with these two. Someone needs to keep the peace."

While he led the others off to the Bar, Nick and Katie headed back to Cripps. As they crossed the Bridge of Sighs, they passed students dressed in their gowns heading for Hall.

"So what time's your outing? Must be pretty cold on the river, first thing."

"Didn't Annabel tell you? They've promoted me to W2. I'm rowing afternoons now."

"Congratulations, I didn't know."

"Thanks, but W3 should do well with Brett coaching them. Are you going to watch them in Bumps?"

"Probably," he said, reluctant to talk about how things were with Annabel. "Listen, Katie, I'm going to head off now."

"Oh, OK."

"Thanks again for tonight."

"No problem. Hope your game goes well. Who's it against?"

"Jesus. Semi-final."

"If you win," she said, "I'm planning on coming to the final."

"No pressure, then."

Katie turned and headed off down the cloister. "*A bientôt*, Nichola!"

Nick made his way back to A staircase. He had just flicked his room indicator to IN, when Annabel came hurrying down the steps, adjusting her gown.

"Oh! Hi," she said, stopping in front of him.

"Hi," he replied.

There was an awkward silence.

"I see you're going to Hall," he said.

"Yeah. We try to go once a week. The crew, that is."

"Right," said Nick, imagining her sitting next to Brett. He noticed her gown was hunched up on one shoulder. "Your gown, it's… crooked."

"Oh," Annabel said, craning her neck as she tried to adjust it. "Could you?"

"Sure."

Nick reached forwards and unfolded the fabric, conscious of how close she was.

"There," he said, stepping back.

"Thanks." She studied him for a moment. "Nick, there's something I've been meaning to ask you."

"Right," he said, thinking, *Here we go.*

"Ash and Brian were wondering if you could help them move the punts back on the river?"

Surprised, he wasn't quite sure how to respond. "Sure."

"Thanks, they'll be thrilled." She tucked a strand of hair behind her ear, something he knew she always did when she was nervous.

"There was something else," she said.

Nick braced himself.

"Do you think some of the Redboys might help with the punts too?"

"Oh," he said. "I can ask Trevor, I suppose."

"That would be super," she said. "Thanks."

"No problem."

Again a long pause.

"Well, I'd better go," she said. "You know, Hall."

"Of course," Nick said. "Have a good time."

Annabel hurried off, her gown flapping behind her. Nick watched her go, and wondered how long she would stay mad at him for Christmas. Perhaps he'd ask his little brother, next time he saw him. Then again, he knew what Charlie would say. "Women!"

Chapter Sixteen

Giles glared at Ying. "You have caused me to lose my temper: a thing that has hardly ever happened to me before. I prefer to say nothing more tonight. I am going to bed."

Ying glared back. "You'd better leave a note for the Housekeeper about the coffee; she won't be told by me."

"Damn the housekeeper," Giles railed. "And damn the coffee, and damn you, and damn my own folly in having lavished my hard-earned knowledge and the treasure of my regard and intimacy on a heartless guttersnipe."

With that, he spun on his heels and strode for his study door. Ying flicked a V sign at his back as he slammed it behind him.

There was a long moment of silence.

Then the others began clapping.

"Bravo!" exclaimed George, while Pippa blew a most unladylike wolf whistle.

Ying turned and frowned. "Do you think the V sign works?"

"Definitely," said Pippa. "If anyone had called me a guttersnipe, that's the least he'd have got."

"I mean, was it around in the 1920s?"

Giles stepped around the door frame nailed to the stage floor.

"Some people think it was used by English archers at Agincourt. But you're probably safer with cocking a snoop." He put his thumb to his nose and waggled his fingers. "Or you could stick your tongue out." This he did too.

"Careful Professor," said Ying, "or I might just knock your block off!"

"Method acting my dear, nothing more. Now, where are my slippers?"

Pippa laughed and Giles headed for the stalls. Stuffing the script in his backpack, he looked around at the others.

"Ying, are you heading back to College?"

"No, Pippa and me are talking costumes over a cocktail at Vodka Revs. You're welcome to join us."

"Think I'll give that a miss. Not sure my liver could keep up with you two ladies."

"Me?" Ying thrust her hands on her hips. "I'm a good girl I am!"

Giles just raised an eyebrow.

"Mostly," she added, fluttering her eyelashes.

After saying goodbye to the others, Giles left the ADC a good deal wearier than when he'd arrived. With only four weeks to opening night, Ying had been ramping up rehearsals to five nights a week. And with litter picking, lectures, Supervisions and his dissertation, he'd had no time to find out what Gupta was up to in the College Library. But he hoped that that was all about to change.

The lights were still on in the Great Gate Lodge when he stepped inside and found the new female Porter behind the counter.

"Evening, Shirley. I had an email saying there's a package for me."

"Ah yes, Giles Chamberlain, isn't it?"

"Got it in one."

"Let me have a look for you."

She headed into the post room and returned with a shoebox-sized parcel, which he signed for.

"Thanks, Shirley!"

Leaving the lodge, he headed across First Court with the package tucked under his arm. Inside would be the video camera he'd ordered—the sort of device used in the Zoology department to observe animals such as badgers at night. Movement activated, it could be left in place outside a den for weeks on end, recording the comings and goings of its occupants.

The subject Giles had in mind for this particular study was a secretive creature which frequented the alcoves of the Old Library.

"The lesser-known Gupta," he said as he entered Second Court, and glanced towards the Professor's room in the far corner of the square.

Giles stopped and stared. There, above the top floor windows, something was moving on the roof, a dark outline against the tiles, peering over the ramparts. He frowned. So far as he knew, there were only three members of the illicit night-climbing club in College: him, Trevor and Ying. And while the latter was currently knocking back cocktails in town, he doubted Trevor would be attempting the "Circuit of Second Court" on his own. Which meant that a new practitioner was traversing the College's aerial routes.

"And they haven't even paid their subs!" he muttered.

His professional pride piqued, Giles strode across the court, eyes fixed on the far corner of the roof. The crenelated rampart made it difficult to get a clear view. So when he reached the Professor's staircase, Giles listened instead. There was a faint whispering sound, intermittent and coming in short bursts. He tried to work out what it could be, but there was only one thing he could think of. Sniffing.

Taking a few steps back, he looked up and called out.

"Hey! You there!"

The sniffing stopped.

Giles stared at the gap between the ramparts and thought he could make out a dark shape. Someone was there, peering down at him, their features covered in shadow. No, not a shadow, more like a hood. Yes, that was it! And beneath that hood the face was…

"Giles?"

Spinning around, he saw a hunched figure no more than ten feet away. Heart hammering, it took him a moment or two to recognise the familiar crumpled jacket and sagging shoulders.

"Professor?"

"This is an unexpected pleasure," said the old man, approaching. "What brings you here?"

Giles glanced up at the ramparts. The hooded shadow had gone.

"I think I just saw someone up there."

"On the staircase?" said Gupta, staring at the landing window.

"No, the roof."

The other raised his gaze. "A fellow night climber perhaps?"

The Professor was well aware of Giles's rooftop activities.

"I thought it might have been," he conceded, "but I'm not so sure now." He scanned the rooftops. "It was making… well, a strange noise."

"Strange?"

"A sort of sniffing sound."

"A cold maybe?"

Giles turned and saw that the Professor was smiling at him.

"Yeah, I know. Sounds far-fetched."

"A little, perhaps. Are you all right? You're looking a bit pale."

"No, I'm fine Professor, it's just…" He looked up again at the roof, remembering the face and those eyes. "Professor, there's no way that some sort of creature could be up there, is there?"

"No, Giles. I told you. That door has been sealed."

Giles turned back to him and found the smile gone.

"I just wondered, you know, if anything else might have come through as well."

"If it had, I think we would have noticed before now, don't you?"

Giles remembered the trail of animal carcasses left by the

last creature. He hadn't found so much as a bone on his morning litter picks.

"I suppose. I just wondered, that's all."

"Giles, trust me. Whoever you imagine you saw tonight, they could not have come from there."

There was a finality to that statement that brooked no argument.

"Fair enough, I had to ask."

"Yes, well," the Professor sighed, "I don't know about you, but it's been a long day."

"Certainly has," Giles agreed. "And another one tomorrow, no doubt."

"You're not overdoing it, are you?"

"What me?" Giles scoffed. "No. Nothing that a trip to the Library won't fix."

"In that case, I'll say good night then."

Giles watched as the old man clicked his room indicator to "IN" and disappeared up the stairs. The sound of his footsteps faded, and silence descended on Second Court.

Glancing one more time at the ramparts, he turned and headed back to his room. As he did so, Giles felt a shiver down the back of his neck that had nothing to do with the night air.

Chapter Seventeen

Ravi climbed to the first-floor landing and paused to peer through the leaded window. He watched the blonde-haired figure disappear into the staircase on the far side of the square.

Turning, he took the rickety staircase to the top floor. As he climbed, he noticed that it was getting colder the higher he went. The ancient wooden treads creaked under his weight as he gained the top step. The doors leading off the landing were all shut, but one of the leaded windows he saw was wide open.

Reaching inside his coat, his fingers touched the metal haft of the old ruler. Reassured by its presence, he crossed to the window and listened for the sniffing that Giles had said he'd heard.

Nothing.

Ravi was about to close the window when he noticed grains of sand on the sill. Reaching down, he rubbed the gritty powder between his fingers and thumb. Frowning, he turned and saw that there was more on the mat by his door.

Removing the ruler from his pocket, Ravi reached for his

keys and unlocked the door. Stepping inside, he held the ruler in front of him until he found the light switch. The central pendant light flickered into life, casting a dim glow over the familiar surroundings of his room.

There were the faded sofas and armchair around the coffee table with its antique astronomical devices. So too the bookcases lining the walls, their shelves sagging under the weight of journals and books. As far as Ravi could see, all was as it should be. He crossed the room and pushed open the door to his kitchen. Save for the mugs in the drying rack from this afternoon's Supervision, everything was in its usual place.

Returning the ruler to his pocket, Ravi refilled the kettle and a few minutes later, he returned to his desk with a steaming mug of tea. He eased himself into the old leather chair, and thought back to the conversation he had just had with Giles.

The boy clearly had seen somebody on the rooftops that evening. Part of Ravi wanted to believe it was nothing more sinister than a night climber with a cold. But why would such an individual try to access the roof via the landing window? That wasn't a recognised route as far as he was aware. Besides, using conventional staircases to access the rooftops was frowned upon by any self-respecting member of the night-climbing community.

No, they must have been trying to gain access to his room, and it wouldn't be the first time someone had broken into his office. Last term, it had been Schiller, intent on discovering what Ravi knew of Robert's research.

And there had been that other time, of course, almost half a century ago. When someone Ravi had trusted had sought to uncover his secrets. But she had been more subtle, more patient, playing the long game. Playing him and Robert for the fools they were.

Ravi stared into his tea as the memories of the past swirled into view.

******

A lean, fresh-faced Ravi sat at the small circular table in Fitzbillies tea shop, and looked out the window. He had timed his arrival to beat the morning rush of long-haired students returning from lectures. While listening to conversations about nuclear disarmament and Rag Week antics was entertaining enough, Ravi had more pressing concerns. Four years into his research with Robert, he had uncovered a new line of inquiry that was both intriguing and concerning. He needed time to think about the best way forward, and for him, that meant tea.

"A penny for your thoughts?"

Ravi looked up and was dazzled by the winter sunlight pouring through the shop window. Blinking, he held up a hand against the glare and could just make out the outline of a figure in a fur-lined duffel coat.

"Sorry?" he said.

"I didn't mean to startle you," said the woman. "It's just that you looked a bit lost there for a minute."

"Oh, right. Well, not lost exactly."

He rose from his chair and recognised the new research

assistant who had joined the Cavendish at the end of the last term.

"Please don't get up on my account," she said. "I saw you sitting here and thought I'd say hello."

"Please join me."

"Only if it's not too much trouble."

"Not at all. Here, take a seat."

She placed her tray on the table and smoothed back her dark, shoulder-length hair.

"I'm Mary by the way," she said, holding out a hand.

Ravi shook it.

"Nice to meet you, Mary. I'm Ravi."

"I've seen you at the Cavendish, I think."

"That's right," he said, resuming his seat.

The young woman removed her coat and hung it on the back of her chair. She was wearing a tight turtleneck sweater, which clung to her slim frame. As she sat down opposite him, her short suede skirt rose up her long stockinged legs. Ravi took a sudden interest in his tea and began stirring it assiduously.

"It's freezing out there," said Mary. "I should have worn a jumper like yours."

Ravi looked down at the knitted Fair Isle sweater.

"It was a present," he said.

"Well, she has good taste."

"What? Oh, no, it was from Robert."

"That big chap with the broken nose?"

He smiled at the blunt but accurate description of his friend. "Yes, I stayed with him and his family in Edinburgh over Christmas."

"Cold, was it?"

"Perishing!"

Mary smiled. "I've been meaning to say hello at the Cavendish, but you always seem so pre-occupied."

"Really?" he said, surprised she'd noticed him.

"You two must be working on something exciting. You seem to be there all hours."

"Oh, you know, this and that."

Ravi never liked discussing their work in the lab. Not just because their unconventional approach might leave them open to academic ridicule. He and Robert didn't want to attract the attention of certain government agencies, both domestic and foreign, known to be active within the university.

"Well, you can't be working on anything as dull as I am," Mary continued. "I've spent so long doing planet spectroscopy studies that I'm thinking of quitting and taking up a career in advertising."

"Why would you want to do that?"

"Oh, I don't know. Looking through a lens at human bodies isn't so far removed from celestial ones. And at least that way I can afford to pay the heating bills."

Ravi remembered how cold it had felt the first time he had come to Cambridge, and this winter had been a particularly harsh one.

"You're not in College accommodation then?"

"No, digs in town. My landlady still thinks there's a war on. I mentioned that rationing had ended more than a decade ago, but she looked at me as if I was soft in the head. The lab is like a sauna by comparison." She raised her cup to her lips and peered at him through the rising steam.

"I'm sorry to hear that," he said, trying to erase the mental image of Mary in a towel.

"So, what accommodation do you boys have at John's?"

"How do you know I...?"

She inclined her head towards the neatly folded College scarf on the chair next to him.

"Oh, of course." He smiled. "I'm lucky enough to have a room in Second Court. Just above the Library."

"Nice. No skinflint of a landlady, then."

"We have no women in College at all, I'm afraid."

"That's right. I'd forgotten. A bastion of bachelorhood."

"I think the phrase is a community of scholars."

She laughed. "Oh, I almost forgot." Twisting in her seat, she reached for something in her coat pocket. As she did so, her sweater rose slightly, and Ravi caught a flash of bare skin above the band of her skirt. Aware of the colour rising in his cheeks, Ravi dropped his eyes to study the contents of his cup.

Her hand slid across the table and placed something in front of him. When her slim fingers withdrew, he saw a penny laying there. Looking up, he found Mary watching him, a quizzical smile on her lips.

"I'm sorry," he said, "I don't understand?"

"Well," she leaned forwards to place her elbows on the table and rest her chin on her hands, "I promised you a penny. So, now I'd like to know your thoughts."

Ravi found himself staring into those pale green eyes, and heard his voice say, "I was thinking that it would be nice to invite you to dine in Hall one evening."

Her eyes widened.

"With Robert and me," he added, his courage faltering under her gaze. "To continue our discussion of spectroscopy, and save you from the superficial, though well-rewarded, world of advertising."

Mary blinked.

"Wow!" she said. "That was a penny well spent."

Ravi stared back at her, feeling as surprised as she looked.

"I think, Ravi, you just asked me out to dinner. Albeit with a chaperone."

"What? I mean, yes, dinner." The cafe felt very warm all of a sudden. "But I thought Robert would enjoy hearing more about your work. As will I, of course."

Mary laughed. "With or without Robert, I am delighted to accept your kind invitation. Though I have to warn you," her expression became serious, "that you'll need compelling evidence to counter the allure of advertising."

"Challenge accepted," he said, raising his teacup.

Mary did the same and, as the bone china clinked together, Ravi felt a thrill in the pit of his stomach. Gazing across the table into those bright, intelligent eyes, it dawned on him that he had just invited this dazzling girl on a date.

******

Half a century later, a much older and wiser Ravi sat in his leather chair and stared at the contents of his mug. The tea had long-since gone cold, and so had his feelings for the woman he had met all those years ago. Had he known then what that encounter would set in motion, Ravi would never have extended that invitation to dine. Even so, he wondered if it would have made any difference.

"She played you for a fool," he said, needing to hear it aloud to stiffen his resolve once more.

If someone wanted to snoop around his room, this time they would find him better prepared. Picking up his ruler, he rose from the desk and, turning off the lamp, headed for the sofa.

Ravi lay there for a while, unable to shake the feeling that something, somewhere, had shifted, and that otherworldly forces were closing in once more. What and how, he couldn't yet determine, but it was with this sense of foreboding that he slipped into an uncomfortable and troubled sleep.

Chapter Eighteen

Annabel woke to see sunlight reflecting off the ceiling of her Cripps room. She frowned and wondered what it was doing there. Then a terrible thought occurred to her.

"Oh, no!"

Jerking upright, she grabbed her phone and stared at the time.

"8.00am? You're kidding!"

She swung her legs out of bed and stared at the screen again, willing it to be wrong. That was when she saw which day it was. "Oh, thank goodness," she breathed, laying back down.

Sunday morning. No early outing. No lectures. No Supervisions. Sure, a stack of assignments to complete, but those could wait. Annabel wrapped the duvet around her and savoured the moment before considering how she might spend this blessed day of rest.

The Buttery didn't open until lunchtime, so that meant tea and toast in the communal kitchen. Not a bad option as things went, depending on who else was up and about.

But then a shadow darkened her thoughts. Tall, leggy,

and with a designer dressing gown. Her neighbour Naomi. And if last night's bed-thumping was anything to go by, Nick would be there too. The warm glow began to fade.

Come on, girl! Annabel chided herself. *Happy thoughts!*

What about Chapel breakfast? She'd been a couple of times with Katie last term. A full English in Hall for anyone attending the early morning service.

Good thought.

And wasn't Brett a regular churchgoer? With no outing, might he be there too?

Excellent thought, she decided as the warm glow returned.

Ten minutes later, dressed in jeans, a fleece and her College scarf, Annabel hurried over the Bridge of Sighs. Save for a few crows on the lawns, the courts were deserted, and she arrived in Chapel Court just as Canon Walker was closing the large oak door.

"Hold up!" she called out as she ran towards the Chapel entrance.

The Chaplain's careworn features creased into a smile.

"Annabel! Lovely to see you again."

"So sorry, Canon Walker. I hope I'm not too late."

"Not at all," he said, ushering her in. "Take a pew."

Annabel stepped inside and headed over to the alcove at the North end of the antechapel. There, chairs had been arranged in a semi-circle around a small altar, most of them already taken. But she saw Katie sitting on the stone bench along the wall. Her former crewmate smiled and shuffled up to make room for her on the long cushion.

"Morning," she whispered, sitting down.

Annabel looked across and saw Brett beaming at her from his chair on the opposite side. Returning his smile, she lowered her head to pray.

Thank you, Lord.

******

The early morning service took just over half an hour. Brett gave one of the readings, his confident voice echoing around the vaulted space. Following communion, there was a quiet time for prayer, and memories of Annabel's late family came flooding back to her. They did most days, of course, often triggered by the simplest thing. But here, in a place accustomed to grief and surrounded by others facing up to their own doubts, she found it easier to bear.

After the service was over, Brett came to join her.

"Good morning, Annabel. I thought you'd be enjoying a lie-in this morning."

"I was tempted," she said. "But this has its attractions too."

"Chapel breakfast, you mean? Definitely worth getting up for."

"Can't argue with that," said Canon Walker, joining them. "Can I suggest we head over before the Choir get there? It's like a plague of locusts when they arrive."

They wandered out into First Court to find the sun shining over the Great Gate ramparts. Walking next to Brett, Annabel decided that things were looking pretty good all round.

"So, Annabel. I hear you're helping out with the punts this morning," he said.

"Oh," she said, having completely forgotten that the punt society meeting was today. "Yes, that's right."

"And Nick's coming too?"

"Yeah," she said. "I asked him to bring the Redboys along."

"That's great, I'm looking forward to meeting him."

"Right," said Annabel, wondering how that would go. "Should be fun."

Breakfast had been set up at the far end of Hall on the two Fellows' tables. These lay under the portrait of Lady Margaret Beaufort who looked down on the scene with what Annabel felt was stern approval. A look that was also shared by the woman standing behind the Fellows' servery.

"Good morning, Aurelia," said the Chaplain as they approached.

"Good morning, Canon Walker," replied the waitress. "Is a beautiful day."

"It certainly is. Come on everyone. Get it, while it's hot."

Annabel loaded her plate with eggs, bacon, sausage and beans, and joined Katie and Brett on the table near the bust of Bishop Fisher. The morning sun streamed in from First Court through the huge oriel window, its stained-glass crests projecting a mosaic of colours over the polished oak table. Canon Walker said grace and they all tucked in as the first of the Choir members strolled into Hall.

"Heaven be praised, we made it in time," he said, with a grin.

As the conversation flowed up and down the table, Annabel was glad she'd left the warmth of her bed to come here.

"So, how do you think you're going to do in Bumps?" Katie asked.

"Depends on who we're behind on the river," said Annabel. "But as far as the crew is concerned, it feels like it's coming together."

"Couldn't agree more," said Brett. "Once you got the balance right, everything else started to flow."

"Like life in general," said Canon Walker, who had come to join them. "Take the Choir, for example. Twenty hours practice a week, and yet their grades are some of the best in Cambridge. It's the same for the sports teams. How many hours are you doing a week?"

"At least twelve," said Katie.

"Annabel?"

"Something similar," she replied.

"And when you're not training, what are you doing?"

"Working," she said, thinking about the pile of assignments on her desk.

"Precisely," said Walker, waving a fork with a sausage stuck on the end of it. "But at least then you're ready for it, aren't you?"

"I suppose so," she agreed.

"Balance, that's the secret to doing well here," said the Chaplain. "You mark my words."

Later, when they filed out of Hall, Annabel thanked Canon Walker.

"Always a pleasure, Annabel. I hope to see you again soon. And good luck in Bumps. Give them hell!"

Laughing, she joined Brett and Katie and they headed towards Cripps.

"He's a great guy, isn't he?" said Brett.

"You should hear him talk about cricket," said Katie. "That's his other religion."

"What is it with that game?" said Brett. "You play for days, and still don't get a result."

"You're close to committing blasphemy, there," said Annabel.

And as they wandered through the courts, she and Katie did their best to explain why a draw in cricket could be just as exciting as a win. By the time they made it to B Staircase, Brett held up his hands.

"OK, I guess I'm just going to have to see a game for myself."

"Well, I'm sure Canon Walker will be delighted to take you," said Katie.

"Don't you mean convert me?"

"Probably. Listen, I'm off. Good luck with the punts and give my best to Nick. Tell him, I thought he was brilliant yesterday."

Annabel stared at her, confused.

"You know, Cuppers," said Katie. "The Redboys have made it through to the final."

"Right, of course."

Annabel watched her go, wondering how she'd forgotten about Nick's game.

"You OK?" Brett asked.

"Yeah, fine. Come on, we'd better find this the punt pool."

They headed down the steps and emerged onto a jetty

overlooking a murky stretch of water between Cripps and Magdalene College. Save for a pair of Swans watching them from the bank of a small island, they were alone.

"Looks like we're the first ones here," Brett said, looking around. "Hold on, there he is. Hi Brian!"

The diminutive figure stood inside a large rectangular doorway set in the concrete wall. He was wearing an oversized fleece with SJC PUNTS printed on the front.

"Hi, you two," he said.

"Any sign of the others?" Annabel asked.

"That sounds like them, now," he said.

She heard the sound of footsteps on the stairs and, looking up, she saw a familiar face appear around the corner.

"Hi, Annabel," said Nick.

******

Seeing Annabel standing by the punt pool with the tall, good-looking American shouldn't have come as a surprise to Nick. Still, he felt his stomach tighten as he led Trevor and the rest of the Redboy volunteers down onto the jetty.

Their numbers had been thinned by injuries from the previous day's game, but Trevor and Gareth had managed to drag Aden along, though the latter still looked half asleep.

"So, where do you want us?" Nick asked Brian.

"We're just waiting for Ash," he said.

Moments later, there was a flurry of footsteps and Ash's gangly frame hurried down the steps carrying a canvas shopping bag bulging with packs of Jaffa cakes.

"Hi everyone," he said. "Wow! What a great turnout!"

"They were just asking where we wanted them," Brian said.

"Come inside, and we'll show you what we're doing!"

Ducking through the doorway, Nick went down the ramp after him into what appeared to be a concrete bunker. The others followed, but not before Aden managed to bang his head on the lintel.

"Don't worry," said Gareth. "He's a forward, so no damage done."

"And the building?" Trevor asked.

"That's another matter."

Brett's deep laugh echoed around the cavernous basement.

"So, this is the punt store?" Nick asked.

"Or the Bat Cave as we like to call it," said Ash.

Nick stared around at the low ceilinged basement, which was crisscrossed with pipework, under which Brett and Gareth had to stoop. Storage cabinets and workbenches lined the walls, each filled with vices, planing tools and offcuts of wood. Cans of paint and varnish were stacked in one corner, and there was a heady smell of chemicals and sawdust in the air. But the space was dominated by row upon row of upturned wooden hulls stretching all the way back to the far wall.

"I take it, these are the College punts," said Brett, patting one of the flat-bottomed vessels. "How many are there?"

"Ten in total," replied Ash.

"They look pretty heavy," said Trevor. "You'd better tell us how you want to shift them."

Ash, with the occasional prompt from Brian, launched

into an enthusiastic briefing on the morning's plan of action. Once he had finished. Brian disappeared up the steps to organise wooden rollers on the quayside while Ash led the rest of them over to the first punt. He positioned Nick and Gareth opposite Annabel and Brett towards the stern, and spread the others along either side.

"Nick, isn't it?" said Brett, offering his hand across the upturned hull. "I've heard a lot about you."

"Likewise," said Nick, shaking it.

"I'm Gareth," said the big Welshman.

"Brett."

The two giants shook hands.

"OK, everyone," said Ash. "Let's see if we can lift her."

The punt was as heavy as it looked but working as one, they were able to lift it without too much difficulty.

With Nick, Gareth and Brett using their height to good effect, they hoisted it up the ramp and slid it onto the rollers that Brian had laid out for them. While Ash took hold of the mooring chain, they rumbled the punt along the jetty and launched it into the water.

"Brilliant," he said, leading it around to the mooring points. "I'll just tie her up while you go back for the next one."

As they headed inside, Nick found himself walking next to Brett.

"So, Nick, I hear you boys played yesterday?"

"Yeah, it was against Jesus."

"A good win?"

"In the end. Aden got the winning score," said Nick,

nodding towards his teammate. "Which is why he was looking a little worse for wear this morning."

"Nick forgets to mention the two tries he scored," added Gareth.

"I see," said Brett, eyeing him with interest. "No celebrations for you, then?"

"Maybe after the final," Nick said. He'd been teetotal since that first brutal training session in the snow.

"When's that, then?" Brett asked.

"Tuesday week."

"You should come along," said Gareth. "It's played at the University ground under floodlights. Should be quite a crowd."

"Maybe we can get the girls along, eh, Annabel?" Brett suggested.

"Sure," she said. "Good idea."

Though Nick didn't think she sounded overly enthusiastic about it.

"OK, one down, nine to go," announced Ash. "Ready?"

After four more punts, they stopped for tea, which was served in an eclectic collection of mugs that had seen better days. But there were no complaints when Brian handed out the Jaffa cakes. These seemed to revive Aden, who managed to finish off two packs himself. After the break, he led a chorus of "A pirate's life for me" as they hauled the next punt up the steps.

"You see what we have to put up with in the forwards," Gareth quipped. "Heaven forbid he scores another try."

It didn't take long to shift the remaining punts, much to the delight of Ash. Even Brian seemed happy, joining Aden in a good piratical YAARGH when the last punt launched into the water. The Punt Committee made a point of thanking everyone in person at the end.

"Thanks so much for bringing everyone along, Nick," Ash said.

"No problem."

"Are you joining us for lunch?" Ash asked. "We're going to The Punter just across the road."

Nick didn't think his budget would stretch to a pub meal. "Thanks, but I've got essays to write."

"Oh, OK," said Ash.

"Don't worry," said Aden, "more for us, eh, Brian?"

He clapped his new crewmate on the shoulder, almost sending him into the water.

Looking around, Nick spotted Annabel standing on her own, staring across the punt pool. After saying goodbye to the others, he headed over to join her.

"Hey," he said.

At first, she didn't reply, and when she did, her voice sounded distracted.

"Nick, did you see two swans out there earlier?"

Nick looked towards the distant island, which was empty save for a cluster of feathers at the water's edge. He thought back to when he'd arrived but couldn't remember anything beyond the sight of her and Brett together.

"Can't say that I did."

Annabel scanned the surface of the water, while Nick stood there, thinking *You really don't want to talk to me, do you?*

"Well, I'm heading off now."

"Oh?" she said, turning as if noticing him for the first time. "So, you're not coming to the pub then?"

"No, Library."

"Right. Of course."

Just for a moment, Nick thought she was going to say something, but Brett laughed, and Annabel turned towards the sound.

"I'll see you around," he said and made for the stairs.

"Nick?"

He paused and turned back to her.

"Thanks for bringing the others."

"That's what friends do," he said.

And before she could reply, he headed up the steps, two at a time.

Chapter Nineteen

Ravi entered the Senior Combination Room for lunch with some trepidation. For years he had preferred to take his main meal in the evening before visiting the observatory on Madingley Road. However, he'd been forced to vary his usual routine to avoid the constant attention of Gabrielle Dutour, who dined in Hall most nights.

Seeking him out in the Green Room, she would accompany him to High Table and have him trapped for an hour or more. There she would press him to discuss his earlier research with Robert, something he had done his best to discourage, with little success.

This far into term, Ravi had run out of polite ways of saying no. Instead he had resorted to the ignominious tactic of avoiding her wherever possible.

Standing in the entrance to the seventeenth-century long room, he scanned the heads of those sitting at the extended, mahogany table for her distinctive bob and glasses. What he saw were the usual mix of early diners, senior Fellows seeking to avoid the one o'clock rush of returning lecturers. Of Gabrielle, there was no sign.

Relieved, Ravi made his way along the table to take a seat next to a burly Fellow with a ruddy complexion. Henry Winterbottom was a former Professor of veterinary science, who'd spent many years advising farmers on poultry production.

"Hello, Ravi, not seen you for a while."

"Indeed, Henry, how are you keeping?"

"Can't complain. A bit creaky here and there, but aren't we all? Water?"

It was a dining convention at John's to attend to your neighbour's glass, a tradition that was scrupulously observed.

"Please," said Ravi, studying the menu card. "So, what's on the menu today?"

"The tomato soup is good," said his companion, leaning back to allow the waitress to collect his plate.

"And for you, Professor Gupta?"

Ravi turned and found himself staring up at Aurelia.

"Oh," he said. "Why yes, tomato soup please, followed by the Arnold Bennett omelette."

"Of course."

"I'll have the same," said a familiar voice next to him.

Turning, Ravi found Dominic Lester settling into the adjacent chair.

"Good afternoon, Master."

"Good afternoon, Ravi. You're looking well."

"I still try to walk most mornings, Master. Especially now the snow has gone."

"Ah, yes. I had no idea we had so many talented sculptors in College."

"Indeed, Master." Ravi reached for the jug. "Some water?"

"Thank you."

Ravi poured as Lester nodded at the other Fellows who continued to file in, filling the long table.

"I haven't seen you in Hall recently," Lester remarked.

"I thought I would give lunch a try. Good to sit with some different fellows, now and again."

The Master chuckled.

"Someone was missing you last night."

"Really?" Ravi said as Aurelia returned with their soup.

"Gabrielle Dutour was asking after you."

Ravi may have imagined it, but he noticed a thud as the waitress placed the bowl down in front of him. "Oh?"

"A forceful woman," said the Master, smiling at him. "Gabrielle Dutour, I mean."

"I was going to say intellectually curious."

"Well, she's certainly curious about your research, Ravi," said Lester, reaching for a bread roll. "She even asked me about it."

Ravi put the spoon to his lips but said nothing as he sipped the hot liquid.

"Of course, I explained I knew little of your work," Lester said. "So, instead, I decided to press Gabrielle on the details of her own research."

"And what did you discover?" Ravi knew how effective the former spy was at distilling information from people.

"It proved to be a fascinating conversation. Gabrielle has been doing some remarkable work on the practical applications of space/time theory."

"So I understand." Ravi remembered his conversation with her in the Buttery.

"She has some radical ideas about how these might be used for the benefit of mankind."

"How so?"

"An ecological lifeboat might be a fair summary."

Aurelia returned to remove their plates as Ravi stared at the Master.

"Anyway, Gabrielle seems intrigued by your reluctance to speak with her. She called you her enigma."

Despite the thick Persian carpet, Ravi could feel the floorboards vibrate as Aurelia stomped away with their plates.

"Tell me, Ravi, did you know that Gabrielle is the beneficiary of a very generous research grant?"

"I should imagine so. Practical applications rarely come cheap."

"This one appears to have some particularly deep pockets. So much so that I did some digging."

Lester paused to smile at a couple of younger Fellows heading for the far end of the table.

"As Master, one is always on the lookout for potential benefactors," he continued. "You'd be surprised by how persistent our Development Office is with its enquiries."

"I had heard," said Ravi.

The College's Development Director had an intelligence network that could rival that of a small country.

"Hidden behind the various funding organisations, many of which had labyrinthine ownership structures, we found an entity that you might be familiar with. Indeed, one that was good enough to fund a project of yours."

"Sorry?" said Ravi, confused. "My research does not rely on any external funding at the moment."

"I wasn't referring to your research," said the Master, as Aurelia returned with their main course and laid the plates in front of them.

"I don't understand?"

"Your schools' programme," said Lester. "In Nepal."

"I..." but then Ravi understood, and his stomach churned.

"Quite," said Lester, noticing his discomfort. "It turns out that if one looks far enough behind her network of support bodies, Gabrielle Dutour's work is funded by the Schiller Foundation."

Ravi stared at Lester, who looked back at him, his face a mask.

"You're sure?"

"As eggs are eggs."

"Is Gabrielle aware of this?"

"That is something I was hoping you might discover," Lester said. "Something for you to discuss the next time you dine with her on High Table, perhaps?"

The Master turned to his other neighbour.

"Peter, could I trouble you for the salt please?"

Ravi looked down at his omelette, his appetite gone. Instead, he stared out the leaded window at the distant rooftops of Second Court, digesting this new information. A voice murmured in his ear.

"I'd be careful there if I were you."

Startled, Ravi turned and found Henry Winterbottom looking at him.

"Sorry?"

The vet indicated the omelette.

"Can't be too careful with eggs," he said, tapping his nose. "Parasites, you see. Difficult to eradicate."

"Oh? Right."

As he watched the old Fellow tuck into his beef stew, Ravi felt a deep sense of unease at this latest development.

The idea that Schiller could be using Gabrielle as his mole was disturbing, though not unprecedented. He had encountered other moles in College before. The last time, he'd been young and naive. So much so that he'd not seen it coming. Not, he remembered, until it was way too late.

******

Robert's good-natured laughter echoed across the Hall, and Ravi smiled as Mary giggled into her glass of wine.

"You can imagine how ridiculous I looked," said his friend, "standing there with my face sporting a charcoal moustache, protesting my sobriety to the Porters. Needless to say, I got Deaned."

"What was the punishment?"

"On that occasion, I had to polish the Chapel floor by hand. Though to be fair, I had some assistance from the cleaning staff who took pity on me."

"Bribed more like," said Ravi.

"A few bottles of beer may have changed hands,"

admitted Robert. "It was either that or nobble my knees before the varsity match."

"So, when you boys aren't tormenting Porters," asked Mary, "how do you spend your time?"

Ravi saw Robert's eyes twinkle, and before he could intervene, his friend leaned forwards and whispered. "That, my dear, is a closely guarded secret. Only to be shared with trusted collaborators."

"Sounds mysterious," she said with a grin. "Are girls allowed, or is this just another bastion of male privilege?"

Ravi wanted to change the subject, but flushed with wine, Robert ploughed on.

"Hardly. Membership has to be earned. A minimum of six months hard labour down at the Cavendish, peering at distant objects without giving up the will to live."

"I meet two of those for sure. Does hanging on by one's fingernails count for the latter?"

Robert took her hand and examined it.

"I see what you mean," he said.

"Hey!" she said, pulling them away. "Seriously, though. I could do with something a bit more challenging. I spend most of my time at the lab doing data entry."

"That's because you made the mistake of showing you can type. Always fatal. Like making a good cup of tea, eh Ravi?"

"Robert's tea is undrinkable," he confirmed.

"You see? The good news is that Ravi here is something of a tea sommelier, so you won't be required to perform that essential role."

"So," she dropped her voice, "what exactly is involved in this secret society of yours?"

"Perhaps we can show you Mission Control. What do you say, Ravi?"

Ravi found them both staring at him, the two people he most wanted to please in the world. Their faces, alive with mischief, were as intoxicating to him as the bottles of wine they had polished off over dinner.

"We could show you, I suppose," he said as Mary gazed at him. "But it's not very glamorous."

"Glamorous? It's downright hideous," said Robert." But it's all the College would give us at the time. Do you have the key, Ravi?"

"You're not thinking of going now, Robert?"

"Why not?" He turned to Mary. "Are you wearing sensible shoes?"

"I'm sure I'll manage," she said, her eyes sparkling with excitement.

"Good girl," said Robert approvingly. "In that case, we have something special to show you, my dear."

After finishing their wine, they headed out of Hall and across Second Court towards the river. Ravi found himself following the other two, who were laughing and joking as they crossed the Bridge of Sighs, oblivious to his presence.

It was only when they reached New Court's B Staircase that his friend turned to him. "Of course, all this would not have been possible without Ravi here. The man's a genius. He was Senior Wrangler in our final year."

Robert was referring to Ravi getting the top grade in the

Cambridge mathematics tripos across the University.

Mary arched an eyebrow and gazed at him.

"Was he indeed?"

Ravi felt his cheeks flush. "I wouldn't pay much attention to that sort of thing."

"You're too modest as always," said Robert, holding the lobby door open for them.

Aware of Mary's eyes on him, Ravi hurried past her towards the cellar door.

"You mark my words," said Robert, "my good friend is going to change the world one day."

Ravi was so flustered that he dropped the keys before finding the right one and opening the door. Turning on the lights, he said, "Watch your dress, Mary. The walls can be damp in places."

"The damn place is always flooding," explained Robert. "Below river level, you see."

"How exciting," she said, following him down the stairs.

Ravi closed the door and hurried after them.

Robert strode through the labyrinth of tunnels, the route second nature after all these months. They came to a long corridor with openings on either side, and they halted before the last door on the left.

"Is this it?" Mary asked.

"Certainly is. This is the end of the road," said Robert, giving Ravi a wink, "so to speak."

Ravi gave him a sharp look while selecting the key. "I'm sorry for the long trek."

"Don't apologise," she replied. "It has only added to the suspense!"

Seeing the eager, almost hungry look on her face, Ravi wondered if they were about to make a terrible mistake. He tried to catch Robert's attention. But his friend only had eyes for their guest and appeared to be enjoying her reaction.

"Go on then, Ravi," he said. "Let's not keep the lady waiting!"

With a strange sense of foreboding, Ravi inserted the key and unlocked the door. Robert reached past him and found the switch.

The overhead light bulbs illuminated the room in which they'd been working these past months. Some twenty feet long, its arched roof was just high enough to accommodate Robert's six-foot frame. Racks ran along the sides of the cellar, their shelves filled with boxes of equipment and files. But it was the far wall which drew their guest's attention. Mary crossed the room and paused in front of it.

The brickwork had been painted from floor to ceiling with blackboard paint, which was covered in numbers and diagrams.

Ravi watched as his two friends stood side by side, facing his life's work.

"Welcome to Mission Control," said Robert.

******

"Professor?"

Ravi closed his eyes and the memory faded.

"Professor," said Aurelia, "have you finished?"

Looking around, Ravi found that he was sitting alone on the long table, the last of his lunchtime companions now heading for the Combination Room door.

"Would you like some fruit or cheese?"

"No, I'm fine, thank you, Aurelia. Don't let me keep you."

Rising from his chair, Ravi gave her an apologetic smile and left the room.

Passing the portraits of former Masters on the stairs, he remembered that the current incumbent had just instructed him to re-engage with Gabrielle and report back his findings. Not wishing to encounter Lester in the Green Room again, he decided to forego coffee and head back to his room for a cup of tea instead.

A gust of wind buffeted him as he stepped out into Second Court. Keeping his head down, he made his way to the sanctuary of his staircase. Thrusting his room indicator to IN, Ravi had just begun stomping up the stairs when he heard a voice call him.

"Professor?"

Turning, he peered down at the entrance, where a small figure stood staring up at him.

"Annabel?"

"Sorry, Professor, is now a bad time?"

"No, I was… pre-occupied, that's all."

"I can come back later if you want?"

Ravi noticed how pale and drawn she looked.

"There's no need for that, Annabel. How can I help?"

She hesitated, and he saw her lip tremble.

"How about a cup of tea?" he suggested. "I daresay I might even have some chocolate somewhere."

"Haven't you just eaten?"

"Over the years I have found that there's always room for chocolate."

Annabel smiled. "Always."

"Come on then," he said, setting off up the stairs. "Let's put the kettle on."

Chapter Twenty

It was late when Giles returned to his room and deposited his script on the desk next to the well-thumbed Roof-Climber's Guide.

Since seeing the mysterious figure above Professor Gupta's staircase, he'd made several night-time forays over the College's rooftops in the hope of another sighting. So far, he'd only managed to startle an owl above First Court and stumble upon a pair of students smoking from their Third Court windows. Tonight, he planned on staking out the Shrewsbury Tower above Second Court.

Opening his wardrobe, Giles slipped on a pair of rock shoes and his climbing jacket before pulling a buff around his neck and a charcoal beanie over his blond hair. From a backpack, he retrieved a much-scuffed LED torch, which he stuffed into his trouser pocket after checking the battery. With no one to belay for him, he ignored the harness, ropes and carabiners in the bottom of the bag. That just left the ice axe.

It lay in the corner of the wardrobe, its notched metal blade winking at him in the glow of the ceiling light. Of course, there was no technical reason to have something like that with him, no sheer-sided ice cliffs to scale. And if he was caught by a Porter, even he might find it difficult explaining why he had an axe with him.

But Giles still remembered that strange sniffing noise from the ramparts, and he knew from bitter experience that there were worse things than Porters prowling the rooftops at night. Picking the faithful axe up, he clipped it to his belt.

"Can't be too careful," he said to himself.

With everything he needed, Giles reached up to the window set high in his wood-panelled wall and swung it open. Cold air seeped into the room as he pulled himself up and onto the ledge. Outside, all was quiet, and after checking below, he lowered himself onto the Buttery roof.

The 1960s self-service canteen hadn't been built when the Roof Climber's Guide had been written. It now provided a much easier starting point for an avid reader planning on completing "Route B: Circuit of Second Court".

Giles made his way along to a sturdy iron drainpipe and used it to shimmy his way up to the narrow ledge that ran along the Southside of the sixteenth-century roof. Once there, he looked across the moonlit lawns of Trinity, which were spread out before him. There were a few lights visible in buildings beyond, but he doubted any of their occupants would spot his catlike form at this distance.

Turning towards the river, he climbed over window gables and behind tall chimney stacks until he reached the Third Court roof. This was where he'd almost been spotted the previous week by the illicit smokers reclining on the ledge outside their room.

Tonight, however, there were no glowing red dots visible, so he headed north over the tiles towards the Shrewsbury Tower. Here, he found the drainpipe described in the guide that gave him access to the roof. After a brief climb, he emerged onto the relative safety of its turreted crown, hidden from prying eyes in the courts below.

Standing here beneath the moon and stars, he could well understand why in the nineteenth-century the College's astronomers had chosen this location to house an observatory. Though those old telescopes had long since been relocated to various museums, the tower still afforded commanding views over both Second and Third Courts.

Giles heard voices and footsteps below, and he shrank back into the shadows of one of the turrets. A pair of night Porters emerged from the archway beneath him. They strolled between the moonlit lawns before turning towards Chapel Court.

By their relaxed demeanour, they appeared to be at the end of an uneventful patrol. No doubt heading back for a warming cup of tea in the Forecourt Lodge. Still, he waited until they'd disappeared into the passageway before stepping out from the shadows and staring out across the court.

In the far corner, the Chapel Tower rose into the night sky, its sheer sides pale and forbidding. The surrounding sixteenth-century buildings looked dark by comparison, save for the mullioned windows of Hall, which glinted in the moonlight. All appeared still, and though he watched for some time, he could detect nothing moving among the chimneys and gables.

Turning, he crossed to the opposite side of the tower and looked out across the river towards the distant pinnacle of New Court. The golden weathervane glinted in the gentle breeze, and Giles remembered that moment last term when he'd leapt from that very spot to escape the harpy.

Though terrifying at the time, he couldn't deny it had been exhilarating too. Perhaps he'd been hoping for something similar after spotting the shadow above Gupta's room. But despite his night-time forays, there hadn't been so much as a sniff from the mysterious stalker. After another uneventful patrol this evening, maybe it was time to switch focus.

Earlier that week, he'd managed to deploy the surveillance camera in the Old Library. After several failed attempts, he'd found a place on top of a bookcase that gave an excellent field of vision, while concealing the camera behind a benefactor's crest. He hoped he now had some footage to explain what the Professor had been doing up there.

Giles glanced towards the Old Library, its long-ridged roof looking skeletal in the moonlight. At its far end, two tall pinnacles rose from a carved gable, and between these stood a statue staring out across the river.

He blinked.

The Old Library didn't have a statue. At least, not as far as he could remember. Staring at the motionless shape, Giles wondered if he was mistaken. But then he saw the figure crane forwards to peer down at the water far below.

"Gotcha," he whispered.

Whether it heard him or sensed it was being watched,

Giles would never know. But in that instant, the figure spun around and glared back at him. They both stood perfectly still, eyeing each other across the rooftops.

Then, it started to run. One moment, it was standing by the gable, and the next, it was sprinting at breakneck speed along the roof.

"Oh no, you don't!"

Giles rushed to the other side of the tower in time to see the figure leap from the Library towards the Second Court roof. As it flew through the air, the folds of the cloak swept back just for a moment, but it was enough. There was the fleeting glimpse of a long flowing dress before the figure landed on the sloping roof and disappeared from view.

"Clever girl," he said before peering over the parapet.

There was the top of the drainpipe. Swinging his legs over, Giles used it like a fireman's pole, sliding down to the roof below. As soon as his feet touched the tiles, he set off in pursuit.

Taking the inside track around Second Court, he scrambled over the window gables, all the time keeping track of the footsteps of the figure doing the same on the Chapel side of the court. As they neared the final section of the roof, known in the Night-Climber's Guide as "The Dean's Highway", he wondered if the other person would slow down. If anything, though, the footsteps sped up.

Desperate not to lose her now, he vaulted over the final two gabled windows and clambered around Dr Jones's staircase turret. Panting, Giles stared along the pitched roof of the Hall. Nothing stirred in the pale moonlight.

Where the hell had she gone?

Careful not to make any noise, he lowered himself onto the narrow walkway at the bottom of the slope and pulled the torch from his jacket pocket. He swept the beam over the steeply rising tiles before directing it at the set of false gables that ran along the inside of the court. Each of these had an archway cut into them to allow access to the bell tower halfway along the roof.

Giles edged forward, keeping the torch trained on the first of these openings, expecting at any moment to see the shape appear. He paused on the ledge above the Dean's staircase, known as Gunning's balcony. Named after one of the College's earliest night climbers, he could just make out the carved inscription in the lead flashing.

PETRUS GUNNING ELIENSIS, HUJUS COLL: ALUMNUS FEB 19TH 1734.

"So, Peter," he asked under his breath, "where did she go?"

That was when he heard a hiss behind him. Giles spun around and just caught sight of a pale fist before a blinding pain exploded in his cheek.

The next thing he knew, he was lying flat on the leaded roof with the hooded figure looming over him. Still groggy, he felt around for the torch, but it was nowhere to be found. Instead, a hand grabbed his jacket and lifted him from the floor. The figure leaned in, and Giles heard a familiar sound. Only this time, and this close, it made his skin crawl.

Sniff.

"What's going on out there!"

The voice came from the Dean's window, and for an instant, the figure above him froze. When it turned towards the noise, Giles felt the pressure on his chest ease a fraction. He reached for the clasp holding the axe to his belt.

"I'm warning you," the voice called out. "I've called the Porters!"

A light went on in the Dean's window, and a blurred outline appeared in the frame. Still gripping the front of his jacket, the figure flinched from the glare and Giles seized his chance. He tugged the ice axe free and swung it at the arm holding him.

How she sensed it coming he never knew. In a blur, she twisted to block his blow with her hand, before grasping the blade and ripping the axe from his grip. Moments later, Giles found himself flying across the roof and slammed into the parapet wall.

For a moment, he lay there, too stunned to move as she strode towards him. Even as her pale hands stretched towards him, a bright beam of light shone up from the court below. The figure gave an angry hiss and crouched down behind the parapet, shielding her face from the glare.

"You there!" A voice demanded. "What the hell do you think you're doing?"

The cowl looked towards Giles, and he heard that hiss again. Then the figure turned and ran back along the walkway, disappearing into the shadows.

From the turret window, he heard the Dean's voice call out. "Bert? Is that you?"

"Dr Jones? What's going on?"

Stifling a groan, Giles levered himself up and peered over the rampart. Two Porters, both wielding flashlights, were standing on the Second Court lawn.

The Dean called down. "There are people climbing on the roof!"

A beam swung in Giles's direction, and he ducked behind the wall.

"There's one!"

He recognised Shirley's voice.

"We'll be right up, Dr Jones!" Bert replied.

Groggy as he was, Giles knew he had to get moving.

Groping around, he searched for the ice axe, but there was no sign of it. Instead, his fingers closed around the stubby torch. Thankfully, its beam was no longer shining to give his position away. Stuffing it in his pocket, he heard the thump of footsteps coming up the turret stairwell.

"Time to go," he said, getting to his feet.

Keeping his head down, he headed for the Bell Tower, ducking through the gable archways as he tried to put as much distance as possible between him and his pursuers. Once past the tower, he had to clamber over more window gables until he reached the turret above his own staircase.

That was when he heard the thump of an access door somewhere behind him. Glancing back, he saw two beams of light probing across the Hall roof like wartime searchlights.

Sod this for a game of soldiers, he thought, and began scrambling up the final incline. At the top, he was greeted by the welcome sight of Trinity College laid out before him once again. Swinging his legs over the ridgeline, he glanced back in time to see a bright beam of light sweep towards him.

Letting go, he slid down the roof until his feet hit the ledge at the bottom of the slope. There he stood, his forehead pressed against the tiles as the beams passed back and forth overhead.

"And that, ladies and gentlemen," he panted, "is a wrap."

Shortly afterwards, Giles lowered himself through his bedroom window and felt the reassuring creak of old floorboards beneath his feet. Pulling the window shut, he staggered across the room and collapsed into his armchair.

"Well, that was eventful," he said with a smile.

He reached up to touch his cheek and winced at the lump forming there. Whoever that night climber was, she packed quite a punch, and was quick too. He doubted the Porters would catch her. Though where she'd run off to was anyone's guess. Back along the Dean's Highway perhaps? He made a mental note to check the Guide to see if there was another route down from the roof that he'd overlooked.

What worried Giles more was the loss of the ice axe. If it could be traced back to him, he'd be Deaned for sure. And after clambering over her roof, he doubted Dr Jones would go easy on him this time.

Feeling battered and sore, he rose gingerly to his feet. What he needed now more than anything was a shower, and a stiff drink. And not necessarily in that order.

Pulling off his climbing jacket, he felt in the pocket for the torch. "At least I got you back," he said, taking it out to inspect the damage.

"Holy crap!" he yelled, dropping it on the floor. It landed with a thud and rolled down the slope of his room until it came to rest by the leg of his bed.

Giles stared in horror. It wasn't a torch at all. It was a finger. And this one was made of stone.

Chapter Twenty-One

Giles spent most of the next day down at the Sedgwick site, examining the finger at the Museum of Earth Sciences. He ran a whole series of tests on the stone, so it wasn't until late afternoon that he headed back to College on his lime-green bike, pursued by a peloton of other cyclists returning from lectures.

Rising from the saddle, he accelerated up Sydney Street, past the closely packed shops, and merged with the traffic from Jesus Lane. Only when he neared the sweet shop on the corner, did he slow down for a family using the zebra crossing, the mother smiling her thanks as she ushered her children across.

Turning left into St John's Street, Giles called over his shoulder to the bikes behind him, "We'll call that a tie, guys. I'm feeling generous," before parking his bike in Forecourt. When he entered the lodge he was greeted by Bert, who looked unusually serious for once.

"Evening Giles, what have you been up to then?"

The Head Porter indicated the bruise on Giles's cheek.

"Occupational hazard," he said. "You know us drama

types, Bert. Fight scenes and all that."

"I don't remember too many of those in Pygmalion."

"I don't know. That Eliza Doolittle can be quite feisty."

"I see," said Bert, not sounding convinced. "Anyway, I was wondering if you could help us with something." He reached under the counter and produced Giles's ice axe. "We found this embedded in the Second Court lawn. The Dean's been asking who it belongs to."

Giles stared down at the notched blade and then at the Head Porter. Their eyes met and Bert offered the handle to Giles.

"I'd keep it out of sight if I were you," he said. "This too." He placed a battered LED torch on the top as well.

Giles hesitated a moment before stuffing the axe inside his backpack, and pocketing the torch.

"Thanks, Bert."

"I wouldn't want Ying to be without her leading man. Not after I've bought tickets to the show. Mind how you go, young man."

"Will do, Bert."

Slipping his backpack on, Giles hurried out the door, and almost collided with the College rugby team coming the other way.

"Sorry boys! Didn't see you there."

"Easy to miss, I suppose," said Gareth, holding the door open. "You coming tonight, Giles?"

"Cuppers final? Are you kidding? Ying cancelled rehearsals especially." He stepped out of the way as the others filed past. "Where is Trevor anyway?"

"Bringing up the rear," came a familiar voice.

He saw his friend carrying a net of rugby balls over one beefy shoulder.

Giles grinned. "All set?"

"Will be. Just heading down early to practise some drills."

"I see you're playing your B team." Giles nodded at Gareth.

"Yeah, well, we were short of players."

In the distance, Giles heard the Library door thump open, and saw Nick jog across the court, kitbag in hand and face set.

"Looks like this one's got his game head on."

Trevor snorted. "Yeah, I wouldn't want Woody tackling me tonight."

"You and me both," Giles agreed. "Listen, Trev, I just want a quick word with young Nick here. I'll catch you later."

"I'm counting on it."

As his friend headed off, Giles turned to greet the last member of the squad.

"Don't look so cheerful, Nick," he said. "It may never happen."

The younger student smiled. "Hi, Giles. Are you coming later?"

"Do bears crap in the forest? I'll be there."

Nick frowned. "What happened to your face?"

"That's what I wanted to talk to you about."

"Now's not really a good time."

"I was thinking after the game."

"Sure. Nothing serious is it?"

"I think the Professor's got a rooftop stalker."

Nick's expression darkened. "Does he know?"

"I was on my way to see him now."

"Try the Old Library. He's been there all afternoon."

"How do you know?"

"The law section overlooks it."

The lodge door opened, and Trevor called out. "Woody, are you coming or what?"

"On my way!" He shouldered his kitbag. "Better run."

"Can you bring Annabel with you?"

"Annabel? Why?"

"She needs to know too."

Nick hesitated. "Sure, if I see her."

"Woody!" yelled Trevor.

"Coming!" he replied. "Sorry, Giles, gotta go."

"OK, I'll see you later. Have a good one."

Nick headed off to join his teammates and Giles glanced at his watch. It was already five o'clock. Hurrying across the court, he made his way to the Old Library, where the archivist looked up and smiled.

"Evening, Giles. What brings you here today?"

"Evening, Andrea. I was wondering if Professor Gupta was around?"

"Well, yes, he's upstairs. Though I'm not sure that he wants to be disturbed."

"It won't take long, I promise."

"Well, I was about to let the Professor know we'll be closing shortly."

"In that case, I can save you the trouble."

He went over to the visitor book to sign in. As he did so, he saw that Nick was right. The Professor had been there most of the afternoon. Leaving his backpack by the table, Giles entered the lower library, wondering what the Professor had been up to all this time.

The rattle of his footsteps on the iron staircase announced him better than any doorbell, and he half expected to find the old Fellow waiting for him at the top of the stairs. Instead, the upper library appeared deserted. Peering along its length, he was aware of how dark it was, the early evening light barely penetrating the screened windows. The place was also quiet as a grave.

Giles walked down the carpeted aisle, checking each of the alcoves as he passed. When he reached the stone archway leading to the original entrance, he noticed the sliver of light. It was coming from a hidden door set back in the wood-panelled lobby.

Standing outside, he listened for a moment before tapping his knuckles against the frame.

"Professor Gupta?"

There was the scrape of a chair and the creaking of floorboards inside. The brass knob gave a metallic squeak, and the door opened a fraction.

"Giles?"

"Hello, Professor."

"What are you doing here?"

"There's something I need to show you."

"I'm rather busy. Can it wait?"

"Afraid not."

The old man studied him.

"Very well. Come in."

Giles stepped through the doorway into a cramped office with arched windows, a large stone fireplace, and bookcases lining the walls. On the table lay a leather book, which Gupta closed, though not before Giles saw that the pages were covered in symbols and geometric patterns.

The Professor slipped something in his pocket and turned to face him. As he did so, Giles noticed a giant canvas scroll hanging on the wall behind him.

"Is that the Mappa Mundi?" Giles asked.

The old man turned and looked at the medieval illustration of the known world.

"It is," he said, "though not the original Hereford version, I'm afraid."

"I didn't know we had one."

"You'd be surprised what the College has in its archives," said the Professor, meeting his gaze. "Still, Giles, I'm sure you didn't come here to talk to me about maps."

"No," he said, reaching into his pocket. "I've got something to show you, Professor."

Giles pulled out a red-spotted handkerchief. "I found this the other night and thought you should see it."

Peeling back the layers, he held out the stone finger.

Gupta stared at it. "Where did you get that?"

"From a statue, I think."

"You think?"

"It's made from Ancaster stone, like many of the statues

here. Except that this particular one tried to throw me off the Second Court roof."

The Professor stiffened. "When was this?"

"The other night. I didn't get a good look at her, I'm afraid."

"Her?"

"I'm pretty sure she was female, but it was difficult to tell under the hood."

"Did she say anything?"

"No," he said. "Just sniffed."

"Sniffed?"

"Remember when we met below your room?"

The old man stared at him. "She wore a cloak, you say. You're sure that's what it was. Not a pair of…?"

"Wings?"

"Well, yes."

"No. This one had arms and legs, and the agility of a cat. Once she spotted me, I could barely keep up with her. And when it comes to rooftops, Professor, I'm no slouch."

The old man nodded. "So how did you get this… sample?"

"You remember the ice axe? Must have happened when I took a swing at her. Though you'd never have known. She didn't even flinch."

The Professor indicated the handkerchief. "May I?"

"Be my guest."

Reaching down, Gupta picked up the finger and examined it.

"So what do you think?" Giles asked. "Were there human

creatures in the other world?"

"No," said the Professor. "Not to my knowledge."

Giles waited for him to say more, but the old man just kept staring at the finger. Trying a different tack, he asked, "Professor, do you still have that talon you recovered last term?"

"From the harpy, you mean?"

"That's the one. Perhaps we could compare its composition."

Gupta shook his head.

"After we destroyed the creature, all that was left was a pile of dust. That's what happens when the creatures die."

Giles looked at the severed finger. "Which means this one's still alive."

The Professor placed the finger back on the handkerchief. "I think so, yes."

"Then we had better find her," Giles said, "before she does any harm."

"Tell me, Giles, where exactly did you see her?"

"I first spotted her on the Old Library roof."

"Above here?" Gupta glanced up at the ceiling.

"Yep, at the far end. It looked like she was staring down at the river."

"Have you told anyone else yet?"

"No." Giles omitted to mention that he had arranged to speak with Nick and Annabel later.

"For the moment, can I ask you to keep this to yourself? There's someone I have to speak to first."

"The Master?"

Gupta shook his head. "Not yet at least. No, someone who's been showing an unhealthy interest in Robert's research."

"Professor Mackenzie's, you mean? You think this person may have something to do with our hooded friend?"

"That's what I intend to find out."

A knock on the door made them both jump. Giles wrapped the finger in the handkerchief and stuffed it in his pocket. The door creaked open and the archivist peered through the gap.

"Sorry to disturb you, gentlemen, but I'm about to lock up."

"Of course, Andrea, my apologies," Gupta said. "I think Giles and I were just finished."

"Yes, Professor, thanks for your help. I look forward to hearing how you get on with that research."

"I'll be sure to let you know. Andrea, if you don't mind showing Mr Chamberlain out, I'll just tidy up here and be down shortly."

Leaving him in the office, Giles followed the archivist between the tall bookcases, their crested ends standing sentinel as they passed. The old man had been his usual secretive self, of course, but there was no doubt the finger had spooked him. The question was, what would he do next?

We'll soon find out, Giles thought, glancing up to where the surveillance camera lay hidden. Gupta may have tried to conceal the title of the leather volume he'd been reading, but by tomorrow night, Giles would know where to find it.

They arrived at the old metal staircase, and Andrea was

about to head down when a deep rumble of thunder shook the building.

"Sounds like a storm's coming," she said.

Giles stared out through the Oriel window, and saw dark clouds rolling towards the College from the West.

"You're not wrong," he replied, before following her down the steps.

Chapter Twenty-Two

Once Giles had gone, Ravi leant against the table in the Old Library office and considered his next move. When he'd found the young man standing outside his hidden sanctuary, he'd been worried. But the sight of the severed finger had confirmed his worst fears. Something had come through the portal. The question was how? Or, more to the point, when?

He thought of Robert. Now more than ever, he needed to know what his friend had been doing last summer. And that meant speaking to the one person who had access to his research, Gabrielle Dutour. If the Master was right and Schiller was funding her work, Ravi had to find out exactly what she knew.

Ravi picked up the leather-bound volume he'd been studying and checked to make sure the pieces of parchment were safely inside. With a final glance at the map on the wall, he turned off the office light and hurried down the carpeted aisle to the last alcove on the right. He was about to return the book to its shelf when a flicker of lightning illuminated the bookcases. Ravi hesitated and glanced around, unable to shake the feeling that he was being watched.

His eyes settled on the pale face of William Wordsworth, staring back at him from across the aisle. The life mask sat in its glass cabinet by the oriel window, as it had done for two hundred years. Ravi shook his head.

"Jumping at shadows."

He slid the book into place and headed for the spiral staircase. When he arrived back at the Old Library reading room, he found the archivist waiting for him with her coat on.

"My apologies, Andrea."

"All done for the evening?"

"One's work is never done, it seems."

"In that case, I hope you have a productive night."

"Oh, I intend to," he said. "Good night."

After leaving the Library, Ravi headed straight for the Forecourt Lodge, where he found Bert reading the Cambridge News.

"Evening, Professor. Will you be heading down to watch the rugby later?"

"I'm afraid not, Bert. Something has cropped up. I was wondering, do you have the Fellows' dining list for this evening?"

"Of course. Though I don't remember your name being on it."

"No. I was hoping to catch up with Dr Dutour, and wondered if she was dining tonight."

"I believe so," said the Head Porter, returning with a typed menu card with the names of the fellows planning to dine. Sure enough, Gabriele's name was there at the bottom of the list.

"Excellent. Many thanks." He handed it back.

"Oh, and this came in for you earlier, Professor."

Bert handed him a pale blue envelope. Ravi looked at the Yorkshire postmark with his address in neat flowing script. Reaching inside his jacket pocket, he drew out the old ruler and slit it open. There was a single sheet of paper inside.

Dear Professor Gupta,

I trust you are well. The weather here in Yorkshire is wet but considerably milder than a few weeks ago. Annabel tells me the daffodils are coming through on the Backs, a sure sign that Spring is on its way. I'm so glad she can be there to enjoy it with her friends.

Annabel mentioned that she had been to see you recently and found your advice invaluable as always. I just wanted to thank you once again for all you do for her and your other tutees. It is a source of great comfort to me that you are there should she need a cup of tea and a chat. For that, I am truly grateful.

I plan to travel down to Cambridge for the last day of Bumps, and it would be lovely to thank you in person if you were around on that Saturday. I understand The Plough is an excellent place to watch the action. Still, I'm sure you are more experienced in these matters than I. Rest assured I shall be buying the first round. It is the least I can do by way of thanks.

Yours as ever,

Patricia Hamilton.

Ravi thought back to that moment in All Saints Passage when he'd witnessed this formidable woman disable an attacker and dress a gunshot wound in the space of a few minutes. Though he didn't usually socialise with his Tutees' families, he decided that this wasn't someone who'd take no for an answer. Though the words "first round" sounded ominous. He wondered just how many she had in mind.

The sound of the Trinity bell brought him back to the present. Glancing up at the clock behind the lodge desk, he was surprised to find that it was already six o'clock. If he was going to catch Gabrielle Dutour before supper, he needed to go now.

"Everything all right, Professor?" Bert asked.

"What? Oh, yes, fine, thank you. Have a good evening."

"I daresay we'll be busy with the Redboys, but nothing we can't handle. Good night Professor."

Ravi left the lodge and hurried across Chapel Court to Gabriele's staircase. After climbing to the top floor, he paused on the landing to gather his breath before knocking on her door. There was no reply, so he tried again, louder this time. Still no response.

Frowning, Ravi wondered if she wasn't back from the Cavendish yet. But when he tried the door, he found it unlocked.

"Hello? Is anyone at home?"

The room was silent. Ravi stepped inside and stared around at the tasteful apartment. Save for a faded wine stain on the carpet, it was immaculate. A far cry from the shabby confusion of his own room. Its owner, however, was nowhere to be seen.

"Gabrielle?"

Still no response, though he thought he heard a faint rattle in the distance. Moving through the apartment, he passed a small kitchenette and entered a short hallway leading to another room. Peering inside, he saw it was her study. A white desk ran along the far wall, covered with files. Next to these sat a computer with a screensaver of snow-capped mountains. This provided the only light in the otherwise darkened space.

Just then, a gust of wind fluttered a stack of papers, and Ravi heard that same rattle again, though closer now. He saw that one of the large windows facing the river was open, its blinds swaying back and forth in the breeze.

Ravi approached the opening and peered outside. He found himself looking out onto a flat roof bordered by a low parapet of brickwork. Beyond this, he could make out the boxy profile of the Cripps building through the swaying branches of a plane tree. And to the right of that lay the Master's Lodge, its chimneys jutting up towards the blackened sky.

But it was the figure standing on the edge of the parapet that caught his eye. It stood motionless with its back to the window, the long hooded cloak flapping in the breeze as its wearer stared out over the Master's Garden towards New Court.

Heart racing, Ravi reached inside his jacket pocket and withdrew the ruler. In doing so, his arm knocked the blind, which rattled against the window frame. The figure spun around, and he saw a pale face with huge eyes staring back at him.

"*Zut alors*!" Gabrielle cried, stepping back in surprise.

The woman's foot struck the low wall. The cigarette she had been holding flew into the air, its glowing red tip spinning end over end. Gabriele's mouth opened wide, forming an O as, arms wheeling, she toppled backwards.

How Ravi made it out through the window, he never knew. One moment, he was standing on the plush grey carpet, and the next, he was lunging across the roof for her. Gabriele's flailing hand grabbed his wrist and yanked him towards the edge. His leather shoes skidded across the leaded surface until his heels caught on a welded seam, arresting his momentum.

For several heart-stopping moments, they tottered there, Gabriele's body hovering over the sheer drop and him straining to hold her back. Then gravity, a capricious friend at best, for once lent him a helping hand. Ravi felt its blessed pull as he staggered back, dragging her with him. They fell in a heap on the floor, with Gabrielle landing on top of him.

"Ooof!" he gasped.

There was an awkward moment as he stared up at her, their faces inches apart, noses almost touching. Then Gabrielle rolled off him. They both lay side by side, staring skywards, skin glistening with sweat, chests rising and falling like exhausted lovers.

"*Merde.*"

"Quite," he replied, turning his head to look at her. Beneath the dishevelled hair, her skin looked ghostly white.

"Are you all right?" he asked.

"*Oui*," she said. "You?"

Ravi wondered. Apart from a racing heart and a near dislocated shoulder, his backside felt like one enormous bruise.

"I'll live," he said, thinking it could have been a lot worse.

That dreadful image of Robert's lifeless body at the foot of New Court came to mind. What would the College gardeners have made of finding Ravi and Gabrielle lying dead in each other's arms among the Master's roses, he wondered? Or Lester finding them, for that matter? Ravi shuddered at the thought.

"Are you cold?" she asked.

"No, it's just... Well, I mean, perhaps we should head back inside."

But before he could get up, her hand clasped his arm, and he found her staring at him through those large lenses.

"*Merci*, Ravi. I am very grateful."

"You're welcome, Gabrielle."

For a moment, he thought she was going to say something else, but instead, she let go of him and began getting up.

"*Mon Dieu*, if ever I needed a cigarette it is now." But when she saw the look he gave, she relented. "OK, a drink then?"

"That's probably a better idea."

"*Bon*, come."

Heading back inside, Gabrielle removed her cloak and hung it on the back of the study door.

"Cognac?"

"Sounds good."

"Please, take a seat."

Ravi returned to the living room, and lowered himself into a Swedish-looking armchair. Gabrielle reappeared carrying a bottle and a couple of brandy glasses, which she deposited on the coffee table. Pouring two generous measures, she handed him one and took hers over to the sofa.

"*Santé*," she said, raising her glass.

Ravi did the same and took a sip. The burning sensation came as a shock, though not an unpleasant one. He settled back into his chair, noticing that Gabrielle had finished hers in one gulp, and was pouring another. Catching his eye, she shrugged.

"I had not had such an experience before. To feel that all is about to end, and your existence hangs by a thread, that is rare indeed."

Not as rare as you might think, Ravi mused.

"Will you tell the Master?" she asked.

"About what?"

"My secret."

Ravi stared at her.

"The smoking," she said. "It is not permitted in rooms."

"As I recall, Gabrielle, you were not in your room."

She appeared to consider this. "That is true."

"Besides, I feel sure the Master has more important matters to occupy him. Though the maintenance department might appreciate you removing the cigarette butts."

"Really?"

"Blocked drainpipes," he explained. "Third Court in particular. I believe the students refer to it as Marlborough Country."

"I am not surprised, I have seen them myself."

"You have?"

"Of course. On the Old Library roof."

Despite the Cognac, Ravi felt a sudden chill, though he tried to keep his voice even. "When was this?"

"Oh, I often see figures climbing there."

"And you didn't think to mention it to the Porters?"

"Why? I am not a hypocrite."

"Were they smoking?"

"Why else would they be there?"

"Why indeed?" said Ravi.

Gabrielle drained her glass and poured her third.

"So, tell me, Ravi, what brings you to my room?"

Straight to the point as ever, he thought.

"I was wondering if those papers I sent you proved useful in the end?" he asked, knowing full well that his early work on Einstein-Rosen bridges was a well-argued but circuitous blind alley. It was clear from Gabrielle's answer that she felt the same way.

She spent the next twenty minutes summarising the essential threads of his work before dismantling each one with contemptuous ease. When she offered him another drink, he declined and watched as she refilled her glass.

"Of course, Ravi, my own research leads me to consider Visser's work of greater interest."

"In what way?"

Gabrielle launched into the possibility that cosmic strings created traversable wormholes between parallel universes. Whether it was the cognac talking, he couldn't be sure. Still, the more she spoke, the more animated she became, her voice speeding up and running sentences together so that her argument was hard to follow at times.

Ravi did his best, listening for the faintest hint or slip that might indicate that she had uncovered something significant. Still, he couldn't help but be impressed by her brilliant and insightful mind. He could well understand how she had persuaded others to fund her work.

Then, she stopped and stared at him through glasses that teetered on the edge of her nose.

"Ravi?"

"Yes?"

"*Je suis pompette*," she announced.

"Sorry?"

"Tipsy," she added, beginning to sway, "very tipsy..."

"Careful," he said, reaching forwards to catch her empty glass as it slipped from her hand.

"I think I might need to lie down," she added.

Ravi grabbed a cushion and managed to lay it under her head before she slumped onto the sofa, dislodging her glasses.

"Let me take those," he said, putting them on the table before hurrying to the kitchenette for some water. Returning with a tumbler, he found Gabrielle curled up on the sofa, one shoe on and the other hanging off her toes. Removing both, he set them down on the floor.

"I have some water here if you want it."

Gabrielle said something unintelligible but didn't open her eyes. Looking around, he found a cashmere shawl hanging from a hook behind the front door and laid it over her, though she didn't seem to notice.

Ravi picked up the brandy glasses and half-empty bottle of Cognac and returned them to the kitchenette. As he did so, he caught sight of the computer screen glowing in the next room and hesitated.

You're not going to get a better chance than this, he thought.

Checking that his host was still asleep on the sofa, he entered the study and crossed to the desk. Flicking on the Anglepoise lamp, Ravi began sifting through the stack of papers, noting with increasing apprehension how many were Robert's.

As he leafed through these, he examined the underlined sections and spidery annotations in French, some ending in exclamation marks. These increased in frequency with the most recent papers, most of which Ravi had never seen before. But it became clear that his friend had been circling closer and closer to revealing the existence of the portal. And then Ravi found it.

It appeared as a footnote in a draft paper prepared by Robert some two months before his death. There were three words, which Gabrielle had circled in a red pen, with a large question mark next to them.

See Gemini Passage.

Reading the name that he and Robert had given to the portal in black and white was a shock. It felt to Ravi as if a cold hand had just reached inside his chest and gripped his heart.

"You fool, Robert," he breathed.

Fighting down his rising panic, he rifled through the rest of the stack, looking for a folder with that name. There was none. Nor could he find another reference to those words. Just one entry, but Gabrielle had seen it. The question was, what had she done then. More importantly, who had she told?

Ravi's hand brushed against the computer's mouse. The screensaver flickered and was replaced by a password-protected home screen with a stunning image of a mountain range as a background. But it was the group of skiers captured in the foreground that drew his attention.

The figures were standing in a line, their sunburnt faces and bright ski jackets in sharp contrast to the snow-covered slopes behind them. In the middle of the group was Gabrielle, looking relaxed and happy alongside her companions, none of whom he recognised. Save one. Standing at the end of the row, his bronzed features bearing that same pencil-thin smile that never reached his eyes, was Julian Schiller.

Ravi stared at the photo, and the fist around his heart tightened its grip. Lester had been right. Gabrielle was not only funded by Schiller, but knew him personally. She had to be his mole. And if so, the Schiller Foundation might already know about the Gemini Passage.

How long would it be before they discovered its location? he wondered. Had they already done so? Did that explain the mysterious stalker prowling the grounds?

A feeling of dread settled in Ravi's stomach. He now knew where he needed to be, and it wasn't here. Switching off the desk light, he headed out through the living room and past Gabrielle lying asleep on the sofa. Letting himself out, Ravi hurried down the stairs with one thought in mind. To seal the door whose location had been known to three people only, two of whom were now dead.

As for the hooded stalker, if it was from the other world, then he would have to deal with that later. It was his responsibility to clear up Robert's mess. And if that meant sealing the gate and hunting down its transgressors, so be it. He, after all, was now the sole surviving gatekeeper.

Back in Gabriele's room, the inebriated scientist slept on, oblivious to the departure of her guest. Nor was she aware of the silent figure that appeared outside her window. It bent down to pick up the old metal ruler lying among a pile of discarded cigarette butts. After examining the oxidised surface, it held the blade to its nose and sniffed. Then the figure rose and, tucking the blade inside its long robes, disappeared once again into the shadows.

Chapter Twenty-Three

Down by the river, Annabel stood in the cramped coxes' room on the first floor of the College boathouse. Lady Margaret W3 had just had their final outing before Bumps, and her fingers were still cold from their time out on the water.

After struggling to undo her life jacket, she hung it up and removed her headset and digital cox box from around her neck. These she plugged into the wall sockets to charge overnight, adding to the hum of the other devices stored there.

Annabel thought back to Brett's debrief after the crew had put the boat away. All in all, it had been a pretty good outing, and even Clarissa had offered little by way of criticism. The downer had come with Brett's closing remarks.

"So, who is coming along to the rugby tonight?"

Clarissa, always alert to an opportunity, had asked, "What time is it starting?"

"Seven-thirty, isn't it, Annabel?"

"Erm... I think that's right."

"In that case," Brett said, "I'll see you all there! Don't forget to wear something red!"

The truth was that Annabel hadn't planned on going to the match. The thought of seeing Naomi there, cheering on Nick, made her stomach churn. But if Brett and Clarissa were going with the rest of her crew, she couldn't very well miss it.

I'm damned either way, Annabel thought.

With a sinking feeling, she walked through the weights room, barely noticing the pungent smell of sweat still lingering in the air. But when she reached the top of the stairs, Annabel saw an old friend waiting for her at the bottom of the steps.

"Hi, you."

"Katie?"

Her former Stroke, still rosy-faced from her outing with W2, looked up at her.

"I thought I'd wait for you."

"Oh, thank you," Annabel said, heading down the steps. "You didn't need to."

"Well, we don't see each other so much any more, so I thought I'd find out how life is treating you."

Annabel gave her a hug, grateful to have her friend there.

"Are you on your bike?" Katie asked.

"Yes. It's outside."

"Me too. Come on." Katie glanced towards the workshop, where the College boatman was working on an oar. "Good night, Blades!"

He glanced up from the workbench. "Good night, ladies.

See you tomorrow. Make sure you get a good night's sleep."

"You sound like my mum, Blades," said Katie.

"More like my Gran," said Annabel.

"Enough of that," he said. "Be off with you!"

They headed outside, and Annabel looked up at the storm clouds overhead.

"We'd better head back before the rain starts."

"Is that good or bad for the Redboys?" Katie asked. "What does Nick think?"

Annabel sighed. "I don't know."

Katie gave her a look. "Annabel, can I ask? Are you guys OK?"

Annabel thought about giving her the same old line about them both being busy. But then she remembered her cup of tea with Professor Gupta the previous week, when she'd opened up to him about how confused she felt about Nick. What was it that he'd said?

"Honesty may not get you a lot of friends, Annabel, but it will get you the right ones."

So, here goes, she thought.

"I think Nick's seeing someone else."

The words hung in the air between them. Annabel waited for Katie's reaction, expecting shock, outrage or sympathy. Instead, her friend burst out laughing.

"What's so funny?" Annabel asked, bewildered.

"Nick? You're kidding, right?"

"No, I'm not."

"Oh Annabel," Katie smiled.

"I've seen him…" Annabel insisted, "with Naomi Clarke."

Katie laughed again.

"I'm serious," Annabel said. "She's in the room next to me. They've been at it like rabbits."

"I think you'll find that was Colin."

"Colin?"

"Naomi's boyfriend, Colin Philby," Katie said. "Though why she's still with him, beats me. He's a complete git. I saw him dump Nick in it at a Tutorial. I'm surprised your boy didn't flatten him."

She stared at Katie, trying to process this. "So, Nick's not with Naomi."

Katie snorted. "More like her minder, from what I hear."

Annabel thought back to when she'd seen the pair together. And then remembered all the things she'd thought and said to Nick.

"Annabel, are you all right?" Katie asked. "You're looking a little pale."

"It's... just a lot to take in."

"Come on, you can do that on the way. We'll need to hurry if we want to be there on time."

Annabel stared at her.

"The match," said Katie, mounting up. "You are coming, I take it?"

"Oh, yes," she said, grabbing her bike. "Of course."

After a wash and a change of clothes, they joined the rest of the John's supporters streaming through the Eagle Gate out onto the Backs. Pretty much everyone had a red hat, top or College scarf. Someone had managed to get hold of vuvuzelas, and the atmosphere was noisy as they made their way to the University Rugby Ground on Grange Road.

On arrival, they discovered that the Queen's supporters, bolstered by what seemed like most of the other colleges, had taken up residence in the main pavilion stand. The John's contingent headed for the "Red Shed", the old wooden stand on the far side of the pitch.

Annabel could see that Brett was already seated there, flanked by Ash and Brian, relegating Clarissa and the rest of her crew to the row behind. Ash spotted her and waved with his usual enthusiasm.

"Annabel! Over here! We've saved you a seat!"

Sitting down in the empty space next to Brian, she introduced Katie to her friends and stared around.

"Wow, there's a big crowd already. When do they kick off?"

"They've just finished the warmup," said Brian. "They'll be out shortly."

On cue, a huge roar went up as Trevor, wearing his red and white hooped top, came running down the steps of the pavilion, followed by the rest of the John's team. Among them, Annabel saw Gareth, towering above the others, and last of all Nick, peeling off to sprint towards his own posts.

"Yay! Go, Nick!" yelled Ash, though his voice was drowned out by a loud blast from the vuvuzela section in front of them.

If Annabel thought the noise was loud for the Redboys, it was nothing compared to the cheers that greeted the team in green. The massed crowds on the far side rose as one when the star-studded opposition ran out on the pitch.

"Queen's, Queen's, Queen's!" rang out from the stands, and a brass band did its best to drown out John's vuvuzelas. With it came the chant, so beloved of opposition sides against the teams in red.

"We'd rather be at Oxford than at John's,

We'd rather be at Oxford than at John's,

We'd rather be at Oxford,

Rather be at Oxford,

Rather be at Oxford than at John's!"

But even as the last trumpet faded, a blond-headed figure rose in front of the John's stand. Giles, his face covered in red warpaint and wearing a scarlet tee-shirt with the logo "ST JOHN'S COLLEGE – WELL RED!", held up his hands like a conductor. Pausing to soak up the cheers, he put a megaphone to his lips.

"Let's hear it for our boys in red!"

To the tune of You'll never walk alone, the Red Shed sang their hearts out.

"Walk on! Walk on!

With hope in your hearts,

Because you'll never be at John's!

You'll never be at John's!"

As the chorus finished, the vuvuzelas struck up again, and Annabel joined in with the rest of the stand.

"John's, John's, John's!"

Hundreds of feet came down in unison, the chant thumping out like a drumbeat from the stand as the teams lined up. Next to her, Brian was bouncing up and down, his heavy boots beating out the rhythm with the others. Those on the other side of the pitch matched it with their own chant.

"Queen's, Queen's, Queen's!"

As the noise rose to a crescendo, the referee raised an arm above his head and gave a long shrill blast on his whistle. The Queen's fly-half kicked the ball high into the floodlit sky, and battle commenced.

The previous term, Annabel had seen Nick play in the league for John's, and she was used to the sight of bodies crashing into one another. But nothing had prepared her for the speed and intensity of a Cuppers encounter.

Not only were both teams psyched up for the highlight of the College calendar, but with University Blues eligible to play on both sides, the added power and pace made the initial collisions brutal.

The moment Trevor caught the ball from the kickoff, he was flattened by a wave of Green bodies. Groans rose from the John's supporters. Annabel saw Ying cover her eyes until, shaken but unhurt, the Redboy Skipper picked himself up and headed back into the fray.

The big hits kept coming, and there were as many groans as cheers from the Queen's fans. The action continued, fast and furious, but it soon became evident to Annabel that the Redboys were up against it.

Queen's had two international forwards, both post-grads studying MBAs, and it was all Gareth, Aden and the others could do to hold them at bay. Even so, it was John's who were the first to score just before half time.

In a pre-planned move off a line out, the ball was

switched to Nick coming at pace off his wing. He burst through a surprised Queen's defence to score in the corner.

The crowd around Annabel erupted, everyone jumping up and down and screaming as the vuvuzelas started up again. Then came the song from Giles's megaphone.

"Walk on! Walk on!"

This was taken up by the other Well Red supporters as Nick and the others jogged back to the halfway line. Though Kyle missed the conversion, John's finished the first half five points ahead, much to the delight of Brett, who turned to Annabel, his face alive.

"How about that! What a game!"

Next to him, Ash yelled, "Great score by Nick!"

Annabel gave him a thumbs up before noticing Clarissa lean forwards and start chatting with Brett.

"Good game," said Katie, "but I thought Queen's looked strong."

"Yeah," agreed Annabel. "What do you think, Brian?"

"I concur," he said before reeling off a series of statistics that would have made a sports channel proud.

While Katie listened in bewildered amazement, Annabel found herself looking around the stand. It was then that she spotted Naomi sitting a few rows back, next to a good-looking boy who was talking to his friends. While her boyfriend held forth, Naomi glanced around, and their eyes met. Her Cripps neighbour gave Annabel a warm smile, which she returned, feeling guilty after all the things she'd thought about the girl.

Turning back to the pitch, Annabel saw Giles standing

on his seat. Holding the megaphone to his mouth, he was beckoning to a group of students clad in gowns and red scarves by the entrance.

"Over here, Gents!"

Katie, who seemed glad of a distraction to Brian's half-time analysis, stared.

"Isn't that the Choir?"

"You're right," said Annabel, remembering them from Chapel breakfast. "They must have finished evensong."

Justin and the others made their way over and were greeted by Giles, who issued them all with "Well Red" tee-shirts. By the time the two teams returned to the pitch, the John's contingent responded with a much more tuneful version of Walk-on, Giles conducting the new arrivals with a vuvuzela-shaped baton.

All harmonies were forgotten after the restart as both sets of supporters got behind their teams with more earthy shouts of encouragement. In the second half, Queen's threw everything at the boys in red, and their two internationals began to dominate the contest. The stand opposite grew more vocal as they sensed the shift in momentum, while the John's crowd became more subdued with less to cheer about. It was then that it began to rain.

At first, there were just a few drops, barely noticed by any save those on the pitch. But when it began to come down in earnest, umbrellas started appearing in the opposite stands, and the players' shirts became plastered to their mud-splattered bodies.

As conditions deteriorated, the red defence became ever

more desperate in the face of the relentless waves of green. The powerful Maori winger was getting more and more ball as the game progressed, and Nick had his work cut out to nullify the threat.

Heart in mouth, Annabel watched as, time and again, the Redboy used his superior speed to drag his man down or bundle him into touch. Each time, Giles's megaphone kicked in, and his jibes of "Give him a chance, Woody" began getting to the Queen's player.

The opposition winger's mounting frustration showed with ten minutes to go, when he received the ball close to the John's line. Rather than trying to run around his marker, he decided to bulldoze his way over instead.

Annabel thought she caught a flicker of a smile on Nick's muddy face before the two wingers came together. The impact was sickening. One moment, the Queen's player was charging for the line, and the next, he was being hammered backwards with Nick's shoulder buried in his midriff. As he hit the ground, the ball spilt from his hands, and the Red Shed erupted.

Amid the din, Annabel saw Nick pick himself up and extend a hand to his opposite number. The Queen's winger, who was lying on his back looking winded, reached up and took it. Rising to his feet, he limped back to join his teammates as Giles began a chorus of "Walk on" once more.

Any euphoria the John's supporters felt though was short-lived. The Queen's forwards won the resulting scrum, and, driving back the tiring Redboy pack, pushed them over the try line to score. This time it was the crowd on the far side of the pitch who went wild, their band striking up "We'd rather be at Oxford" to add insult to injury.

The stand around Annabel went quiet. Even Giles seemed lost for words, the megaphone hanging forgotten by his side. Glancing along the row, she could see Brett looking stony-faced and Ash on the verge of tears. Beside her, Brian had his head in his hands.

While the Queen's kicker prepared to take the conversion to put them in the lead, the John's players gathered in a huddle under the posts to listen to their captain. Whatever Trevor said was drowned out by the cheers from across the pitch as the ball sailed between the uprights, and the scoreboard registered "Queen's 7 - 5 St John's".

As the Redboys jogged back to the halfway line, Annabel turned to Brian.

"How long to go?"

"One minute, thirty-eight seconds."

Annabel felt her heart sink. That wouldn't be enough time. After all that effort, to come this close to winning and lose it in the dying seconds was cruel. Then she noticed Trevor come running across to the touchline to speak with Giles. The two friends exchanged a few quiet words before the John's captain headed back to join his forwards.

"What was all that about?" Annabel asked.

"No idea," said Katie.

Putting the megaphone down, Giles turned to face the stand and stared at the expectant supporters. Then, holding his hands out wide either side of him, he brought them together above his head in a Viking clap.

"Woody!" he yelled.

Then he repeated the gesture, this time with the Choir and some of the nearby rows joining in.

"Woody!"

Again, and again, the clap was repeated, increasing the tempo as, row by row, the Red Shed did the same.

"Woody! Woody! Woody!"

Annabel looked down at the touchline below them. Nick was poised like a sprinter on the starting blocks, staring at his opposite number. The whistle blew, and Kyle launched the ball high in the sky towards the Queen's Winger. As it hung in the air, the chants of "Woody, Woody!" had grown to such an ominous rumble that it sounded like thunder itself. Only this time, the bolt of lightning was wearing a red shirt.

Nick had begun running as soon as the kick had been taken. Sprinting down the touchline, he left the chasing Redboys in his wake as he arrowed towards his opposite number. Even as the ball descended, Annabel knew there was no escape for the unfortunate receiver. The Queen's player must have known it too.

As chants of "Woody! Woody!" reached their crescendo, the winger took his eye off the ball and glanced towards Nick – just for a split second, but it was enough. The ball bounced off his outstretched fingers and, as he fumbled to keep hold of it, Nick hit him square in the chest.

The momentum of the tackle lifted both players off the ground, their bodies almost horizontal as they flew through the air. When they came crashing down to earth, the ball was sent coughing upwards, and all eyes followed its trajectory as it tumbled end over end towards the Queen's try line. Green-shirted players began scrambling back, but the Redboy forwards, following up Nick's do-or-die charge, were already there.

Gareth dived on the bouncing ball, knocking away the flailing boot of a desperate defender. Aden arrived seconds later, slamming into bodies to clear them away. Then Trevor pounced and, picking up the ball, rolled out of the melee to dive for the line. A long arm grabbed for him, but the Redboy captain would not be denied. Shirt ripping, Trevor lunged and grounded the ball over the line. There was a moment's pause before the referee's hand went up, his whistle blew, and the Red Shed erupted.

In the explosion of noise, Annabel found herself jumping up and down with Katie, both hugging each other as others did the same. Along the row, Brett was trying to high-five Ash, who was bouncing so high he looked like he was about to take off. Even Clarissa seemed caught up in the moment, screaming with the rest of W3 as everybody in the stand went crazy. All except one.

Amid all that commotion, Annabel felt someone tug on her coat. Still bouncing, she looked down at Brian, peering at her through his long lank hair. It looked like he was mouthing something, but with all the noise, she could barely hear herself think let alone understand what he was saying.

"What?" she shouted.

"Look, Nick…!"

But his voice was drowned out by Ying, who had grabbed Giles's megaphone and was yelling, "I love you, Trevor!"

"I can't hear you," said Annabel, grinning.

"Nick's hurt!" Brian yelled.

Annabel stopped jumping and stared at him.

"What?"

Brian pointed towards the pitch. She turned to look, but couldn't see over the heads of the other supporters.

"Here," he said, lifting her up onto the bench. Annabel stared out across the pitch.

Over by the posts, a scrum of Redboys had mobbed Trevor, his mop of curly hair just visible among the scrum of red and white shirts. But some twenty feet back from the celebrations, she saw another group of players, including Gareth and the Queen's winger. These were squatting down next to a John's player lying face down on the turf. On the back of the muddy shirt, she could just make out Nick's number.

As the Choir began singing "Walk on, walk on", Annabel was already running for the stairs.

Chapter Twenty-Four

The blinding white light made Nick flinch.

"This is purely precautionary," said the female voice, "but I have to ask you some questions. Do you know where you are?"

Nick blinked and peered at a woman in her thirties, her hair still damp from the rain.

"Grange Road."

"And what's my name?"

"Dr Osborne."

"Very good."

She adjusted the angle of the pencil torch and lifted his head to examine the nasal passageways. Nick stared at the ceiling of the treatment room while she completed her examination. When the doctor stepped back, he saw that her lips were pursed.

"OK, I've completed the Head Injury Assessment. The good news is that there are no indications of a concussion. The bad news is that you've broken your nose. Fortunately, the passageways are still clear, and it looks pretty straight. Have you broken it before?"

"No, first time."

"Well, there's been a fair bit of bleeding, but that's stopped for now. I think it's safe to leave it to heal on its own. You'll need to go to a pharmacy in the morning and get some painkillers. No strenuous exercise for two weeks and no rugby for six."

"Six weeks?"

"As a minimum," she said, fixing him with a look. "Let your GP know if the nosebleed persists, or if you get headaches and blurred vision. Do you have a car?"

Nick snorted and regretted it immediately as blood splattered over his muddy top.

"Sorry," he mumbled.

Dr Osborne retrieved a wad of cotton wool from her medical pack and handed it to him. "Here."

"Thanks," he said, pressing it under his nose.

"Do you have a first aid kit back at College?"

"The Porters will have," he said.

"Well, here's some ibuprofen to get you through the night, and some arnica cream for the swelling. No alcohol for 48 hours, and no aspirin. That will just make your nose more likely to bleed. Understood?"

"Got it," he said, stuffing them into the pocket of his shorts.

"I'll write all this up and forward it to your GP. I can organise a taxi if you want, but I believe there's someone waiting to take you back."

Nick wondered who that would be. "So I'm free to go?"

"Yes, we're all done here."

Nick eased himself off the couch, aware of how heavy his legs felt.

"Doctor?"

"Yes?"

"What was the final score?"

"Don't you remember?"

Nick wasn't going to tell her that he had no recollection of anything beyond that final desperate tackle.

"I was a bit pre-occupied with this at the time," he lied, indicating his nose.

Dr Osborne pursed her lips. "12-7, to John's."

Nick felt such a surge of elation that he half-expected his nose to erupt again. Still, he managed to control himself and said, "Yeah, I thought so."

The doctor studied him for a moment longer before opening the door.

"Take care, Nick. And remember what I said about headaches."

"Got it. Thanks."

He stepped outside and waited until after the door swung shut before punching the air. His muted celebration over, he felt the elation ebb away and a wave of weariness wash over him. Leaning a hand against the wall, he limped down the corridor, his studs clicking on the wooden floor. When he emerged into the Pavilion lobby, he saw Giles, his face still covered in red warpaint, was waiting for him.

"Hail, the conquering hero comes!" he cried. "Battered but unbowed, I see."

Giles inspected Nick's nose. "Very battered, by the look of you," he added.

"That bad, eh?"

"Oh, I don't know. It has a certain rugged charm, I suppose." He turned to the other person waiting there. "What do you think?"

Annabel emerged from the entrance looking very bedraggled. There were dark smudges under her eyes, whether from the rain or not, he couldn't tell.

"Hi," she said.

"Hi," Nick replied.

There was an awkward pause as they stared at each other. Given how strange she had been with him that term, Nick was relieved Giles was still there. The last thing he needed right now was another angry tirade from Annabel. But when she began striding towards him, he wondered if that was what he was going to get.

Instead, Annabel flung her arms around him and buried her face in his chest. Nick just stared down at the top of her head, not sure how to respond. He looked across at Giles, who gave him a wink.

"I'll just give you two a minute. I'll be outside."

For some time, Nick and Annabel stood in the empty lobby, surrounded by faded photographs of rugby teams. Only when Dr Osborne appeared, carrying her medical bag, did Annabel release him.

"Ah, I see you found each other," she said.

"Err, yes," said Nick, realising now who she'd meant earlier.

"I'll say goodnight, then."

"Right, good night. Thanks for your help."

She gave them both a brief smile, and headed out the door. Nick turned to Annabel and found her wiping her face with her sleeve.

"You OK?" he asked.

"Me? Yes, fine."

"That's good," he said. "Only Giles, he's…"

"Waiting. I know."

Nick hesitated. "So, shall we join him?"

"Yes, let's."

And that was it. No words. No explanation. No blow by blow account of what he had, or hadn't, done. Instead, Annabel headed for the door. Bewildered, but relieved, Nick collected his kitbag and followed her outside. They found Giles standing in the shelter of the stand, watching Dr Osborne hurry through the rain towards her car. He raised an eyebrow.

"All good?"

Nick nodded.

"Excellent. I've taken the liberty of ordering us a taxi."

"Thanks, Giles," said Annabel.

"So, while we're waiting for that, I wanted to talk to you both about what happened at the start of last term. There's been a development."

Annabel stared at him. "What sort of development?"

"Another close encounter."

"What?" she said, her eyes wide. "Where?"

"Above Second Court."

"Another harpy?" Nick asked.

"Not exactly. This one was wearing a hooded cloak, and

she packed a punch like a heavyweight boxer." He indicated the swelling on his cheek.

"One of Schiller's goons?" Nick suggested, remembering the team who had ambushed the Professor.

Giles shook his head. "I don't think so. She left this behind."

He removed a red handkerchief from his pocket and unwrapped the object inside.

"What is it?" Annabel asked, leaning forwards to look.

"Her finger."

"Giles!" she said, recoiling.

"Don't worry. It's made of stone."

Nick tensed and they all exchanged a look. "How did you get it?"

"Remember my ice axe?"

"You're kidding," Annabel said.

"Usually, yes, but not this time."

Nick stared at the severed digit. "So where is its owner now?"

"No idea." Giles folded the handkerchief and stuffed it back in his pocket. "She disappeared into thin air."

"Have you told Gupta?" Nick asked.

"Yes, but as usual, he wasn't exactly forthcoming. You know what he's like. It's like getting blood from a stone... excuse the pun."

"He's just trying to protect us," said Annabel, sounding defensive on her Tutor's behalf.

"Did you show him the finger?" Nick asked. Giles raised an eyebrow. "You know what I mean."

"Yes, I did. The Professor asked me to keep it quiet for now. Said he wanted to speak to someone about Mackenzie's research."

"Why?" Nick asked.

"I think Gupta's worried his old friend may have left some research papers behind about the portal."

"Where it is, you mean?"

Giles shrugged. "Or how to open it." He stared out at the rain-swept car park. "What I'd give to find those papers."

Something stirred at the back of Nick's mind. "You could try his trunk."

The others turned to look at him.

"What trunk?" Annabel asked.

"Mackenzie has a trunk in the New Court cellars. I saw it at the start of term."

"You're not serious," said Giles, his face lighting up.

"Why didn't you say?" Annabel asked.

"I've only just made the connection. It had Mackenzie's initials on the side."

"RTFM," said Giles.

Nick looked at him, impressed.

"He Deaned me enough times. I have a whole stack of summons from him."

"Yeah, RTFM was stencilled on the trunk."

Giles beamed and turned to Annabel.

"Annabel, if you don't marry this boy, I will."

"Giles!" She scoffed. "We're just…"

"I know." He rolled his eyes. "Just friends."

Annabel's cheeks went pink, but Giles ignored her.

"So, Nick, how do we find this trunk of yours?"

"We could ask the Porters to open up the cellar."

"Won't they want to know why?" Annabel asked.

Giles frowned. "They're not going to be happy about us removing something that's not ours."

"There is another way in," said Nick.

"Really? Where?"

"From the river. There's a loading bay near the Bridge of Sighs. The door's pretty much rotted through."

"Sounds promising," said Giles, "but how are we going to get there?"

Nick hadn't thought of that.

"By punt," said Annabel.

Giles stared at her, and she shrugged. "We returned them to the river the other day."

"But will the Porters let us take one out at night?" Nick asked.

"Ash and Brian are on the Punt Committee," she said. "They'll have a key."

Giles knelt down and took both her hands in his.

"I take it all back, Annabel. Dump Nick, and shack up with me."

"As if," she said.

At that moment, headlights swept into the car park as their taxi pulled into view.

"Can't say I didn't try," said Giles, getting to his feet. He set off across the car park in the rain. "Come on, then. Looks like a perfect night for a bit of punting."

Nick shook his head but as he did so, he noticed the

distant headlights begin to blur. Then the ground seemed to shift under his feet, and he had to grab the back of the nearby seating to steady himself.

"Nick?" Annabel asked. "Are you all right?"

Nick waited for the fuzziness to clear, and saw her face come back into focus.

"Yeah, I'm fine."

"You're shaking."

She was right, his legs were trembling.

"Just a bit cold, that's all. Could do with a hot shower."

"Of course," she said, wrapping an arm behind him. "You must be freezing. We need to get you out of those wet clothes."

Across the car park, Giles was standing by the taxi, peering back at them through the rain.

"Come on, you lovebirds. We haven't got time for that."

"Ignore him" she said, giving him a gentle squeeze. "He's just jealous."

And before Nick could respond, she led him through the puddles to their waiting ride, while lightning forked overhead.

Chapter Twenty-Five

Ravi stood outside the entrance to the New Court cellars on B Staircase, listening for anyone moving on the landings above. Other than the distant sound of thunder, the place was eerily quiet, with so many students out watching the rugby.

Looking down at the duplicate set of keys that he and Robert had made all those years ago, he doubted even Bert knew of their existence. Ravi had not used them for half a century. Until now, he thought the same had been true of Robert, but perhaps he'd been wrong on that score.

Unlocking the door, Ravi was greeted by the familiar musty smell, its long-forgotten aroma unchanged over all this time. Turning on the lights, he closed the door behind him and descended the steps.

The salt deposits and damp patches on the brickwork were still there, as were the cobwebs clustered in the corners of supporting joists. But the cable ducting that ran along the walls looked modern, as did the fluorescent light fixtures.

The passageways themselves hadn't changed much, save for the odd section of repaired brickwork, and it wasn't long before Ravi arrived at his destination. Walking down the long narrow corridor, he glanced at the open doorways on either side, their contents now lying in darkness. The only sound this far below New Court was that of his footsteps echoing through the empty passageway.

When he reached the end, Ravi turned to the nondescript door in the last alcove on the left. This, like him, was showing its age. The red paint had faded and was peeling in places. There was evidence of dry rot towards the bottom, no doubt caused by flooding over the intervening years.

Still, he found his fingers were shaking as he fumbled with the keys, and it took a couple of attempts to insert the correct one in the lock. The key turned smoothly, and as he pushed the door open, he noticed a dry, dusty smell that was very different from that in the corridor. Flicking on the light switch, he found himself looking at a room much altered from before.

Gone were the table, chairs and shelf units that had filled their working space. So too the boxes of files and equipment. To the untrained eye, it looked like any other cellar beneath the nineteenth-century building. For Ravi, though, the otherworldly signs were unmistakable.

Stepping inside, he felt the crunch of red sand under his shoes, the sound travelling further than the dimensions of the room should allow. Then there was the dryness in the air that was at odds with the damp of the cellars. And, finally, there was the far wall.

Of the blackboard paint, there was no sign. Nor had the render survived. It lay in a fine dust on the floor, like exfoliated skin, exposing the brickwork beneath. This was unremarkable, save for the fact that the terracotta bricks were untouched by salt, moss or spiders' webs. As if nothing from this world could survive on their surface. Or beyond.

Ravi took a steadying breath and removed the piece of chalk he'd slipped in his pocket in the Library. Then he started walking towards the wall, much as he had done on that fateful night in 1969, when it had all begun.

******

Ravi watched as Robert stared at the blackboard, chalk and eraser in hand. Row upon row of calculations covered its surface, from ceiling to floor, their outline shrouded in dust that hung in the air from the multiple revisions. His friend had led the effort, and his hands and forearms now looked deathly pale beneath a fine patina of chalk. There were similar streaks in his hair, where he'd run his fingers through in exasperation.

"It's no good, Ravi. I can't see any way this is going to work. There's something we are missing, but what, I just don't know."

He tossed the piece of chalk onto the pile of worn stubs filling the tobacco tin on the table. Ravi had known for some time that this had been a doomed effort, but he'd indulged his friend, waiting for the moment when Robert would reach the same conclusion. Now that it had arrived, he couldn't help but feel a tingle of excitement, and perhaps fear, at what he was about to do.

"I think you're right, Robert," he said, weighing his

words carefully. "There is something we are missing."

"Well, it beats me, laddie."

And Ravi thought that for once his friend really did look defeated.

"There is something we might want to consider," he said, trying to keep voice level.

"Go on then, man. I'm open to anything right now."

"You know the work of Sir John Herschel?"

"Of course I do. One of your Victorian heroes, wasn't he? Did all that work on binary star systems."

Ravi placed a folder on the table.

"What's that you've got there?" Robert asked.

"I found this among Herschel's papers in the College archive," he said, extracting a piece of torn parchment, its edges faded and worn from age.

"You removed that from the Library? Are you mad?"

"You yourself said that we were missing something."

"Gods, man. The Librarian will have your hide for this."

"I'm not even sure he knows of its existence. It is not catalogued anywhere."

Ravi laid it on the table. Robert stared at the ancient document with its astrological symbols, diagrams, and Latin text.

"That's all very interesting, Ravi, but it's torn in half. I can't make head nor tail of it."

"Nor me," he agreed, "until I began looking through John Couch Adams's papers."

"The Fellow who discovered Neptune?"

Ravi nodded, putting another folder on the table. "I

found this in one of his journals." He removed another piece of parchment and placed it alongside the first.

Robert stared. "But they're the same manuscript," he said, moving the two halves together.

"Indeed they are," Ravi agreed, pointing to the header at the top of the document. "*Ad viam prodeat duobus Geminis.*"

"Meaning?"

"To the Gemini passage."

Robert frowned. "That's all very well, Ravi. Two astronomers have different parts of the same manuscript. Fine. But look at it, man. It's all hocus-pocus. Some sort of mystical, occult nonsense."

"Maybe," Ravi said, "But it got me thinking. Why would two of the greatest astronomers of their day have in their possession a manuscript like this? Not only that, but one that has been separated deliberately."

"Let me hazard a guess. Because even in Victorian times, having something like this was likely to get you drummed out of College?"

"Magic, you mean?"

Robert stiffened at this. "Steady Ravi, we don't use the M-word around here. Not if we want to retain any semblance of academic standing."

"Yet how much of what was once considered magic has now been explained by science? Why shouldn't that be true with this? Isn't that why we are here, after all? To uncover the secrets of the universe?"

"No, Ravi, we are here to *explain* the secrets of the universe. There's a big difference. We can't just apply for research funding without a viable scientific theory or some sort of academic proof. Are you going to stand before the College's governing body and wave a piece of parchment in the air and say, 'We don't know how it's going to work, but we'd like some money to dance in a circle under a full moon?' We would be a laughingstock. And not just us, mind you, the College too. Could you imagine what the University would say if they found out?"

"Fine, but sometimes the ends justify the means. We're talking about winning the space race here. Some people are revisiting Einstein and Rosen's theories on wormholes."

Robert snorted. "I think Einstein was on a flight of fancy there."

"Similar things were said about Darwin."

"Until he produced compelling evidence. And that, my friend, is something we cannot do. We've been working on this for close to four years now with nothing to show for it. Are you prepared to pin your hopes and our reputations on some sort of arcane text that looks like gobbledegook?"

"Like computer code looks to anyone who doesn't understand programming, you mean?"

"It's not the same, and you know it. We are talking career-ending stuff here. The College Council would send us off to the funny farm."

Ravi raised an eyebrow.

"OK, fair enough," Robert said. "There are plenty of others they'd probably send before us. Still, I'm not about to spend the rest of my academic career having people whisper about me behind my back. That's no way to live."

Ravi looked at his friend and saw a side of him that he'd never noticed before. This handsome, talented, larger than life personality was more interested in how others thought of him than in pursuing the truth. This realisation came as such a shock that Ravi felt a crushing sense of disappointment. It must have shown on his face because Robert sighed and gave him a weary smile.

"Listen, old man, we're both tired. We've been pushing it pretty hard the last few months. Why don't we call it a day and speak about it in the morning?"

Ravi resisted the urge to say yes to his friend. He *was* tired, of course, but he was also frustrated. He'd imagined Robert would be as excited as him to pursue this new line of inquiry to salvage something from their work, no matter how unorthodox it might be. Ravi might still have tried to say something, had Robert not checked his watch.

"Hellfire, is that the time?" He reached for his jacket. "Sorry Ravi, I've got to dash!"

"You're not dining tonight?"

"Afraid not, rugby training."

"Oh," he said, thinking his friend had been doing a lot of that recently.

"Think about what I've said, Ravi," said Robert. "I know you're keen to pursue this thing, but let's keep it to ourselves for now."

"What about Mary?"

Robert stiffened. "What about her?"

"Shall we ask what she thinks?"

"No." A shadow seemed to cross his friend's face. "What

I mean is, I'd rather not tell her just yet. Not until we've discussed it in the morning, eh?"

Ravi nodded. "Very well."

"Good man. I'll see you tomorrow."

Robert hurried off, his footsteps echoing through the cellar. Ravi sat there for a while, wondering about his friend's erratic behaviour. It wasn't like Robert to be so defensive or hostile even.

These must have really spooked him, he thought, eyeing the two pieces of parchment on the table.

Though unattributed, Ravi had a fair idea who had penned them. He believed that the document came from another of the College's great minds. One whose name had attracted a certain amount of notoriety over the years.

John Dee had once been considered the greatest thinker of his age. His library, and scientific standing, had been impressive enough to attract the attention, and patronage, of Elizabeth I. Until that is, his pursuit of knowledge had drawn him into the realms of the occult and supernatural.

Indeed, his great work, the *Monas Hieroglyphica*, was still regarded with suspicion by many. So much so, that if the College possessed a copy, there was no record of it in the archive. The same, he believed, was true of this document, its contents so arcane that its existence might ruin the reputation of anyone seeking to use it.

Was he, Professor Ravi Gupta, in danger of doing that now? Delving into a field of study that would bring more than just professional damage to him personally, but to his beloved College also. Is that why Herschel and Couch

Adams had made sure that the two halves of this mysterious manuscript were separated all these years ago?

While logic told him he should return the pieces of manuscript to the Library where he found them, part of him knew he would always want to know what secrets they could unlock. That's when Robert's impassioned words about the need for evidence came back to him.

"Well, my friend," he said under his breath, "there is only one way to find out."

Rising, Ravi picked up the chalk and strode towards the blackboard.

******

Half a century later, Ravi stood before that same wall, chalk in hand, and closed his eyes. The days when he'd needed to read from the manuscript were long gone. The portal's activation glyphs were now as familiar to him as the Latin of the College Grace. These last weeks in the Old Library had seen to that. Poring over those two torn sheets of parchment for hours on end, he doubted that he would ever forget those symbols again.

With firm, confident strokes, he drew from memory, just as he had practised on the wall behind the map in the old Librarian's office. The chalk scraped over the rough brickwork, sending dust into the air as Ravi reproduced the hieroglyphs depicted in the manuscript. Only when he finished the last symbol did he step back and open his eyes.

He stared at his creation, which covered most of the far end of the cellar, checking each glyph to ensure nothing was askew. Happy they were all as they should be, he began the incantation, reciting the Latin aloud just as he had done all those years ago.

With each completed sentence, he felt the occult energies in the room grow. What he now suspected might be dark matter drawn from the elements around him, coalesced onto the chalk symbols. First came the two half-moon shapes, one facing down, the other facing up. These were joined by a pair of vertical lines that ran from floor to ceiling. Together they formed a pulsing red symbol some six feet high and three across.

The Gemini Gate.

There it was, for all to see. Hidden in plain sight, on the cellar wall. Ravi stared at the shape, mesmerised as he had been that first time.

Then the crash of splintering wood broke the spell.

Ravi spun around, eyes wide, staring at the doorway as the distant noise echoed through the cellars. For a while, he stood there listening, wondering what it could be. Had someone entered the cellar and dropped something? Some students perhaps? If so, where was the warning shout of a Porter?

Frowning, he crossed the room and paused in the doorway to peer down the empty corridor. For a while, everything remained quiet, and he began to wonder if he'd been mistaken. But just as he was about to return to the portal, he heard another noise. Again a long way off, but there was no doubt what it was.

Breaking glass.

Ravi stepped out into the corridor. "Hey! What's going on?" He imagined, somewhere in the cellars, a group of shocked students staring at a dropped crate of beer bottles. "I suggest you clear that up," he called out, "before I call the Porters!"

That should be enough to send anyone packing, he thought. Sure enough, he heard the sound of footsteps. Only these weren't moving away. If anything, they were getting nearer.

Smash! Smash!

"I'm warning you," he called out again.

Smash! More footsteps.

"I mean it!"

Smash! And still, they came on.

A growing sense of dread crept over Ravi. He found himself backing away towards the door as the archway at the other end of the corridor became darker. Then, with the next tinkle of glass, he understood. Those weren't bottles being broken. They were fluorescent tubes.

Ravi was about to turn for the Gemini room when the far light shattered, and the junction fell into darkness. Long seconds passed as he stared at the shadows, sensing rather than seeing a figure looking back at him.

That was when a pale hand emerged from under the archway. It stretched up towards the ducting that ran along the ceiling. Bony white fingers gripped the cables and yanked them down. There was a flash of blue and white sparks, and the cellar went black.

The slow, deliberate treads began again, stalking towards him. Fighting down his panic, Ravi felt for the doorway, and slipped inside the room. Shutting the door behind him, he pressed his back against the heavy wood panels and fumbled in his pocket for the keys. Ravi fingered each one in turn until he found what he hoped was the cellar key and thrust it into the keyhole.

The footsteps stopped outside, and there was a long silence.

Ravi imagined that pale hand reaching for the doorknob. Twisting the key, he felt it catch, and for a terrifying moment he thought he'd selected the wrong one. Desperate, he tried again, and this time it turned, emitting a welcome clunk as the bolt slid into place.

Ravi rested his head against the wood, weak with relief. It lasted less than a second.

With a shuddering boom, the door exploded inwards.

One moment, Ravi was leaning against its sturdy timbers, and the next, he was flying across the room in the dark, arms and legs flailing. How far he was thrown, he couldn't tell, but when he landed, the impact drove all the air from his body.

Skidding along the floor, Ravi hit the far wall, pain blossoming in his head. Then the heavy cellar door landed on him, and the world went black.

Chapter Twenty-Six

Annabel hurried along the covered walkway beneath Cripps, glad to be out of the downpour. The storm had well and truly broken now, and she could barely see the School of Pythagoras on the other side of Merton Court through the rain.

After arriving back in College, the other two had headed back to Nick's room while Annabel went in search of Ash and Brian. Though it was hard to tell beneath all the mud, Nick had looked pale in the taxi, and she was pleased that Giles had offered to stay with him while he got himself cleaned up. While he claimed he was fine, she suspected that the injury was troubling him more than he made out.

"Typical," she said. "As soon as I go caring about someone again, something bad happens to them."

It had started with her sister and parents. Then Brett, and the porter, Cummins. When she thought about it now, it was a miracle that the Professor and Gran hadn't been killed as well. It was as if Annabel had become a Jonah, her bad luck rubbing off on everyone she touched.

Don't go there, girl, she thought as she arrived at the

bottom of H staircase. *Think positive thoughts.*

Looking up at the sign, she saw that both Brian and Ash were IN.

"You see?" she said. "Come on!"

Annabel ran up the stairs and emerged on her friends' floor to find the landing quiet. She suspected many were over in the College Bar, celebrating the Redboys victory.

After trying Ash's room without success, she knocked on Brian's and was relieved to hear the sound of footsteps. The door opened a fraction to reveal Ash peering around its edge, a set of noise-cancelling earphones around his neck.

"Annabel?" he said. "What are you doing here?"

"Hi, Ash. I'm not disturbing you, am I?"

"Erm, no, not really."

"I need to ask you and Brian a favour."

"Oh, OK?" He hesitated for a moment longer before opening the door. "In that case, you'd better come in."

"You're sure this isn't a bad time?" she asked.

"No," he said, closing the door behind her. "We're just getting started."

He led her down a short hallway and paused outside the door.

"I'd better go in first," he said. "You might need to shield your eyes."

"Sorry?"

Ash pushed the door open, and light streamed out of the room. Annabel held up a hand against the glare as he disappeared inside. Peering through her fingers, she saw a bright sun shining down from a cloudless sky over a settlement of crumbling buildings. Even as she looked, Annabel saw figures running for the safety of the forest, pursued by multi-limbed creatures that scuttled across the ground. One of the alien shapes rose up before her, and she was about to cry out when a burst of pulsing green light blew it apart.

Ash turned on the room lights. "Brian, we have a visitor."

Annabel stared at the enormous plasma screen and the leather chair in front of it, where Brian sat, console in hand.

"Hi Annabel," he said, removing his headgear.

"Hi," she said, looking from him to the stack of matt black servers in the corner of the room. "What is all this?"

"Our gaming setup," said Ash. "Well, Brian's really. Mine's not nearly as good."

"It's incredible."

"Thanks," said Brian.

"It's for eSports, mainly," Ash explained.

Annabel looked around and saw trophies filling the shelves. "So, these are?"

"Brian's. They pay for all this." Ash indicated the screen and computer drives.

"Tuition fees too," added Brian.

"He's terrific," Ash said, smiling at his friend. "On Fortnite, where are you ranked now?"

"Twenty-third."

Annabel stared at Brian, who peered up at her from his chair.

"Anyway," said Ash. "Can we get you a cup of tea? I think we might have biscuits somewhere."

"No," said Annabel, "I have to get back. Listen, I need to ask you guys for a favour."

"Of course. What sort?"

"I need to take out a punt."

"Sure. When were you thinking of?"

"Like, now, maybe?" Ash stared at her. "If that's possible, of course."

"I'm not sure the Porters would allow that, Annabel."

"I wasn't planning on telling them."

"I see," he said, turning to Brian.

"I'll bring it back in one piece," she said. "Promise."

"The trouble is the punt keys are in the Porters' Lodge," said Ash.

"You don't have a spare set?"

"We don't, I'm afraid."

Annabel felt her shoulders sag. She'd been so sure they'd have some.

But then, Brian swivelled his chair to face Ash.

"An interesting scenario," he said.

"Very true," said the other.

What happened next was so strange that Annabel could only stare in bemusement at her friends.

"If the punt keys are in the Porters' Lodge," said Ash.

"Then, we'll need to create a diversion," Brian replied.

"One of us could say we'd locked ourselves out of our room," Ash continued.

"And ask the Porter to let us in."

"That would give Annabel time to enter the lodge."

"And remove one of the punt keys."

"Number 10 would be best as it's half-hidden by the willow."

"Less likely to be noticed."

"Agreed," said Ash.

They both paused as Annabel looked on.

"How long to take the key and unlock the punt?" Ash began again.

"Two minutes?"

"Those locks can be tricky."

"OK, three minutes."

"And paddle clear of the punt pool before the Porter notices?"

"That depends."

Ash turned back to Annabel. "Have you used a punt before?"

"I used to paddle dinghies with my father," she said.

Ash turned back to Brian. "So, experienced."

"And with no one else on board, there'll be less drag."

"Making it faster through the water."

Brian nodded.

"Distance to the river?" Ash asked.

"Say a hundred feet."

"Provided you don't hit the bank."

"Annabel's a cox," Brian pointed out.

"So, let's say four minutes to the river."

"Bringing the total to seven minutes," said Brian.

Ash nodded. "How long will it take the Porter to walk from the lodge to H staircase and back?"

"Five minutes."

"If we offered to make them a cup of tea."

"Would they accept?"

They turned to Annabel.

"Which Porter is it?" Ash asked.

Annabel remembered the face peering at her as she walked past the lodge.

"Shirley."

Brian frowned.

"I could ask her to wait until I found the key?" Ash suggested.

"That works."

They both nodded and turned to face her.

"OK, Annabel," Ash said. "We have a plan."

She stared at them. "You're sure?"

"Pretty sure. It's like role-play, only without the beards and pointy ears."

"Yes, that stuff is weird," Brian agreed, making a strange gurgling noise. It took her a moment or two to realise he was chuckling.

Ten minutes later, Annabel and Brian stood on the first-floor landing of Cripps D Staircase, waiting for Ash's signal. It wasn't long before they heard someone pass underneath whistling the Mission Impossible theme song. Brian gave her the thumbs up. A few seconds later they heard the door of the Cripps Lodge open, and Ash speak in a loud voice.

"I'm so sorry, Shirley. Could you help me? I've locked myself out of my room."

Shortly afterwards, they heard footsteps coming back.

"It's not like me," Ash said in a loud voice. "Don't know

what I was thinking. I'll forget my head next!"

As the footsteps faded, Brian led her down the stairs. In the distance, Annabel saw Ash in dressing gown and bare feet disappear around the corner with the Porter.

"Go!" Brian said. "I'll keep a lookout."

"Thanks, Brian," she said and ran for the lodge.

Once inside, Annabel lifted up the countertop and stepped through the access gate. Then she crossed to a set of numbered punt hooks on the far wall. Here she selected the wooden float marked 10 and headed out in the rain to the punt pool.

The College punts lay moored along the quayside, their long hulls nestling side by side. Annabel made her way to the last punt by the willow tree and squatted down next to its mooring. A chain ran from the punt through a metal ring and back to a brass padlock attached to the punt pole and paddle. Pulling the hull towards her, Annabel inserted the key and popped the shackle open, almost dropping the lock in the process.

Stuffing it safely in her pocket, she headed back to the lodge. It was only after she returned the key to its hook that she noticed the flaw in their plan. A trail of wet footprints ran from the door, past the counter, to where she stood. And she knew there'd be another set going back. There was no way Shirley could miss those.

Desperate, she saw the hunched figure of Brian watching her from D Staircase and waved for him to join her. Glancing briefly towards Ash's staircase, he came hurrying over.

"Brian!" Annabel said, pointing at the floor. "We need something to wipe this up!"

For a moment he stared at the footprints. Then without saying anything, he began pulling his coat off.

"What are you doing?"

"Go," he said, stripping off his black tee-shirt. "I've got this."

Annabel stepped outside and watched as Brian ran to the hooks in the corner and dropped to his knees. Then he began mopping up the footprints with his shirt, working his way back towards the door, his thin arms scrubbing back and forth. Realising there was nothing she could do to help, she blew him a kiss he would never see and headed back to the punt pool.

While the rain continued to lash down, she pulled the chain free of the ring. Then, placing her hands on the bow of the punt, Annabel pushed off from the quayside and stepped on board. For a few heart-stopping moments, she wobbled before squatting down in the bows. Wet fronds of weeping willow brushed over her face as the punt glided away from its mooring and into the open water.

Looking back at the Porters' Lodge, she just caught sight of Brian's pale body as he stood up by the door, grabbed his coat and ran for D staircase. Annabel hoped he'd remembered to replace the countertop, but knew there was nothing she could do about that now.

Turning back to the punt she saw the stern heading straight for the looming wall of Magdalene College.

"Oh, no!"

Reaching down, she grabbed the paddle, and after a few frantic strokes, managed to arrest its momentum sufficiently to avoid a collision. Then as Annabel got into her rhythm, she turned its nose towards the river.

Whatever Ash and Brian had thought of her boating abilities, manoeuvring a twenty-four foot punt was a lot harder work than she'd expected. It seemed to take forever to build up any sort of headway. By then, Annabel could feel sweat mingle with rainwater running down her neck. It was only when she was gliding out through the punt pool entrance that she risked a look over her shoulder.

The nine remaining punts were lined up in a neat row along the quay, a picture of serenity after the frantic activity of earlier. Beyond them stood the Porters' Lodge. Framed in its window was the squat outline of Shirley staring out across the water.

Annabel froze, not daring to move, expecting to be spotted at any moment. Instead, she saw the Porter raise a mug to her lips before turning back towards her desk. Seconds later, the lodge disappeared from view as the punt drifted out into the river, with its wet, and very relieved, stowaway on board.

Chapter Twenty-Seven

Nick stood in his room and stared at his face in the mirror. Two panda-like bruises were forming either side of his swollen nose, which, thankfully, had stopped bleeding. But the throbbing in his temples was getting stronger, and he reached for the painkillers the doctor had given him.

"How is it?" Giles asked from the armchair in the corner.

"OK." He popped two pills in his mouth and took a drink from the tap.

"OK as in 'I've had worse' or OK as in 'It hurts like hell, but I'm not going to moan about it'?"

Nick smiled but said nothing as he padded over to his desk. His right shoulder and neck were sore too, but he felt more human after the shower.

Giles looked out the rain-splattered window towards New Court.

"How long has Annabel been gone? I thought she'd be back by now."

"Maybe the others aren't in and she's gone to look for them."

"Do you think I should call her?"

Just then, Giles's phone vibrated, and he grabbed it off the table.

"It's her," he said. "She's downstairs."

"Did she get the punt?" Nick asked.

"Certainly did," said Giles, grinning back at him. "As I said, if you don't marry that girl, I will!"

They grabbed their coats and headed for the door.

Located next to the river, Cripps A Staircase had been designed with a series of stepped terraces running down to the water's edge. At the bottom of these, Annabel's head could be seen poking above a NO MOORING sign.

"There she is," Giles said, as they hurried down to join her.

Nick found Annabel kneeling on the bow of the punt, holding it against the bank.

"Hi. How'd it go?"

"Ash and Brian were amazing," she replied. "We owe them a drink, big-time."

"Anyone see you?"

"I'm not sure. Shirley, maybe. Any sign of her?"

Nick looked towards the lodge, which appeared quiet.

"Not so far."

"No point in waiting to find out," said Giles, springing into the back of the punt and reaching for the long wooden pole, laid lengthways between the seats. With deft movements, he raised and planted it into the river before stepping up onto the aft deck.

"All aboard for tonight's magical mystery tour."

"Keep it down, for goodness sake!" Annabel hissed from the bow.

Even in the darkness, Nick saw the flash of white as Giles grinned back. The third-year was clearly an old hand when it came to punting. He looked like a professional tour guide as he stood there leaning on the pole.

Growing up in the Midlands, Nick had never spent much time in or around boats. He preferred having solid ground beneath his feet, and he was a lot more tentative as he stepped on board. The punt dipped under his weight, sending rainwater lapping up between the duckboards as he squatted down on the damp seat.

"All set?" Giles asked. "Who brought the champagne?"

Annabel glowered back at him through dripping hair.

"Cast off there in the bow," he said, leaning on the pole. "Full speed ahead!"

Annabel pushed them off from the bank, and the nose of the punt swung towards the Bridge of Sighs. Water slapped against the hull as Giles propelled them upstream.

Above him, Nick saw the branches of the Master's plane tree sway and groan in the wind. A strong gust whipped spray into his face, and he suspected that Annabel was having an even worse time of it in the bow.

What with the rain and water seeping into his trousers, their first time together in a punt was a long way from the balmy sunny outing he had once envisaged. Though he liked to think that after tonight's reconciliation, the prospects of one day doing so had improved considerably. But when Annabel looked back at him, her bedraggled face bore no resemblance to the serene tranquillity of his imagined summer outing.

"Nick, where's this door of yours?"

Nick peered through the driving rain at the New Court building looming over them. He pointed to a dark outline in the wall on their right. "There!"

Annabel nodded and indicated with her paddle. "Giles, can you get us alongside?"

"Aye, aye, Captain!"

The punt shifted direction.

"Looks like there's a mooring point next to it," she said, reaching forwards and catching hold of a large iron ring set in the wall.

While Annabel used the punt chain to make them fast, Nick squatted in front of the shadowy archway. The outline of the door was visible in the darkness, its timbers finishing just above the waterline.

"So, what's the plan?" Giles asked after stowing the pole next to the seat.

Nick thought back to the beginning of the term. "There are steps on the other side of the door."

"Is there a lock?"

"Yes, but the wood is pretty rotten."

Nick leaned forward and gave it a tentative push. To his surprise, the door swung inwards, and he almost tipped into the water. Giles grabbed him and hauled him back.

"Whoa, steady!"

Nick swayed, feeling nauseous. *Not a good sign*, he thought.

"Nick, are you OK?" Annabel asked.

"Fine. Just not great in boats." He pointed at the

splintered frame. "It wasn't like that before."

"Well, saves us having to do it," said Giles. "Probably got hit by a tourist punt."

"At this time of year?" Annabel asked.

The sound of loud voices from the Bridge of Sighs made them all turn. A group of students, their red tops visible through the arched windows, crossed the river, singing "Walk on, Walk on" as they disappeared into New Court.

"That was close," said Annabel.

"Not sure they'd see us in this rain," Giles said. "Still, no point in hanging around. Nick, are you happy to lead as you know what's on the other side?"

"Sure," he said, pushing the door open more carefully this time. The entrance was pitch black, and he tried to gauge how far it was to the steps.

"Do you need a light?" Annabel asked.

"Not sure that's a good idea," said Giles as more singing could be heard approaching the bridge.

"I'm fine," said Nick.

Standing on the edge of the punt, he took a deep breath and jumped into the dark. His foot slipped, and he pitched forward, cracking a shin against one of the steps.

"Oh! You bast…!"

"Nick?" Annabel cried. "What is it?"

Nick gasped, his leg on fire. Easing himself upright, he hobbled around to see their worried faces peering in through the doorway.

"I'm, fine," he said. "Just watch yourself on the steps. They're slippery. Come on. I'll catch you."

Annabel looked doubtful, but he gave her a reassuring smile and held out his hand. She took a moment to set herself on the edge of the punt, and then sprang across the gap.

Whether it was because the punt was lighter now, Nick couldn't be sure, but the hull seemed to dip as she jumped and landed in the water.

"Nick!" she cried.

"I've got you," he said, grabbing her top and hauling her up onto the steps. For a moment, she just clung to him. "Are you OK?"

"I think so," she said, looking down at her soaking trousers. "As if I wasn't wet enough already."

"Oh crap," said Giles.

"What is it?" Nick asked.

"Vuvuzelas!"

"What?"

"Coming through!"

"Wait, we're not..." he began, but it was too late.

Giles leapt across the gap, collided with Annabel and rebounded into the water. The resulting splash sent a wave surging up the steps. Struggling out from under Annabel, Nick saw Giles floundering next to the punt.

"Here," he said, reaching down and grabbing Giles's outstretched hand. Flexing his knees, Nick dragged his friend clear of the water as Annabel scrambled out of the way. Giles and Nick stood cheek to cheek on the step, like a couple of dancers.

"Thanks for that," said Giles.

"No problem," Nick said, feeling something hard pressed against his leg.

Giles smiled. "Torch."

"What? Oh, right. Good to know."

They disentangled themselves as more noise came from the bridge.

"Sorry about that," Giles explained. "The vuvuzela section decided to have a pissing contest from the Bridge of Sighs."

"You're kidding," Annabel said.

"Afraid not. Brings a whole new meaning to the Bridge of Sighs, don't you think?"

"Did they spot the punt?" Nick asked.

"By the state of them, I doubt it," said Giles, digging the torch out of his pocket. "Besides, there's not much we can do now. Might as well crack on and find Mackenzie's trunk. Hopefully, we can get the punt back before anyone notices."

Giles turned his LED on and shone the beam up the steps. Above them, Nick saw Annabel pull her phone out and activate its torch app.

"Have you got a phone, Nick?" Giles asked.

"No, I don't have one."

Annabel stared at him. "What do you mean?"

"I broke it," he said, "on Christmas Eve."

"Why didn't you tell me?"

He shrugged. "You didn't ask."

"And you didn't get another one?"

Nick looked at her. "I couldn't afford one."

The tunnel went silent, and the dawning comprehension

on Annabel's face only made it worse. Nick could feel his face flush, the blood pounding through his head. The thumping behind his temples was so loud that it took him a moment or two to realise Giles had spoken to him.

"Sorry?"

"I asked if you remember where the light switches are? You know. When you last came down here?"

Nick closed his eyes, willing his head to clear.

"Yeah, they were on a panel by the entrance from B staircase."

Giles handed him his torch. "In that case, you'd better lead as you know the way."

"What about you?"

"You'll look after me, won't you, Annabel?"

"Sure," she said, her voice very quiet.

Nick took the torch. and climbed up to the landing where Annabel waited for him.

"It's this way," he said, not wanting to meet her eyes, and set off down the steps. He heard the others follow him and tried not to think about the looks they were probably sharing right now. Nick was so preoccupied with his thoughts that he never registered the set of large wet footprints that preceded them into the cellars.

Chapter Twenty-Eight

Ravi woke to find himself sitting in absolute darkness, back propped against a wall, his legs stretched out in front of him. Blinking to check that his eyes were open, he tried looking around but stopped as pain lanced through his shoulder. When it subsided, he realised that his left arm hung useless at his side.

Memories came flooding back of approaching footsteps, the sound of breaking glass, and a door exploding inwards, throwing him across the cellar and then… nothing. Was that where he was now, he wondered, beneath New Court, with the…?

Sniff.

Ravi stiffened.

Sniff.

Closer this time.

He held his breath, staring into the blackness. The figure, he knew, was right in front of him. Perhaps it had been there all along, its hooded face inches from his own, waiting. For what?

Just for a moment, Ravi's will wavered as his desperate

situation became clear. Here he was, alone, wounded and with a creature that could smash aside a heavy wooden door. No one even knew that he was here.

But then a memory came back to him from long ago of a cold, disoriented boy from Nepal. Standing outside the Great Gate on a chill October night. Staring up at the imposing edifice of this venerable seat of learning – dark, impenetrable, and steeped in mystery.

Ravi hadn't given in to his fears then. And he wasn't going to do so now. Somewhere deep inside, a spark of courage still flickered. It kindled a flame of defiance that burned within him, driving back the all-pervading gloom.

"What are you looking at?" he said, barely recognising his own rasping voice.

There was a long pause, but Ravi didn't flinch, refusing to be cowed by the presence looming over him. The sniffing began again, only this time, the inhalation took longer. Ten, fifteen, twenty seconds… Way beyond anything a human lung could inhale. Proof, if any were needed, that the entity before him was not of this world.

Ravi waited for the sound to stop, and when it did, he spoke again, stronger this time.

"Satisfied?"

The exhalation that followed was like the expulsion of air from a crypt. So cold and soulless that it was all Ravi could do not to wither before it. On and on it went, forcing him to avert his gaze, while the lifeless breath washed over him. When it stopped and fell silent, he opened his eyes and gasped.

Two orange orbs stared back at him, their pinprick pupils locked on his. After the darkness of the cellar, it took Ravi a while to adjust to their presence. And when he did, the face in which they sat became visible. Its features were as still and unyielding as stone.

That was when Ravi knew where he'd seen it before. On Christmas Eve, with the Master, staring up at the Chapel Tower. This face had looked back at them from an alcove set high in the wall. The face of a woman who had died five hundred years earlier. Lady Margaret Beaufort.

The stone statue of the College's founder had peered down on Chapel Court for centuries. Then last year, it had seen a harpy fall, an egg shatter, and an alien life force swirl around the cloister, looking for a new host.

Ravi cursed himself for not realising the danger sooner. He and Robert had witnessed similar transformations happen on Gemini. Harpies preyed on one another, not for flesh alone, but to absorb the life force of their victim. The same alien energy that allowed them to reanimate their calcified bodies.

Only what Ravi now saw before him was the result of the dying spirit of a mother and the life force of her egg. She had taken possession of the very statue Giles had hung from, high above Chapel Court, all those months earlier. And it was those same amber eyes that had glared at him across the Chapel roof that stared at him now. No longer staring out from the head of a harpy, but from the face of the College's founder reborn.

These thoughts passed through Ravi's mind in a

heartbeat. A heartbeat that faltered as he realised the enormity of what he had allowed to happen. And with it came an understanding that he, and he alone, had to put matters right.

Taking a deep, steadying breath, he said, "Why are you here?"

For a while, the statue did not respond, as if considering his question. Then a haunting voice escaped its mouth.

"For… you…" it said.

Ravi blinked. "I don't understand."

After another long pause, it repeated its answer, firmer this time.

"For you."

"Me? But why?"

It raised a pale hand that was missing one of its fingers, and pointed at him.

"You… open…"

"Sorry?"

It reached down and gripped the front of his jacket, lifting him off the floor like a child picking up a doll. Pain coursed through Ravi's damaged shoulder. He gasped and its chill breath filled his nose and mouth, numbing his brain.

"You open…"

"I can't…" he moaned.

This time it shook him, his legs swinging clear of the floor. Ravi's broken arm flapped back and forth, the pain excruciating.

"Stop," he yelled, "please, stop!"

The shaking ceased, and the glowing eyes studied him

from beneath their hood. Blinking away the sweat that ran down his face, Ravi forced himself to meet their unrelenting gaze.

"What is it you want me to open?"

"Gate..."

"Never."

The blow almost took his head off. Pain exploded down the side of his face, and he felt something shatter inside his mouth. Ravi spat blood and what he suspected were teeth into the dark. At that moment, he would have welcomed oblivion, but consciousness refused to leave him.

"Open gate..." it said, spinning him around. The bones in his broken shoulder grated and Ravi thought he might pass out with the pain. Weeping, he peered at the pale, chalky outline of the Gemini, just visible in the orange glow of the creature's eyes.

"No, I can't..." but his protest was cut as the creature shoved his face forwards, pressing his cheek against the brickwork.

"Open... gate..." it hissed in his ear.

At any second, he expected another blow to fall. But he still had one more trick up his sleeve. His last throw of the dice. With his back to the creature, Ravi slipped his good hand inside his jacket and felt for the ruler. And found the breast pocket was empty.

Trying not to panic, he thrust his fingers deeper inside as he replayed his movements that evening. He'd had it with him in the Old Library and also in Gabriele's room when he'd... stepped out on the roof.

"No!"

The creature spun him around and its glowing eyes narrowed into what might have been a smile. It reached inside the folds of its cloak and withdrew an object, which it held out in the palm of its hand. It was his ruler, the sharpened blade glinting in the orange glow of his tormentor's gaze.

Ravi moaned, unable to believe how stupid he'd been. To lose his one weapon, tonight, of all nights, when he finally had need of it.

The creature hissed again. "Now… open… gate…"

Ravi stared up into those eyes and felt the anger grow inside him. Anger at Schiller. At Mary. At Robert. But most of all, at himself for allowing things to come to this.

Through broken teeth, he said, "I will…"

He paused for a fraction of a second as the grip on his neck relaxed. "…NOT!"

Ravi lunged with his good hand for the ruler. He almost made it too. Fifty years ago, he might have done. But even as his fingers closed around the blade, the creature's hand clamped over his and crushed his bones against the metal. Ravi opened his bloodied mouth and screamed.

Chapter Twenty-Nine

Giles kept close to Annabel as Nick led them through the cellars, using the beam of his torch to light the passageway ahead. It wasn't long before their footsteps developed an echo, suggesting that they were approaching a larger space. Sure enough, they emerged into a hallway with archways leading off in different directions and a stairwell disappearing above them. Here they paused, and Nick shone his torch up the steps.

"That's the entrance from B staircase," he said. "Wait here while I turn on the lights."

"Good idea," Giles said to Annabel, as Nick headed upstairs. "We don't want to make the classic horror movie mistake."

"Which is?" she asked.

"Groping around with torches in the dark when there's a perfectly good lighting system overhead."

Nick's footsteps stopped and they heard a series of clicks.

"Guys?" Nick called down. "Is anything happening?"

"Not yet," Giles replied.

"In that case, we have a problem."

"What is it?" Annabel asked as he came back down.

"Fuse must have gone. We'll have to use the torches after all."

Annabel shot Giles a look.

"What?" he said. "How was I supposed to know?"

"So, how do you want to do this?" Nick asked.

"I suggest we split up..." Giles began. Annabel's head whipped around.

"Only kidding!" He held up his hands. "Just a joke, OK?"

She glared at him. "Seriously unfunny, Giles."

"We stick together, OK? Find the trunk, recover anything of interest, and then get out of here. Agreed?"

"Agreed," said Annabel.

"Nick?"

But the latter was directing his beam at the ceiling.

"I think I know why the lights aren't working."

Giles looked up. Protruding from the overhead light fitting were the jagged remains of the fluorescent tube.

"What about the others?" Annabel asked.

Nick's torch illuminated shattered filaments in each of the fittings. "A power surge?" he suggested.

Giles shook his head. "The fuse would have blown first." He thought back to the shattered doorframe. "Come on. We can report all this to Maintenance later. Where's that trunk, Nick?"

"This way," he said, pointing to a passageway.

"Lead on, MacDuff."

Annabel didn't look happy, but she kept quiet as Nick

led them through the maze of tunnels, their feet crunching on the glass littering the floor. Every now and again, he paused, shining his torch around a room to find the next doorway. But when they came to a four-way intersection, Nick leaned heavily against the wall as he tried to remember the way.

"Nick, are you all right?" Annabel asked.

"Fine," he said, looking around and pointing at some pipework. "It's this way."

Annabel headed after him, and Giles was about to follow when a noise made him stop. It came from one of the openings. Just a murmur, from a long way off. Giles was about to call the others back, when he heard Nick cry out.

"Here it is!"

Following their excited voices, he found Nick and Annabel in a large cellar lined with tall wooden racks. They were standing in the far corner, their lights pointing at a dark rectangular shape. It was an old travelling trunk, similar to the one he'd had at school.

"Where've you been?" Annabel asked.

"I got distracted."

"It's locked," said Nick.

Giles squatted down next to him and fished in his pocket for his keyring.

"That's the great thing about being sent to a boarding school," he said, selecting one of the many paperclips hanging from the loop. "You soon learn where to store contraband like cigarettes and alcohol."

Bending the end of the clip, he inserted it into the lock.

"And no self-respecting prefect would conduct a dormitory inspection without mastering the art of unpicking a trunk's factory settings."

There was a click, and the clasp sprang open.

"Giles, that's criminal," said Annabel.

"That's a bit harsh," he said, "I prefer to call it resourceful. Now, let's see what old Mackenzie was hiding in here."

Whatever Annabel's doubts about his methods, when Giles lifted the lid, both she and Nick crowded forwards to shine their torches inside. The contents appeared to be divided into three sections: journals, cardboard boxes, and a stack of tartan blankets.

Reaching for the journals first, Giles saw that they dated all the way back to the 1960s. The opening page on each one had the same entry in the former Dean's flowing script.

"The Gemini Club," he read aloud.

"What's that?" Nick asked.

"Not sure, but these appear to be workbooks," said Giles, flicking through the pages. They were filled with notes, diagrams and those strange hieroglyphs he'd seen in that book Gupta had been reading in the Library.

"What's in those boxes?" Annabel asked.

Taking one of the older ones, which was also marked 1969, Giles opened the lid. He found a crumpled collection of newspapers inside, each contained a fine white powder.

"Is that what I think it is?" Nick asked.

"It may have been the sixties," Giles said, "but I don't think Gupta and Mackenzie were dealing."

He dabbed a finger in the powder and licked it, grimacing at the acrid-tasting sediment.

"Calcium."

Annabel's eyes widened as she stared at the other boxes. "All of them?"

Giles picked up one of the newer ones and lifted the lid. This time when he prised the paper apart, he saw a pair of curved conical shapes, over six inches long.

"Tusks?" he suggested.

Annabel stretched a hand towards them, but as soon as her fingers touched their surface, they crumbled into that same white powder. "Sorry"

Giles thought back to his conversation in the Library. "The same thing happened to that talon the Professor found in his jacket last term. Once the creature died, that too crumbled to dust."

He replaced the box and noticed a strap sticking out from under the tartan blanket. "Hello, what's this?"

Pulling it out, he found it belonged to an old canvas rucksack, its khaki fabric faded with age.

"Well, well, well," he said, examining it.

"Is that the one they took to the other place?" Annabel asked.

"Oxford, you mean?"

Nick snorted.

"Looks like it," Giles said, indicating the red dust deposits on the material.

Reaching inside, he produced a coil of rope, a battered metal canteen, and a pair of Carl Zeiss binoculars.

Rummaging around at the bottom of the bag, he also found an old Zippo lighter, which worked the first time.

"That's interesting," he said, examining the brass casing.

"What is?" Annabel asked, leaning in closer with her torch.

"The engraving."

"It's that same symbol, isn't it?"

"The Gemini, yes," Giles said, turning the lighter over, looking for an inscription. "Here we go. 'To Robert, love Mary.'"

"Who's Mary?" Annabel asked.

But before he could reply, the silence was shattered by a scream. Giles spun around.

"What the hell was that?"

"Whoever it is, they're in trouble," said Nick, running for the doorway. "Come on!"

"Nick! Wait!" Annabel yelled, running after him.

"Guys! Wait up!" Giles said as their lights disappeared down the passageway, leaving the room in darkness.

"Great," he muttered, clicking on the lighter. The orange glow illuminated the contents of the trunk once more.

"I'll see to you lot later," he said, closing the lid. Then he sprang to his feet and, holding the flickering flame before him, ran after the others.

Chapter Thirty

Nick ran from the trunk room, following the pipework back to the tunnel crossroads. There he paused, ignoring the throbbing in his head as he tried to decide which passageway to take.

"Nick, wait up!" Annabel cried.

But then he heard another scream from the archway to his left.

"This way!" he said, setting off again, the beam of his torch bouncing up and down as he followed the noise.

Turning a corner, he came to a two-way junction. This was where he and Shirley had got lost at the start of the term. Some way behind him, he heard Annabel calling for him.

"Nick?"

"Here!"

He waited until he heard the sound of her footsteps crunching over broken glass and saw the glow of her phone light appear.

"It's somewhere up ahead," he began, but Annabel interrupted him.

"Don't you ever do that again!"

"What?"

"Run off like that. We stick together, OK?"

"I didn't want to lose him, that's all."

Annabel glared at him, but then they heard Giles's voice.

"Where the hell are you two?"

"We're here!" Annabel called back.

They waited until the guttering glow of the lighter appeared.

"There you are," Giles said, clicking the flame off. "Found anything?"

Nick, turned towards the two archways. "It came from one of these. Listen." He closed his eyes, but the thumping in his temples was louder if anything.

"There!" said Annabel, pointing at the opening on the right.

Nick shone the LED down the long corridor, noticing that there were no shards of glass littering the floor. Instead, tendrils of cabling hung from torn ducting in the ceiling.

"You're sure you heard something?" he asked.

"It sounded like a moan," she said.

Nick focused the beam on the shadowy doorways running along both sides of the corridor.

"Anyone there?"

They waited for a response but heard nothing.

"Come on," he said, stepping forwards.

"Wait!" Annabel said. "What would make someone scream like that?"

Nick pointed at the cables. "Electric shock, maybe?"

"Then why isn't he lying here?"

Nick's head really was throbbing now.

"I don't know. Look, we go from room to room. If we don't find anything, we'll come back and check that other passageway. OK?"

"Works for me," said Giles.

Annabel didn't look too sure, but nodded.

Nick headed for the nearest doorway, the others following. Standing in front of the opening, he shone his torch inside. The room was some twenty feet long with an arched ceiling and a brick wall at the far end. Swinging his beam from left to right, he could see that there was nothing there except shelves of empty racking.

"Clear," he said before crossing to the opposite side and doing the same.

Annabel kept her mobile trained along the corridor while Giles kept an eye out behind them.

"Clear."

As Nick headed for the next doorway, the corridor began to sway. Reaching out, he grabbed hold of the doorframe to steady himself before pointing the LED inside.

"Clear," he said, wincing as the pain intensified behind his eyes.

"What was that?" Annabel said in a hushed voice.

Blinking, Nick turned to see both her and Giles peering down the corridor. Then, even he heard the groan.

"There!" Annabel said, "Come on!"

The other two hurried forwards with Nick following on behind. When they stopped in front of the last doorway on the left, Annabel gasped.

"My God. What is that?"

Nick caught up with them and stared. There in the beam of their torches, he saw a huge mystical symbol covering the far wall.

"That, if I'm not mistaken," said Giles, "is a Gemini."

For several seconds Nick stared at the shape, the lines and surrounding symbols making his head hurt. He lowered the beam and, as he did so, noticed a crumpled heap at the foot of the wall. The others saw it too.

"Professor Gupta!" Annabel yelled, running into the room.

Giles followed her in, but Nick had to steady himself against the doorframe, fighting down a wave of nausea.

"Quick guys," she said. "He's hurt!"

Annabel was crouching over the body. As he came closer, Nick could see that the old man was in a bad way. Blood ran from his mouth, and his arm hung limp at his side. Even the fingers of his hand were bent at an odd angle.

"Oh, Professor," whispered Annabel, her voice wavering. "What's happened to you?"

The Professor's head lolled back, and he peered up at them with listless eyes. His cracked lips split open, and Nick could see broken teeth behind his bloody gums.

"What was that?" Annabel said, leaning in.

The Professor tried speaking again, but all Nick could hear was a rattling wheeze. Tears were running down Annabel's face now.

"I can't understand you, Professor. Say it again."

Giles squatting down next to her.

"He doesn't look good, Annabel. We need to get him out of here."

"But Giles, we can't move him like this."

Nick saw the Professor's eyes blink open. His lips began to move again.

"I think he's trying to say something," he said.

"Professor. It's Annabel. You'll have to say that again."

"Safe..."

"Yes, Professor," she said. "You're safe now."

The old man groaned, but Nick didn't think it was from pain. It was frustration. Then his hollow eyes opened wide and he stared at the doorway.

"Not... safe!"

That's when Nick heard the crunch of sand behind him. But as he began to turn, the room started to spin. The last thing Nick remembered seeing was a hooded shape standing in the doorway before the shadows closed in.

Chapter Thirty-One

Annabel was still holding the Professor when she saw Nick topple backwards.

"Nick!" she cried.

But then Giles was there, throwing himself under Nick's bulky frame to cushion the fall and grunting as the Redboy landed on him. Nick's torch fell from his grasp and rolled against the wall.

Annabel called out, "Giles! Are you all right?"

But before he could reply, she heard the sound of heavy footsteps stalking towards her. Looking up, she saw the shadowy outline of the hooded figure approach, lit by the distant glow of the torch. Shrouded in robes, it had a spectral appearance, save for the crunch of sand beneath its feet.

Supporting the Professor with one arm, Annabel scrabbled around for her phone. The figure came to a stop a few feet away, and she saw glowing amber eyes stare down at her from under the cowl. Their unnatural stillness sent a chill through her, but she held its gaze.

"What do you want?" she asked.

The baleful eyes considered her. Then the hidden face

leaned in closer and emitted a hiss so full of menace that Annabel felt her resolve fade. Had the figure reached for the Professor then, she'd have been powerless to intervene.

Instead, a bright light lit up the room, and they both flinched. Annabel peered over at the wall and saw Giles cradling Nick and pointing the LED at the hooded figure. Annabel looked up and caught a fleeting glimpse of a woman's face before a robed arm shielded it from the light. That's when she noticed the missing digit of the raised hand and knew that this was Giles's rooftop stalker. He must have seen it too.

"You again."

Still shielding its face from the glare, the figure turned towards him. Behind the cowl, Annabel heard a long rattling sniff, the sound so unnatural that it made her skin crawl. If Giles felt the same way, he didn't show it. He slowly extracted himself from under Nick while keeping the beam pointed at his adversary.

"Light a bit bright, is it?" he asked as he eased himself to his feet.

There was another menacing hiss from the creature as the two began circling each other, Giles careful to keep the torch between them.

"Remember me, do you?" he said, moving around to put himself between the prone body of the Professor and his hooded stalker.

Annabel eased the old man back against the wall, and he let out a moan. The figure paused, and for a moment, she thought it might lunge for them. But Giles intervened.

"Why so shy?" he said. "We all know why you're here, sniffing around."

The creature hissed, but he had its attention again.

"You're looking for something, aren't you?" he continued. "Been looking for a while, I expect."

Out of the corner of her eye, Annabel noticed Nick raise his head.

"And maybe I can help you with that."

The room became very still.

"I'll tell you what, why don't we play a little game? Seeing as we're all here for a while."

He patted his pocket, and though its face was still shielded, the hooded shape leaned forwards a fraction.

"Here we are," he said, producing the red handkerchief with a flourish. "Something I borrowed from you the other night. Now seems a good time to return it."

What is he up to? Annabel thought.

Giles peeled back the material and held out his hand. "I give you… the finger!"

With an angry hiss, the stalker lunged for its missing digit. But Giles was ready for it. He whipped his hand away just in time and threw the stone finger out into the corridor. "Fetch!" he yelled.

As plans went, it wasn't great, but Annabel could see what he was trying to do. The trouble was, so could the stalker.

It lashed out with its arm, sending the LED flying across the room. It smashed against the wall, and the cellar fell into darkness, save for the dull orange glow of the creature's eyes.

Annabel heard a stifled groan as Giles was lifted from the floor. She then sensed rather than saw movement as Nick charged across the room.

"Nick, no!"

Annabel watched the Redboy barrel into the hooded figure, the two coming together with a sickening thud. But the creature didn't so much as flinch, and this time it was Nick who staggered backwards. He would have hit the floor, but a robed hand reached out and grabbed him.

Gripping both students by the neck, the figure turned to face her. With inhuman strength it extended both arms out wide in a grotesque parody of a crucifix. Then it lifted her two struggling friends clear of the floor. Annabel felt her courage falter, awed by the creature's power and menace.

"Annabel...."

Turning, she saw the Professor staring at her.

"Here..." he wheezed, looking down.

Annabel saw her phone was in his mangled hand.

"Light..." he said, "face..."

She nodded. Reaching down, Annabel took the phone from the Professor's broken fingers. Rising to her feet, she turned and faced the hooded figure.

"Let them go."

The room went still. The hiss, when it came, was dismissive.

"I warned you," Annabel said, raising her arm and shining the torch app into the hood.

The creature hissed, twisting and turning in anguish. But Annabel saw its face clearly for the first time.

"Lady… Lady Margaret," she said under her breath.

As she watched, those familiar features begin to stiffen under the intense beam of light. The amber eyes closed, and for a moment, Annabel felt a brief surge of triumph. But then Nick and Giles began to convulse, their faces contorting as the pale hands squeezed their necks.

"No," she said, looking from her struggling friends to the hooded figure, its face now a stony mask.

Annabel stood there, holding the phone in front of her, wondering what to do. If she lowered her arm, she might save her friends. For now. But wouldn't the creature just torture them again anyway? Use them to force the Professor to open the portal? What if he couldn't?

A terrible thought struck her. *Or wouldn't?*

Images of her dead parents and sister came flooding back. This was her fate, she realised. To see everyone she cared for die. This was her curse. To bring death to everything she touched.

Annabel blinked.

Everything she touched…

Time seemed to stand still as she stared into the unseeing, unfeeling face before her. An idea formed in her head, small at first, but growing in strength and conviction. To draw on her curse and turn it from a weakness into a weapon. If only she could use it, and channel it into a force to save her friends. Annabel lowered her arm and thrust the light under her own chin, lighting up her face like a demon.

At first, the hooded figure didn't move, its eyes remaining closed and its body rigid. Then the eyelids flicked open, and the two pools of amber stared out at her. As they did so, Nick and Giles stopped gagging, and began sucking in deep gasping breaths.

The pale lips of Lady Margaret parted in a thin smile.

"Open... gate..." she said.

Annabel took a step forward. "First, let them go."

The smile didn't waver.

"Open... gate."

She shook her head and took another step. "Let them go."

The eyes glared at her.

"Open... gate!"

"That's not going to happen."

"Then... they... die..."

Annabel heard her friends begin to moan again, but she didn't break eye contact. Instead, she placed her free hand against Lady Margaret's chest.

What Annabel expected to happen, she couldn't say. But she felt the creature flinch and look down. She did the same and gasped.

The Professor was lying face down at their feet. Somehow, he had dragged his broken, bleeding body over ten feet of flagstone floor. One arm lay useless at his side. The other was stretched out towards Lady Margaret. And gripped in his mangled, twisted hand was the old metal ruler, its blade buried in the statue's foot.

Then Annabel heard a click. Turning, she saw Giles, face glistening with sweat, suspended from the outstretched arm. In his hand, he held the zippo lighter, its flame poised beneath the Lady's hanging sleeve.

"Light, anyone?" he said.

There was a whoosh as the pale fabric caught fire and a blue flame raced along the arm. Even before it reached the hood, the screech began, so loud and piercing that Annabel had to cover her ears.

Flames spread over the folds of the robe, coursing down the pale forearm towards her hand. For a terrible moment, Annabel thought that they would wash over Giles's exposed face. But then he was falling, the fingers releasing him just before the fire engulfed them.

Still, the screeching continued as flames framed Lady Margaret's face in a halo of fire. On they rushed, down the other arm, and then Nick was falling too, collapsing in a heap on the floor. The figure tried to drag the burning cowl off its head, but by now its fingers were ablaze. It screeched again, thrashing around wildly as the long skirt ignited. Even then, it stood there, writhing in agony, its foot pinned to the floor by the ruler, the Professor's blistering hand still gripping the metal.

"Professor!" Annabel cried, grabbing hold of his legs.

"Giles! Help me!"

Still choking, Giles crawled over to join her, and together they dragged his limp body back against the wall.

"Stay with him!" Annabel said, scrambling towards Nick.

He lay where he'd fallen, inches from the screeching, blazing figure above him. Grabbing his arm, Annabel heard him groan as she hauled him back across the floor.

"Come on, Nick," she yelled, and she felt him start pushing with his feet as they backed away from the flames.

They collapsed against the wall next to Giles, the three of them staring up at the blazing effigy of the College's founder. Annabel saw the wild amber eyes stare at her as the screech reached a pitch too high to register. Nick gripped Annabel's arm, and Giles leant over, covering the Professor's face.

"Watch out!" he shouted.

Lady Margaret exploded.

One second she was there, and the next she was an expanding ball of fire. Annabel closed her eyes and waited for the flames to hit, but they never did. Instead, she was blanketed by a hot wave of ash that filled her nostrils, making her cough and choke. She heard the others splutter too, and, peering through half-closed eyes, she caught sight of a cloud of pale dust whirling above their heads.

When the maelstrom finally died down, an eerie silence fell over the cellar, broken by the occasional cough from Nick or Giles. Annabel reached for her phone and shone the torch around the room. Of Lady Margaret, there was no sign. Just a pile of white powder around the blackened ruler, protruding from the flagstones.

Chapter Thirty-Two

Alfonso fled through the labyrinth of tunnels, the leather bag thumping against his back. His pursuers bounded after him, their angry grunts echoing through the confined space. Twisting left and right, he ran past his markers carved into the walls, not needing them now, the passages so familiar after all these months.

Behind him, he could hear that his pursuers were gaining, scrambling over one another to get at him. Fighting down his fear, Alfonso focused on avoiding the fallen rocks and fissures that littered the floor. Any slip would mean certain death, the chasing pack on him in seconds.

Keeping up his blistering pace, he recited the upcoming turns in his head. *Left, right, right, left*, counting each one off as he jinked this way and that. Thighs burning, chest heaving, he pushed himself off the walls and leapt over obstacles.

Sweat stung his eyes, but he dared not wipe it away for fear of losing his balance. Even so, his blurred vision began to make out a dim light seeping into the passageway ahead. It grew brighter with each gasping metre, and, with it, so did his hope.

But his pursuers must have noticed it too. Their scrabbling was becoming more urgent, and their pace increased. A blood-chilling chitter echoed through the tunnel. The lead runners had caught sight of him. The staccato sound of claw on rock became even more frenetic as the pack made its final dash.

Alfonso pumped his arms harder, his dust-coated feet slapping over the dusty floor. Up ahead, the last bend came into view, its wall glowing scarlet in the sunlight. *One more turn*, he thought, *one more. This time, I'm going to make it.*

Behind him, the snarls died away, his hunters saving their breath for the final leap, when they would drag him down and rip him to shreds. Alfonso careered around the corner into the corona of white light. Blinded, he continued to run, not missing a stride until… Wham!

The blow flung him against the wall with tremendous force, the air driven from his lungs by the impact. His momentum carried him down the tunnel, his body bouncing over the rough surface.

As he came to a stop, a cloud of red dust billowed up around him, filling his nose and mouth and blotting out the sunlight. Coughing, he tried to get to his feet but was slammed back down by a massive claw. Pinned to the ground, he peered up through streaming eyes at the hulking shadow towering over him, its wings spread in challenge.

"Quiet!" it hissed.

That was when the hunting pack came leaping around the corner. Alfonso caught a glimpse of albino bodies and glowing red eyes that widened as they saw what awaited them. There was a flicker of panic among the lead runners as, too late, they realised their peril.

Then the second shadow dropped over them.

Terrified squeals erupted in the tunnel. Claws blurred through the air, tearing through pale torsos in arcs of crimson blood. The floor shook with the thump of heavy objects as bodies were slammed against walls or crushed underfoot. The dreadful crunch of bones was followed by mewling screeches as the sound of butchery continued, reverberating around the confined space.

Alfonso covered his eyes and ears, willing the noise to stop. Still, the memory of those images and sounds continued long after the tunnel fell into shocked silence. When he opened his eyes, he had to blink away the red dust that had settled over his face. Looking up, he saw the claw still planted on his chest and the broad wings flared in a protective arc around him. Above these, two dark eyes glared down at him.

Through dust-caked lips, he panted, "I could… have made it!"

The pressure on his heaving chest increased as the creature bent down and hissed.

"You think?"

Alfonso met her stare, biting back the retort that would only cause him more pain. Even so, he knew this small act of defiance might cost him dear. But before his minder could administer punishment, the sound of clapping echoed down the passageway, followed by a cackling laugh.

"Very good, my daughters," came the familiar voice.

"You timed that well. We can't have this fool getting himself mauled just yet."

The sound of approaching footsteps was accompanied by the rhythmical thud of an object against the floor. The hunched figure of Mary appeared, leaning on her staff, as she paused to peer down at him.

Then from the tunnel, another monstrous form appeared, arched wings and angular head splattered with blood. Two amber eyes surveyed Alfonso with predatory interest, and he felt his stomach tighten.

"All good, Olga, my dear?" Mary asked.

The creature tore her eyes from his and inclined her head at the woman.

"Good enough. There were more this time. The molevin must like this one's stench."

The old woman cackled again. "Maybe next time, he can entice one of the dominant males."

Alfonso reached for the bag slung over his shoulder, and he felt the pressure on his chest increase as Katya pressed her foot down. Glaring at her, he unslung the strap and tossed the package at Mary's feet.

"Here," he grunted.

"A present? How thoughtful," she said, poking at it with her staff. The severed head of a molevin boar appeared from between the folds of leather, the bloody puncture mark visible behind its ear where Alfonso had stabbed it with his bone stylus.

Mary snorted.

"Well, well. It seems our young pup is learning after all."

Alfonso saw Olga glance at the grisly bundle, unimpressed.

But he felt the pressure on his chest ease a fraction, and he looked up at Katya, who was staring at him, her dark eyes unreadable.

"Not many pickings on that, though," said the old woman. "If you want to impress me, boy, you'd best bring the whole carcass next time."

Alfonso flinched, expecting a blow for disappointing her, but none came.

"If it wasn't for your guardian angel here," Mary said, indicating Katya, "it would have been your head, not porky's, lying there. My daughter must have a soft spot for you."

Alfonso winced as the claw tightened once more, though whether this was deliberate or just anger at being mocked, he couldn't tell.

"You wanted him alive," Katya said.

Mary studied him. "For now."

The pain in his chest grew, and he struggled for breath.

"Oh, release him," said the old woman, "before he starts crying."

"As you wish, Mother."

The pressure on his chest eased, and Alfonso gasped, sucking in deep sobbing breaths. The old woman's leathery skin creased into a smile.

"I trust you learned something useful today," she said. "It is we who rule here, boy. That is the true order of things, and don't you forget it."

Alfonso stared up at the woman and saw both conviction

and madness there. A combination that made her all the more frightening.

"Come, girls," said Mary. "All this sport has made me hungry."

Pulling the hood over her bleached white hair, she strode towards the entrance to the tunnel, each stamp of her staff throwing up puffs of red sand. Alfonso was about to rise when a shadow loomed over him. Looking up, he saw Olga standing there, her amber eyes glowering.

"Tomorrow, we play a new game," she said, her long tongue licking blood from her pale lips. With that, she turned and headed after her mother, calling over her shoulder. "Bring supper."

Alfonso sagged onto the sand, relieved to have escaped so lightly. Feeling his bruised but intact ribs, he glanced towards his minder. But Katya was not looking at him. Instead, she was staring after her sister. The hostility in that look was unmistakable. In that moment, in the charnel house of the tunnel, a flicker of hope kindled in Alfonso's heart. It didn't last long.

"You heard Mother," the harpy snarled. "Get up, or I'll drag you through the dirt like the worthless pup you are!"

Alfonso laboured to his feet and, retrieving his bag, shuffled before her towards the light.

Chapter Thirty-Three

Alfonso stood on the flat top of the stone column, watching the first sun slip below the horizon. Its orange glow fought a losing battle with the pursuing rays of its twin, chasing it from the sky.

Mary and her daughters sat some way apart, crouched in a circle around the fire. Alfonso had lit this earlier under the watchful gaze of Katya, using flint and molevin gut as tinder. The flickering flames danced inside a brazier of calcified bones, throwing disturbing shadows across their faces as they conversed together in hushed tones.

Alfonso couldn't make out what they were saying. Olga's occasional glance in his direction suggested that his fate must figure to some degree in the conversation. Keeping his head down, he strained his ears. But try as he might, he only caught the odd word, and not enough to learn what was being planned for him.

The family council, if that is what it was, had been going on since supper. The three had eaten their fill of the molevin boar from his latest foray underground. The skull and carcass lay discarded on a nearby rock, the meat picked clean by Olga. Mary's eldest daughter had taken particular delight in breaking the bones in front of him and sucking at the marrow inside.

Still, the rich aroma of roasted meat hung in the air, and Alfonso's stomach cramped in response. Not that he was fool enough to sneak a bone for himself. To do so would invite at best a beating and more likely several days without food. No, his place was to wait until nightfall, when Katya would return him to the ledge, tossing him the scraps Mary deemed his performance had merited that day.

So, he remained standing, taking what pleasure he could from the last rays of sunshine before night closed in once more.

"Boy!"

The shout was so unexpected that Alfonso flinched. He stared around, wondering for a moment if they were under attack. But with the sun still visible, they were safe for now.

"Boy!" Mary repeated, her voice rising. "Here!"

Alfonso looked at her, and saw the others were staring at him too. Even then, he hesitated, not wanting to incur their wrath.

"Are you deaf or just stupid?" Mary said.

Keeping his head bowed, he approached the circle, stopping a few feet away, wondering what new trouble he was in. The matriarch studied him.

"We left you the eyes."

"Sorry?"

"The eyes, boy. They are for you." She indicated the discarded remains of their meal.

Alfonso glanced towards the glassy sockets of the grinning skull.

"Well? Are going to eat them or not?"

The ominous threat in her voice was all too clear.

"Of course," he said, and bent down to pick up the skull. The bone was still warm and sticky to the touch. After surviving on dry scraps for months, Alfonso found his mouth salivating.

"Thank you," he mumbled. He was about to return with it to his place when Mary surprised him again.

"Sit and eat. I have something to say to you."

Careful to remain just outside the inner circle, Alfonso squatted down with the skull in front of him. Its glazed eyes stared up at him, and he sensed that these weren't the only ones watching him.

"Go on then," said Mary. "You're hungry, aren't you?"

It was a test, he knew. Everything else had been so far, and why should this be any different? Reaching down, Alfonso dug his fingers into the socket and scooped out the lukewarm orb. It was the size of a boiled egg and, with that thought in mind, he stuffed it in his mouth, bit down and began to chew.

Mary chuckled, but he ignored her, drawing on the memories of his father, mother, and sister as he reached for the second eye. He thought back to those balmy summer nights in Porto Pollença, sitting on the veranda as dusk fell over the bay, sharing tapas and watching the dogs play. When he had finished, he looked down at the sightless skull.

"Needs must, eh, boy?"

"Sorry?"

"How do you think I survived here? Do you think I could have turned down a morsel like that in this world?"

"I don't know what you mean."

"You are not the only one who had to crawl through tunnels in search of food. I too know what it is like to hunt molevin in the depths. To creep into the dark, not knowing what waits beyond the next bend. To run before the pack, their hot breath on your heels."

Alfonso gaped at her, understanding for the first time the origins of his brutal training regime.

"Only I had no guide, boy. No guardian angel." She nodded at Katya. "I had nothing when they abandoned me here."

"Who?"

Mary turned from him and stabbed the fire with a curved rib bone, sending sparks spiralling into the air.

"Gupta and Mackenzie. The worst of your kind. Ran for their lives and left me here to die. They are the ones who abandoned me."

Alfonso had no idea who she was talking about. But rather than ask, he waited. And for once Mary seemed inclined to speak. Not to him or her daughters, but to herself, her voice quiet and almost reflective as she continued.

"They must have known. After I disappeared. Where else could I be? We'd studied together, worked together, dreamed together. Why would I leave them?"

Again the pause, her face creasing into a frown.

"Sure, they wanted me back in Moscow. Yuri never

believed their theories as I did." Her voice adopted a perfect Russian accent. "*Gimnazisty*, he called them. Schoolboys, Mariya! They'll convince you magic is real!"

The old woman went quiet for a while, the only noise coming from the crackling flames. When she spoke again, the bitterness was back.

"And then, after all that, they went through without me. Me! Good enough to sleep with, eh Robert? But not to take with you? And as for you, Ravi, what would you know about women? You barely know yourself."

Alfonso stared at Mary, wondering who she was talking to. Whose faces danced and flickered in the flames before her? Whoever it was, there was no doubting the pain they'd caused. He'd never seen her look like this, and it touched him in a way he hadn't expected.

Glancing at Katya, Alfonso saw her face stricken with sadness at her mother's words. But when he turned to Olga, he flinched. Those awful amber eyes were glaring back at him. It was as if she held him responsible for what these two men had done.

"Mother?" Katya's voice broke the spell. "Night falls."

Alfonso looked towards the horizon and was startled to see the second sun turning to gold as it dipped from view.

"My, how time flies when one has company," said the old woman, rising to her feet.

Alfonso was about to do the same when he felt the staff rest on his shoulder.

"I said I had something to tell you." Mary peered at him along its length.

After hearing more in one evening than he had in the past months, Alfonso wondered what else was coming.

"Tomorrow, we depart for the plains."

"The plains?"

"What, you thought this was all there was?" She gestured at the surrounding cliffs with the staff before bringing it back to hover in front of his nose. "This is but an isolated and, for now, overlooked corner of the Western realm. The perfect training ground for your next task."

Alfonso felt his stomach tighten, and it had nothing to do with his recent meal.

"There is an item I wish you to... obtain for me. It is some way from here, and you will leave first thing in the morning."

"Leave?"

Alfonso thought of the markings on the cave wall, which he had carved with such care. The names of his mother, father, and sister had seen him through those long nights when the harpies fought to get at him. His anguish must have shown on his face because Mary tutted.

"Don't you go fretting yourself. I am sending one of my daughters to keep you safe."

Alfonso saw Olga glare at him, and all thoughts of his family were driven out by the fear he felt at that moment. Mary glanced towards her elder daughter and laughed.

"Not Olga, she is too important for this task. Katya will accompany you instead."

It was all Alfonso could do not to sag with relief, but with the staff still pointing between his eyes, he forced himself to remain upright.

"We will rendezvous in two days, once you have completed your task. And be in no doubt, boy: this is something you will complete. If not, I will be disappointed. So disappointed that I may have to ask Olga to administer punishment. What do you say, my dear?"

Her elder daughter licked her lips.

"My pleasure, Mother."

If Alfonso hadn't been kneeling, he felt sure his legs would have buckled.

"What is it... you want me to do?"

"Oh, I wouldn't want to spoil the surprise. Katya will tell you on your journey. It will give you something to talk about."

The shadows were lengthening, and Alfonso heard the sound of wings flapping in the lee of the tower.

"Now, don't let me keep you up," said Mary. "You have an early start, remember."

And with that, she lowered the staff and strode towards the edge of the precipice.

"Come, my dear. I find long goodbyes so overrated."

Olga grinned at Alfonso before glaring at her sister.

"Two days. Don't be late."

"I won't be," said Katya, the edge in her voice unmistakable.

If Olga noticed, she paid it no heed, leaping into the air and banking towards her mother. Mary stepped off the edge and onto her daughter's back as she swept past. The last Alfonso saw of them was their winged outline flying towards the distant sunset. Katya followed their progress until the speck disappeared into the darkening sky.

"Come," she said, "I must get you to your cave before nightfall."

He rose and followed her to the edge of the stone column.

"What about your supper?" Katya asked.

Alfonso glanced back at the sightless skull, lying by the embers of the fire.

"I'm not hungry."

Katya said nothing. Instead, she leapt into the air and, gripping his shoulders, bore him out over the shadow-filled valley. As they banked towards his ledge, Alfonso saw that the tower's steep sides already bristled with movement – a reminder, if he needed one, of what the night would bring.

Chapter Thirty-Four

Alfonso rose with the first sun, making what he expected would be his last entry on the wall. One hundred and sixty-nine grooves in total, each one an inadequate record of the nights of horror he had endured on this world. Leaning forwards, he dug a final time into the red surface, carving his initials, before stowing the stylus in his pocket. Then he slung the leather bag, containing his flints and molevin gut, over his shoulder, and he stared down the valley, waiting for his ride.

It wasn't long before he saw Katya's winged outline soar above the distant cliffs and sweep towards him. Stepping back, he waited for her to land, her wings blowing up loose sand before she settled on the ledge. In one clawed foot, she held a crumpled bundle, which she tossed his way.

"For you," she hissed. "Take it."

Alfonso glanced from her to the package, wondering if this was another trick, a final test before their departure. But when he picked it up, he found that it was a patchwork cloak made of animal hide and stitched together with gut string. Inspecting it, he saw that the hood was trimmed with feathers, and there was a clasp at the neck formed from shards of bone. It was crude, but to receive anything other than a beating from Mary and her daughters was nothing short of miraculous.

Alfonso looked from the cloak to Katya, not knowing what to say.

"You will need it where we are going," she said.

"It is cold there?" he asked.

"You will see."

Alfonso looked into those fathomless dark eyes.

"Thank you," he said.

She snorted. "You will not be thanking me by the end of the day. We have far to travel before night falls and we stop only for water and food."

Still, Alfonso felt something stir inside. Something he hadn't felt for so long that it took him a while to recognise what it was. Gratitude.

Then Katya was springing into the air. "Come! We must be away before the second sun rises. We have dawdled long enough."

Angling his face against the rising dust cloud, Alfonso slipped the cloak around his shoulders. He just had time to tie the bone clasp together before she grabbed him in her powerful claws and hoisted him into the air.

The wind rushed past his face as Katya climbed above the column, her wings beating hard. The valley floor fell away below them, and Alfonso felt his insides lurch as she banked away from the rising sun and followed the line of the river heading west.

It was impossible to say, how far they travelled that morning. Alfonso found it hard to take it all in as they flew over countless valleys, gorges, and sheer-sided cliffs. Between these, the tall columns of stone stood like fossilised trees, their branches long since lost through time.

As the hours passed, he found that his attention waned, the features becoming blurred in his mind while the shadows shortened, and the twin suns rose higher in the sky. Suspended beneath Katya, Alfonso was protected from the worst of their rays by her broad wings. However, he could feel the heat radiate up from the russet-coloured cliffs.

Katya used the warm thermals to gain height before gliding to save energy in the sapping heat. Even so, by the middle of the day, he could hear her breathing become laboured.

"I must stop for a while. Your body grows heavy, and we have far to go today."

Dipping her wings, she dived into the valley, the thin thread of the river broadening into a ribbon of green and blue that wove around the columns.

Katya angled towards a spur in the river, formed by a collapsed tower of stone, and as she spread her wings to arrest her speed, Alfonso braced his knees for landing. Still, after all that time suspended in the air, when she lowered him onto the ground, he stumbled and fell on all fours. For a few moments, he remained like that, eyes closed against the swirling dust as Katya climbed away.

"Stay here while I get us some food," she called back, circling around and heading along the valley.

Alfonso waited until the noise of her beating wings had faded before looking at his surroundings.

The cliffs were some fifty yards away. Scanning their sheer sides for movement, he could see no sign of harpies, dormant or otherwise, clinging to their walls.

Instead, there were patches of vegetation in the lee of the rocky outcrops, where there was a measure of shade. Dark green stains were also visible in the river itself, which flowed around the bend just below him. Listening to the sound of running water, Alfonso realised just how parched his mouth was.

Easing himself to his feet, he spent a minute shaking out the stiffness in his legs before climbing down the broken sections of rock to the water's edge. The red sand was hard-packed where he knelt down and dipped his hands into the stream. The water was fresh, and after splashing some against his face and neck, Alfonso cupped his hands to drink.

Had he closed his eyes, he would have died. As it was, Alfonso caught sight of the dark shadow beneath the water moments before a monstrous serpent struck. The thick, sinewy tree-trunk of a body burst from the water, and not one but two heads lunged for him. The twin snouts opened wide to reveal rows of teeth that scythed towards his head and neck.

Months of brutal training in the molevin tunnels had honed Alfonso's reflexes. Still, he barely escaped. Ducking to the side, he felt one set of jaws brush his ear, the serrated teeth ripping it open in a gout of blood. Continuing to roll, he heard the thump of the massive body landing on the bank where he'd been kneeling moments before.

Alfonso's back slammed into a rocky outcrop, preventing him from rolling further. Two ugly snouts twisted towards him, tendrils beneath their chins quivering in the air as they sought his location. Even as he tried to get up, the hydra lunged again. He raised his arms in a defensive block, though he knew it was hopeless.

But the blow never came.

Instead, a shadow fell over the monster, and a split second later, Katya's claws tore into the nearest head. Deflected by the sudden strike, the other snout smashed into the rock, inches from his face, fragments of stone and broken teeth peppering his cheek.

Unable to arrest her momentum, Katya pitched into the river, her claws embedded in the monster's head. The brute's mottled green body followed her in as they both disappeared beneath the surface.

Scrambling to his feet, Alfonso saw Katya struggling to rise clear of the water, her massive wings beating on the surface to lift herself free. But even as she began to climb, a grotesque head reached up and grabbed her leg, tugging her below once more. For a moment, her dark eyes locked on his, and then she went under.

Too stunned to move, Alfonso stared at the turbulent water as the two creatures grappled beneath the waves. A wing rose from the river, and he saw Katya's head break the surface long enough to gasp for air before disappearing again beneath a thrashing, scaly body.

At that moment, he knew she was doomed. Without the

advantage of flight, a harpy's wings were a liability, whereas the hydra was in its element. It was only a matter of time before it crushed the life from Katya, and then… and then, Alfonso realised, he would be free.

Staring at the frothing surface, he knew that the loser of the contest would never be seen again. When they didn't make the rendezvous, Mary and Olga would never find the body to discover that he'd escaped. This was the moment he'd been waiting for.

After all these months of captivity under Mary's relentless gaze, suffering Olga's vindictive punishments, he now had a chance of escape. He could head out along the valley on his own, travelling by day and holing up at night, until he made his way back to the cave where the portal was located.

Once there, he might be able to eke out an existence until an opportunity presented itself to slip back through. Or until someone, his sister perhaps, could find a way to rescue him.

And yet… Alfonso hesitated, fingering the stitching of his cape, imagining Katya's dark eyes peering down at the tough hide as she threaded the sections together with her claws. Had she really done that on Mary's orders? Or had the creature fighting for her life in front of him chosen to do that? If so, why? He would never know, if he left now.

"*Merda*!"

Ripping off the cape and bag, Alfonso reached in his pocket for the stylus. Clamping it between his teeth, he took two running steps and dived into the river. Plunging through the cold water, he felt himself back in Pollença Bay, diving for squid off the beach. But when Alfonso saw the writhing bodies ahead of him, any thoughts of home were banished. He struck out for the tangle of limbs.

The hydra had coiled itself around its victim. Had one of its heads not been knocked senseless against the rock, Katya would be dead. As it was, she was struggling to keep the remaining jaws from her neck.

Alfonso kicked with his feet and arrived just as the hydra pulled back for a strike against her unprotected face. Grabbing a handful of tendrils, he took the stylus from his teeth and stabbed it down into the monster's skull. Inky black blood gushed from the wound as the creature convulsed, its body shuddering and spasming in a frenzy of bubbles and gore.

Alfonso pulled his weapon clear, and saw Katya tear herself free from the writhing serpent. They struck out for the surface and, moments later, their heads emerged, gasping for air. Looking around, he saw that they had drifted downstream during the struggle, and the river was picking up speed as the valley narrowed.

"Here," he spluttered, grabbing a fistful of feathers and tugging her towards the shore.

Kicking hard with his legs, he side-stroked them towards the bank until his fingers dug into the wet sand. Alfonso staggered upright and, sliding both arms under her wings, hauled her free of the water and up onto the bank. Then, he dropped to his knees as she lay there, gasping.

"Are you OK?" he asked.

She nodded, unable to speak. Looking down at her drenched body, Alfonso could see deep lacerations down one leg, where the hydra had dragged her under.

"Your leg," he said, and crawled over to the water's edge to inspect it.

"It's fine," she panted, "I... Alfonso!"

Her warning came just in time. Turning, he saw the hydra lunge from the river, one head limp but the other opening its jaws wide, revealing rows of broken teeth.

Alfonso didn't even blink. Batting the head aside with his forearm, he plunged the stylus through its eye socket and pinned it to the ground. The creature spasmed for a few more seconds until, with a final, quivering shudder, it lay still.

Alfonso stared down at the two mutilated heads leaking dark blood onto the red sand.

"What is that thing?"

When she didn't reply, Alfonso turned and found Katya studying him. As always, her expression was unreadable. Then, she glanced at the lifeless body at their feet.

"Lunch," she said.

Chapter Thirty-Five

Katya's wounded leg prevented her from carrying Alfonso on the next stage of their journey, and she allowed him to ride on her back instead. Mary had made mounting look simple with Olga. Still, as he stepped off the rocky outcrop, he almost slipped off.

"Watch it!" she hissed as he grabbed hold of her feathers to stop himself from falling.

"Sorry," he said, hauling himself higher up her back.

"Don't squeeze so tight."

He relaxed his knees.

"And stay low, I don't want you creating more drag than you need to."

Alfonso did as he was told, lowering himself against her, so that his head was just above hers.

This seemed to satisfy Katya for now, though he sensed she was far from happy. She began beating her wings with long, powerful strokes, the muscles in her back flexing beneath him. Higher and higher she climbed until they were clear of the valley and she was able to benefit from the warm thermals rising from the surrounding cliffs. The twin suns beat down on Alfonso's back as they followed the river course towards the distant plains.

Over the following hours, he watched the landscape change beneath them, the steep red cliffs broadening out into a wide valley. The sloping sides were strewn with boulders and scraggy vegetation. The tall columns at its centre became fewer and farther apart, many of them no more than tumbled mounds of red stone.

As nightfall approached and the land cooled, Katya had to work harder, to keep them aloft, her wings beating constantly. And when the second sun began to dip behind the horizon, it was clear she could go no further that night.

"Now, I must land," she said. "Hold tight until the end. A fall from twenty feet is as fatal as from two hundred."

Alfonso clung on as she glided down to a low cliff face, which was all that remained of the red river valley. Angling towards a fissure in the rock, Katya landed on its narrow ledge, arching her back to allow him to dismount. The cleft opened up into a cave that was more than big enough for them both to rest for the night.

They had seen no sign of other harpies on their descent. Still, Katya was taking no chances, instructing him to light a fire in the entrance. This he did, using his flints and molevin tinder, before cooking the slabs of hydra flesh that they had brought with them.

Since their struggle with the monster back at the river, Katya had said very little. Now, she stared into the fire without a glance in his direction. Alfonso could understand her being tired after bearing him all that way. But he sensed that something else was behind the troubled expression on her face. Pain from her wound, perhaps? Or shame for being rescued from disaster by her captive?

Either way, he decided not to interrupt her thoughts, and kept his head down as he chewed on the tough meat. It wasn't until the end of the meal, when she tossed the leathery scraps into the flames, that Katya broke her silence. What she had to say was anything but reassuring.

"Tomorrow we reach our destination. When we arrive, it will be guarded, so I will not have time to brief you there."

"Guarded?"

She glanced towards him. "You are not on a training ground anymore."

If the nightmare of the molevin tunnels was no more than a training exercise, he feared what the dawn would bring.

"You need to know what your task is," she continued, turning back to the flames. "So you can prepare yourself."

Katya had his full attention now, and Alfonso waited in silence.

"At the far side of the lowlands, there is a column," she said. "It is much larger than those you have seen before. We call it the Hive."

"Like bees?"

She turned to him, a frown on her face. "Bees?"

"Flying insects... small, like this," he said, indicating with his thumb and forefinger. "We call their colonies, a hive."

Katya considered this.

"Similar, I think, though this Hive was inhabited for many years by molevin. As their population grew, they needed more space and built larger chambers and tunnels throughout the core. Too large, as it turned out. A host of harpies entered the upper levels and were able to kill or enslave them."

"How many harpies are there?"

"Close to a thousand, but they have grown stronger in recent years."

Alfonso shuddered at the thought of that many creatures concentrated in one place.

"And we are going there tomorrow?"

"Before nightfall, while they are still dormant. I will drop you off there and leave."

"Leave?"

"Harpies are territorial. If they saw me hanging around the entrance, they would kill me."

"And why would they not kill me?"

"Because they will not know you are there. We know of a tunnel where you can gain entry to the Underhive."

Alfonso stared at her. "The Underhive?"

"The network of molevin runs beneath the foundations. They are too small for the harpies to enter."

"So, they are empty?"

Katya shook her head.

"That is where the harpies keep their slaves. The molevin who maintain and repair the Hive."

Alfonso stared at her, realising that she meant for him to infiltrate a tunnel system full of molevin and guarded by their masters. Katya met his eyes.

"Why do you think we've been training you all this time? You can navigate their underground warrens as well as them. Besides, you now smell like one."

"What do you mean?"

She indicated the cloak, and Alfonso looked down at the stitched sections of animal hide.

"Its scent will help you avoid detection."

So, what he wore over his shoulders had not been a thoughtful gift to protect him from the elements. It was a disguise to help him evade the molevin patrols. He stared at Mary's younger daughter, and thought back to that moment by the river when he could have escaped.

"Don't worry," she said, mistaking his look. "My mother has a distraction planned as well."

"A distraction?" he said, still reeling.

"There will be an attack on the Hive tomorrow night, led by Mary and her bodyguard. You can be sure that the Hive dwellers will fly out to meet them in force."

"What, all of them?"

"Enough to allow you to locate what we seek."

"Which is what?"

Katya looked at him, her dark eyes once more impenetrable.

"An egg."

"What sort of egg?"

Katya paused for the slightest moment before continuing. "That doesn't concern you. All you are required to do is collect the egg and return it to me."

"And then?"

"Then, we leave."

Alfonso looked at her as if she was mad. "How am I to find an egg in this Hive? A place I have never visited before?"

"Simple, you go towards the light."

"What light?"

"For the egg to incubate, it needs warmth. The Hive has a central shaft to allow sunlight for the nest during the day. At night it remains open, and there will be a full moon. Wherever you are in the tunnels, you will be able to see the glow. Head towards it, and you will find the egg."

Alfonso wondered at this. No such feature existed in the molevin tunnels in which he had trained. He had learnt their layout by trial and error, mapping out the network of passageways over many weeks. If there had been a light source, that would have made navigation straightforward. Still, he didn't fancy his chances, even with such a reference point.

"What if I say no?"

Katya sighed. "Then I will kill you myself."

To Alfonso, it seemed that the air inside the cave had gone still, the only sound coming from the crackling of the fire. That was when he understood the real reason why Katya placed herself close to the opening. It wasn't to protect him from any creature discovering their overnight lair. It was to stop him from escaping. Even if he could slip past her, he doubted he would make it down the scree slope without breaking his neck.

"You do not mean that," he said, trying to hide the tremor in his voice.

Katya didn't trouble herself with an answer.

"You had better get some rest," she said. "We fly at first light. We need to reach the tunnel entrance before nightfall."

A thought occurred to Alfonso.

"What will you do while I am inside?"

"Wait for you to return."

"And if I do not?"

"You have until dawn. After that, I'll assume you're dead or captured. Either way, I will leave."

"You will not rescue me? Like today?"

Katya looked at him, her dark eyes impassive.

"If you cannot obtain the egg, why would I need to?"

Now he understood. Her life would be forfeit too if they did not complete this task. That was why she had saved him from the hydra. To preserve her own life rather than his. Alfonso felt like the air had been sucked out of body, and with it any flicker of hope.

Katya leant against the wall, stretching her wounded leg in front of her.

"Enough talk," she said. "Get some rest. I will wake you before dawn."

Not wanting to look at her, he rolled over, tugging his molevin cape around him, all too aware now of its lingering smell. Lying there, curled up on the floor, Alfonso stared into the deep recesses of the cave, as dark and inescapable as his future.

Chapter Thirty-Six

The final leg of Alfonso and Katya's flight to the Hive took most of the next day, and they stopped only for a lunch of dried hydra meat. Mary's daughter never let Alfonso out of her sight, although they both knew that there was little he could do to escape.

Her wounded leg had stiffened during the night and was not strong enough to carry him, so he rode on her back as before. As he clung to her shoulders, Alfonso was all too aware of the sharpened stylus in his pocket, and no doubt she was too. But to attack her while so far above the ground would mean certain death to both of them.

So, they travelled in stony silence, the land flattening as it rolled away beneath them. Over time, its surface became covered by green scrub, the meagre vegetation fed by waterways, branching off from the meandering river like unruly hair.

It wasn't until one of the twin suns began dipping below the horizon, that Alfonso caught his first glimpse of the Hive. A distant flat-topped structure, jutting up from the low-lying landscape. And as they drew nearer, he became aware of just how massive it was.

Half a mile wide, its sheer-sided walls rose hundreds of feet into the air, the surface scored by vertical furrows in the red stone. Within these he could just make out patches of shadow in the fading sunlight. These were the molevin caverns that had allowed the harpies to gain access to the mountain and root out its former inhabitants. Entry points that would now be guarded against rival flyers attempting the same.

Surrounding the colossal column were foothills of fallen rock, their misshapen slopes darkened by a covering of trees. It was for these that Katya swooped, keeping the dipping sun behind her to avoid being spotted. Coming in low and fast, Alfonso held on tight as the ground rushed past, his eyes smarting from the wind that buffeted his cloak.

Katya never slowed, even as the outlying tree line rose up to meet them. Sweeping back her wings, she darted between their grasping branches, leaving them whispering in her wake. Alfonso clung on as they jinked from side to side, the forest rushing past in a dizzying blur. Then, without warning, she came to a juddering stop before a vertical wall of rock and shrugged him from her back. After so long in the air, Alfonso's legs were stiff, and he stumbled against a fallen tree stump.

"Hush," she hissed.

He raised a hand in apology while waiting for his balance to return. Katya glared at him but said nothing, before scanning the trees for signs of movement. Alfonso listened for cries of alarm or other indications that they had been spotted, but the woods were silent.

Looking around, he found that they were in a small clearing, surrounded on three sides by trees and on the fourth by the crimson rock face. Katya limped towards what looked like a fissure in its surface. Turning, she nodded that he should join her.

Creeping forward, he peered into the crevice that ran deep inside the rock and disappeared into the darkness. The gap was narrow, too tight for a harpy. But Alfonso had squeezed through worse during his many months of training.

"Here?" he asked.

She nodded. "It leads to the warrens."

"How do you know this?"

Katya indicated his cloak. "Where do you think we obtained those?"

All part of the plan, he realised.

"There is one more thing I must tell you," she said. "Molevin gut is highly flammable, but so too are harpy feathers."

"And that helps me how?"

"All harpies fear fire. A sun may render their bodies dormant, but fire will destroy them."

Alfonso remembered those nights by the campfire, when the creatures had left them alone. Then, a thought crossed his mind. "What about you and your sister?"

Katya gave him a grim smile. "We are our mother's daughters. Neither sun nor flame has power over us."

Then what does? he wondered. Mary had created two of the most formidable predators on the planet. Was there any force that could withstand them? Perhaps tonight he would find out.

"During Mother's attack," Katya continued. "The egg will be guarded. Fire will give you the opening you need."

The prospect of lighting a fire underground, surrounded by inflammable objects, filled Alfonso with dread. But that was the point Katya was making. Any harpies left in the Hive would find its presence terrifying. He felt in his pocket and found the pouch of flints and molevin gut nestled alongside his stylus.

"So, where will you be when I return?"

Katya nodded towards the trees.

"Waiting for you here."

"Won't they spot you?"

"With the Hive under attack, I doubt many will be checking the tree line. Besides, if any see me, I'll deal with them."

Alfonso didn't doubt it.

Behind her, he noticed that the shadow of the trees had risen high up the rock face. She must have seen it too.

"You must go! Head for the core. Once you find the nest, lie low until the attack has begun. You will get only the one chance."

Taking a steadying breath, he adjusted the strap of his bag and stared into the crevice. It looked dark and forbidding.

"Alfonso," she said, and he turned to find her staring at him. "All your training was for this moment. You can do this."

Though he resented Katya for playing him, Alfonso could not help but be stirred by her words.

"This egg had better be worth it."

With a final glance up at the blood-red tower, he slipped the hood over his head and disappeared into the shadows.

******

Alfonso knew he was being stalked long before he heard the first patter of claws behind him. Weeks of probing tunnels in absolute darkness had heightened his senses to such a pitch that he could detect the faintest sound or shift in the air.

Not long after leaving Katya at the entrance, the hairs had risen on the back of his neck in warning, alerting him to another presence. What he couldn't understand was how the creature had got behind him.

Since entering the abandoned molevin run, he'd taken care to check each opening and side passage as he made his way deeper into the labyrinth beneath the Hive. Some of these had been too long to explore, and Alfonso suspected that his pursuer had been lurking deep within one of these, waiting for him to pass before emerging to track its prey.

Now that the tunnel had started to climb upwards, he sensed that his stalker had begun creeping closer. The faint sound of displaced sand became more noticeable, and he found himself glancing back over his shoulder every few steps.

Removing the stylus from his pocket, Alfonso pressed on. The prospect of being trapped between harpies ahead of him and this unseen stalker behind was an unenviable one. And while part of him wanted to confront the creature, he'd rather know what he was dealing with before doing so. If Katya was right, somewhere up ahead he would find a glimmer of light, and maybe then he'd find out who or what was tracking him.

Alfonso was so busy checking for movement behind him that he didn't notice the tunnel broaden out into an underground chamber. Only when he reached out to a wall that was no longer there did he realise that he was standing in a much larger space. Confused, he stopped to check his bearings, and that was when it happened.

The first indication that he was under attack was a shift in the air from the tunnel behind him. The thrumming of steps came moments later, but Alfonso was already moving. One second he was staring around at his new surroundings, and the next he was diving to one side as something exploded from the tunnel, missing him by inches.

Alfonso landed on the sandy floor and rolled to absorb the impact, keeping a firm hold of the stylus in his fist. Squatting low to the ground, he looked up in time to register the enormous presence adjusting its point of attack. With a blur of jointed legs, the giant centipede circled around the chamber, its articulated, chitinous plates flexing as it angled towards him. Two whiplike tentacles probed the air, fixing his location as its blunt head rose, mandibles opening wide to emit a challenge of angry clicks.

Alfonso tensed, ready to spring away, but even as he did so, he heard another sound. The scrabble of many claws. The centipede must have heard them too because, for a split second, it hesitated. Pale shapes appeared out of the gloom, converging not on Alfonso but on the coiled monster in front of him.

Clicking in surprise, it swung to face the new threat. But quick as it was, the molevin were faster. Chittering in excitement, the pack fell on their prey, their pale forms leaping at its flanks and smothering it in a mass of writhing bodies.

Crouching on one side of the chamber, Alfonso was forgotten, though he knew this wouldn't be for long. There was a whimper of pain and a sickening thud as two molevin landed at his feet. One had its neck twisted at an unnatural angle, the other was pumping dark blood onto the floor. More shrieks and clicks rang out across the chamber as the vicious battle continued.

Looking around, Alfonso realised why he was able to discern the desperate melee in front of him. Against the far wall was a circular opening, from which came a pale glow. Moonlight.

As more shapes entered the chamber, he got to his feet and ran towards the light. Whether it was the cloak or not, he couldn't be sure, but the molevin ignored him as they headed in the opposite direction to join the fray.

Covering the last couple of yards at a run, Alfonso ducked into the opening. He found himself in a long, empty tunnel illuminated by a pale glow in the distance. It was coming from a hole in the wall, which was emitting more than just light. A cloying reek of something so foul and rotten that it made him nauseous the closer he came to its source.

Reaching the opening, he gripped his stylus and peered around the corner. As his eyes adjusted to the glare, Alfonso saw that he was at the base of a shaft that rose upwards at a steep angle for hundreds of feet. At the far end, the unmistakable glow of moonlight shone down on him.

Turning, he looked back down the passageway. Someone would emerge victorious from the life or death struggle in the chamber, and he didn't plan on waiting to find out who it was. Stowing the stylus in his pocket, he ducked into the opening and began to climb.

Chapter Thirty-Seven

Alfonso inched his way up the shaft, the stench getting worse the higher he climbed. But that wasn't the only thing that made his skin crawl. Over his laboured breathing, he heard a sound. A strange keening noise that came echoing down the passageway, setting his teeth on edge.

Harpies. Lots of them. So many that their dreadful calls mingled together into one continuous wail. By the time he reached the top, he could barely hear himself think. But this was nothing compared to the sight that greeted him when his head emerged above ground.

"*Deu meu*!"

Above Alfonso rose a vast dome, hundreds of feet high, hollowed out from the centre of the Hive's core. At its peak was a circular aperture open to the night sky, through which shone the bright moonlight. This was the source of the glow Alfonso had seen from the shaft, and it revealed an interior that he could only stare at in wonder.

Sheer-sided walls ran from floor to vaulted ceiling, their pale red surface disfigured by row upon row of pulsing grey blisters. Harpies, clinging limpet-like to the rock, in numbers he had never seen before. Most were stretching and flexing their wings, but many had already left their perches, the narrow ledges lying empty.

While he watched, more of the creatures leapt into the air, spreading their wings and emitting dreadful screeches before disappearing through the roof into the night. Katya was out there somewhere, and he hoped for both their sakes that she was keeping well out of sight as the exodus continued.

Dropping his gaze from the departing flyers, Alfonso noticed a tower, some twenty feet tall, in the centre of the floor. Circular in shape, it lay beneath the aperture, its top bathed in silvery light. In that glow crouched an ominous grey shape, its massive frame dwarfing any of the creatures he'd seen so far. Broad wings spread out in a protective umbrella over the summit. And though the monster's head was hidden from view, Alfonso didn't need to see the face to know who it was. This had to be the Hive Matriarch, sitting on her nest, and beneath her enormous body would be the egg he had come to steal.

Staring across at the tower on which she lay, Alfonso noticed that it wasn't made of the same smooth, red rock as the rest of the dome. Its surface was rough and white in colour. Studying it for the first time, he realised that it wasn't made from rock at all. The entire structure was a composite of another material, which also covered the entire floor of the chamber. It was bleached bone.

With mounting horror, he looked around at the thick carpet of shattered carcasses and grinning skulls that filled the space from one side of the Hive to the other. Over these, tattered fragments of skin flapped like grotesque confetti in the downdraft of circling wings. This was the source of the smell, and its cloying stench made his stomach lurch. Unable to stop himself, he heaved his half-digested hydra rations down the shaft.

Cries of alarm erupted above him, and Alfonso imagined hundreds of harpies turning towards him. Instead, when he looked up, he found that all were staring skywards, where a shadow was drawing a dark veil over the moon.

As the light in the Hive dimmed, the Matriarch stirred. A hideous raptor's head emerged from under her wing. It turned towards the aperture, and gleaming yellow eyes stared towards the heavens. Alfonso followed her gaze and saw the shadow for what it was. Like a murmuration of starlings, a massive horde of raiding harpies was banking in front of the moon, and swooping down towards the Hive. Mary was launching her attack.

Seeing the danger, the Matriarch opened her beak-like maw and emitted a screech that echoed around the chamber. The surrounding walls erupted into life as harpies leapt from their perches in a cloud of flapping wings. The creatures whirled around the circular walls with dizzying speed, a vortex forming in their centre, through which the veiled moon became visible once more.

The Matriarch sprang from her nest, wings thumping with percussive force, scattering discarded bones across the floor. Gaining speed with every wingbeat, she rose through the ring of harpies, her talons flexing beneath her as she climbed. With an ear-shredding shriek, she shot from the

Hive. The whole colony followed, uncoiling like a snake to strike at the descending storm of raiders.

This was the moment Alfonso had been waiting for. His one chance to get to the egg while the nest was unguarded. Scrambling from the shaft, he set off across the floor, leaping over mounds of discarded carcasses as he headed for the tower. The sounds of bones crunching underfoot echoed around the empty chamber, but Alfonso paid them no heed. The time for stealth was over, and he hadn't a second to lose.

When he reached the column, he looked up at the skeletal structure. Bones jutted from its steep sides, providing plenty of hand- and footholds for anyone desperate enough to use them. Alfonso didn't hesitate. Jamming his fingers into a spine of calcified vertebrae, he began to climb, ignoring the leering skulls in the wall in front of him.

His only moment of panic came as he reached the summit, when a femur on which he was standing snapped under his weight. For a heart-stopping moment, Alfonso wobbled, arms flailing, before grabbing a ribcage and hauling himself forward onto a bed of crushed feathers and bone.

For several seconds, he lay there, panting, waiting for a cry or a screech of alarm. But none came. There was complete silence in the Hive. The only reaction to his clumsy arrival came from the warm, smooth object he felt pressing against his cheek. It twitched.

Alfonso froze, hardly daring to breathe. He peered out of the corner of his eye. There, less than an inch from his nose, was the smooth, marbled surface of an egg. Except that this one was the size of a football.

Heart racing, Alfonso backed away to get a better look.

The egg lay on a bed of feathers and strips of hide, cushioning it from the cradle of bones beneath. It was, if anything, larger than he first realised, easily as big as... as the heads he'd been trained to retrieve from the molevin tunnels.

Alfonso thought back to that night when Mary and her daughters had sat around the campfire and offered him the skull of the molevin boar he'd hunted that day. An object bulky enough to represent the objective of his mission now.

They played you for a fool, he thought, staring down at the egg that he had been sent here to retrieve.

For one insane moment, Alfonso felt like smashing it, hurling it from the tower, just to spite their plans. But what hope did he have of getting away from here then? Like it or not, Katya had made it clear that the egg was his only ticket out of here. Without it, his life, and probably hers, was forfeit.

That realisation steeled his resolve once more and he reached for his prize. As he did so, Alfonso noticed a shaft of light settle on the back of his hand. Looking up, he saw moonlight shine through a gap in the Hive's protective cloud of harpies. A gap formed by a winged shape that had broken formation and was diving towards him.

One of the harpies had finally noticed the intruder. And it was not alone. Others had peeled out of the cordon and were following in its wake.

"*Merda,*" he breathed.

Alfonso turned back to the nest and, slipping his hands underneath its smooth sides, picked up the egg. He was about to place it inside his leather bag when the first harpy burst into the Hive. Screeching in alarm, it made straight for him, claws extended. Knowing it would be on him in seconds, Alfonso used the only thing that could protect him. He thrust the egg above his head like a talisman.

Not wanting to slam into the colony's most prized possession, the harpy pulled out of its dive and banked away. Its warning cry alerted the others to the danger as they swept into the atrium, their angry screeches filling the air.

Some twenty feet off the floor, Alfonso knew that he couldn't risk jumping from the tower. Not only was he likely to break his neck, but if he damaged the egg, its outraged guardians wouldn't hesitate to kill him. They were already circling the nest, eyeing him with undisguised hatred, waiting for their chance to attack. No, there was only one thing for it.

Alfonso squatted down and tucked the egg inside his bag. Pulling the leather pouch from his pocket, he grabbed a discarded tibia bone and wound the molevin gut around one end. Then he picked up the flints and tried striking them together over his makeshift torch. His hands were shaking so much that he dropped one. Had it fallen through the haystack of splintered bones, he would have been finished. But it landed on the bed of broken feathers, and he was able to retrieve it.

"Come on!" he muttered.

At the fourth attempt, a bright spark shot onto the tightly

wound gut. A pale blue flame rose from the spot and traced its way around the haft of bone, igniting the waxy material. Offering a silent prayer of thanks, Alfonso stuffed the flints back in his pocket and slung his bag containing the precious egg over his shoulder. Then he thrust the burning torch into the mattress of harpy feathers.

The nest burst into flame, scorching Alfonso's face as he scrambled back. The angry cries from the circling harpies turned to panicked shrieks as they wheeled away, desperate to escape the fire. They soared towards the aperture, and were met by more of their number returning to protect the nest. In the narrow confines of the entrance, bodies slammed into each other with bone-jarring impacts. Creatures began tumbling from the air, their keening wails adding to the dreadful din.

Seizing his chance, Alfonso swung his legs over the edge of the tower and began clambering down. The summit was already ablaze, the flames, fanned by the downdraft of flapping wings, spreading through the structure. But fire wasn't his only concern.

Alfonso was still some way from the floor when he spotted a harpy, its wing broken by an aerial collision, spiralling down towards him. Realising the danger, he turned and jumped clear, his feet landing on the carpet of bones just as the stricken flyer crashed into the flaming tower. There was a moment of shocked silence before the creature's body exploded. It sent a mushroom cloud of burning feathers into the air, enveloping the nearest harpies.

Alfonso didn't wait to see what happened next. Getting

to his feet, he picked up the torch and ran, his bag with the egg inside, bouncing against his back.

That was when the Matriarch arrived.

With a roar that drowned out all other noises, she smashed through the canopy of burning flyers. Flaming bodies fell from the sky, exploding like incendiaries on the bone-strewn floor. Alfonso kept running as she swept towards the nest, which was now burning like a funeral pyre. Its owner let out a soul-wrenching scream that reverberated around the atrium, the noise so shrill that it was all Alfonso could do not to cry out.

Still running, he glanced over his shoulder. The monstrous creature was hovering just above the burning tower, her head twisting and turning as she scanned the floor. Then her hunter's gaze settled on him.

"*Santa Mare*," he breathed.

Alfonso fled, dodging between fires and blazing bodies as the roar began again. He didn't need to look back to know that she was coming for him. Up ahead, the entrance to the tunnel was just visible through the smoke. He sped towards it, knowing that one stumble now and it would be over for him.

Driven on by terror, Alfonso covered the last few yards at a sprint, the approaching roar so loud that it drowned out his own scream. It was still ringing in his ears when, clasping the bag to his chest, he leapt feet first into the shaft and plummeted into darkness.

Chapter Thirty-Eight

The sound of his footsteps echoed along the tunnel as Alfonso ran through the Underhive, the bag containing the precious egg slung over his shoulder. There was no sign of the molevin, and he wondered if the acrid smoke leaking from the upper chamber had driven them to seek shelter in the lower warrens.

Alfonso made good progress, and he started to believe he might actually make it to the dell after all. Would Katya be waiting for him, he wondered? Or, seeing the flames rising from the Hive, had she given him up for dead? If so, Alfonso wouldn't have blamed her. It was a miracle he'd made it this far.

He reached the final junction and, finding it deserted, he hurried on, his feet splashing through puddles, heedless of the noise. Then, an uncomfortable thought crossed his mind, and he skidded to a stop.

In the guttering flame of the torch, Alfonso saw more puddles up ahead. He thought back to when he'd come this way earlier. There had been no water then. Unless, of course, he hadn't come this way.

Doubts formed in his mind. In his eagerness to escape, had he taken a wrong turn back there? Had his fear-clouded memory betrayed him? Was he now deeper underground than he thought, nearing the water table maybe?

Stop it! he told himself. *Something's wrong, but not your sense of direction. Not after all this time.*

Alfonso lowered the torch and stared at the puddle in which he stood. Then he lifted one foot and saw that it was not covered in water but something much darker.

Blood.

Stifling a cry, Alfonso pressed himself against the tunnel wall, staring down at the dreadful steam filling the passageway. Fighting the urge to run, he raised his torch and peered ahead.

The glistening surface continued for another twenty feet or so. It appeared to be coming from an opening in the wall. Beyond that, the tunnel continued, and, in the distance, he fancied he could see a pale sliver of light coming from the entrance to the dell.

Alfonso knew he was now only a few hundred feet from safety. But between him and the clearing was that opening. And somewhere inside, his tunnel stalker lay in wait. Wounded and bleeding, it had somehow made its way back there, to where it had first picked up his trail.

As he debated what to do, the torch began to splutter. Alfonso looked at the flame and saw that it had almost burned itself out. Any moment now, he would be plunged into darkness.

What he needed was molevin gut, or even harpy feathers

to rekindle the flame. He patted his pockets, and his fingers brushed the rough stitching of his cloak.

His cloak!

Careful not to drop the torch or the bag, Alfonso removed his cloak and wrapped it in a tight bundle. Then he held the feather-lined hood over the flickering flame. There was a faint blue glow, followed by a whoosh as the feathers caught alight.

In seconds, flames were racing over the tightly bound molevin hide, the intense heat scorching his hand. Wincing, he hurried forwards, splashing through the puddles of gore, heedless of the noise. When he reached the opening in the wall, he hurled the blazing cloak inside. A terrified clicking noise came from the tunnel, followed by a desperate scrabbling of claws.

Ignoring the pain in his blistered hand, he leapt past the opening. As he did so, he caught a glimpse through the flames of the terrified centipede, backing away from the fireball. And then he was past, running for his life towards the distant tunnel entrance, the sound of the monster's desperate clicks fading behind him.

Alfonso reached the narrow crevice and paused just long enough to tuck the precious bag under his arm before squeezing sideways through the gap. Then he was outside, standing beneath a night sky that looked impossibly large after so many hours underground. For a moment, he stood there, staring at the heavens, before looking around at the clearing.

"Katya?"

No response.

"Katya?" he said, louder this time as he scanned the empty treetops.

A winged shape swept overhead, so fast that all he saw was a dark shadow in the night sky. Alfonso called out.

"Katya! Here!"

The shape banked and swept back. As it did so, it emitted a screech that Alfonso had never heard either of Mary's daughters utter before. Eyes wide, he saw the hostile harpy dive towards him, its claws swinging forward to strike.

Katya appeared from nowhere, her wings swept back as she hammered into his attacker. The harpy's body slammed into the rocky outcrop with a sickening thud, and fell senseless to the ground.

Katya swooped over him, tufts of feather still clutched in her claws.

"Idiot! What were you yelling for?"

"I'm sorry," he said, still too stunned to move. "I thought it was you."

In the distance, came a cacophony of warning cries. Looking up at the Hive, Alfonso saw a cloud of dark shapes descend towards them.

"Quick," Katya said, wincing as she landed beside him. "Climb on!"

Alfonso saw dark patches of blood on her flank. "You're hurt!"

"Never mind that! Get on!"

He clambered onto her back, doing his best to avoid her wounds. The next moment, they were airborne, her wings beating powerfully as they rose up and over the trees.

"Do you have it?" Katya asked, grunting with the effort as she built up speed.

"The egg, you mean?"

"No, a kiss from the Matriarch," she said, skimming the treetops. "Of course the egg!"

"*Sí*, yes, I have it."

"You do?"

Alfonso could hear the surprise in her voice.

"*Sí*, here in my bag."

Katya grunted. "That must be why we have half the Hive on our tail."

Looking over his shoulder, Alfonso saw a shadow spread across the night sky, all but blotting out the funeral pyre of the mountain.

"Not half," he said, seeing hundreds of harpies, swooping after them. "It is all of them, I think."

And at their head was a creature that he knew only too well. The Hive Matriarch, her enormous wings pumping up and down, was leading the pursuit. When her eyes fixed on Alfonso, she opened her maw to let out a blood-chilling screech that made even Katya flinch.

"You need to go faster," he said.

"I will if you keep your damn head down. Lie flat!"

Alfonso did as he was told, dropping his head to her neck, like a jockey on a galloping horse. Feeling her blood-stained feathers against his chin, he realised what it had cost Katya to wait for him. But she had kept her promise, just as he had done in returning to her.

Now, with the egg slung across his back, there was nothing more he could do. Both their fates depended on her strength and endurance. Leaning close to her head, Alfonso repeated what she had said to him all those hours ago.

"You can do this."

On they flew, the ground rushing beneath them in a black and white showreel, with the occasional glimmer of moonlight reflecting off a meandering waterway. The cries of the chasing host, which had been incessant at first, became fewer as the minutes passed, then died out completely.

Alfonso risked a look over his shoulder to see if they had given up the chase. But the Hive dwellers were still there, no more than half a mile back, wings a blur as they pursued their prey in silence. He saw some of the smaller harpies had moved ahead, allowing the Matriarch to follow in their slipstream.

"Stop fidgeting," panted Katya.

Alfonso tore his eyes away from their pursuers and faced forwards.

"They are getting closer," he warned. "They are taking turns to lead."

Katya didn't say anything, but Alfonso sensed her wings increase in tempo. Though he was tempted to look back and see if this made a difference, he kept his head low to avoid adding more drag.

Occasionally, he would feel a twitch from the bag nestled under his arm, as if the egg could sense the presence of its chasing mother. Of more concern to Alfonso was the growing dampness against his leg, which came from the wound in Katya's side.

How much blood she had lost was impossible to say, but it couldn't be helping that the injury was still weeping. Their one hope was for dawn, knowing that their pursuers would be unable to fly in sunlight.

"How long before sunrise?" he asked.

"Long enough," she said through gritted teeth, the strain beginning to tell. "But first there is the point of no return."

"The what?"

"When they turn back for the Hive or are left stranded in the lowlands."

Alfonso remembered the look on the Matriarch's face.

"And what if they don't turn back?"

"Then we all die," she said.

There was nothing more to be said, and he peered towards the distant horizon, where he prayed that they would soon see the sunrise. If they lasted that long.

On they flew in silence, Katya never faltering, her wings beating a high tempo as they raced over mile upon mile of the shadowy landscape. With no thermals to aid them, it came down to raw speed. Carrying a payload as she was, Katya was at a clear disadvantage.

Alfonso wondered whether there was anything more he could do. He had his stylus and flint, but there was nothing combustible to burn. Even if he had something, he doubted he could manage it with the wind rushing past. Besides, any movement from him risked unbalancing Katya further.

No, his only other option was to drop the egg and hope that the Matriarch would abandon them to save it. If he did that, his life would be forfeit, though Mary may spare her daughter, Katya.

Alfonso thought back on their time together. Whatever her motivations, Katya had saved him from the hydra and the harpy. That she had come back to the Hive for him, not knowing if he had the egg was reason enough to be grateful. Even now, though wounded, she was still fighting to keep them both alive.

Si, Alfonso thought, when the moment came, he would save her. If he could. He owed her that.

"How close are they?" she asked, bringing him back to the present.

Alfonso glanced over his shoulder, and felt his heart falter.

"Less than a hundred yards."

"How many?"

"A dozen or so."

"And the Matriarch?"

"Not far behind, with the rest of the Hive."

Katya went silent.

"Why do you ask?"

"We went past the point of no return some time ago."

So, the Matriarch and her brood were not returning to the Hive after all. She would hunt down her prey or die in the attempt. All that could save them now, was the dawn.

Staring ahead, Alfonso imagined that he could make out the jagged profile of cliffs, no more than a thin, dark outline on the horizon. Was the sky getting lighter, he wondered, or did his mind just want it to be so? He closed his eyes and looked again. The uneven line of cliffs was still visible.

"Katya," he said, trying to keep his voice calm. "I can see the horizon."

Katya did not respond at first, save for her breaths, which seemed shorter and shallower than before.

"I see it," she panted. "But so will they."

At that moment, the egg began to twitch, and Alfonso heard the drumbeat. At first, he thought it was a distant rumble of thunder. But it came again and again, with a steady rhythm that no storm could replicate. Glancing over his shoulder, he saw the Matriarch power through the spearhead, brushing them aside. Some tumbled from the sky, either exhausted or beaten senseless by her brutal wingbeats.

"She's coming," he said.

Beneath him, Alfonso felt Katya increase her tempo a fraction, grunting with the effort. He knew that she was almost spent. The egg, by contrast, came alive, its twitches becoming ever more frequent. Looking back, he saw the Matriarch closing the gap with every wingbeat, and he realised that there was no way they could outrun her.

Reaching for the strap of his bag, he unslung it from around his neck.

"What… are… you… doing," gasped Katya, angry at his sudden movement.

"It's the egg she wants," he said.

"Don't…" she said. "Mary…"

"Will kill me, I know," he said, "but you, I can save…"

"No!" she cried in frustration.

Without warning, she angled her wings and Alfonso had

to cling on with his hands and knees as they swept upwards into the ever lightening sky.

There was a screech as the Matriarch swept underneath them, caught unawares by Katya's unexpected move. But it was only a temporary respite. Driven by anger and desperation, she arched her neck and soared up after them, wings beating furiously.

"What are you doing?" Alfonso asked, clinging onto Katya's feathers as she continued to climb, her shoulders straining. They couldn't hope to outrun the Matriarch – she was too strong.

Knowing they only had seconds to live, he let go of Katya with one hand, and, gripping the vibrating bag, held it out by its strap. The Matriarch's screech was so close now that he almost dropped it in fright.

"The egg!" he yelled.

"Wait…!" Katya cried, her wingbeats faltering, her strength almost spent.

Twisting, he looked back into the Matriarch's dreadful face. Her maw opened revealing razor-sharp teeth that gleamed in the sunlight.

He blinked.

The sunlight!

Alfonso stared at the monstrous head. It was so close now that he could reach out and touch it. And, if he did, there would be nothing the Matriarch could do. Because her jaw, eyes and neck were already turning pale as the living tissue transformed into stone.

That was when Olga hit her.

Mary's elder daughter slammed into the Matriarch with such force that she tore the creature's head from its body. One moment, Alfonso was staring into those wild, staring eyes, and the next, he saw the headless torso thump into Katya.

The impact almost unseated him, and it was all he could do to keep hold of the bag as he clung on. For a few bizarre seconds, the two flyers hung there, one still flapping to escape, the other now inert as sunlight played over the Matriarch's broad wings. The long grey feathers turned to white as the creature's body lost its fight with gravity and began slipping back towards the earth. Picking up speed, it fell towards the chasing brood, knocking the leaders from the sky.

Of those that escaped, a few were so enraged by their mother's death that they continued to climb until their wings too fell prey to the sun's deadly rays. Bodies calcified in shocked silence before tumbling away, unable to revive before smashing into the ground far below.

Others, seeing the fate of their sisters, turned for the distant cliffs, fleeing for the sanctuary of the shadowed slopes. From his high vantage point, Alfonso could see that they wouldn't make it. As the sun crept over the horizon, one by one the doomed creatures fell to their deaths. Within minutes, all that remained of the once-mighty colony was a trail of shattered bodies strewn across the plain.

Beneath him, Alfonso felt Katya shudder and let out a low sob as she stared at the calcified stain across the land.

"Katya? Are you OK?"

For some time, she didn't answer. When she did, her voice sounded dull and lifeless.

"The egg, is it safe?"

Alfonso felt the bag clasped under his arm, now lying quite still.

"*Si*, I think so."

"Then, it is done."

Dipping her wings, Katya glided down to join her sister, who waited with the Matriarch's pale head still gripped in her claws. Olga glanced up from the killing fields below them, a triumphant gleam in her eyes.

"Sister!" she called. "You have the egg?"

"We do," Katya replied.

Olga gave Alfonso a sharp look, before turning and wheeling away.

"Then, we must hurry," she said, heading towards the distant cliffs.

"But why?" Katya called after her.

Olga's reply brooked no argument.

"Because Mother is dying!"

Chapter Thirty-Nine

Olga led them towards the distant cliffs, following the line of the river as it meandered across the remaining lowlands. Though they had rested for a brief spell after reaching the valley, Katya was already lagging behind her sister, drained by the long chase and loss of blood.

Carrying him could not have helped, but they both knew that there was no way her older sister would allow him to ride her, even if Katya asked. Nor did Olga show any inclination to ditch the Matriarch's severed head, which she still gripped in her claws. So, Alfonso kept quiet and hoped that it would not be long before they reached their destination.

The river became narrower as they neared the cliffs, threading itself through rocky outcrops that grew into valley walls. They soon passed the cave where Alfonso and Katya had spent their last night before the raid on the Hive. And as they did so, he saw that the valley beyond had been transformed since they'd passed this way.

Before, the sheer sides had been an unblemished red. Now they were covered with clusters of grey blisters. These,

Alfonso realised, had to be the survivors of the raiding force that Mary had used to assault the Hive. The ones who had made it back across the plain before the sun rose.

He wondered how many had been lost in the assault and withdrawal. The hundreds gathered here gave an indication of the scale of the undertaking. All unleashed to secure the object contained in the leather bag under his arm.

As they swept around a bend in the river, Alfonso caught sight of the first vertical tower ahead. It rose from the valley floor like a tombstone, its red core covered in a carapace of harpies. At its top was a structure he had not seen before.

It was some sort of stone pavilion, formed by a circle of columns with a domed roof. However, there was something about its structure that unsettled him. And as they drew closer, he understood why.

Each column was a tall harpy, standing in a circle with their broad backs turned outwards to the world. Above them, their long-winged arms curved forwards so that they touched in the centre, forming a canopy of feathers. Each must have adopted this stance as the sun rose, for their bodies had calcified in this shape, creating this living pavilion of stone.

"*Santa Mare de Déu.*"

"Do not say anything," Katya said. "And stay close to me."

"*Si,*" he whispered.

"Whatever happens," she added.

Olga made straight for the top of the tower, and Katya followed, gliding the last few yards. On landing, Alfonso was quick to alight from her back, to protect her damaged leg, though he too stumbled, his limbs stiff and sore after so long aloft.

Looking down, he saw that his clothes were covered in dried blood from Katya's wounds. He marvelled at her strength, realising what that desperate flight must have cost her. But as instructed, he said nothing and kept his head down.

Not that Olga paid him any heed as she strode towards the rigid ring of honour guards without so much as a backwards glance. Katya, her face drawn but stern, indicated that he should follow, which he did, keeping a firm grip on the bag containing the egg.

Olga dipped beneath an arch formed by the upraised arms of the two nearest harpies and disappeared inside. Alfonso followed, noticing for the first time the damage that the creatures had sustained in the battle. Rents in their wings and missing feathers indicated that it had been a brutal encounter, and this impression was only reinforced when he stepped into the segmented shade of the canopy.

The frozen faces of the surrounding guardians, many disfigured by horrific scars, stared at the form lying in the centre of the circle. Mary lay on her back on a makeshift mattress of molevin hide. Her staff was clasped in front of her, and he saw that one end had been snapped off, its shaft stained dark with dried blood. The long cloak was torn, revealing a dreadful wound that ran down her body, where claws had opened her from neck to hip. The old woman's leathery skin looked sallow, and there was an ugly blue tinge to her lips and eyelids, which remained closed.

Behind him, Alfonso heard a sharp intake of breath from Katya. She started forwards, towards the recumbent figure. But Olga was there first.

“Mother,” she said, blocking her sister. “I have brought you something.”

Alfonso saw the death mask turn towards them, the eyes fluttering open. Like her white hair, Mary’s face was splattered with blood, though he couldn’t tell whether it was her own or someone else’s. Still, a fire flickered into life in those green eyes when she saw the calcified head of the Matriarch, which Olga held before her.

“Excellent, my dear,” she said with grim satisfaction. “I knew I could rely on you to take down that upstart.”

Alfonso felt angry that Olga would take credit for the kill, when it was Katya who had lured the Matriarch to her death. Nor could he understand why the younger sister remained silent. But he kept his mouth shut, wondering if Katya had expected this.

“And the Hive?”

“All dead,” confirmed Olga with obvious relish, “their remains scattered over the plain. A lesson for all who challenge us.”

Mary gave a weak cackle, and Alfonso noticed flecks of blood appear on her lips. “I expected no less from you.”

“Mother,” said Katya, her voice soothing, “we have something else for you.”

Mary turned her head as if noticing her other daughter for the first time.

"Katya?" She frowned, trying to focus on the figure standing only a few feet from her. "So, you made it back, did you?"

"We did."

Olga scowled at her sister's use of the word "we", but Katya ignored her and turned to Alfonso, indicating that he should give her the bag. Slipping it from his shoulder, he handed it over, and, stepping forwards, she held it out to her mother.

Mary stared at it.

"You have the egg?"

"Yes."

"And it is intact?"

"Yes."

There was a moment of silence as the old woman digested this. Looking around the pavilion, she caught sight of Alfonso, and her eyes rested on him. There was no warmth in her gaze. It was, if anything, curious. Turning, she looked up at Katya.

"Thank you, my dear. You have done well."

"Mother," said Katya, bowing her head.

"Now hand it to Olga."

Alfonso saw Katya stiffen at this, and when Olga reached for the bag, she didn't move. For a moment, both sisters stared at each other, their eyes as stony as the harpies looking on. Then Katya's softened, and she passed the egg over.

"Now help me up," said Mary.

Katya turned to her, a look of concern on her face.

"Mother, do you think that's wise? You're..."

"Stop blathering, girl. This has to be done."

Mary held up a blood-stained hand, and Katya took it. With the other, she reached for her staff before remembering it was broken. Alfonso stepped forwards, and took the old woman's hand.

There was a moment of shocked silence as Mary looked up at him, her green eyes burning into his. Behind him, Alfonso sensed Olga's amber gaze boring into the back of his head, but while she still held the egg, there was nothing she could do. However, Katya could, and he waited for the blow to fall. Instead, she just stared at him, her expression unreadable.

Alfonso felt Mary's grip tighten and, hissing in pain, she levered herself upright. Glancing down, he saw fresh blood seep from her wounds and fall in droplets on the floor. The old woman swayed for a moment, leaning on him until she had gained her balance. Then, he felt the pressure of her grip ease and she let go.

"Leave us," she said.

Alfonso looked from her to Katya, who tore her stricken gaze from her mother and nodded.

Turning, he found Olga glaring at him, but she made no move to intervene. Giving her a wide berth, Alfonso headed under the overlapping arms of the silent guardians and out into the bright sunlight.

Looking back through the winged arches, he saw that Mary was still upright, though her broken body was stooped now more than ever. Katya held her hand, her head bowed as if in prayer. In front of them stood Olga, who had removed the egg from its bag.

"You know what to do," he heard Mary say.

Katya looked up, and Alfonso saw the distress on her face. But Olga only nodded and, spreading her wings, raised the egg high above her head.

"From death to life!" Mary intoned.

"From death to life!" Olga repeated.

Then, she hurled the egg down, and the world went white.

One moment, Alfonso was staring into the stone circle, and the next, he was bathed by a corona of brilliant light. It burst through the gaps between the standing guardians, beams strobing across the valley like a multifaceted lighthouse.

Caught in the intense glare, Alfonso averted his gaze, crouching down to protect his sight. As he did so, the wind began its scream. It was no more than a low whistle at first, like that of a boiling kettle, but as he listened, it grew in intensity. His tattered clothes began to flap, warm air buffeting his face, hair, and body as the sound rose to a howl. As it grew stronger, he found himself being dragged across the surface of the rock, his fingers unable to find purchase as he was sucked towards the stone circle behind him.

Gasping for breath, he slid into the legs of one of the guardians, which he clung to in desperation as the wind whipped past him and joined the whirling vortex in the centre of the pavilion.

Looking back through slitted eyes, he could just make out the shadowy outline of the three figures standing in the eye of the storm. Their shapes, illuminated by the bright light at their feet, were distorted by the whirlwind of air and sand. They appeared unmoved by the force of the wind, which grew wilder with every second. It took all of Alfonso's remaining strength to cling to the statue as the noise rose to a piercing shriek. And then, the storm broke.

The light went out, and the circle fell dark. In that instant, the vortex of air exploded outwards.

Had Alfonso not been holding onto the stone guardian, he would have been swept from the top of the tower. Instead, his legs were flung outwards by the wind rushing from the ring and out across the valley. There, it swirled around the column until, like a spent tornado, it finally blew itself out. All that was left was a cloud that hung in the valley like mist before settling over its walls, floor, and river, covering everything in a fine layer of dust.

Alfonso lay there for some time while the ringing in his ears faded. Opening his eyes, he waited for the corona of light imprinted on his retinas to fade. When it did, he saw that any loose sand and rock that had once been on the top of the column had gone. All that remained on its surface was the canopy of stone guardians, and himself, still grasping the stone ankle.

Letting go at last, he eased himself to his feet and wondered what, if anything, would be left of the other three. Alfonso stepped through the arched arms of the guardians and froze.

Olga and Katya stood there, their backs to him, wings furled, and heads bowed as if in prayer. Despite the tornado that had ripped through this space, their feathers were unruffled. Even the deep lacerations down Katya's side had gone, as had the scarring on her leg.

"*Mare de Déu*," he breathed.

"What have I told you about speaking that nonsense!"

The two sisters parted to reveal the figure standing before them.

Mary glared at him, the green fire blazing in her eyes brighter than ever. The stooped frame was gone, so too the deep wound down her front. Instead, the woman stood tall, without the aid of a staff. Though her hair was white, it hung in long locks over her shoulders, framing a face whose skin glowed with vitality.

"*Santa Maria*!" he cried, dropping to his knees.

Mary strode across the circle as he looked on her in wonder.

"There you go again!"

She backhanded him with such force that Alfonso was sent sprawling across the floor. Wincing, he turned to stare up at her.

"How… how is this possible?"

Mary rolled her eyes.

"The egg, you fool. Its life force restores us. Look around you."

Alfonso did so. The mute honour guard stared straight ahead, their calcified faces proud and unmarked, the damaged plumage pristine once more.

"From death to life," she said, echoing the phrase he had heard earlier.

Alfonso shook his head in disbelief but said nothing, his mind racing as he thought back on all that had happened.

The training, the mission, the escape, and now this. They had used him to destroy a Hive, assassinate a Matriarch, and wipe out its population. And the egg he'd stolen had been used to restore this tyrant and her protectors to full strength. It made him feel sick. No, worse than that. Ashamed.

Mary turned to her daughters.

"We must go. It's time to return to the Citadel. We have important matters to discuss."

"And him?" Olga asked.

Mary studied Alfonso as he knelt there, struggling with his emotions.

"I had my doubts at first, but he's proven more useful than I expected."

She turned to Katya. "Bring him. I have something else in mind for this one."

With that, she stepped outside the circle.

"Come, the rest of the force can follow later."

Olga stared briefly at Alfonso, before setting off after her mother. Katya turned to him.

"You heard Mother. It's time to go."

"And what if I don't want to?"

"Then, all of this will have been for nothing."

Alfonso looked at her. The life force of the egg had restored the nobility of her features, removing much of the pain and anguish he'd seen earlier. There was still a careworn expression in those dark eyes, as if the things she had seen and done could not be forgotten. This added something to her face, a quality that he had not noticed before and that was hard to define. And then he had it.

Humanity.

"I'll see you outside," she said.

Alfonso watched her go before rising to his feet. His blistered hand was healed, and his aches and pains were gone. Reaching into his pocket, he found that his stylus was still there. Running his finger over its sharpened edge, he looked at Mary's retreating form, and then around at the fixed faces of her personal honour guard. They stood, staring at him with sightless eyes, bound by the sun and unable to move before shadowfall.

At that moment, an idea formed in his head. One so terrifying that he almost dismissed it. But he didn't. Instead he stored it away at the back of his mind, like those names carved in the deep recesses of his cave. To be drawn upon when needed. His time would come. Where and how he did not know. But when it did, he'd be ready.

Standing tall, he left the stone pavilion and stepped into the sunlight. Ahead of him, Katya stood at the edge of the tower, staring at the dwindling shape of her sister, who was bearing her mother towards the distant horizon. As he approached, she lowered her broad back for him to climb aboard.

"I thought your leg was healed," he said.

"It is," she replied, without turning.

Alfonso smiled but said nothing as he reached for her shoulders and settled between her wings. Katya launched herself into the air and they soared after the others.

Chapter Forty

Ravi woke to feel fresh, dry sheets over his body and a soft pillow beneath his head. Breathing in, he smelt disinfectant in the air and heard quiet conversations nearby. For a while, he just lay there, enjoying the sense of peace around him.

The sound of approaching footsteps made him tense, and sharp spasms of pain shot through his shoulder.

"Aah," he groaned.

"Is all right, Professor," said a soothing voice.

Ravi squinted up at the face looking down at him.

"Aurelia?"

"No, is me, Professor. Raquel Vidal."

"Raquel?" he said, confused. "What are you doing here? Where am I?"

Footsteps approached the bed, and Ravi saw a mop of unruly blond hair appear over him. "Addenbrookes, Professor. Glad to see you're awake."

"Giles! Thank goodness," he said. "And the others?"

"All fine, Professor. Nick and Annabel were here earlier but had to leave. Last day of Bumps, you see."

Ravi tried to process this.

"It's Saturday? How long have I been here?"

"Three days now. We've been taking turns checking in on you."

"Three days?" He blinked and looked at Raquel. "And you…?"

"I came yesterday, Professor. To see Giles." She smiled. "And you, of course."

"I see," said Ravi, beginning to piece things together. As he did so, a terrible thought occurred to him.

"My dear, could I trouble you to get me a glass of water?"

"*Si*, of course."

While she headed off down the ward, Ravi whispered, "Giles, is it…?"

"Safe?" The young man smiled. "Yes, everything is back to normal."

"There's nothing left to see?"

"Strangely enough, my last community service involved sweeping out the New Court cellars. So, no, Professor, there's nothing to see."

Ravi sagged back on the pillows. "Thank you, Giles."

"Oh, and while tidying up, I found these."

He held out the old ruler and Ravi's set of cellar keys.

Ravi took them in his bandaged fingers, and they exchanged a look. Keeping his voice low, he asked, "How much do people know?"

He heard approaching footsteps.

"About your fall, Professor?" Giles said, louder now.

"Fall?" Ravi asked, tucking the returned items under his sheets.

"Down the cellar steps."

Raquel arrived with a plastic beaker.

"The steps," said Ravi, "of course."

Raquel offered him the beaker, and he took a sip.

"It was lucky we found you when we did," Giles said. "You'd really taken quite a tumble."

"So, that would explain...?"

"Your injuries. But don't worry, we've reported the faulty lighting."

Ravi nodded. "That's good to know."

"Still, it might have been better if you'd waited for us, Professor," said Giles. "We'd have been happy to help."

Ravi looked at him. "I didn't want to trouble any of you."

"No trouble, Professor. Besides, it was probably too much for one person to handle. The trunk, that is."

Ravi stared at him. "Trunk?"

"The one you were trying to get up the stairs, Professor. When you fell."

"Right..." said Ravi, not having a clue what trunk Giles was talking about.

"Don't worry, we've since moved it to your room for safekeeping. What with the cellar being so damp and all."

"That is good to know," he said, now having enough information to deal with anyone asking questions. "Thank you, Giles."

"Don't thank me. I couldn't have done it without the others. Annabel especially. She was amazing."

"I'm glad to hear it," came a woman's voice.

Ravi turned and saw the compact but formidable

presence of Annabel's grandmother standing at the end of the bed. "Patricia," he said, trying to sit up but stopping when a spasm of pain shot though his shoulder.

"You lie still," said the former nurse, "I don't want you disturbing those bandages."

"Forgive me," he said. "I didn't expect to see you here."

"We were hoping to meet at The Plough, if you remember," she said. "But when Annabel told me about your accident, I thought I might pop in to see you here. How are you feeling?"

"A bit battered and bruised, I'm afraid."

"These things happen as we get older," she said, turning to the others. "As for these youngsters... Hello, I'm Annabel's grandmother."

"I'm Giles."

"Of course! Finally, I get to meet you. Annabel has told me all about you."

"Really?"

"Quite the climber, I hear."

"Oh... I've done a bit, here and there."

"Mainly here, from what I understand."

Giles looked surprised, and Ravi rather enjoyed seeing him on the back foot for once.

"And you must be...?" she said, turning to Raquel.

"Raquel Vidal."

"Raquel!" Mrs Hamilton took her hand in both of hers. "I was so sorry to hear about your brother, my dear. How are your family?"

"Is difficult... but we stay strong."

"That's all any of us can do. It is how I kept myself going after losing Annabel's parents."

Raquel smiled and turned to Giles. "And I have good friends."

"I should hope so. And are you here for Bumps too?"

"Bumps? No, to see Giles's play."

"*Pygmalion*," explained Giles.

"At the ADC, if I'm not mistaken," came a voice from behind them.

They turned to find Dominic Lester standing there. "My, my, this is quite a reunion, isn't it?"

"Master," said Mrs Hamilton, thrusting out a hand. "Good to see you again."

"And you, Mrs Hamilton. Here for the rowing, I take it?"

"That's right. Thought I'd see how Annabel's getting on."

"My spies tell me they were unlucky not to bump Newnham yesterday. But I have high hopes today."

Always with his finger on the pulse, Ravi thought.

"And Miss Vidal," he continued. "What brings you back to Cambridge?"

"To watch Giles tonight."

"Ah yes! Professor Higgins, isn't it?"

"It is, Master," said Giles.

"Of course. In my youth, I once played Colonel Pickering."

"You're an actor too then, Master?"

He arched an eyebrow. "Aren't we all? Still, I'm looking

forward to tonight's performance."

"You're going then?"

"I invited the Master of Trinity. With two Johnian leads, I thought she might enjoy it."

Then, he turned to Ravi. "Dear me, look at you, Ravi. What have you been up to?"

"An unfortunate accident."

"In the New Court cellars, I understand."

"I took a tumble down the stairs."

"It must have been quite a fall," Lester said, studying the bruising around Ravi's face.

"I don't remember much about it, I'm afraid."

"I see," said the Master, turning to Giles. "Fortunate that you, Nick, and Annabel were on hand to help."

"You know how it goes, Master. Right place, right time and all that."

"Remarkably fortuitous," said Lester.

"I'll say," Giles continued. "Given the state of that lighting. It's lucky the Professor wasn't killed."

"Sorry, the lighting?"

"Shocking, Master. I can't imagine what Health and Safety would say if they ever heard about it."

Their eyes met, but the younger man never flinched. Ravi made a mental note never to play Giles at poker. The boy was a natural. The awkward silence was interrupted by Annabel's grandmother.

"Master, I wonder if I might trouble you for directions to The Plough? I don't want to be late for the first race."

"The Plough?" said Lester, his smile returning. "It's a

good way from here, Mrs Hamilton. Are you sure you don't want a taxi?"

"My pensioners' travel card doesn't extend to taxis, I'm afraid. Anyway, it'll be good to stretch my legs after all that time on the train."

"In that case," he said, "perhaps I could offer you a lift. I have my car downstairs."

"That wouldn't be the Morris Minor, would it?"

"Bilbo?" His face brightened. "Why, yes, it is!"

"How exciting," she said. "I haven't been in a Moggie for years!"

"You won't be disappointed. The old fellow runs like a dream."

"Excellent," said Mrs Hamilton, escorting him towards the door.

Ravi smiled as he settled back onto the pillows. The way Patricia had handled Dominic Lester had been nothing short of… masterful.

"We should probably go too," said Giles. "We still have to pack for tomorrow."

"You're going away?"

"Thought we'd go for a climbing holiday."

"Somewhere warmer than Cambridge," Raquel added.

"Good idea," said Ravi. "Well, take good care of each other."

"We will," said Giles. "We may even send you a card, Professor!"

Ravi watched them go. Once he was alone again, he took the keys out from under the sheets and placed them in the drawer by his desk. Then he examined the ruler.

Except for the scorch marks, it looked almost the same as before. One side worn to a sharp edge, the other still showing the inch markings along its length. In a couple of these, he spotted a tiny residues of white powder lodged inside the grooves. Ravi stared at the deposits for a moment. Then he took the blade in his bandaged fingers and began to polish it clean.

Chapter Forty-One

Holding three glasses in a triangle between his hands, Nick backed through the doorway of The Plough, careful to avoid spilling their contents on his new Redboy jumper. Presented to him at the Rugby Club dinner the night before, it had survived a boisterous evening with no major damage, helped by Nick sticking to water, as per the doctor's orders.

Down by the river, he could see students clustered in groups against the wind, watching the boats row by. Making his way over the damp grass, he approached a pair of figures standing some distance from the others.

"Here you go."

"Thanks, Nick!" said Ash, reaching for his lager shandy. Brian's hand appeared from the hidden depths of his coat to take the Guinness.

"Least I could do, after your help with the punt."

"No problem. It was rather exciting, wasn't it, Brian?"

Brian made an odd grunting noise, which might have been a chuckle.

"Anyway, cheers," said Nick, raising his pint of water.

"Any sign of Annabel yet?"

"Not yet," said Ash. "They shouldn't be long now."

"I think you'll find that's them now," Brian said, looking along the river.

Nick turned and saw a red prow appear around the bend, with matching blades beating a steady rhythm through the water. LMBC was clearly visible on the backs of the crews' tops as they moved back and forth as a unit. In the stern, he could just make out Annabel's College beanie pulled down tight over her ears.

"There's Brett," said Ash, pointing to the far bank.

The tall American was following his crew's progress from the towpath, riding a muddy-looking bike. He wore the same LMBC top as the others but had a Yale cap perched on his head. Riding behind, with the crew's kit bag slung over his shoulder, was the imposing figure of Gareth, his distinctive University rugby fleece drawing admiring glances from other spectators.

Annabel brought the boat to a halt, and they sat midstream with their blades in the water while Brett issued instructions from the bank.

"Looks like they are going to practice a start," said Ash. "Brett says that in Bumps the start is critical as there's only a length and a half between each boat. If you can close that gap, and panic the crew ahead of you, then..."

"Bump time," said Brian.

"Got it," said Nick.

They watched as Annabel issued instructions into her microphone. The crew came forwards on their seats, arms stretched out in front of them. Brett began counting down from ten and, when he reached five, Annabel gave the command.

"Square blades!"

The red blades dipped below the water.

Seconds later, Brett yelled, "Gun!"

The crew exploded into action. Hauling on the oars, they slid backwards and forwards in a series of rapid strokes, accelerating away from the standing start. Spray whipped through the air as they came sweeping past The Plough.

"Go, Maggie!" yelled Ash.

For a fraction of a second, Annabel's eyes flicked towards them. Nick saw the hint of a smile before her focus returned to the boat and she called out the rhythm. Her intensity was mirrored on the faces of her crew as LMBC W3 powered its way down the Cam.

"That's good, ladies!" Brett shouted from the towpath, eyes focused on their blades as he and Gareth followed on behind.

"What are they rating?" Ash asked, turning to Brian, who was consulting his digital watch.

"Thirty-six."

"That's good, is it?" Nick asked.

"Brett says they've been up to thirty-eight," said Brian.

"But in these conditions?" Ash asked.

"They're probably holding back to avoid the risk of crabbing," agreed the other.

"Right," said Nick, deciding not to ask what that meant after being warned by Annabel about Brian's lengthy monologues. His thoughts, though, were interrupted by a breathless voice behind them.

"Am I too late?"

Turning, Nick saw Annabel's grandmother hurrying towards them.

"Mrs Hamilton," he said, "you found us."

"Hello, Nick," she said, pausing to get her breath back. "And Ash and Brian too, I see."

"Hello," said Ash. "Don't worry, you've not missed anything. They've just gone down to the start."

"Thank goodness!" she said. "What a carry-on."

"What's happened?" Nick asked.

"Would you believe it, the Master's car broke down!"

"The Master?"

"Dominic offered me a lift, bless him. Then his radiator blew. I had to leave him by the side of the road, and leg it the rest of the way."

What a girl, Nick thought. "Can I get you a drink, Mrs Hamilton?"

"You are a saint, Nick. I'd murder a pint."

"Right," he said.

"I'll tell you what, set up a tab." She handed him a card. "We can get a taxi home."

On the last day of the Bumps, the bar was rammed. So, by the time Nick had made it back, the spectators were already lined up along the bank. Ash turned and waved at him to join them.

"Hurry, Nick! The start gun has just gone off!"

Careful not to spill her beer, he headed over to join them.

"Here you go, Mrs Hamilton," he said, handing over her pint.

"Thank you, Nick," she said, taking a hearty swig before wiping her lips with the back of her hand. "Champion!"

A ripple of excitement ran through the crowd.

"They're coming!" said Ash, peering over Brian's head.

Mrs Hamilton muscled her way in front of a group wearing Girton scarves for a better look.

"Can you see them yet?" she asked.

Nick looked down the river, where three boats were heading their way, oars rising up and down as they cut through the choppy water. There were no red blades among them. A peloton of bikes appeared around the far bend known as Grassy Corner. Nick recognised the blue, grey, and gold Newnham scarves. Then he spotted the distinctive tops of Brett and Gareth pedalling after them.

"I see them!" yelled Ash, and Nick spotted a flash of red in the water.

Although the distance was some eighty yards away, Nick could tell that LMBC had already closed the gap behind the Newnham boat. Above the roar of the crowd, he could hear the sound of whistles.

"That's two whistles!" shouted Ash.

"What does that mean?" Mrs Hamilton asked.

"Maggie has closed the gap to half a length," translated Brian.

From this distance, the red blades seemed right behind those of the Newnham crew. It wasn't long before two whistles became three, and the cries of encouragement became more frenetic. Ash was jumping up and down now.

"We're closing!" he yelled.

"How exciting!" said Mrs Hamilton, her pint forgotten.

From what Nick could see, the Newnham boat was throwing up a lot of spray. In contrast, the red blades moved up and down in perfect unison. The whistles became continuous.

"Overlap! Overlap!" screamed Ash.

"Oh my," cried Mrs Hamilton as the boats came ever closer.

"Go, Maggie!" Nick roared, caught up in the chase.

And that's when it happened.

One moment, it looked like Lady Margaret were about to bump, and the next, their boat shuddered and slewed to one side. Red blades disappeared underwater on stroke side, and the girl in front of Annabel was flung back in her seat. The Stroke just managed to duck under her oar handle before it whipped over her head.

A gap opened up between the boats as Newnham pulled clear and LMBC veered towards the bank. Nick saw Annabel tug on the rudder lines to no effect. Oars banged into one another and spectators leapt back as the scything red blades flashed across the towpath. Then the prow ploughed into the bank with a juddering thud, throwing most of the crew off their seats.

There was a moment of stunned silence as everyone lining the river stared at the crippled boat and its shocked crew. Annabel, her face pale, reached forwards to check on the Stroke, who batted her hand away as she struggled up from her seat. Others began picking themselves off the floor of the boat or rubbing ribs where oar handles had thumped into them. Nick saw Brett and Gareth dismount from their bikes and hurry down the bank to check on everyone. Then the sound of whistles began again.

"Coming through!" came a call from a nearby Marshall as more boats headed up the Reach. While the crowd at The Plough turned their attention to the continuing action, the small huddle of Lady Margaret supporters was left to watch the sorry scene on the far bank.

"I can't believe it!" said Annabel's grandmother.

"They were so close," moaned Ash, crestfallen. "What happened?"

"Rudder failure," said Brian.

"What?" Nick asked.

But further conversation was drowned out by the cheers of the Girton supporters, whose crew rowed by at that moment. Nick looked across the river and saw Annabel sitting in the stern, staring down at the guide ropes hanging limp in her hands. The girl at Stroke stared stony-faced at her, while Brett crouched down, saying something that Nick couldn't hear over the din.

"What do you think, Nick?"

"Sorry?"

He saw Ash and the others looking at him.

"Do you think we should head over to the boathouse to commiserate?"

Nick glanced towards Annabel.

"If it was me," he said, "I'd want some space just now."

"You think?" Ash asked.

"Yeah. Brett will want to talk with them. Use it as

motivation for next term. We'd just be in the way."

Mrs Hamilton considered this.

"I think Nick's right," she said. "Besides, they all have a Boat Club dinner to go to. And I'm buying the next round."

"You're sure?" Ash asked.

"Definitely!"

"They're getting ready to go," said Brian.

Brett and the Marshall were pushing the boat off the bank. Its prow was covered in mud, and some of the riggers had vegetation hanging off them. But the crew were back in their seats with their oars ready. Nick saw Annabel sitting in the stern, looking pale but determined.

"I meant to ask you, Nick," said Mrs Hamilton, turning to him. "Are you and Annabel… back on good terms?"

"I think so," he said, not sure where this was heading.

"In that case, I was wondering if you'd like to visit us in Yorkshire over Easter. Unless you've got other plans."

"No," he said. "I mean, no I haven't got any plans. So, yes, that would be great."

"Excellent." She smiled. "Annabel will be thrilled. She never complains, but it can't be much fun having just me for company."

"I'm not sure about that," he said, thinking Mrs Hamilton would be pretty good company, but decided to stop while he was ahead.

"Looks like they're ready!" said Ash.

Mrs Hamilton turned back to the river. "That's good."

Nick watched as the red-topped rowers moved forwards on their seats. Annabel gave the command.

"Square Blades!"

"Yeah, Maggie!" Nick called out.

Annabel looked towards the bank and their eyes met. She gave him a grateful smile, and turned back to her crew.

"OK, ladies, let's make this a good one. Light pressure, go!"

And with that, LMBC W3 set off on their final row of the term.

Chapter Forty-Two

Annabel trudged up the steps of Cripps A staircase feeling emotionally and mentally drained. It had been a long time since she'd felt this low. Not only had the race been an unmitigated disaster, but the journey back to the boathouse had been a cox's nightmare.

With the rudder not working, she'd had to vary the pressure between bow and stroke side to navigate through the meandering turns of the river. On three occasions, they'd had to stop to let other boats past, suffering the stares of their crews at their stricken vessel. When they finally pulled up on the Maggie slipway, it was a relief to put the battered boat away, until Blades could inspect the damage.

In the post-race debrief, Brett had done his best to lift their spirits, giving them a rousing pep talk about how proud he was to have coached them and how unlucky they had been.

"Remember this feeling, ladies," he said. "So that next term, we come back stronger."

It was a good speech, but the others' expressions said it all, and Clarissa's face had looked like thunder throughout.

To catch a crab in front of the crowd at The Plough was humiliating enough. But for an experienced Stroke like her, it must have been mortifying.

What is more, from the glare she gave Annabel it was clear that Clarissa held her responsible for the sudden swerve across the river. And, as cox, she could understand why the others might think that too.

By the time Annabel was back in her room, the prospect of facing them all at the Boat Club dinner was filling her with dread. Rather than a celebration, it felt like she was going to a wake – and she'd had enough of them to last a lifetime.

If Nick had replaced his phone, or if Gran had possessed one, she might have called them there and then. *And what?* she thought. *Join them in the pub?* In the mood she was in, she'd only ruin their evening too. Besides, what would her crew think? That it had been her fault after all? She could almost hear Clarissa expressing her opinion on that subject to the others, and it didn't bear thinking about.

No, Annabel thought, she should be there for Brett. After all that he had done for them that term, she owed him that.

"Come on, girl!" She scolded herself. "Shit happens."

And always to me, a little voice said in her ear, but she ignored it.

Grabbing her dressing gown, Annabel headed off to the communal bathroom for a shower. When she emerged on the landing ten minutes later, hair wrapped in a towel, she caught sight of Naomi disappearing into her room. With only half an hour to dinner, Annabel was relieved that the girl hadn't seen her. The last thing Annabel wanted to do right now was answer questions about the race.

Returning to her room, she dried her hair and put on the simple black dress that she'd worn for her matriculation photograph. Then, she picked up her new red blazer. Like many coxes, she'd bought hers from St John's College School, home to the Chapel's choristers. This had the same red design as the LMBC but was a good deal slimmer and cheaper.

Annabel was just checking herself in the mirror when she heard a commotion outside. Someone was thumping on one of the landing doors.

"Naomi! I know you're in there! Come on out! We need to talk!"

After a pause, he continued again.

"Naomi, I mean it! I'm not going anywhere!"

Annabel heard her neighbour's muffled response through the wall.

"Go away!"

Big mistake, girl, she thought. *You should have kept quiet.*

Sure enough, the thumping began again – harder, if anything.

"Naomi, come out now! I'm serious!"

"Leave me alone!"

There was another pause, and this time, when the voice spoke again, it was softer.

"Don't be like that, Naomi. Come on, let me in. I just want to talk."

Don't do it, Annabel thought.

"Go away, Colin. It's over."

The hammering began again. "It's not over! Now open this door!"

Right, thought Annabel, *I've had just about enough of this.* Reaching for her mobile, she activated the video app and strode to the door. Yanking it open, she stepped outside.

Colin was on the landing, hammering on Naomi's door.

"Hey!" Annabel said, glaring at him. "She said no."

For a moment, the look of surprise on his face was almost comical.

"Stay out of this!" He turned back to the door. "Naomi, let me in!"

Her reply was clearly audible through the wood.

"No, Colin, I told you. Leave me alone!"

Grabbing the handle, he began rattling it.

"No means no, Colin Philby," said Annabel, pointing her phone at him.

The boy stopped and stared at her.

"What the fuck are you doing!"

"Recording this," said Annabel. "Now leave that girl alone."

"Or what?"

"Or I send this to the Porters."

Colin stared at the phone for a moment. Then, without warning, he lunged for it. Annabel was so surprised that he'd grabbed her wrist before she could react.

"Give me that," he snarled, his face inches from her own.

"Get off me!" Annabel grunted, struggling against him.

A door banged open. Then Naomi was there, grabbing his arm. "Colin! No!"

He swung an elbow back and caught her in the face. Naomi groaned and staggered backwards.

"Hey!" came a voice from the stairs. "What's going on!"

Colin turned, distracted for a moment. This was all Annabel needed. Planting her left foot on the ground, she drove her right knee up. It caught him square between the legs with such force that he was lifted off the ground. Screaming, Colin released her wrist and collapsed on the floor.

Panting, Annabel turned to look at the figure who'd just arrived on the landing. Immaculate in her scarlet blazer, Clarissa stared at the scene open-mouthed.

"What the hell?"

"Oooh," moaned Naomi, holding her mouth.

"Naomi," Annabel said, rushing to her side. "Let me see."

The girl removed her hand to reveal blood pouring from a split lip.

"We need to get someone to have a look at that."

"Would someone tell me what's going on?" Clarissa asked.

"That's my ex," mumbled Naomi, looking down at Colin. "I tried to break it off today."

Clarissa stared down at the writhing figure. "It looks well and truly broken now."

"Bitch…" he moaned.

Clarissa ignored him. "Come on. Let's get you down to the sickbay."

Naomi gave them a weak smile. "I'll just get my shoes, I'll be with you in a minute." She headed inside her room.

"What about him?" Clarissa asked, looking down at Colin.

"We can send one of the Porters," Annabel said. "I saw Shirley in the Cripps Lodge."

Clarissa smirked. "I wouldn't want to be in his shoes then."

Colin glared up at them through watery eyes.

"I'm going to… press charges…"

Annabel held up her phone. "Really?"

"You… assaulted me…"

"Oh, shut up, dick for brains," said Clarissa. "She's got witnesses too."

Annabel smiled at Clarissa as Colin continued to whimper. "Glad you came by when you did."

"Felt I had to," she said with a shrug. "To apologise."

"What for?"

"Today," the older girl said. "It wasn't your fault."

Annabel didn't know what to say.

"After you left, Brett and I had a look at the boat," Clarissa continued. "The rudder had sheared away."

"It what?"

"Ripped clean off. He's never seen anything like it."

Annabel stared at her.

"Anyway, I just wanted you to know."

"I see. Thanks."

The door opened again, and Naomi stood there. Even with a bleeding lip, the girl looked fabulous.

"I'm ready," she said.

Annabel turned to Clarissa.

"Shall we?"

"You're in charge," said her Stroke.

Annabel smiled. "OK, ladies. Let's go."

The three of them set off down the stairs, leaving Colin behind them.

Chapter Forty-Three

Ying strode towards him, eyes blazing, and Giles took a step back. But before she could reach him, they both heard a door open. They turned to see Pippa standing there, staring at them.

"The carriage is waiting, Eliza," she said, pulling on long white gloves. "Are you ready?"

Ying paused, squaring her shoulders and lifting her chin.

"Quite ready. Is the Professor coming?"

"Certainly not," Pippa scoffed. "He can't behave himself in church. He makes remarks out loud all the time on the clergyman's pronunciation."

The audience laughed, and Ying nodded.

"Then I shall not see you again, Professor Higgins. Goodbye." Turning, she glided across the stage.

Pippa followed. "Goodbye, dear."

"Goodbye, mother," said Giles, watching them go. Then, as if on impulse, he called out.

"Oh, by the way, Eliza!"

Ying paused by the door, and turned to look back at him.

"Order a ham and a Stilton cheese, will you?" He waved

a hand in the air. "And buy me a pair of gloves and a tie to match that new suit of mine." He peered at her over his glasses. "You can choose the colour."

Ying regarded him with disdain.

"Buy them yourself," she said and swept out.

Giles looked at Pippa, who shook her head.

"Never mind, dear," she said, heading after Ying. "I'll buy you a tie and gloves."

"Don't bother..." But it was too late. They were gone.

Frowning, Giles stood there alone. Glancing around the stage, he spotted something by the armchair. Walking over, he picked up a pair of slippers and stared at them.

"She'll buy them, right enough..." Then, almost to himself, he added, "Goodbye."

The lights went out, and he held his breath. There was a moment of stunned silence, before the audience erupted.

Giles let out a long sigh and stood there amid the thunderous applause. In the darkness, he became aware of the other cast members hurrying on stage. Ying grabbed his hand and squeezed it.

The lights went up, and Giles led her forwards to take the first of her many bows. In the front stalls, he could see Raquel on her feet, her face radiant as she joined in the applause. Standing a couple of rows behind was the Master with his guest from Trinity, both clapping enthusiastically. Giles gave him a wink and Lester beamed. Whoops and whistles rang out from the back, where Trevor and a host of Redboys were gathered.

Giles took a bow, and as he rose, he spotted a lone figure

by the exit who was not applauding. To his surprise, he realised it was Jane. She was standing in the aisle and staring at a person in the stalls in front of him. Following her gaze, he realised that she was looking at Raquel.

"Giles!" whispered Ying, bringing him back to the present. "Last time, so let's make it a good one."

They stepped forwards again and went down for one final bow. And when he rose, the figure at the back of the auditorium had gone.

Half an hour later, Giles walked out through the doors of the ADC theatre with Ying on his arm. Trevor and Raquel waiting for them. Ying was in high spirits after consuming half the bottle of Champagne that Giles had bought for the cast.

"Trevor!" she said, letting go of Giles and flinging her arms around her boyfriend.

"Been celebrating, have we?" he asked.

"What makes you think that?" she said, wrapping a leg around him.

Giles, in his best Professor Higgins voice, said, "She's so deliciously low, so horribly dirty."

"Oy!" said Ying. "I heard that."

"So, did you enjoy it?" he asked Raquel.

She kissed him full on the mouth.

"I'll take that as a yes," he said.

"Thank you, Giles."

"For what?"

"For tonight. It was perfect."

"My pleasure," he said, and he meant it.

"Are you two love birds joining us at The Maypole?" Trevor asked.

Giles gave him an apologetic smile.

"Sorry, we have an early start in the morning."

"That's never stopped you before," said Ying, hanging off Trevor's arm.

"What can I say?" said Giles. "I'm a reformed character."

Ying snorted. "Yeah, right. Well, your loss. I was buying."

Reaching over, she gave Raquel a hug.

"Good seeing you again, Raquel. Glad you could make it."

"I would not have missed it. I liked Eliza."

"Yeah well, she had a good Professor." said Ying, taking Giles's face in her hands and giving him a big sloppy kiss before grimacing.

"Blah! Too much champagne."

Wheeling around, she hurried over to her boyfriend. "Come on, Trev, I need something to wash away the taste."

"See you two around," said Trevor. "Have a great holiday."

"We'll try," said Giles.

"And don't forget to pack your slippers," called out Ying, playing Eliza once more.

Giles watched them and the rest of the cast head off for what would no doubt be quite an after-party. Turning to Raquel, he bowed.

"Can I walk you home, my lady?"

"*Si*, Professor. That would be nice."

Taking her by the arm, he led her along Jesus Lane to All Saints Passage. At this time of night, it looked like the quintessential lovers' lane with its old-fashioned streetlamps casting a golden glow over the Victorian shopfronts.

Raquel leaned against him as they walked arm in arm, their footsteps echoing on the flagstones between the tall buildings.

"You OK?" he asked.

"A bit cold," she said with a shiver.

Giles smiled and began to hum.

"All I want is a room somewhere,
Far away from the cold night air,
With one enormous chair,
Oh, wouldn't it be lovely?"

They turned by the railings and headed towards the College.

"Lots of chocolate for me to eat,
Lots of coal making lots of heat,
Warm face, warm hands, warm feet
Oh, wouldn't it be lovely?"

"Sounds good," said Raquel, squeezing his arm.

They walked up to the Great Gate, and Giles pushed the wicket gate open. As Raquel went inside, he glanced back the way they'd come and paused, peering into the darkness.

"Giles?" said Raquel. "What is it?"

He waited a little longer for the shadow to move again, and, when it didn't, he smiled.

"Nothing," he said. "Just looking forward to a holiday."

Giles ducked through the opening and, linking her arm in his, set off across First Court.

******

Jane waited in the shadow of the doorway until the gate swung shut. She lifted a cigarette to her lips and lit it.

"They're back in the College," she murmured into her wrist mike.

"Do you think Chamberlain knows?" the voice in her earpiece asked.

Jane blew out a plume of smoke.

"Probably."

"What will he do, do you think?"

She stared at the laminated ADC flyers attached to the railings. Giles's Professor Higgins grinned back at her.

"What we least expect," she replied.

There was a grunt from the other end. "So, are you logging off then or what?"

Placing the cigarette to her lips, she took another drag and said, "Yeah. Out."

Jane tossed the cigarette away and deactivated the microphone. Turning from the College, she walked back up the alleyway and began to hum.

"Someone's head resting on my knee,
Warm and tender as he can be,
Who takes good care of me,
Oh, wouldn't it be lovely?"

Behind her, the cigarette glowed in the night air until it too faded to black. Soon all that lingered in the little tree-lined square were shadows.

Epilogue

As the taxi pulled away, Ravi stood in the Forecourt, gazing around at the familiar surroundings. Little had changed during his time in hospital. The trees in the small square had more foliage perhaps, and there were fewer bikes in the racks now that the Easter holidays had begun. But the formidable iron gates and imposing Victorian Chapel were as reassuring as ever.

Though the bones in his shoulder had knitted together remarkably well, the surgeon had insisted on Ravi wearing a sling. He adjusted this before picking up his leather briefcase and heading for the lodge. The automatic doors swung open, and he saw a familiar figure standing behind the counter.

"Good morning, Professor," said Bert. "Glad to have you back."

"It's good to be back, Bert. I hope you are well."

"Better than you, I suspect," said the Head Porter, peering at him over his glasses. "We thought it would be some time before we saw you again, eh Shirley?"

His colleague appeared from the back office and stared at Ravi in surprise. "Professor Gupta. Welcome home."

"I was just saying how well he looks," said Bert.

"Certainly does," said Shirley, approaching the desk. "That was quite a beating you took, Professor, on those stairs."

Ravi met her eyes. "It probably looked a lot worse than it was," he said. "I'm well on the mend now."

"Pleased to hear it."

"By the way, Professor," Bert said, "I wonder if you can help us clear up a bit of a mystery?"

Ravi felt his stomach tighten. "What would that be?"

"We couldn't seem to find a record of you signing out those keys."

"Sorry?"

"To the New Court cellars."

"Ah yes," he said, aware they were both studying him. "These, you mean?"

He produced from his pocket the set of keys that he and Robert had made all those years ago.

"From my student days, I'm afraid. I suppose I should have returned them some time ago. Would you like them back?"

"Ah, that would explain it," said Bert, glancing at Shirley. "Well, if you have no further need of them?"

Ravi slid the keys across the counter. "No. After this regrettable incident, I doubt very much I'll be going down there again."

The Head Porter picked them up. "Thank you, Professor."

"Well, I imagine my mail has been building up while I've been away?"

"It certainly has," said Shirley, heading for the Fellows' pigeonholes.

"And you've missed a good deal of excitement too," said Bert.

"Oh, yes?"

"I've seen some high jinks over the years, Professor, as you know. I still remember that car under the Bridge of Sighs," he said, shaking his head. "But the students outdid themselves this time."

"Did they indeed?"

"Don't ask me how they did it, but a statue's gone missing."

"A statue?"

"Lady Margaret Beaufort, no less. From the Chapel Tower."

Ravi raised his eyebrows. "How did they manage that, I wonder?"

"Beats me, Professor. That was some feat."

"I'm sure it was," Ravi agreed.

"Mind you, the Dean took a pretty dim view of it, I can tell you. Livid, she was."

"I can imagine."

"All in all, Dr Jones has had a busy time of it. What with that trouble over at Cripps, eh Shirley?"

"A Staircase, you mean?" said the other Porter, returning with a stack of envelopes wrapped in an elastic band. "Yes, some third-year got himself sent down for assaulting two freshers."

"Your Miss Hamilton was one," added Bert.

"What?" said Ravi. "Annabel?"

"Don't you worry, Professor," Shirley said. "She sorted him out. Quite a girl, our Miss Hamilton."

"Like her grandmother," Bert nodded, approvingly. "A chip off the old block."

Ravi stared at them both. "It seems you *have* been busy."

"As I say, Professor, it's been exciting," said Bert.

More than you know, Ravi thought.

He left the lodge and was halfway across Chapel Court when he paused to look up at the tower. The empty alcove where Lady Margaret used to stand was there, high above him. Ravi glanced towards the other statues and gargoyles, who peered down at him in stony silence. Suppressing a shudder, he turned and made his way back to his staircase, where he slid his room indicator to IN with a sense of relief. It didn't last long.

As soon as he unlocked his door, the smell hit him. It was an ancient musty odour that conjured memories of cellars and worse. Putting the briefcase down, Ravi reached inside his jacket and drew out the ruler.

Standing in the doorway, he scanned the room, looking for anything out of the ordinary. All seemed as it should be until he spotted the dark shape lying on the floor next to his desk.

Ravi tensed, waiting for it to make a move. When nothing happened, he peered closer and realised what it was: an old trunk. The conversation with Giles in the hospital came back to him, and he smiled at his foolishness.

After closing the door, he crossed the room to inspect his

new acquisition. It looked vaguely familiar, but when he saw the initials R.T.F.M., it all came flooding back.

Robert's trunk, the one they had lugged up and down all those flights of stairs when they shared rooms as undergrads. Rushing off to lectures, preparing for Supervisions, hosting room parties, and talking late into the night about how the pair of them were going to change the world.

Ravi sighed, staring at the battered old case that had been there with them during those wonderful years. It was only then that he registered the brown paper parcel someone had placed on the lid. There was an envelope too, which read:

Confidential.
Professor R. Gupta.
Open first.

Drawing up his old leather chair, Ravi sat down and did as instructed, opening it with his ruler. Inside he found a handwritten note.

O3 Second Court
Dear Professor Gupta,

I hope you are fully recovered. Here is the trunk we collected from the New Court cellars. It came without keys, so I took the liberty of leaving it open for you. You may wish to add a padlock for additional security. Some things are best kept locked, as I'm sure you'll agree.

I expect that you will find the contents both

illuminating and useful. Should you ever feel the need to share them with anyone, I would be most interested in learning more. However, I leave it to you to decide if and when the time is right.

For now, I have some long-overdue fieldwork to complete, so I have more than enough to keep me occupied.

I wish you a relaxing and enjoyable holiday and look forward to seeing you on my return.

Yours sincerely,

Giles Chamberlain

PS The package contains something to add to the collection.

Ravi re-read the note, his heart beating faster. What had Robert stored in the trunk? More to the point, what had Giles meant by 'adding to the collection'?

The parcel was surprisingly light. Taking his ruler, he ran it down one side and peeled back the paper to reveal a cardboard sample box. Lifting the lid, Ravi peered inside and stiffened. There, cushioned in a red spotted handkerchief, lay a pile of white powder.

******

Reaching for the chalk bag on his belt, Giles dusted his fingertips and stretched up to jam them in a cleft. When the hold felt secure, he raised his left foot onto a ledge and levered himself onto the summit. Adrenalin spiking, he gave a whoop of delight.

"Giles? Are you OK?" Raquel called from below.

"Fine," he said. "Give me a moment, and you can see for yourself."

Giles secured the rope with a restraining cam and belayed until her sweat-soaked bandana appeared above the edge. Reaching down, he grabbed her hand and pulled her up. She wrapped her arms about his neck, and he swung her around.

"Hey," she said, laughing, "put me down."

Giles deposited her back on the ground and gazed into her flushed face.

"So, how was it for you?"

"Tough, but good," she said. "Like my man."

"He's not here right now, but will I do?"

"OK, then," she said and kissed him.

Her lips were warm and salty, and Giles closed his eyes, savouring the moment.

When they finally pulled apart, she looked up at him.

"So, have you seen anything yet?"

"Not so far," he said, glancing around at the summit.

It was some forty feet across, its rocky surface dusty and bare. Still, what it lacked in terms of physical features, it more than made up for in panoramic views. From their hard-earned vantage point, he could see all the way down the steep-sided valley, which cut a swathe through the surrounding cliffs.

On his many overseas adventures with Ying and Trevor, it was rare to find a place as breathtaking as this that was still free of tourists jostling for photographs. Giles felt humbled by its majesty and counted himself fortunate to be able to enjoy it with Raquel.

"Incredible, eh?"

She didn't respond at first, and he assumed that she must be enjoying the moment too. But when he turned towards her, he saw that she was staring off into the sky, her hands shielding her face from the glaring sunlight.

"Giles, you have those glasses?"

"Sure."

Reaching into his backpack, Giles withdrew the Carl Zeiss binoculars and handed them to her. She trained them on a pair of shapes flying towards the sunset.

"And?" he asked.

For a while, Raquel said nothing, but when she spoke, he could hear her excitement. "It's two of them."

"In broad daylight? You're sure?"

Raquel handed him the glasses. "Here, take a look."

Giles focused the lenses on the far horizon. It took him a moment to find the two objects, but when he did, their broad wings were unmistakeable.

"You're right," he said, handing back the binoculars. "Let's see where they're heading, and we can try over there tomorrow."

While Raquel turned to stare after the disappearing flyers, Giles checked the bearing on his compass. As he did so, he wondered how long it would be before the Professor discovered that Robert's backpack was missing. Part of him wondered if he ever would, given how reluctant Gupta would be to discuss the contents of the trunk with Nick and Annabel, the only other ones to have seen the backpack inside.

Of course, Giles had been tempted to take some of Mackenzie's journals with him too. But in the end, he had decided against it. For one thing, they planned to travel light, and for another, he wasn't sure he needed them any more.

After seeing the markings on the wall that night in the cellars, Giles now knew the glyphs needed to recreate the gate. And once he'd reviewed the footage from his camera in the Old Library, it hadn't taken long to locate and memorise the two pieces of parchment the Professor had hidden there.

The only tricky moment had come when Mr Weston had found him returning the leather-bound volume containing the fragments to its bookcase. However, the Librarian had seemed gratified that he was taking his scholar's privileges seriously, and he had wished him luck with his dissertation.

Once the preparations were complete, Giles had taken Raquel back to the New Court cellars using a copy of the keys he'd returned to the Professor. After performing the ritual to activate the portal, he'd led her into the Gemini Passage, taking care to seal the gate behind them. And now they were here, staring at one of two suns dipping below the distant horizon.

"There it goes," Raquel said as the orange glow finally disappeared.

Giles shielded his eyes to stare up at its twin as it began its own slow descent through the azure sky.

"Come on," he said. "I saw a fissure in the rock on the way up. We can shelter there for the night."

Raquel turned towards him. "Giles?"

"Yes?"

"Thank you."

"For what?"

"For doing this. For Alfonso."

He shrugged. "Beats going to lectures."

She punched his arm.

"OK, you're welcome. Now, can we go, please? I may be English, but only a mad dog would stay out here after dark."

Giles led Raquel back to the edge of the towering red column. Roping up, they looked once more towards the distant horizon. Then, they began their descent into the valley of shadows.

GET YOUR FREE SHORT STORIES FROM *CAMBRIDGE GOTHIC*

If you enjoyed *Gate of Shadows* and would like to learn more about the fantasy world of *Cambridge Gothic*, sign up to my mailing list. I'll also send you free short stories:

1. *Come Out to Play* – a creepy encounter for Ying and Trevor from their first term as freshers.
2. *A Late Arrival* – a chilling tale set in the Cambridge admissions week.
3. *A Poisoned Chalice* – a prequel involving Alfonso, Raquel, and their family in Mallorca.

To receive your free stories and other exclusive content, sign up to my *Cambridge Gothic* mailing list at www.marknwells.com

DID YOU ENJOY THIS BOOK?

Reviews are the most effective way of building awareness of a series you have enjoyed. While I'd love to tell more people about *Cambridge Gothic*, the best way to do that is through a committed and loyal group of readers. Honest reviews help bring my books to the attention of other readers.

So, if you have enjoyed *Gate of Shadows*, I would really appreciate it if you would spend just a few minutes leaving a review (it can be as short as you like) on the book's Amazon page.

Many thanks,
Mark

CAMBRIDGE GOTHIC BOOK 1
COLLEGE OF SHADOWS

Cambridge is home to the brightest minds…
and the deadliest monsters.

Working-class rugby player Nick feels out of place at university. The hallowed halls of Cambridge seem impossibly huge and far beyond the Mansfield of his youth. But Nick has much more than fitting in to fear when he's attacked by a creature straight out of his worst nightmares…

Emotionally scarred by the sudden death of her parents, Annabel buries her feelings deep in her studies. But after barely surviving another freak accident, the shy girl begins to fear she's cursed. And when her new friends nearly fall prey to a monstrous beast that shouldn't exist, she's terrified that her bad luck could bring their demise.

As Nick and Annabel plan to trap the creature, they stumble upon a long-held Cambridge secret. And the otherworldly truth is less pass-fail than do-or-die.

Can Nick and Annabel banish the beast before freshers' week becomes their last?

College of Shadows is the engrossing first novel in the Cambridge Gothic YA urban fantasy series. If you like haunted heroes, unspeakable horrors, and mystical magic, then you'll love Mark Wells's atmospheric tale.

Buy *College of Shadows* to watch students school the supernatural today!

ABOUT THE AUTHOR

Mark Wells read law at Cambridge University, and after a varied career, he returned to his old College as a Bursar and Fellow. He has published short stories for Games Workshop's Black Library under the pen name Nicholas Alexander, and is currently writing two new fantasy series set in and around Cambridge:

1. *Cambridge Gothic* follows the fortunes of Alfonso, Nick, Annabel, Giles, and Professor Gupta as they battle dark forces converging on their beloved College. For more details visit www.marknwells.com

2. *The Hidden Tales* is a series of illustrated children's books funded by the Arts Council of England. Readers visit museums, solve puzzles, and decipher codes to find a hidden artefact somewhere in the city. For more details visit www.hiddentales.co.uk

Mark lives in Cambridge with his family and can be found wandering its ancient courts and passageways, plotting...

You can follow Mark on:
Facebook www.facebook.com/markwellsauthor/
Instagram www.instagram.com/marknwells/
Or you can email him at mark@marknwells.com

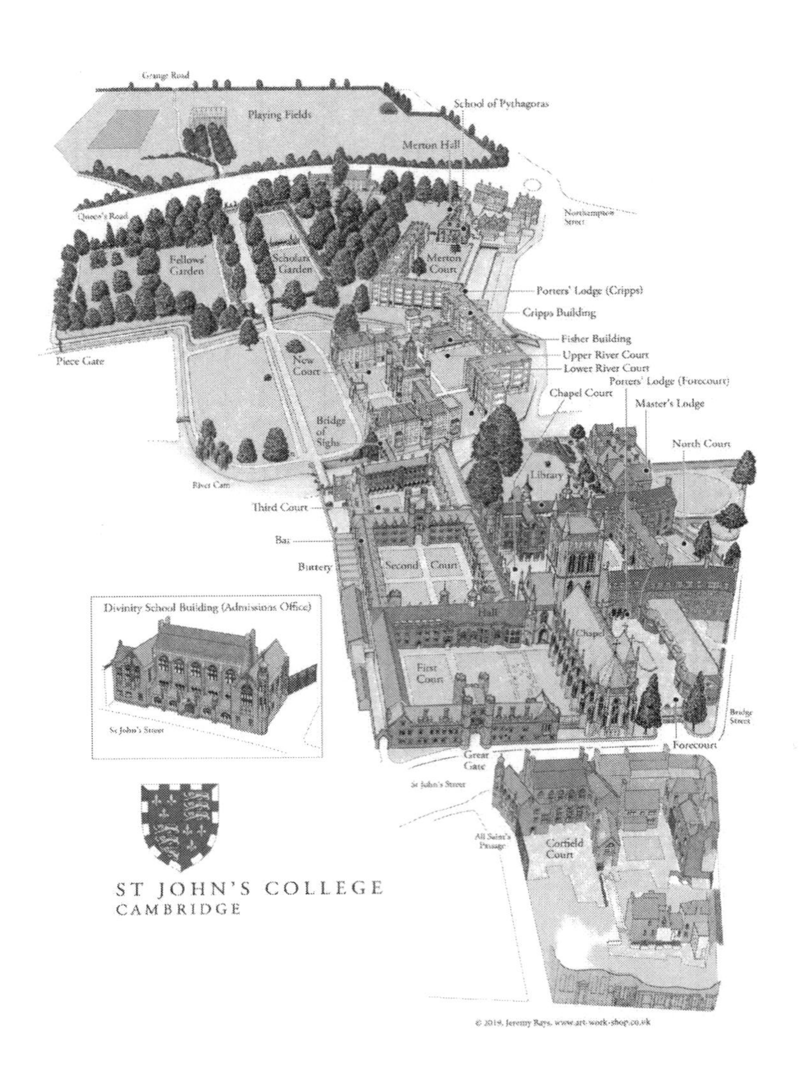

For an interactive map of St John's College visit:
www.marknwells.com/maps